ARMY OF PREY

CALIXTO WAYNE

DARNOLDO PUBLISHING LLC

To my brother, who has believed in me from the beginning.

CONTENTS

1. Chapter 1   1

2. Chapter 2   5

3. Chapter 3   10

4. Chapter 4   15

5. Chapter 5   31

6. Chapter 6   43

7. Chapter 7   52

8. Chapter 8   67

9. Chapter 9   74

10. Chapter 10   91

11. Chapter 11   95

12. Chapter 12   106

13. Chapter 13   114

14. Chapter 14   118

15. Chapter 15   124

16. Chapter 16   131

17. Chapter 17   136

18. Chapter 18   142

19. Chapter 19   154

20. Chapter 20   161

21. Chapter 21   165

22. Chapter 22   170

23. Chapter 23   178

24. Chapter 24   181

25. Chapter 25   189

26. Chapter 26   193

27. Chapter 27   205

28. Chapter 28   211

29. Chapter 29   215

30. Chapter 30   222

31. Chapter 31   227

32. Chapter 32   229

33. Chapter 33   236

34. Chapter 34   244

35. Chapter 35   249

36. Chapter 36   259

37. Chapter 37   269

38. Chapter 38   274

39. Chapter 39   278

40. Chapter 40   281

41. Chapter 41   285

To The Reader   290

About the author   291

CHAPTER ONE

Byron cursed as the missile flew over his head. The bottle shattered against the wall, showering him in red wine and jagged glass shards. He vaulted over the bar and hunkered down, seeking a momentary respite from the chaos consuming the common room of the tavern.

"Byron! Nice seeing you here," exclaimed Dalton as the tall slender blonde boy took a swig from a bottle of red wine, while crouched behind the bar in what looked like an uncomfortable position. "Want some?" he asked in a too steady voice. "It's from Kelon. Pre-destruction."

Byron glowered at his friend. "No. I'm kind of in the middle of a fight," he said with a scowl. "A fight that you should be a part of."

Dalton gave him a sidelong glanced as he tried vainly to arch a single eyebrow. "Why would I do that?" he asked. "Didn't you hear me say that this is a fine red wine from Kelon? Why would I abandon such luxury for a tavern brawl?"

A table shattered against a wall of the inn. "Oh, maybe because your friends are caught up in that brawl?" retorted Byron acidly.

Dalton shrugged unconcerned as he took another sip. "Well then maybe my friends shouldn't flirt with attractive bar maids."

Byron's scowl morphed into a roguish grin. "But then it wouldn't be a night out on the town."

A gangly well-dressed man tumbled over the bar landing in Dalton's lap. The slender boy yelped and dropped his bottle of wine. It shattered on the ground, the red liquid quickly seeping into Dalton's clothes. His eyes widened in outrage as he promptly threw a seated punch at the groggy intruder.

"That's the spirit," chortled Byron as he hurtled back over the bar and into the thick of the melee. It was not his fault that a merchant and a minor noble both grew upset with the bar maid paying him an inordinate amount of attention. He could be quite charming when he wanted.

"You enjoy violence way too much," grumbled Dalton as he appeared next to Byron, his hands pressing against his wet clothing as he tried vainly to force the liquid out of the fabric. "Just once could you not take every situation as a competition? I don't think my body can handle much more of this."

Byron brushed the comment aside as he scanned the room for Jeron. The olive-skinned boy was like a brother to him, and he was not about to leave him alone during a fight. They were similar in height with Byron having broader shoulders and Jeron having arms that would make a blacksmith jealous.

Across the room, Jeron's fist was busy burying itself into a merchant's ribs. Jeron's dark black hair and his mane were both soaked through with sweat. A feathered man interrupted Jeron's fun as he leaped onto Jeron's back, squeaking as he tried to gouge Jeron with his talons and beak.

Jeron roared in pain as he struggled to remove the man from his back and end the furious onslaught of pecking and scratching. Byron calmly picked up a chair, strode across the room, and broke it across the back of Jeron's assailant. The man fell off of Jeron, his head striking the ground with a wet thump. The feathered man lay on the ground unmoving as his avian features slowly retreated beneath his skin as his body reverted back to its human form.

"Good fight, huh?" asked Byron as he slapped Jeron on the back.

Jeron responded by slapping him upside the back of his head. "What is wrong with you?" he demanded. "Why did you have to hit the nobleman?"

Byron shrugged. "He annoyed me," he said simply as a man leapt at them and threw a wild punch. Byron dodged it effortlessly. "And hitting him was fun."

"And the bar maid?" asked Jeron as he struck their assailant in the face.

"Are you kidding?" said Byron as he connected with his own punch, dropping the man to the floor. "Did you see how pretty she was?"

Dalton threw a bottle at an angry unshaven man who was blindly swinging a chair leg around. "She was that," he confirmed reluctantly.

Jeron scowled briefly at the two of them. "So what? I can't see Byron's father or mother approving of a bar maid."

Byron rolled his eyes as he tackled a drunk combatant to the floor. "I wasn't planning on marrying her," he called out as he rolled across the floor, entangled with the drunkard.

Jeron's reply was drowned out over the sound of the drunkard's fists pounding an unsteady rhythm upon Byron's head. Lights exploded and sparkled across his field of vision in the aftermath of each blow. The drunkard was none other than the possessive nobleman who desired the bar maid. Fangs now glistened in the man's mouth, and fur covered his face. The man was fully in the grip of some sort of dog or wolf totem.

Byron tried to block the strikes as they rained down upon him. He only needed to hold the lout off until Jeron or Dalton could pull the man off of him.

They never got that chance. The door to the inn burst open as a squad of palace soldiers wearing the orange and blue of the duke poured into the common room.

The soldier at the head of the column was an average sized man carrying a great axe in his hands. "In the name of the Duke, and the Prince, everyone stop what they are doing!" he bellowed at the top of his lungs.

Everyone ceased fighting. Immediately. They stared at the man for an instant before darting for the nearest exit. Byron heard a few loud shattering sounds as men made their exits through windows.

The nobleman that Byron was fighting also bolted. How disappointing. Most of the clientele in this establishment had reputations. Reputations which would not be enhanced by spending time in the duke's jail. Byron let the man leave without a struggle. It just was not worth the effort.

Byron sighed and let his head fall back onto the floor with a resigned *thunk*. There was no where he could escape to in his condition anyway.

A shadow fell over Byron's body as the soldier and his great axe hovered above him. "Well, what do we have here?" asked the soldier with a delighted smirk on his face.

Byron groaned. "Heya Renaldo," he said with forced cheer. "What are you doing here?"

Renaldo shrugged nonchalantly as the soldiers and patrons continued to run, shout, and wrestle. "I was sent to find the duke's no-good, irresponsible, troublemaking son." He spread his hands out wide in a sarcastic welcomingly gesture. "And look at my good fortune! All I had to do was follow the sounds of drunken idiots. What was this brawl over?"

Byron winced as he pulled himself into a seated position. His body and his head both ached. The sign of a successful night out on the town. "A bar maid's affections," he said with an unapologetic grin.

The smile left Renaldo's face as he shook his head sadly. "A woman? Really?" he asked with disappointment. "I know your brother has offered to introduce you to a number of fine young ladies. He'll be disappointed in you."

Renaldo extended a hand and Byron accepted it gratefully, pulling himself up off of the wooden floor with all sorts of extra dirt and debris embedded within his clothing. "I'm devastated," he replied drily. "And the last I checked, he isn't married either, and he's not here. So I don't have to deal with that judgmental look of his."

Renaldo smiled wickedly in response, and Byron felt his stomach plummet. "Oh no. He's here, isn't he?" Byron asked horrified.

"He's just outside," Renaldo said cheerfully as he steered Byron towards the inn door. "Didn't you hear me announce that we were here in the name of the Prince?"

"I thought you meant me," grumbled Byron.

"Well, I didn't," said Renaldo as he opened the inn door, holding it open for Byron. "Now go have a conversation with your brother, Your Highness. While you do that, hardworking soldiers such as myself, will spend our evening tending to your friends and cleaning up the mess that you have made."

"Good man," said Byron. He straightened his torn shirt, brushing off a few ragged splinters and stepped into the night.

Chapter Two

D arik Villa was not known as a warm passionate man. He kept his emotions internalized where they belonged. That restraint had not been passed down to his little brother. Byron had gone too far this time, but he was not going to get a rise out of Darik. The immaturity was amusing for a while, but the act had grown stale with age.

If Byron would not accept responsibility, then Darik would thrust it upon him.

His little brother exited the inn in a deplorable state. His shirt and trousers were stretched and torn. Bruises stood out starkly against his pale skin and high cheekbones.

Byron shared a similar but not identical build with Darik. Both were taller than average, although Byron was not as tall as Darik. Both brothers had broad shoulders and narrow waists, a common trait in the Villa family, but again, Byron was slightly slimmer.

Darik knew that the physical differences bothered Byron. The pair were constantly being contrasted against each other by every noble in in the duchy. And given Byron's condition, the comparisons were rather vicious. Venomous whispers stalked his little brother every day, and as a result, Byron gave the people what they wanted.

A brutish princeling regarded as a failure to the family.

Byron beamed at Darik as he crossed the street, a sparkle in his eyes. "Hey big brother, what are you doing here?"

Darik stared at him blankly. He had anticipated a poorly constructed joke rife with juvenile humor. But nonchalance? As if the entire situation did not exist and everything was fine? That was new.

Darik could feel his skin coloring slightly as his anger rose. Responsibility. Byron would stop acting like a fool. "My brother sneaks out of the palace and instigates a brawl among the merchants and minor nobles?" snapped Darik. "Where do you think that I would be?"

Byron shrugged, the shadows dancing wildly upon his face in the courtyard. "At dinner with one of many fetching ladies. Faces painted and powdered as they coyly try to think of ways to ask you to marry them?"

"Enough," growled Darik. "This isn't about me"

"Oh Prince Darik," sang Byron in his high-pitched childish impression of a vapid brainless courtier. "Did I tell you that I was in attendance when you came back from Ochandor?"

"Byron. Enough."

"Oh, you looked so splendid and radiant," continued Byron. "The way you arrived in the morning, armor covered in a dew. Oh, did you sparkle. Like a jewel-"

"Enough!" roared Darik as he grabbed Byron by the front of his shirt and propelled him up the road towards the palace. The streets grew silent as people gawked at the brothers. Darik's men studiously looked in every direction but at them.

Anger clouded Byron's face. He had a quick temper, and for some reason always cared what other people thought about him. A ridiculous weakness. But a weakness nonetheless.

The anger vanished as quickly as it had arrived. A taunting victorious grin replaced it. "And everyone says I'm the temperamental one," quipped Byron. "So who was she?"

Darik exhaled in exasperation. "No idea," he admitted softly. "I left the palace the moment I heard you three had snuck out."

"Convenient."

Darik shrugged as he pushed his temper down. "Sometimes your immature behavior is to my benefit."

"You know you'll have to get married eventually," said Byron as he wobbled unsteadily on his feet.

Darik gripped his little brother's arm in an attempt to steady him. If it left a bruise, well, that was Byron's fault for carousing so much. "I know," Darik admitted. "But it will be to someone that I choose."

Byron snorted. "And I bet you'll choose someone whose family would support you to be king."

Darik hesitated before answering. "That would be beneficial," he admitted. "But we're not talking about my responsibilities. We're talking about yours."

"We are?" asked Byron quizzically. "I could have sworn we were talking about your courtships."

Darik steered the pair onto a cross street, avoiding a throng of people out enjoying the Antierian nightlife. "You don't understand," said Darik gravely. "This was the last straw. Not just for me, but with mom and dad as well."

Byron narrowed his bleary eyes in suspicion. "What are they going to do?" he asked. "Try to marry me off? No one will agree to that until I find my totem."

"Oh, I agree. Believe me, I agree," said Darik. "Which is why I finally convinced them to throw you out of the city."

"You did what?" asked Byron, his temper rising again.

Darik rounded on his little brother and began poking him in the sternum with his index finger. "You don't find your totem because you don't want to," said Darik. "That takes work. And soul searching. You're a smart man, and I say this because I love you, but you rely on your brains to get you through life with the least amount of work and resistance possible."

"No longer," continued Darik as he propelled his simmering brother back up the road. "You're leaving for training tomorrow."

"I don't leave for another three months," said Byron with a smirk.

"Tomorrow," replied Darik as he returned the smirk. "Jeron and Dalton will accompany you. They could use some growing up too."

"And what am I supposed to do at Raven's Perch for three months?" asked Byron in disbelief.

"Train, study, and push yourself to your limits," answered Darik. "You're nineteen years old. Time to start acting your age. Who knows, with a little sweat and some reflection, maybe you'll find your totem in no time."

"And if I don't?" asked Byron uncertainly.

Darik shrugged as the palace came into sight. "Well then at least you'll be useful to your family, friends, and duchy."

"I am useful to the duchy," grumbled Byron. "I'm the greatest joke it's ever seen. Antier's morale has never been higher."

Darik slapped Byron in the back of the head. "You're a joke only because you let yourself be one," he hissed. "Stop caring about what other people think of you. I guarantee they are laughing and talking behind your back. Guess what? They do that to me too. Learn to ignore it, move on, and stop obsessing about it."

Byron rubbed the back of his head as they passed the first guard post. "And am I supposed to leave you alone in Antier without any distractions to rescue you from the teeming hordes of damsels?"

Darik hesitated and bit his lip. He had been hoping Byron would not think to ask about his own plans. "No," he said softly so that any passing noble, soldier, or servant could not overhead. "While you're gone, I'll be leading a force to Fort Hope."

"Fort No Hope?" hissed Byron, his temper rising again as he referred to the fort by the name employed by the men-at-arms. "Are you insane?"

It was a fair question. One that Darik had asked himself numerous times. Fort Hope was a heavily militarized installation on the far western border of the duchy of Antier. The middle of nowhere. It truly was the frontier of the Kingdom of Ochandor. The closest village, or ruins of one, was days away from the fort and the two passes it guarded.

Beyond those passes lay the land of the beasts. To Darik's knowledge, that land did not have a name. Not that anyone could actually talk to its inhabitants. Centaurs, cyclopes, minotaurs, and other terrible creatures inhabited the land,

and they were not much for conversation. All the Antierians were able to piece together about the monsters was that they desired to invade Ochandor and kill its inhabitants.

But that was mostly guesswork. Since Antier had been settled, Darik's ancestors had thrown the beasts back at Fort Hope, preventing them from spilling into the kingdom and its duchies.

"I don't have much choice," said Darik softly. "According to the reports, the fighting has grown worse. Maybe the worst it has been in a decade." Darik paused lowering his voice even softer. "And with the king lacking an heir, my being out in the middle of nowhere may prove beneficial."

Byron staggered along in silence for a few paces. "And if we're both out of the city, we'll be more difficult to kill," he said in resignation.

Darik grinned. Impetuous and reckless. But not stupid.

"Yes," said Darik. "Now grow up. And do it quickly, or you may not get the chance to do it at all."

Byron groaned. "Had I known that, I wouldn't have drank so much tonight."

"Too bad," said Darik without a trace of sympathy. "Go to your room, get some rest, and pack a bag. You leave at first light."

CHAPTER THREE

J eron tried to suppress a grimace as Raven's Perch came into view on the horizon. It was a small military outpost as such things went. In generations past, well before settlers from Ochandor began flocking into Antier, Raven's Perch had served as the site for numerous conflicts between the local hill tribes. That trend had continued with the settlement of Antier, and the fort's reputation had not faded until the western boundary of Antier was established at Fort Hope.

Nowadays Raven's Perch served as a training facility for the children of the Antierian nobility. It was located out in the countryside of southern Antier in the gentle rolling hills east of the thick frontier forests.

Raven's Perch was remote enough that the noble children could learn to control and employ the powers of their totems, generally significantly stronger than those of the common populace, without causing damage to anything, or anyone, of importance. Also, it was isolated enough so that the students' parents could not impose their influence, political and otherwise, upon the trainers and masters at Raven's Perch.

Those masters played an integral role in the fabric of the Kingdom of Ochandor. Many professions were segmented into societies with members spread throughout all of the duchies. Their numbers included many of the most powerful totem wielders in the kingdom. Power usually resulted in wealth and titles, and Antier was no exception to that rule. The result was that the societies drew predominantly from the young nobility to bolster their ranks.

During training there would be a draft, with societies selecting trainees and offering them membership in their ranks. Jeron dreamed of becoming a paladin like Duke Cedric and Prince Darik. It was a noble profession, and his family had been members of the Church in his youth.

"You have to be kidding me," said Dalton looking crestfallen. "That's Raven's Perch?"

"Yeah. Looks similar to Darik's stories," confirmed Byron.

"But where do they eat?" exclaimed Dalton. "There doesn't seem to be a tavern or inn in the entire place!"

"Hmm. It's almost as if someone doesn't want us going to taverns and inns," commented Jeron wryly.

"Who cares about that!" exclaimed Dalton. Horror entered his eyes. "They have wine, don't they? Tell me that they have wine."

"It is a place where young men are turned into soldiers, and if they are lucky, have the opportunity to join a society and expand their skills and prospects for themselves and their families," recited Byron in an overly formal voice. "They never mention wine."

Dalton spluttered out a variety of half curses causing Jeron and Byron to exchange quick smiles. Raven's Perch, like every other military installation, could count on receiving nobles on their travels. Jeron was certain that there was wine within the premises. Locating and procuring a bottle would be the difficult part.

"Who knows," said Jeron with a shrug of his shoulders. "Maybe they have ale."

"Ale? *Ale?!*" exclaimed Dalton in a manic voice that rose in pitch with each repetition. "I'm in hell. Truly. Hell. Ale." The blonde man shook his head in disgust. "And to think that I should have had another three months partaking in the luxuries of the city."

Jeron tried not to laugh. Dalton professed a love for the "finer things in life," but Jeron doubted that Dalton truly knew what that meant. Dalton had become a ward of Duke Cedric only a few years after Jeron. The three of them had similar childhoods, and rarely did the duke bestow upon them any of the things that

Dalton considered as "the finer things in life." That was a newer affectation of Dalton's. Doubtlessly picked up at an inn while trying to impress women with his worldly sophistication.

"I'm more concerned with what we are going to be doing for the next three months," remarked Byron.

"Probably getting a head start on our training and studies," said Jeron as he scanned the countryside. Banditry was always a threat, even this close to a military outpost. There was no need to be sloppy and careless.

Byron snorted as he gazed out over the distant fields. "Sure. Because that sounds exactly like my brother," he said. "Go take the next three months off. Kick your feet back, relax, and take it easy."

Jeron winced. "We're in for a lot of hard work, aren't we?" Byron nodded in agreement.

"How hard of work?" asked Dalton cautiously.

"You'll be begging for some ale," said Byron dimly.

The boys rode in sullen silence as the fort grew closer. It may have been Jeron's imagination, but he could have sworn that he caught members of their small honor guard smirking at them.

Raven's Perch was surrounded by a sturdy stone wall topped with ramparts and crenellations. It would not protect against heavy siege weaponry, but against smaller forces belonging to local lords or bandits, it would prove more than adequate. The gates stood open, and a group of men stood inside waiting for them.

At their head was an unpleasant looking captain with a receding hairline and a mouth made for scowling. A group of lieutenants and soldiers stood spread out behind him. A welcoming committee. Set up by Darik. Fantastic.

Jeron tensed as Byron trotted his horse ahead of the rest of the group. Hopefully, his friend kept his wits about him and did not do anything stupid. The last thing they needed was to live up to their dubious reputations on their very first day.

"Hello, captain," said Byron in a pleasant and borderline respectful tone. "I am Prince Byron Villa, and with me are-"

"It doesn't matter who they are or who you are," interrupted the captain. "At Raven's Perch you are trainees and I am the captain. You will address me as Captain, Captain Levren, or sir. Do you understand?"

Byron's jaw slid to the left as the muscles in his neck tightened. Resignation gripped Jeron as he waited for his friend's ego to assert itself.

"Just show us to the stable," said Byron crisply and coldly.

Captain Levren walked forward towards Byron, a small smile on his face. Right before he reached Byron's horse he sprinted forward and without warning grabbed Byron's boot and pulled. The prince yelled as he tumbled from his startled horse.

Jeron drew his axe while Dalton flailed for his spear. The captain's men already had a variety of weaponry, bows included, pointed in their direction. Byron's honor guard did not so much as move a muscle, or even acknowledge that their charge had been assaulted and was lying upon the ground.

It was a curious reaction, and one that made Jeron think that events were deliberately arranged to have transpired in this fashion. Captain Levren wanted to make a point, and they were supposed to learn it. Jeron lowered his axe and received a curt tight nod of approval from the captain.

"Very good," said Captain Levren. "At least one of you isn't a worthless ruffian. Now tell me son. What did the young trainee do wrong?"

"Byron did not call you sir, sir," replied Jeron.

"Correct," said Captain Levren with a condescending smile. The older man dashed forward and flipped Jeron out of his saddle. "But a trainee dismounts before answering a superior officer that is on foot."

Dalton groaned and rolled his eyes at the captain. Jeron winced in sympathy as Dalton tumbled to the ground. "And they do not disrespect their superior officers," declared Captain Levren with a self-satisfied smile on his face and a malicious glint in his eyes.

"Now I want you boys to run ten laps around the perimeter wall of Raven's Perch," barked Captain Levren. "These fine soldiers will see that your mounts and men are properly provided for. Now go!"

Jeron stumbled to his feet and half dragged Byron into a stumbling run before his brother in all but blood, could lose his temper for a second time. Three months was a long time to be on the bad side of a superior officer, and Jeron's gut screamed that running was the least inventive punishment that Captain Levren had in his arsenal.

Regardless, Jeron found himself already wanting that ale.

CHAPTER FOUR

"**B**yron!" hollered Jeron and Dalton as they burst out of the stairwell and onto the walls of Raven's Perch.

The red-orange evening light cast a warm glow on the nervous, yet excited faces of the boys as night began to descend on the surrounding countryside. Byron was standing on the ramparts with his hands resting on the stone wall as he enjoyed a rare moment of silence, watching the sun set over the distant mountains.

His hair was a dark brown, yet rays of light from the departing sun revealed plenty of red hairs dispersed throughout his thick mat of wavy hair. Byron Villa was above average height with a set of broad shoulders, making him appear to be larger and more intimidating than he actually was. Despite his frame, he was not built with large, thick, and heavy muscles. Instead, after a few months of Captain Levren's tyrannical training regimen, his arms shone with lean muscles giving him a toned chiseled look, and a narrow waist that spoke of a combination of power and speed, and not raw brute force.

"I seriously doubt that His Lordship decided to send the trainees out to war this late in the evening," remarked Byron as he continued to gaze out at the sunset. "Why, that would border on sheer absurdity, considering the lack of a war to fight at the present. That being accounted for, I can only come to one conclusion that would send the two of you scampering up to the walls." His hazel eyes had a spark of mischief to them as he turned to regard the subjects of his mock diatribe. "The two of you are going to quit training to be soldiers, run off into the night in search of adventure, song, treasure, and women, even if it kills you."

"Hmm," pondered Byron as he tapped a finger against his chin while appraising his friends. "It'll probably kill you," he pronounced. "No, on second thought, it will definitely kill you." He inclined his head towards Dalton. "Oh yes, Dalton, you know it will. No use denying it. Especially since the two of you are up here on the wall with me, instead of being with the rest of the trainees, improving your skills at killing each other politely," concluded Byron with a hint of bitter mockery in his voice.

Dalton, shook his head with a rueful grin on his face. "The art of fencing is a gentleman's sport. Obviously, it is something that a brute like you can't appreciate. What, with your somewhat crude and basic tastes." Dalton paused as he brushed back some straight straw blonde hair from his forehead. He stood slightly taller than Byron but while Byron possessed a broad build, Dalton was of average width with the wiry muscles of an obsessive runner.

"Brawling, bouts of strength, and mock duels where anything goes," continued Dalton, shaking his head in mock disgust. "You two were built for battlefields and street fights, not gentlemanly sport."

"Well, the next time I'm fighting someone I'll be sure to remind them that they aren't fighting fair," retorted Byron. "Why I might even offer him some tea and roses—"

"Are you two finished?" interrupted Jeron with an irritated scowl. Jeron stood just a hair shorter than Byron and noticeably more than Dalton. His eyes were a dark brown whereas Dalton's were a light blue. Jeron had olive skin and black hair. His build was somewhere between Byron's broad frame and Dalton's thinner body. Except unlike the other two, Jeron possessed large muscles on his chest and arms.

"At the moment I don't really care which one of you is the better fighter, or who is more cultured." Jeron looked at Dalton and arched an eyebrow. "Did you forget the reason why we came up here?" Dalton's face reddened in response. "Byron, while you were up here daydreaming and avoiding anything that resembles work, Captain Levren called all the trainees to the assembly hall. Do you know what this means?!"

"Hmm, we're going to get reamed and scolded while suffering numerous insults to our manhood, which will be followed by being drafted by a society which will be responsible for providing us with even more specialized training?" answered Byron.

"Wha-? How did you know?" asked Dalton.

Byron shrugged, "The sun is setting, meaning there is little time left for any real training, and we've almost completed basic training. What else could it be?"

Jeron just shook his head in disbelief. "You know that it is really annoying how quickly you piece things together. Now would you mind if your friends pulled you away from your sunset to see what we will be doing for the rest of our lives?"

Byron flashed a smile and tossed his arms around his friends' shoulders and steered them back towards the stairs. "Well since you asked so nicely. The sun will rise again tomorrow morning anyway." His smile faltered briefly. "Although I suppose I already have an inkling of what my life will entail. But let's hope that I'm wrong."

"It's probably the life of a standard soldier for me," said Jeron as the boys made their way down the hallway lined with bracketed torches and tapestries depicting military scenes. "A soldier's life is a clean life. Honorable too."

Byron smiled inwardly as he listened to his best friend attempts to sell himself short behind a curtain of modesty. Jeron was one of the most intelligent and strongest trainees of the bunch. Byron thought that Jeron just could not wrap his mind around the concept that he was actually smarter than some of his peers, who had always been touted by their instructors as bright young men. There was no question in Byron or anyone else's mind, that Jeron was one of the most capable trainees in Raven's Perch, but when it came to measuring an intangible trait such as the mind, Byron knew his best friend had trouble coming to grips with his own capabilities.

"Nonsense. You're the most qualified out of the trainees who petitioned to join the ranks of the paladins. You'll make a fine knight," assured Dalton as the group passed a tapestry of a paladin in preposterously fine white armor slaying a minotaur with his longsword.

As they walked towards the assembly hall, Byron noticed that more and more of the tapestries portrayed paladins in a noble manner. He saw gleaming shields inscribed with horses running on clouds, jeweled swords, large maces, and mighty axes. All locked in combat and proving victorious over all manner of vicious beasts. Byron doubted that battling those creatures would prove as easy or glorious as the artists assumed.

Jeron looked less than convinced as they rounded a corner and the assembly hall came into sight. "The churches and temples usually prefer their paladin trainees to be skilled in the sword, not the axe. And you guys know that there are a lot of other applicants better with a sword than I am!" Byron looked over at his nervous friend and noticed that sweat was starting to bead on his forehead. Jeron usually did not let his nerves show that much, even around his friends.

"You're not exactly a slouch with a longsword," chuckled Byron. He could clearly see the other trainees filing into the assembly hall as they arrived from other hallways. "Besides, none of them are half as good with a battle axe as you are. That makes you more valuable in the eyes of the different services. They can clearly see your potential. A small improvement in your swordsmanship and you will be deadly proficient in two weapons. What other trainee can offer that? You'll be fine." Byron punctuated his sentiment with a hardy slap to Jeron's back.

"If you say so," replied a thoroughly unconvinced Jeron, sending Dalton and Byron into a momentary fit of laughter at their friend's discomfort. Jeron rolled his eyes at his friend's mirth. He looked less than amused by the situation, and at being the butt of a joke. He flashed a grin that could be called nothing less than predatory at Dalton and said, "At least I didn't stoop so low as to apply to become a cavalier."

Dalton started choking back his laughter as he raised his arms in mock protest and anger. "At least the cavaliers have the nerve to actually attack the realm's foes."

For as long as men had lived in the Kingdom of Ochandor, paladins and cavaliers had been at odds with each other. Both served the same purpose for each of the faiths: vanquish evil and enemies of the realm in the name of their God or gods. The paladins and cavaliers were the militant arm of the faiths. An arm which was always fighting for control of itself. While both were pledged to their gods and to their liege lords, each society had different views as to how to discharge their duty.

The cavaliers were a part of the temple faiths. There edict was to hunt down and root out evil and enemies of the faith. They were proactive in their duty, and were renowned in story and legend for driving deep into enemy territory to slay enemies of the faith. More than one story had been told through the years of a cavalier going on a crusade through lands filled with all sorts of monsters to rescue a maiden locked away in some faraway tower. Those were mainly stories, but like all stories there was some truth to them. Legend also had it that the strongest of cavaliers were able to draw upon their faith and draw some of the strength out of their enemies.

Byron believed those stories mainly to be exaggerations. That the drawing of strength was merely a metaphor used by the cavaliers to cast the unfaithful as cowering in the presence of the righteous. From what Byron could piece together, a cavalier was most likely to lead a charge across a battlefield against another noble's forces. But he had to admit, the monster slaying did add a certain flair to the stories.

Paladin orders were found amongst the Church and the military ranks of the nobles adhering to its tenets. Due to the militaristic nature of their work, paladins were known more as defenders of faith. Songs were sung and stories were told by the hearth of bands of their knights who held forts, mountain passes, and battle lines to the last man. Most proclaimed that they held themselves to a strict code of honor. Byron had spent his life around nobles and knights. Codes of honor were simply a matter of convenience and perspective.

The conflicting nature of their creeds and beliefs had led to numerous conflicts between the paladins and cavaliers. Even when serving within the same military forces, usually in the employ of a duke, each side tended to come into conflict over how to discharge their duties. Over the years, the hatred had tamed down to a somewhat more civil rivalry between those sworn into military service by their liege lords.

However, those serving within the temples and churches were anything but friendly. History chronicled numerous incidents, usually simple bar room brawls, where paladins and cavaliers would side with their brethren of different homelands just for the opportunity to fight their counterparts.

Fearing that the friendly banter between friends might transform into a new chapter in that bitter feud, Byron stepped between the pair. "Great. This is just great. I finally have the two of you ready to break into a holy war and I have no one to bet with!" The two aspiring holy warriors both broke into sheepish smiles while their faces reddened in embarrassment. "Now if your most noble and esteemed selves wouldn't mind, I think we should enter the assembly hall before Captain Levren skins us, well, me, alive."

Byron, Dalton, and Jeron crossed the doorway into the assembly hall, their nerves raw, and stomachs anxious. The assembly hall was less grand than the name implied. Wooden benches lined the large rectangular room in three columns facing a raised stage. The benches all lacked backs in a vain effort to prevent trainees from dozing off during lectures, and force them to pay attention. The room was well lit with torches set in sconces along the walls, as there were no windows in the hall to let in sunlight.

The hall was nowhere close to full, but almost all of the trainees in the current class were present. This batch of trainees was not the normal batch of boys training at Raven's Perch to become soldiers. These trainees were all the sons of nobles in the Duchy of Antier. As a result, almost all of them would receive further specialized training relevant to the society that accepted them. Few nobles were able to pick the society that their son joined. The societies asked for applicants during training, when the nobility were not present, and supposedly selected their new members based off of the merit of their performance and the talents trainees exhibited during basic training.

This structure had been adopted over the years by every duchy in the kingdom to avoid manipulation of the societies by nobles, and as a means of preventing corruption and the consolidation of power within a few families.

It helped matters that the societies were largely independent institutions, capable of generating wealth and social standing for their members. Societies spanned throughout all the duchies and beyond into other countries. Loyalties between society and lord were already a difficult situation without further complications being added by nobles attempting to game the system.

While it was a sound theory, nobles were much like most families throughout the realm. The children grew up following in their parents' footsteps. Butchers raised children who became butchers, and paladins tended to raise children who believed in the same ideas, making them ideal candidates to join the society of their progenitors.

Those few who did not excel enough to be accepted by any of the societies would continue to be trained as soldiers, and if they were lucky, might eventually become officers in the military depending on their skills and family's political positioning. This was not as great an advantage as it would seem, as the more militant societies would also provide similar, if not more extensive training, while also offering their recruits a better chance at promotion due to their added knowledge, abilities, and political connections.

Nervous chatter filled the hall as the gathered boys discussed the odds and options thought to be available to each boy in the class. Every boy there had applied to numerous societies, usually all of them, in order to hedge his odds and be selected to a profession that he would enjoy.

This was the standard procedure, and the process of trainee selection had evolved around it. To say that each society had an equal opportunity to select a recruit was inaccurate. The process worked more as a draft with the resident masters making their selection of recruit. It usually started with the more militaristic societies and working down to the more scholarly pursuits. Upon that selection, the other masters who coveted the trainee would also state their acceptance of the boy, thus leaving the choice up to the trainee which society he chose to join. Each society approached the draft with a set list of which recruits they wanted, or how many they could take. Meaning that the decision of each recruit could vastly impact the fortunes of their fellow trainees. Fortunes had been exchanged between societies as bribes to prevent other societies from offering a boy, thereby eliminating the competition and securing an ideal member. Rumors surrounded the drafting process, and dominated the conversation amongst boys. Especially in a remote fort such as Raven's Perch, where there was little else to do.

A slight stench of fear lingered in the room as the three boys grabbed seats on a bench in the middle of the right column. What was to occur this night would affect them for the rest of their lives, just as much as the actual events transpiring in the outside world. The selection would impact their social standing and that of their families. None of the trainees wanted to have to return home without being accepted into any of the societies. Gossip of that magnitude had a way of dogging a person for the entirety of their life.

"So Byron, which society are you going to join?" asked Dalton as he adjusted his lanky legs in an attempt to get comfortable on the hard wooden bench.

Byron adjusted his pants while mirroring Dalton's leg adjustment. The benches clearly were constructed for shorter people. "I don't know. I haven't decided yet."

"Oh please," snorted Jeron. "You're always thinking ahead. That's why you're in the top of the class. If your training grades weren't enough to judge by, the societies also know your bloodline, which leads me to presume that you'll have offers from nearly every society. Logic also dictates that you know this, and have already made up your mind."

Byron grinned as the boys sitting around them were obviously trying to listen in on his answer. Their chatter became strained and did not flow nearly as quickly as it had before. "Why Jeron, you seem to have forgotten my numerous spats with the good captain. For all the societies know, my tendency to fight like an outlaw, might sound like I actually am an outlaw, after Captain Levren is through talking to them. But still, I think I have narrowed down my choices to two societies."

Byron looked around while he gathered his breath. The surrounding boys had dropped their pretense of talking and were all staring intently. This impacted their lives too. "Which society are you going to pick?" shouted a pudgy blonde hair boy. "Tell us," shouted another. "Please! We need to know!" said another. Some of the boys looked desperate, others angry, and yet some looked eager for a little gossip.

"Give me a break. He's going to be a disappointment." The nasal voice belonged to a tall heavy-set boy. Barith Grannon, was the son of a relatively minor baron, and as a result carried a large chip on his shoulder. He possessed the kind of arrogance that was the sole domain of those who believed they were significantly more skilled and important than they actually were.

Barith styled himself as the best in the class and had a following of two friends who actually adhered to his version of reality. Somehow, Barith also idolized Byron's older brother, Darik, who had led a unit of men to protect the small Grannon estates from a gang of bandits a few years back.

"He is nothing compared to his brother. He has yet to even develop a totem," sneered Barith. "Him and that red headed whelp are the only ones of us yet to develop them to some degree! Remember when skinny Timver was able to knock Byron here square on his back using his totem?" Laughter sprang from the group of boys as they recalled the memory. Their chatter sounded less stressed. The crowd seemed much more confident in their own abilities and odds at landing in a good society after Barith laid out the young prince's deficiencies.

Byron knew where that confidence was rooted. Totems. It always came back to totems.

For as long as humans have told stories, humans have associated certain attributes to animals. Some are based off of the way an animal acts. For instance, a bear is strong, thus a bear symbolizes strength. Other animals get associated with more human concepts due to their appearance, or the nature of their actions. Such as lions, which were commonly associated with nobility, pride, and loyalty. That was the essence that made up totems.

Every human in the kingdom possessed a totem. The totem reflected that which the person believes is inside themself. A person who believed that they were strong, might develop a totem of a bear. While another person may have observed or heard about bears and the way they protect their young, and also developed a totem of a bear. A person's knowledge of the world around them vastly impacted the process.

Despite that, the act of picking a totem was not a conscious choice. A person had no control over the process. It was impossible to lie that deeply to oneself. Deep down, on some instinctual level, every person knew who they really were, and what attributes comprised their soul. The totem merely served as an outward reflection to the world of themself and their beliefs. What they perceived themself to be, or what they strived to be. For most humans, this decision usually was made during their teenage years, as they came to grips with who they were, and what mattered to them.

Totems were more than just a reflection of a person's belief. They were power. A person with a bear totem could draw upon that inner power to harness the abilities of a bear, becoming stronger than a normal person, while a person with a cheetah totem would become much quicker and be able to run faster.

While employing their totem, a person might exhibit some of the features of that animal. Jeron's lion totem constantly bothered him by causing a mane of hair to spring forth from his jawline. The stronger a person and their affinity with their totem, the stronger the gain in physical attributes, and the more they could shift their features to resemble that of their animal totem while harnessing its power. This was most notable among the bird totems, as those people loved to sprout wings and fly freely. The most powerful people, who were few in number, could actually transform into a large version of their totem. Darik was such a person, resulting in everyone in the duchy expecting Byron's totem to be just as strong and powerful as his brother's. However, to date, Byron had failed to bond with his totem, and many in the duchy had little compunction about vocalizing their disappointment in his failure.

Byron knew everyone in the duchy had high expectations for him. From his parents down to the meanest laborer. He just wanted it to be over with. He knew he would eventually get a totem. Every man and woman had a totem. It was not unheard of for someone to take as long to develop an affinity with their totem as Byron. However, given his family history, it was a bit surprising. A bitter smile accompanied the thought. Byron had realized long ago that if he did not have a powerful totem, he would be a source of disappointment and jests for the rest of his life. Everyone else seemed to reach that conclusion only recently.

"And that is living proof why intelligence is underrated," proclaimed Jeron. "And I'm not talking about Barith's use of the word 'ones'." Jeron paused and waited for the few chuckles to subside before continuing. "Byron, you routinely whip all of us in training despite not yet having a totem, and this lout-" Jeron kicked a sitting Barith square in the small of the back to punctuate his statement. Byron grinned and Dalton roared in laughter as Barith leapt to his feet with a high-pitched yelp. Jeron offered a scowling Barith a condescending smile. "-this stupid, smelly-yes, you are smelly. Stop denying it. This moron can't get past the fact that you don't have a totem. And so what?! It didn't stop you from pummeling him in that boxing match a week ago." Byron's grin started to turn into a full-blown smile. Jeron's face was starting to go red with anger as he continued to lay into Barith. As a result, the mane of hair had started to grow around Jeron's chin and cheeks. Byron wondered if his friend was going to lose control of his totem and knock Barith out with a punch to punctuate his argument.

"Sit down Jeron," hissed Dalton suddenly as he yanked on Jeron's arm. "Captain Levren is walking in!"

The trainees all sat down hurriedly and silently faced forward. None of the boys wanted to face the Captain's wrath. He was often a surly and unpleasant man. Students were prone to overhear Captain Levren complaining about training "those stupid noble whelps." All the trainees were hoping to become members of a society within the hour so as to spend fewer hours with the captain. One of the captain's favorite assignments for them was to dispense with night watch duty. It was a thankless task that cut into their sleep. No one wanted to spend the night out on watch patrolling the walls or the courtyard. Especially not with the way the clouds were looking, and with the smells wafting from the kitchen earlier in the day.

Captain Levren stormed up to the platform at the front of the room. He was wearing his dress uniform. The captain never wore his dress uniform in the time Byron had been at Raven's Perch. In fact, he rarely ever was in uniform. He claimed that a uniform was for soldiers who wanted to look pretty; and training boys to be soldiers was never pretty.

A quick murmur swept through the trainees at the sight of the captain, and died just as quickly. There was warm pie tonight, and the night was destined for a downpour. "Listen up boys. Tonight is important. By now you have figured out that you all are about ready to be accepted into a society." Levren's eyes scanned the room as if searching for the one boy who may jump up at any moment and cause trouble. "You're probably thinking that you're done with training under me," said Levren as malice entered his eyes and a wicked smile crept onto his face. "Well my lovelies, allow me to assure you that that is not the case. You all will continue to train with me in addition to learning your new duties in your societies."

Some poor soul on the left side of the room groaned. Byron winced inwardly in sympathy for the poor boy. "WHAT'S THAT?!" shouted Levren. "Talbert! So tell me, when you're out commanding men, real men, professional soldiers who live, bleed, and die and unfortunately for them, you will be in that position due to your daddy humping your mother. Tell me son, as the enemy charges at the end of the day are you just going to say 'Oh I'm sorry but I'm tired right now. I can't lead. Thanks for fighting, enjoy your death'," roared Levren. "Boy, you are going to learn to deal with fatigue and how to think through the fog. All of you are. From the duke's brigand son-" Byron's face darkened and he was vaguely aware of Jeron restraining his right arm "-to the meanest squire's son. All of you will command at some level and it is my duty to see that you are prepared. For their sake as wells as yours. And children, make no mistake, I take my duty seriously."

"Now boys, it's time for the resident society masters to come and make their selections. I expect you all to be on your best behavior, and to be polite if you are lucky enough to have the opportunity to make a decision tonight." Levren paused. "Or there'll be hell to pay."

Captain Levren gestured sharply and the society masters began to funnel into the room and up onto the stage. Byron saw members of the warrior society, different wizard societies, churches, temples, maybe even a representative of the thieves' association. He could not be entirely sure as that lot was rather secretive by nature. Byron noticed his two friends stiffen as the paladin and cavalier representatives stepped on stage. That was when he saw him.

A middle-aged man in his forties wearing a black tunic with a deep blue flame on the center. His pants and cape were also black, trimmed in the same blue as the flame. The ensemble was topped off with a pair of black leather boots trimmed with black fur. This was the man Byron wanted to call his name. The resident master of the Brotherhood of the Dark Flame.

The Dark Flame was a society that worked directly with the nobles. The Brotherhood of the Dark Flame was usually an intelligence unit and rarely took a contract from outside the nobility. Their operatives, called Wraiths, were trained in stealth, ranging from the woods, mountains, desert, river lands, marshes, swamps, and any other terrain, including urban areas. They were also trained in the arts of thievery and assassination. They possessed whatever skill was required to complete the job. As a result, they did not discriminate against fighting styles. While the military was strict, requiring the use of a one-handed weapon with a shield or a large two-handed weapon, the Brotherhood of the Dark Flame did not mind if its members fought with two weapons like outlaws. It was actually encouraged as it would help them blend into less savory crowds. If Byron was being honest with himself, it was for those reasons that he wished to join the society. His strengths would not be viewed as a weakness, or social faux pas, but as an asset.

"Alright boys, time to begin. I hope you have all considered what you want do with your lives, and have given some semblance of thought into your decision. Custom dictates that each one of you will have a maximum of two minutes after receiving your offers to accept one of them," said Levren. He held an arm out towards the men on stage. "I will now turn the event over to the control of the masters," he started to turn and paused as if a thought had just occurred to him. "Oh, and if any of you darling boys decide to cause trouble for the masters or insult them in any way….," he let his voice trail off, the threat dangling in the air as a small sinister smile of all teeth split his face.

Byron watched intently as the man dressed as a thief approached the front of the stage. Byron's brow furrowed as he tried to puzzle out what the man could possibly be doing here. There was no way that Captain Levren would allow a noble's son to become a thief. Many societies were not present at the fort, as the nobles only permitted what they deemed respectable, scholarly, and militaristic professions to be present at the selection gathering. Usually, it was the more martial based societies that went first. Which meant that something unusual was happening.

The ragged man cleared his voice and began to address the assembly. Byron leaned forward as did every trainee, curious as to what the man would say. "My dear boys! How would you like to live a life full of mystery? Where you hold the power to make things disappear from beneath watchful eyes?" It was common practice amongst the societies to boast about what they could offer in order to try to sway the young pliable minds of their coveted recruits. Every master was at least in some small part a salesman and a showman.

Byron glanced around the room again. Every single recruit looked puzzled. Jeron tilted his head slightly toward Byron and whispered, "Yeah, he conveniently forgot to mention that if you get caught, the law will make you disappear just as quickly." Byron stifled the beginnings of a smile and turned his attention back to the ragged man on stage preaching the life of a thief.

"—and when it's all over you can disappear!" With that statement the man threw off his long and ragged cloak and ripped off his battered tunic. Beneath the tunic was a clean shirt with the symbol of the Society of Mirrors. Home of the Illusionists.

The crowd gasped and a few boys let out childlike laughs of glee. The man took out a cloth and slowly wiped the makeup and dirt from his face, revealing a dignified man completely different from the dirty man who had stood on stage just mere seconds before. "Now which of you boys are worthy enough to learn the art and magic of illusions?"

"You mean cheap alleyway tricks and sleight of hand," murmured Dalton.

Byron gave a slight nod of his head in agreement. Magic in the realm was rare and vastly ineffective. The different societies that proclaimed themselves as practitioners of magic did little of the sort. Calling themselves a collection of scholars would be a more apt title. While they studied numerous old tomes of the occult, only the strongest could muster up a ball of fire about the size of a man's hand, and that feat was terribly taxing. Most of the magical societies dabbled in the area of science. Creating new artifacts that to the masses seemed like magic. If they could do more, they did not advertise that to the public. Being burned alive or lynched was a great motivator for secrecy.

The illusionist scanned the room as if he did not know which boy he was going to select. Finally, his gaze fell upon one of the trainees. "Barith! I hereby offer you the position of trainee in the Society of Mirrors!"

The guild master for the warriors stepped forward. "I hereby offer you the position of trainee in the Fist of Steel."

"I hereby offer you the position of trainee in the Valiant Guard," said another.

The ceremony commenced as various society masters stepped forward and offered Barith the opportunity to join them. Barith's face was contorted into a mask of half horror and half jubilation. Tradition held that the first selection by a society was a boy that the societies dubbed a good trainee but not an elite trainee. One who would jump at the opportunity to be able to join the society of his choosing. A trainee that the society masters would like to have, but would not lose sleep if they missed out on. Such was the reasoning behind the system and Barith's reaction. He was embarrassed. He had just been pronounced as slightly better than mediocre before his peers. It was a backhanded compliment that everyone would be sure to remember.

Byron frowned as the situation did not make much sense. Barith was an ass, sure, but mediocre? He was far better than that. And why have the illusionists choose first? Something strange was occurring. Did the masters seek to teach

Barith a lesson? Byron erased the frown from his face and returned his focus to the proceedings.

"I-I choose to join the Fist of Steel," stammered Barith, as he quickly sat down and squirmed uncomfortably on his bench.

The master from the Fist of Steel inclined his head slightly at his choice, satisfied that he acquired a recruit. The ragged Illusionist reacted to the decision with a small smile that failed to reach his eyes. With that rejection the selection process could turn into an arduous labor for him. It would be quite a bit before he was able to make another selection.

It just did not make sense though. Why break with tradition to allow the illusionist to go first? And why would an illusionist select Barith, a boy not widely renowned for his brains? Was some sort of deal brokered between the illusionists and the warriors?

"It doesn't make sense," muttered Byron quietly to himself. Jeron gave him a sidelong glance but said nothing as he was trying to pay close attention to the draft.

The process started to fly by quickly as the first boys that were selected knew exactly where they wanted to go. Roughly a fifth of the boys had been selected. Most of whom were in the middle of the class and fell just short of being included with the upper trainees.

It appeared to Byron that the masters were being conservative with their selections. Acquiring a quality member who would be appreciative and loyal was undoubtedly better in their minds than trying to land one of the best trainees and failing. And then having to deal with the impressionable boys having just witnessed the master being rejected? No. The risks would most likely come later.

CHAPTER FIVE

J eron tried to force himself not to shift and squirm in his seat. He kept his face blank and schooled his features into an expression of indifference. He needed to be professional, act like a man. It would not do to show his nervousness on a day that everyone was sure to remember. Byron would be sure to poke fun at him later if he caught him fidgeting.

The thought of Byron caused Jeron to turn and appraise his best friend's demeanor. Byron sat on the bench with a slight slouch to his shoulders and a cocksure grin on his face. He took confidence to a level bordering near arrogant. Jeron felt the corners of his mouth tug at the sight. Byron was a firebrand if there ever was one. He was a stickler for doing what he thought was right even if it meant breaking the rules, laws, or regulations. However, what was right, and what Byron wanted to do were sometimes indistinguishable to Byron. That difference had led to some rather unfortunate misunderstandings through the years. None of which were resolved by talking.

Before coming to Raven's Perch, the three of them would regularly sneak out of the palace in search of what Byron referred to as fun, or what Captain Levren deemed as brawling. Jeron knew they never actively went looking for trouble, it just happened to find them. They would be out around town and Byron would see something that he just could not abide. A man beating his wife, a mugging, a band of drunkards out looking for fights, or anything else that spelled trouble. It was not their fault that a majority of these encounters happened in taverns or just outside.

Their adventures subsided after arriving at Raven's Perch. There just was not much that passed for fun or trouble in the remote fort. But Byron still found a way to defy authority. The three of them learned that justice for their fun knew no time or place, and apparently neither did the Captain's capacity for creative punishments.

Byron was arguably the most talented out of the trio, but Jeron, despite what he said, doubted the prince would receive that many offers. The scholarly societies did not hold him in too high of regard. They saw him as a man with raw physical and mental power, but lacking in restraint and discipline. That was fine with Byron, as his oft professed point of view of the scholars was that they were stuffy men who pretended to know a great deal about nothing of value.

Jeron did not know what to expect for himself. Dalton said that he was sure Jeron would be overwhelmed with offers, but Jeron was not certain. He had also snuck out and partook in Byron's brawls, but unlike Byron, he had not yet had a personal confrontation with Captain Levren while at Raven's Perch. There was no telling how much weight the societies would place upon those actions. For all he knew, he could be shunned for the fights, or they could be overlooked since he lacked Byron's bloodlines with its inherent expectations, and Bryon's precarious relationship with their gruff commanding officer.

Upon the stage stood a member of the society of wizards describing the wondrous energies that made up their work. Jeron doubted that they would select him. Generally, the societies that specialized in magic drew their ranks from the younger sons and daughters of important nobles. That strategy was designed to gain acceptance of magic by the noble houses, and if something were to happen to the eldest son, have a wizard gain a powerful title. Also, the strategy had proven to open a market to whom the wizards could peddle their gadgets and devices.

Being the fourth child of a relatively minor lord, from an all but dead house, the odds of the wizard calling his name were small. Besides, everyone knew that his heart was set on becoming a paladin. He had not made a secret of that over the years. Jeron allowed himself a slight nervous grin, if anything he should be able to relax and remain unseen until the next battle centric society appeared.

"Jeron!" shouted a voice awakening him from his reverie. "I hereby offer you the position of trainee in the Eldritch Society," bellowed the representative of the wizards.

Jeron was stunned. Could this be happening? He went over the wizard's statement in his head. Everything was said correctly. Only his first name had been used as tradition demanded. Why were the wizards offering him a position? He had little experience in the mystical, unlike Byron who had made it a habit and a game to sneak into their training sessions back at the palace.

Byron.

Jeron allowed himself a mental chuckle. Of course. Byron. The wizards were not stupid. They knew of his friendship to Byron. If they offered Jeron a position in their society, a position that he scarcely even considered growing up, then maybe in the heat of the moment he might accept their offer. If the best friend of the second son of the Duke of Antier joined their society, then maybe the duke's son would accept an offer as well. It was a ludicrous strategy, and not one that would endear the wizards to Jeron if he figured it out.

The other society masters stepped forward and all began speaking at once. Jeron blinked his eyes. He could hardly understand with what they were saying. It was like trying to decipher what a gaggle of pigeons was saying. "What are they saying?" he stammered to Byron. "Which societies?"

"Why all of them," said Byron in grave voice followed by a light chuckle.

"What?!" Jeron could scarcely believe it. He expected a few of the societies to offer him, but not all.

"Well, are you going to accept or just sit there looking like a half-wit?" a smiling Byron chided. "Time's a wasting."

Jeron took a deep breath and stood up, sparing a quick glance around the room. Dalton looked astounded. Awed expressions were set on the faces of the other trainees, and a bunch of nervous society masters shifted their weight as they fidgeted on the platform. The scholars were the worst at hiding their nerves, constantly shifting in stark contrast to fighters that stood stoically beside them on the stage.

"I choose to join The Holy Guard," declared Jeron in what he hoped was a clear, strong, and confident voice.

Jeron sighed and sat down on the bench. He could feel the stress slide off of his shoulders. It was all over, and his dream came true. He was going to be a paladin. A knight in service to the Duke of Antier and the Church. Serve the realm. Protect the weak. That would be enough.

Jeron shifted his weight and attempted to get comfortable, which proved nearly impossible. How was one supposed to sit still when he had just set the path for his future? He could not stop his hands from trembling. What if he had made a mistake? Breathing steadily, he looked up and surveyed the room.

Everyone was staring at him.

Jeron stared back at the crowd. He wetted his lips as his brain raced down the paths of possibilities. He knew that something strange must be going on. Everyone's faces confirmed that fact. Maybe it was one of Dalton's elaborate pranks. Dalton could have convinced everyone ahead of time to stare at him after his selection in an attempt to embarrass him. People liked Dalton. He had an affable nature and a warm personality that people gravitated towards. It was all a joke. Right?

Jeron wrangled his brain, trying to find an answer. Worry slowly started to creep onto his face and he looked desperately towards Byron for aid.

Byron shrugged his shoulders as if the matter was inconsequential, leaned down and whispered, "No trainee in Antier has ever been accepted to *all* societies. Mostly due to the religious differences. Sometimes the person's body or brain is lacking. They're all stunned and a little bit in awe right now. Clearly, they don't know you that well."

Comprehension slowly dawned on Jeron. He sat there stunned trying to process what he had just heard while ignoring Byron's joke. Through some convoluted process of his own talents, and a mixture of societal politics, he, Jeron, son of a deceased minor lord, had just become the most decorated trainee in Antier since...ever.

"No pressure, eh?" said a grinning Byron as he gave Jeron a hearty slap on the back.

Jeron narrowed his eyes. Something was wrong with Byron's face. His eyes looked tight and his smile forced. To the rest of the crowd Byron looked happy, but Jeron could plainly see ill-concealed stress on his friend's face. Jeron knew that Byron was happy for him, but what could be eating at him? Jealously maybe? That did not sound like Byron.

As Jeron stared at his friend, the next society master stepped forward to place his selection. Byron turned his attention back to the stage and eased his body into as relaxed a pose as he could manage with his legs stretched out. Jeron saw Byron's eyes twitch quickly to the side of the stage and then back straight ahead. The time it took Byron's eyes to complete the journey was less than a second, but it was enough for Jeron. He looked to the side of the stage and found his answer.

Captain Levren was leaning against the wall of the room with a satisfied grin on his face. Jeron thought he knew why. Levren was satisfied because no matter how many offers Byron received; it was not going to be enough to match his own. Word would quickly spread through the land that some unknown son of an unknown dead minor noble was accepted to every society. Word would also travel just as quickly that the infamous son of the duke did not manage that feat, and maybe that he did not come anywhere close to that number.

Then the whispers would begin again in every noble's hall, marketplace, and tavern across Antier that the totemless son of the duke was again a disappointment. Some would say that he was just a late bloomer, which was natural among the populace. More would undoubtedly state that every powerful noble's son was an early bloomer, including Byron's own brother. And Jeron knew that was the cause of Byron's distress. Wherever he went the whispers and gossip would start up and the frustration would build up in Byron again. Byron would claim that the pressure and the whispers did not bother him, but Jeron knew otherwise. For years he had seen those pressures eat at his friend and contribute to his willful behavior and shunning of cultural norms. It was one of the main reasons Jeron went out in search of "fun" with Byron. He supported his friend. It was that simple.

Jeron returned his attention back to the stage as some trainee whom he did not know accepted a position within a society. He felt his mirth and excitement begin to die down as the magnitude of the situation set in. While tonight's events would make him famous throughout the duchy, it would also increase Byron's notoriety, and the burden he carried on his shoulders. How could he remain jubilant when the boy who had been like a brother to him for years was going through hell?

Jeron felt the shame wash over him and he embraced it. He was a terrible person to feel happy, and he knew it.

A sharp elbow dug into his side. "Cheer up will you," whispered Byron. "You look like you just got caught stealing a pie from kitchen. Stop feeling guilty over something that you have no control over."

"I am not feeling guilty," insisted Jeron. Byron rolled his eyes. "Okay, fine. But I feel dirty man....and I've never stolen a pie from the kitchen."

"Really?" asked Byron. "Your loss."

The middle-aged wraith stepped forward on the platform and the room went silent. Not even a whisper could be heard amongst the gathered boys. The Brotherhood of the Dark Flame had long served as the intelligence officers for the kingdom. Whispers attached other titles to their names: assassins, warlocks, rumormongers, gamblers, pirates, thieves, mercenaries. They were viewed as an unfortunate necessity to running a duchy. A duke must be aware of what is going on in other duchies as well as his own. Including schemes by other dukes, court intrigue, banditry, and any scrap of information on what the king might do.

Trust was always an issue when dealing with the Dark Flame. The society was employed by the kingdom, individual duchies, societies, merchant guilds, and those wealthy enough to afford their services. The Dark Flame prided themselves on never having a member betray their employer. They had many members though, and many a noble had been found dead under curious circumstances over the years. The trail never pointed to *his* hired wraith of course. And while it was often suspected by the populace that a wraith had murdered his employer, it had never been proven, and everyone politely assumed that a different member of the Dark Flame may have committed the murder. Or the employer could have died of any number of natural causes without the aid of a wraith.

The rumors persisted and the cloud of mystery around the wraiths darkened. And the Brotherhood of the Dark Flame made little to no attempt to stop them. The rumors added to their mystique, and mystique was good for business.

The thought of them made goosebumps spread across Jeron's skin. Assassins that skulked in the night bothered him. A real man would engage his opponent in open honorable combat.

The wraith was a large man built like a bull. He had short cropped brown hair and a goatee that was just beginning to have grey creep in. His face was like granite with deep lines radiating out from his eyes. Those eyes bothered Jeron. They looked as if they were judging and laughing at you at the same time. One surreptitious glance around the room confirmed that belief. Boys who would one day grow up to lead the duchy were fidgeting, biting their lips, averting their gaze, and letting their discomfort show plain across their faces.

Pathetic. They should have learned by now to control their emotions. Jeron's eyes hardened. Letting your guard slip for even a second could cost someone their life. It was weakness, and the actions of prey, not a predator.

That line of thinking was not relevant at the moment, Jeron thought to himself as he refocused his gaze upon the stage. Besides, it looked as if the man was about to speak.

The laughing eyes swept their gaze over the assembly and began to speak in a slow deliberate manner. "My name is Tyson Orgun. I am here to represent The Brotherhood of the Dark Flame in our selection of initiates. And I can see there are so many brave boys gathered here." This Tyson controlled his face so well that Jeron could not tell if he was mocking the group or paying them a compliment. Most likely the former.

"I have observed all of you in your training, as well as asking Captain Levren his opinions of you all, and I have reached a decision." Jeron thought that one particular boy (Atticus perhaps was his name?) looked as if he had just saw a ghost and was praying not to hear his name called.

"Byron! I hereby offer you the position of initiate in the Brotherhood of the Dark Flame!"

This was it! Jeron glanced at Byron expectantly. This was the moment for which everyone in the room was waiting. What was the impulsive youngest son of the duke going to do with his life? Dalton was looking at Byron with a massive smile plastered on his face despite not having heard his own name called yet. Jeron was vaguely aware that his face was a mirror of Dalton's.

If you could not smile for a friend's success, then when could you show emotion, thought Jeron. Besides, it was not like lives were in the balance at the moment. He could afford to let his guard down briefly.

Strangely enough, Byron was not smiling. Why? Jeron glanced to the stage and found the reason why his friend lacked all emotion.

Only two society masters stood on the stage.

A surprised murmur began to rise among the boys as others made the same observation. Dalton was squeezing the bridge of his nose with his right index finger and thumb as if he had a headache. Captain Levren had a self-satisfied smirk on his face. Jeron was making a valiant effort at turning his face to stone. Everyone was looking straight at Byron, and Jeron did not intend to make matters worse with his facial expressions.

The other society master on stage was none other than the paladin society master. Jeron silently cursed. The court gossip would run wild for sure. Only two offers for Duke Cedric's son, and of course one of them had to be from the society that called the duke and Byron's older brother members. It certainly seemed like a pity offer, and a favor to Byron's family.

The room was uncomfortably silent. It seemed to Jeron as if no one was even breathing. As if the intake of breath would ruin the moment and everyone would miss the fiery explosion or embarrassed stuttering that was sure to come. It would be the talk of the duchy for the next decade, and everyone present would be the center of attention at social gatherings. Everyone wanted to hear a good story, especially at the expense of someone else. And the entire room sensed that this would be a good story. Especially considering that the last time Byron lost his temper he wound up assaulting Captain Levren with a spoon. Something had been said about the Captain's mother resembling a pig, a few punches were thrown, and the Captain had received a broken nose. Jeron groaned inwardly at the memory, this was going to be a disaster.

After what seemed like an eternity, maybe six seconds, Byron cracked a large beaming smile. The room seemed to deflate as people exhaled, the tension being chased from the room with a simple smile. However, Jeron's shoulders tensed. The last time Byron smiled like that...merciful God. He started that brawl with those two mercenaries in that tavern. What was it called? The Swinging Lantern? The Coy Maiden? It hardly mattered. The problem was that Jeron could not protect Byron from himself here.

"I choose to join The Brotherhood of the Dark Flame," declared Byron with what could only be described as a wry smirk for the chorus of gasps that met his pronouncement.

Great, thought Jeron. Byron just shunned his father's society to join a band of spies and killers, with a dubious reputation throughout the kingdom. Jeron doubted they would get to the mess hall before Byron found himself embroiled in a fight.

Jeron surveyed the room. A few wide-eyed expressions and slack-jawed idiots greeted his gaze. The idiots probably did not fully comprehend the gravity of the situation. It was all simply gossip to them.

And then there was Barith. Fat and pompous Barith sitting on his bench with a self-satisfied smirk plastered on his face and a malicious glint in his eyes as he looked back over his shoulder at Byron.

Forget the mess hall. It would be a miracle if they made it out of the room without Byron's temper igniting.

And they were going to serve pie tonight in the mess. Too bad.

At least the night could not get any worse.

***

"This night can't get any worse," groaned Dalton.

The masters were filing out of the room as the ceremony came to a close. Only Captain Levren remained on stage. He had a jovial expression and looked as if he had enjoyed the ceremony a little too much.

"You will all meet back here after breakfast for more training so that you won't become too big of disappointments to the ducal army," said Levren. "After lunch you all will meet back here again where you will commence training with your new society masters. You all are dismissed. Try not to get into too much trouble tonight. I would just hate to have to find some sort of punishment for you louts." With that he exited the stage and departed the room behind the society masters.

"This night can't possibly get any worse," repeated Dalton.

"Yes, we gathered that the first time," said Jeron.

"Whining just isn't very becoming of the realm's newest paladin," replied Byron as he nudged Jeron with an elbow and tossed him a wink.

"What?!" hissed Dalton in outrage. "You think this is funny?" His face was starting to turn a shade of bright red. "I was not even offered to join the society that I wanted!" The cords in his neck were sticking out. "It was my dream and those...those...those gods cursed cavaliers didn't even so much as offer me! How could you possibly think this is funny?"

Byron and Jeron broke into laughter at Dalton's indignation. "Well, if you could see your face right now, I'm sure you would agree with us," chuckled Jeron.

Byron chortled and tossed his arm up over Dalton's shoulder and whispered in a mock conspiratorial voice. "Besides, now you can keep tabs on Jeron instead of being forced to kill him for flimsy religious reasons." The crowd had started to thin and the boys began making their way towards the door. "It works out perfectly," continued Byron. "Instead of two friends being twisted into a rivalry by some silly society dispute, you two can remain friends and fight the honorable fights without me."

"Oh, and just where are you going to be?" queried Dalton.

"Well, you know, spy things. Skulking in the dark, midnight rendezvous, engaging in romances with exotic women, and visiting taverns from all over the realms." Byron sighed. "Or spend my time talking to pompous diplomats and visiting with their timid mindless daughters. All while being kept away from military action and strong adventurous women for the sake of the duchy. You know, princely activities."

"Why I do believe that you hath insulted me you lout" sniffed Dalton with an exaggerated aristocratic accent. He stuck his nose up in the air and continued in his most haughty tone. "It will be an apology or your head, sir for that slight. How dare you besmirch our company! A duel I say! But first there must be a banquet! Yes! We shall invite all of the nobles to a grand feast. Ask them to bring their daughters, we'll find you a – oh shit."

"Huh? What?" asked a confused Jeron as he looked around in concern. The corridor emptied out into a courtyard where Barith, Timver, and a pack of other boys had cornered a skinny red headed boy. They were shoving, punching, harassing, name-calling, and anything else that they could think of to make the poor boy's life miserable.

And Byron was almost halfway towards the group. Jeron had not even noticed him leave. "Oh shit is right," whispered Jeron.

"Double shit," swore Dalton.

"What now?" sighed Jeron.

Coming out of a room on the other side of the courtyard was Captain Levren and a few of the masters. Judging by their disapproving expressions they were quickly becoming aware of the situation, and were none too pleased about it. Jeron glanced back at the brewing mess. There were five boys cornering the skinny boy, and they counted Barith among their number. There was no way Byron could take all of them in a fair fight. And judging from the night's previous events and Byron's body language, the last thing on Byron's mind was a fair fight. Still, even with the element of surprise the outcome would be no sure thing.

Barith never even saw the first blow. One moment he was standing above the smaller boy and the next he was bouncing off of the cobble stones as a pool of blood began to spread from his broken nose. Jeron began to sprint towards the fracas. Byron's next blow struck Timver straight in the ribs. There was a loud crack and a gasp as Timver fell to his knees gasping for a breath that would not come.

Jeron was almost to the fight when he heard Levren roaring over the din of combat. He could not hear the words, but he could make out the tone. This was not going to end well. He ducked under a clumsily thrown punch by a stocky boy with dirty blonde hair. Jeron's counter-punch connected with the other boy's eye socket eliciting a most gratifying squeal as the boy dropped to the ground clutching his eye.

There was not even time to look for another opponent. Captain Levren was standing directly behind the fallen boy, murder in his eyes. Jeron spared a quick glance around to survey the action. Byron and the remaining boys had been subdued by the masters. Barith was spitting blood and curses from his mouth while trying to staunch the flow of blood from his nose.

"Oh, you all will regret this," said Levren with a dark chuckle. "I promise you that before this night is over you will all regret this."

High overhead lightning flashed and thunder roared with a rattling clap. Jeron let out a sigh.

And there was going to be pie in the mess too.

CHAPTER SIX

"Your temper is going to get me killed" screamed Jeron as yet another lightning bolt flashed across the night sky, splintering into numerous jagged branches of light.

The rain was pouring down in diagonal sheets, effectively blinding Jeron outside of a few feet. Each drop felt like a small dart striking upon Jeron's exposed face. The wind slashed straight through his armor, each gust a knife carved out of ice. His clothing had long since stopped protecting him from the elements. Worse, they had betrayed him as the fabric held in the rain, making his armor feel twice as heavy and thrice as miserable.

"You didn't have to cheat you know. You could have fought a fair fight and won," continued Jeron. "Well? Are you going to say anything? We are enjoying guard duty in this lovely weather because of you, and frankly, I'm not going anywhere any time soon. For the rest of the night actually. Might as well have a conversation."

"You cheat, you live longer. The math is simple to me." Byron shrugged, "Besides, it wasn't like they were planning on having a fair fight. It was one against, what? Four?"

"Five."

"Fine. Five. Wasn't like they didn't deserve the beating," said Byron.

"I agree. But was it necessary for you to administer it? And hit Timver with those brass knuckles? You broke two of his ribs."

"Timver?" asked Byron innocently.

"Yeah. The skinny kid with Barith. You know, he knocked you down in training a few days ago, and then you broke his ribs a few hours ago? That Timver," said Jeron drily.

"Oh, so that's his name. Never bothered to learn it," said Byron.

"Still find people you deem worthless and incompetent to be beneath you? How...*regal*," mocked Jeron.

"Ouch that stung," chuckled Byron as he placed his hand of his heart as if he had been stabbed, "You wound me though. Brass knuckles? Do you really think I would have to stoop so low to beat those gravel-brained fools in any kind of fight?"

"No. I don't think you *had* to do it, but I think you still did it anyway," replied Jeron. "Care to admit to using the brass knuckles?"

"Nope." A smile started to tug at the corners of Byron's mouth, "Buuut, you have to admit, it was a pretty good punch." Byron removed his left hand off of his spear and twirled a set of brass knuckles around his fingers. "Now where did these come from? What a coincidence." With a flick of his wrist, the weapon vanished as quickly as it had appeared.

Jeron chuckled and shook his head in disbelief. For months he had been trying to figure out where Byron hid the brass knuckles, but he had yet to figure out the trick to Byron's sleight of hand. Yet.

Jeron turned his attention back to the courtyard and tried to focus his mind on making at least a passable attempt at being a sentinel.

It was the same courtyard where the fight with Barith had taken place earlier in the evening. Captain Levren had assigned Jeron and Byron to guard the courtyard as punishment. The ground had long since turned into a pool of water and mud, making the pair's circuitous rounds along the courtyard in their waterlogged gear even more difficult.

Levren said they were protecting the fort against brigands and thugs tonight. Very cute. The captain may as well have said that the fort needed protecting from the two of them. Jeron wondered what punishment Captain Levren had doled out to Barith and Timver. He probably had them keeping watch over the infirmary. Jeron smiled warmly at the thought. Suddenly patrolling the courtyard did not seem so terrible.

"So why'd you follow me?" Byron asked as he kicked a pebble across the courtyard. "You didn't have to join the fight. Especially if you thought I would win."

"To keep you from getting killed. Just because I thought you would win doesn't mean it was guaranteed. All it would take is one lucky punch from one of them and you would have a cracked skull," replied Jeron. He paused slightly before continuing. "And because you'd do the same for me."

"True. I could've handled them though," said Byron.

"Sure."

"Heh. Question for ya. If you fought because I would do the same for you, does this mean that I don't have to step in for Dalton the next time he gets in a fight?" asked Byron.

"Yup, that sounds logical to me," replied Jeron. "That's at least two fights where he has miraculously vanished on us."

"Alright, just checking," said Byron as he kicked another pebble.

"Well, it doesn't sound good to me," said a voice from inside a nearby corridor. Jeron turned to see Dalton standing in the doorway with the small red headed boy they had saved. The boy had a shy smile on his face and was carrying a small bundle in his hands. By the looks of the cloth covering, the package had been hastily assembled. "It's not my fault that I was blessed with the foresight to see that charging straight into a fight wasn't the best plan," continued Dalton. "Besides, if I had gone to fight, I would now be suffering the wrath of dear Captain Levren, and then who would have found and taken care of Cole here?"

"Fair enough," laughed Byron. "It's certainly not the first time you've ran from a fight."

"Or the last," chirped Jeron.

"Yes," Dalton agreed, nodding his head sagely, "I'm wise beyond my years in that regard. Also, I was wise enough to advise Cole here to bring you two diligent sentinels a gift."

"A gift?" asked Jeron. He glanced over at Byron who shrugged, a quizzical expression on his face.

"Why yes of course a gift," continued Dalton. "That's the proper thing to do when being presented before royalty. You see Cole, the one who looks like he thinks he can kill me with a scowl is Prince Byron. Call him Prince, sir, milord, my lord, Highness, or any other title and he's liable to commit a homicide." Dalton swept his arm out before him and bowed in a grandiose fashion usually reserved for nobles in court. "Milord."

"You-" sputtered Byron.

"Yes. I am brilliant. Thank you, Your Highness." Dalton turned back to Cole. "And you see the other one right there is Jeron. I know he's hard to see behind that mangled thing he calls a mane of hair. It truly is hideous. I know. But it only comes out when he gets angry. He must have forgotten to groom himself after the fight."

Jeron reached his hand up to his face. Sure enough, the mane of hair had sprouted from his skin. "Why didn't you say anything?" he growled at Byron.

Byron shrugged, "Didn't really notice it. But I vote we kill Dalton."

"Agreed."

"Quickly, Cole, show them what you brought with you and all will be forgiven," laughed Dalton. "Do it for my sake."

Cole stepped up in the doorway next to Dalton and unfolded his bundle. Inside were the two most glorious meat pies that Jeron had ever seen. The smell of roasted meat and accompanying vegetables made Jeron's stomach growl audibly and his mouth water.

"I thought you two might be hungry so I snatched a pair of meat pies from the mess," said Cole shyly.

Upon second glance Jeron realized that the boy was not all that small. He was of similar height to Byron and of similar build to Dalton. He was just a skinny boy of above average height. He had pale blue eyes and short straight red hair. Cole's complexion was fair, but strangely lacking the freckles that Jeron had grown accustomed to seeing on red haired people. The end result was the boy had haunting sad features with a face that seemed set in a perpetual frown.

"Dalton told me what your punishment was," said Cole. "I felt bad that you guys were out here in the rain because of me. I'm sorry."

"Sorry for what?" asked Byron. "Sorry that Barith was born an ass and thinks with it?"

"But-," stammered Cole.

"Precisely," Jeron interjected. "But that's not what's important Cole. If Barith or any of the other boys try to pick on you again, just come find one us, even Dalton. We'll look out after you."

"Really?" Cole asked hesitantly. He looked rather uncertain to Jeron. As if he was not used to the prospect of trusting the people at the fort, or maybe anywhere else.

"Really," said Byron. He cracked his knuckles, "Besides, it's a rare pleasure to administer a beating to someone who has unquestionably earned it."

"Are you two going to eat those meat pies or talk them to death?" asked Dalton. Jeron and Byron laughed and picked up their respective dinners. "So Cole," Dalton slapped his hand down on the smaller boy's shoulder, "is it true what the other boys say? Are you like Byron here? You a late bloomer totem wise?"

"Dalton!" hissed Jeron midway through a bite of meat pie.

"No, no, it's okay," said Cole. "I'm not like Byron," he shrugged apologetically at Byron, "I do have a totem."

Jeron glanced at Byron out of the corner of his eye. His shoulders had sagged for the briefest of moments. "I just like to keep that fact a secret," continued Cole. "My totem is that of a chameleon. It helps me hide from people. Including the other boys here so they can't beat me. Watch." Cole pressed up against the stone wall and he began to melt out of sight. Jeron blinked his eyes. Where a moment before the boy had stood, now his eyes could only perceive the stone wall no matter how hard he tried to focus.

"Impressive," whistled Dalton. He leaned over and placed his hand where Cole had stood. His hand met resistance before reaching the wall.

"I don't disappear," said Cole as he began to phase back into their vision. "I just blend in to where the human eye cannot discern the difference between me and whatever is behind me."

"Even aided by totems?" asked Dalton.

"Ask the lion," replied Cole.

Jeron felt his brow furrow. Was Cole smirking at him? "No, I couldn't see him. Not even with help of the lion," confirmed Jeron.

"That's how you got the meat pies and avoided Barith for so long," stated Byron. It was not a question so much as him thinking out loud.

"Yes," replied Cole. "It's also why I think I was chosen to be a wraith."

"Ah so you're the other wraith," said Byron as he licked the final crumbs off his fingers. "I knew someone else had their named called, but I was wrapped up in my own situation at the time. So, I know you can hide pretty damn well, but do you know how to fight?"

"Only what Captain Levren has taught us," answered Cole.

"Ahh so you know how to soldier," said Byron. "I'll teach you how to fight."

"Byron, don't," said Jeron immediately.

"Listen to Jeron, Byron. You could cause the kid to get into trouble before we can get him out of it," pleaded Dalton.

"What do you say Cole? Do you want to learn how to fight?" asked Byron as he pointedly ignored his friends' advice.

"Yes, he does," answered a voice from behind Jeron.

Jeron turned around and a mental groan issued through his brain. Standing before him were Masters Tyson and Maxus. They stood still with military calm and silently appraised the boys as the rain ran down their heavy cloaks. After a few moments Master Tyson resumed speaking.

"Cole, with the work you're going to be doing it's imperative that you learn how to fight. Which includes brawling. Your life *will* depend on it at some point. I can guarantee that. Learn everything you can from Byron. In the little free time he'll have of course."

"Um excuse me, sir" asked Byron. "But what do you mean by 'little free time'?"

"What he means is that'll you'll be spending the rest of your free time with me," answered Master Maxus. "You are too big of an asset to this duchy to spend your time being only a wraith. It has been determined from higher on up that you need to grow up. So you're going to be spending the rest of your time training to be a knight."

"You'll be a soldier, a spy, a diplomat, a general, an assassin, or anything else that your brother may require when he takes your father's place," said Tyson.

Byron's eyes narrowed before he spoke, "I have one question sirs."

Jeron closed his eyes. This sort of confrontation never turned out well for Byron.

"And what pray tell is that?" asked Tyson in a deadpan.

"Am I undergoing this extra training because my father asked it as I'm valuable to the duchy, or am I undergoing this oh so *wonderful* honor because my totem hasn't come in yet?" asked Byron. While his face may have been calm, the last words came out as a snarl.

Jeron grabbed Byron's arm. "What the hell do you think you're doing you idiot," he hissed. "Try not to get both of your instructors pissed at you."

"It's okay Jeron. We expected him to be angry," said Maxus. "Given his reputation it was near a certainty. But, Jeron, we're also going to have to work on your behavior as well. It won't do to have one of the Prince's knights constantly grabbing him and correcting him in public. Byron's going to have to learn to control his temper on his own."

Master Tyson stepped forward and placed his hand on Byron's shoulder. "As to your question: No. This duty was not selected for you based on your lack of totem. It *was* picked however because of your importance to the duchy." Tyson placed his other hand on Jeron's shoulder and let loose an evil grin that in Jeron's opinion was not very becoming of a paladin, soldier, or any other decent profession.

"This next bit however *is* because of your lack of a totem," Maxus said as he opened his arms wide towards all of the boys and took a step forward. "Congratulations Jeron and Dalton! You are now Byron's royal bodyguards.

Now now boys, no groaning. We're just making official what has long been an assumed formality. And Cole, don't think that I've forgotten about you."

Jeron looked around and to his astonishment Cole started to materialize next to the door. His face was red and he was looking down at his feet, mortified at being caught up in the situation.

"So-sorry sir. It won't happen again," stammered Cole.

"You're damn right it won't," said Maxus. "I don't allow my knights to be cowardly and bashful."

Cole gaped, "A knight sir?"

Tyson grinned, "Of course, Cole. We can't allow the Prince's Shadow to be out gallivanting around while he's training to be a knight."

"And my knights have backbone in them son," added Master Maxus. "I'll make a man out of you in no time."

"Y-yes sir," stuttered Cole. "Wait! Prince's Shadow?"

"Why of course," said Tyson. "The Prince already has two bodyguards but he will need his own Shadow. His own personal wraith to provide the same services to him as he can provide to his brother. Your similar appearance and build are part of the reason I selected you. However, your martial skills are lacking, and as Prince Byron will almost certainly find himself on the battlefield, you must be schooled in the arts of battle. Your training starts early tomorrow and will last as long as Maxus here deems it necessary. Enjoy the remainder of your guard duty. I expect it will be your last peaceful night for the next few months."

"I'll be expecting the both of you in the evening," said Maxus. His face grew stern and his voice dripped venom. "And if any of you knuckleheads get into another brawl, so help me God, I will make you rue the day your parents met. Young nobles or not, you're under my tutelage now and all of your actions reflect on your brother paladins. And you will represent the paladins with honor. Even if two of you aren't officially members of the order." Maxus gave the boys a curt nod and departed out of the rain with Master Tyson.

Jeron exhaled deeply. He glanced around the courtyard. Cole looked to be caught in a stupor and was starting to glance around looking for aid from any direction. Dalton looked annoyed at the prospect of more duty. And Byron, well Byron no longer seemed to be angry. In fact, he looked like he was amused.

"Byron, are you okay?" asked Jeron hesitantly.

"Yeah I'm fine Jeron," said Byron. He grinned wryly, "I was just thinking that at least we got to have some pie before they send us through hell."

Dalton groaned. "And you sound so happy about that." He turned to Cole. "I told you that we shouldn't have come out here and should have kept the pie to ourselves. All we get out of this is more work and responsibility." Dalton rolled his eyes and punched Cole playfully in the shoulder. "What do you think of that buddy?"

Cole looked up at Dalton dumbfounded. "I'm a knight now?" He asked quizzically.

Jeron could not help it, he burst into laughter as the rain continued to drench him.

CHAPTER SEVEN

C ole stretched his legs. His muscles were sore and had been that way for days. The training the past few weeks was brutal. After the first few days his body had felt rigid, like it was one of those suits of armor on display in the fort. His muscles had refused to straighten to their full length. It had taken nearly a week for him to fully straighten his arms. Now his muscles, while stronger, no longer locked up on him. Instead, they just felt heavy and exhausted on most days like metal ropes dangling from his shoulders.

During the initial training, Cole attempted to avoid fighting as much as humanely possible, and as a general rule of thumb, tried to sneak around whenever it was feasible. But he was finding it impossible to blend in during this new training regimen. Masters Tyson and Maxus seemed to know where he was at all times, and none of his previous tricks worked.

Pain flashed in Cole's right wrist, snapping him out of his momentary reverie and causing his sword to fall, clattering upon the wooden practice floor. Cole rubbed his sore wrist as a sword point was placed at his throat. And at the other end of the blade was Dalton brushing blonde hair out of his eyes with his free hand while directing a very self-satisfied smirk in Cole's direction.

Training to be a paladin was already a pain, and in more ways than one. He had planned to keep his head down, maybe join the military, or a society that could help bolster his social status and maybe, just maybe, restore his family name into something worthy of a modicum of respect.

Instead, Cole found himself spending time with a prince and his bodyguards. Making enemies of people who could squash him like an insect. While Cole wanted more to his name than just an empty title, he also wanted the opportunity to reap the rewards of his work. At this pace, there may not be enough of his body left for even the military to make use of him.

"Never lose your concentration in a fight or you'll lose your head," said Dalton as he lightly poked his practice sword into Cole's sternum for punctuation.

"Sorry, but I've been finding it hard to concentrate with my legs feeling as if they are made of steel," replied Cole.

"The old sore legs excuse," said Dalton with a chuckle. "They're always the first thing to go. Everyone always thinks sword fighting is all about the arms. They never realize how much stress is put on the legs and the lungs. Fighting is tiring if you are trying to win. Usually, the first person to get tired is the one to lose. The body or mind is a fraction of a second too slow and that's the end. Dead. Does not matter how quick or strong you are if you lack endurance." Dalton stretched his neck and began taking a few steps backwards. "Now get back to your ready position and we'll have another bout. Try to stay on the balls of your feet and move lightly."

Cole groaned in protest, but raised his blade to a ready position. "Why do we even have to learn how to use these?" asked Cole as he gestured towards his rapier. "I was doing just fine with a sword when we trained under Captain Levren."

Dalton grinned maliciously at Cole. "Of course you did my precious little chameleon. Any layman can hack around well enough with a broadsword to act the part of a common soldier. But fencing...ahh fencing is the sport of gentlemen. It's the art of the duel. It's graceful artistry. Now en guarde!"

Dalton lunged at Cole and unleashed a fury of cuts and thrusts. The boy talked as if he was a dandy and enjoyed high society a little too much, but he fought with a hunger about him that Cole had only seen in street urchins. While his speech patterns were annoying, the man was simply ferocious with a blade in his hands, and was a good sparring partner and teacher. Dalton already had a height advantage on Cole, and his long arms gave him even greater reach. And his speed. Cole could hardly fathom how someone could be so fast. Dalton flicked his wrist and it appeared as if the blade was moving in three directions at once. It took all of his concentration and skill to track the rapier and parry the barrage of blows that Dalton directed at him.

Cole overextended trying to parry an attack that never came. The next thing he knew there was another flash of pain as Dalton's sword came up beneath Cole's sword hand and rapped the bottom of his wrist.

"Damn it, Dalton! Why do you keep attacking me there!" Cole asked angrily.

Dalton rolled his eyes. "Because you keep forgetting to defend there." Dalton clapped him on the shoulder. "It's a common beginner's mistake. It's natural to focus your thoughts on protecting your torso. There's enough going on that your brain forgets to protect the part of the body that actually holds the weapon." Dalton shrugged his shoulders nonchalantly causing his lanky arms to flap at his side. "Like I said, a common mistake. That is why we practice though."

Cole winced as he rubbed his wrist, "Seems like a lot to learn for some game."

Dalton arched an eyebrow and the carefree grin came back to his face. "Game? Cole, my lad. You're a paladin now. A knight in service to His Grace. A gentleman. Dueling is the sport of gentlemen. Arguments are won by dueling. Reputations are made. Kingdoms are lost. Ladies favor won," continued Dalton.

"I get the idea," groaned Cole. He surveyed the room and saw all the other knight trainees engaged in similar duels with a variety of weapons. To Cole's untrained eye it appeared as if he was the most unfamiliar with the gentlemanly pastime. That did not bother him too terribly much. Cole was accustomed to being the least skilled in martial pursuits. He also doubted he would find himself engaged in many duels. At least if he had any say in the matter.

"Well maybe we'll make a passable gentleman out of you yet," said Dalton as his eyes also scanned the room. "It's just a matter of getting the basics down really. The fundamentals are the foundation..." Dalton's voice trailed off as his eyes focused on something in the distance.

Cole followed his gaze and saw Jeron engaged in a bout with Byron. Both boys were stripped to their waists. Their chests and arms were covered in sweat and welts. The two boys danced back and forth. Their breathing heavy, their sabers whirling. Back and forth they sparred with neither landing a blow.

After a few passes it became clear to Cole where each boy's strengths lay. Byron nearly lost his blade numerous times trying to block the sheer power behind each of Jeron's strikes. And Jeron was nearly skewered numerous times by Byron's uncanny quickness and deft reflexes.

"You'd never tell how close they were by watching them fight," said Dalton as he stared enthralled at the fight. "They're too damned competitive. This happens every once in a while, Cole. One wins a bout, and then without talking they get into a pissing match trying to one up the other."

"A pissing match?" Cole asked quizzically.

"Never mind," said Dalton dismissively.

"Okaaay," said Cole as he dragged the word out. He had yet to figure Dalton out. The boy kept switching between his foppish dandy affectation, but then his language would slip and he would utter a word such as 'pissing.' "But why do they do that?"

"You really don't know?" asked Dalton with an arched eyebrow. For the first time he seemed genuinely shocked by Cole's lack of knowledge. Enough so that the smirk finally vanished off his face. "Everyone in the duchy talks about Byron and by default that means they talk about Jeron as well. By the gods they were nearly brothers growing up! What rock were you under that you didn't hear their story?"

"Umm," stammered Cole as he grasped for words. "My family's holdings are rather small and umm...I'm not really one for talking much. Never heard much gossip." Cole scratched the back of his head and blushed. "Umm Dalton do you think you could tell me the story?"

"Yeah, sure kid," said Dalton absently, his eyes transfixed on the bout. By now the rest of the room had stopped training and was also focused on the fight. Byron blocked Jeron's blade a few scant inches from his scalp and quickly snapped off a riposte that almost struck Jeron upon the side of his own head before he retreated a few steps. Dalton elicited a soft whistle at the exchange.

"You heard of Flintwood Village?" asked Dalton.

Cole frowned as his brow furrowed in concentration. "I think I heard about it once. Maybe a battle or something of the sort?"

Dalton's jaw clenched and his face darkened. "I'd hardly call it a battle. A massacre is the more accurate description of what transpired." Dalton stared stonily ahead as Jeron defended himself as Byron seized the offensive. "Those Loachian bastards snuck through the Flintwood in the dead of winter. You see, Flintwood Village was in the border area between Antier and Loach, and operated the nearby iron mines for the benefit of Antier. Under orders from Duke Camen, his soldiers attacked the village. Without the village there, Antier wouldn't be able to press its claim to the Flintwood iron ore mines. The Loachians would be able to seize control of the mines and establish their defenses before the winter was over. Once spring arrived, Duke Antier and Baron Flintwood would be able to marshal their forces and attempt to uproot the entrenched Loachani from their lands."

Jeron blocked a few more blows and began what looked to Cole to be a weak uncertain counterattack. "The Loachani massacred the village," continued Dalton. "Unfortunately for the raiders, Baron Flintwood was spending a few weeks in Flintwood Village that winter celebrating the successful completion of some expansions made to the local flint-logging and ore operations."

Dalton briefly put his hands over his face and sighed. "It was the Baron and his retainers that 'won' that battle. The Loachani weren't counting on the presence of his troops. The baron killed enough Loachians that it wasn't feasible for them to fortify and defend the mines come spring. So the remaining raiders retreated back to Loach through the Flintwood. It was too late for Flintwood Village though, and most of the nobility in the barony. Smoke from the destroyed village drew people in from the farms to the south. There was only one survivor in the entire village: Jeron."

Dalton sighed again and spared a quick glance to Cole. "Jeron was found in the village long hall surrounded by his dead family members. A slew of raiders' corpses were found around the family including many cavaliers from various temples. Cole, his family, his father, his mother, his brothers and his sisters died trying to protect little five-year-old Jeron. Their bodies were fanned out in a semi-circle around his body. Cole, Jeron was found underneath the body of a

High Cavalier of the Order of Pojomi...with his hand on the dagger that went through the cavalier's heart."

"Wait. Are you telling me that one of the God of the Hunt's own High Cavaliers was killed by a five-year-old?!" asked an incredulous Cole.

Dalton shook his head as the duel continued behind him. "No, that's not what I'm saying at all. All anyone knows is that Jeron was found beneath his body. No one knows what happened except for Jeron. And believe me, he won't talk about it. After being around him for a few years, I gather that he blames himself for something that happened that night. Take it from me, don't ask him about it."

"Okay. I won't," said Cole. "It's strange, but I won't ask Jeron about it. But I have a few more questions."

"Hmm, what are those?" replied Dalton.

Cole scratched his head. "Well you said that Jeron and Byron grew up as close as brothers. How did that happen? I doubt the prince is from Flintwood Village. And why do you refer to the raiders as Loachians and Loachani? What's the difference?"

Dalton chuckled. "That's not a mystery. People from Loach have a mighty high opinion of themselves and couldn't abide using only one moniker. As to the other question, well, after Jeron was found alive, he was an orphan. The Duke's men came to the aid of the barony. The farmers who found Jeron placed him in the custody of the baron who then passed him off to the Duke's soldiers. Jeron was brought to Antier, and as a noble's son was raised as a ward of the Duke."

"The Duke placed Byron and Jeron under the same teachers," continued Dalton. "He figured since Byron and Jeron were the same age that they would get along just fine. He was right, and they've been best friends since."

"Well, that makes sense," said Cole. "But I thought the three of you were all best friends. Where do you fit in?"

A sad look crossed Dalton's face which he quickly replaced with an affable smile. "I wasn't orphaned until I was thirteen," he said simply. At that moment Byron executed a quick feint followed by a swift cut that barely grazed Jeron's shoulder. Dalton whistled and his cocksure grin came back "Well kiddo, now that that's done with it's time to get back to training. You'll have to get my story later. I suggest using wine to loosen my tongue."

"Not bad for a totemless weakling!" someone shouted from across the room.

Dalton groaned and Cole turned and searched for the owner of the voice. Timver was stalking across the room pointing his sword at Byron. "You're nothing more than a sideshow event. Everyone here knows that Jeron would destroy you in a fight if he used even the slightest bit of strength from his totem."

Timver closed the distance and was standing next to Byron. His body was rigid with anger and his eyes screamed pure hatred at Byron. Cole leaned over to Dalton and whispered, "Why does he hate Byron so much?"

"You don't know that either?," asked Dalton incredulously. "Never mind. Dumb question. You seem not to know a lot. Anyway, after the draft when you got cornered and Byron came to your rescue, well Byron kinda sorta broke Timver's ribs. Timver has found it hard to cope with the fact that someone who has yet to recognize their totem could possibly beat him in a fist fight since he is literally as strong as a bear despite his slight frame."

"Well umm, no offense but how *did* Byron break his ribs?" asked Cole.

"What? You don't think he could break his ribs fairly?" said Dalton innocently.

Cole shook his head. "Not if Timver is as strong as a bear."

Dalton smirked at Cole. "Well you're right. Byron hit him with brass knuckles. The only problem was no one could find the brass knuckles after the fight. Timver's ego hasn't been able to cope with the situation."

"But Timver is a cavalier now," Dalton said as his expression darkened. "He shouldn't be at a paladin training session unless he is looking for a fight."

Cole turned his attention back to the brewing situation. The other knight trainees had ceased all pretenses at practicing and had started to gather around the two boys. Byron's face looked like cold murder to Cole. He showed zero expression and his entire being was focused on Timver. Jeron put an arm across Byron's chest, more for show than actually restraining the prince, and whispered something to Byron that Cole could not hear.

Byron's face brightened and then he gave Timver a smile of all teeth. "Well since I'm such a weakling why don't we have ourselves a little match?"

"Let me guess. I can't use my powers?" sneered Timver.

"Oh no," said Byron as he raised his hands up before him. "Of course not. You and all your powers against me. Best to three."

Timver's eyes narrowed in suspicion. "What's the catch? Are you going to sucker punch me again with brass knuckles?"

"Sucker punch you? With brass knuckles?" Byron's eyes widened in mock astonishment. "Jeron whatever is he talking about?"

"Beats me," shrugged Jeron. "Probably can't handle the fact that he got beat in a fight fair and square."

"Beat fairly?!" roared Timver. "I'll show you a beating you whimpering son of a satyr! Let's see how you like having your ribs broken! I'm going to make it so the only totem you could possibly resemble is carrion!"

"How eloquent," muttered Dalton drolly.

Byron let loose a low whistle and nudged Jeron in the ribs with his elbow. "I think he means it," he whispered in a conspiratorial tone loud enough for all of the boys to hear.

"You smart mouthed little sh-" began Timver.

"Yes yes. You're going to beat me to a pulp," interrupted Byron. "We got that part. Now do you want to fight or were you planning on talking me to death?"

"What is he doing?" Cole whispered intently to Dalton. "Timver looks mad enough to try ripping Byron's arms out of their sockets!"

Dalton flashed that infuriating smug grin that made Cole's blood boil. "You don't know this too? Fine. Consider this another lesson. Never-" Timver charged at Byron and unleashed a vicious cut towards his head. Byron ducked and his sword snaked out and bit Timver on his wrist. "-lose your temper when you fight," finished Dalton.

"He went for the wrist!" said an astonished Cole. "That's your move!"

"Why yes it is," replied a very smug Dalton. "It's utter brilliance I tell you. Why I came up with it by-"

"-By fighting Byron and consistently winding up with sore wrists," said Jeron drily as he slid up next to them and out of the way of the fight.

Dalton glowered at the other boy. "But I did learn it."

Timver's bastard sword clashed at an awkward angle against Byron's saber, and a quick riposte again slammed against Timver's wrist.

"That you did," Jeron chuckled. He rubbed his wrist in sympathy. "I think we all learned that lesson the hard way."

Cole glanced back to the fight. Timver's face was beet red, and hair was starting to sprout from his arms whose muscles were bulging and straining against his slight frame. Byron's posture was in stark contrast, looking perfectly calm with the exception of his face where he had a cocky grin stretching the corners of his mouth. Timver charged at him and swung again. He unleashed another high attack at Byron's head. Byron hesitated for a fraction of a second. It seemed to Cole that Byron was not expecting Timver's sword to be swung quite so fierce or in that location. The blade barely glanced off of Byron's sword before slamming into his head.

The totem-powered blow lifted Byron off the floor and he crashed onto the floor with an audible groan. Cole and the others rushed towards the fallen boy. Blood was flowing from a cut on Byron's left temple and his eyes were not focusing well.

"You okay buddy?" Jeron asked with concern etched on his face.

Byron gasped and looked around futilely trying to find Jeron's voice. "Walls...are...spinning," he croaked.

"You sure you can go on?" asked Dalton. For the first time that day, Dalton did not have the boyish grin on his face that infuriated Cole, or any affectations of high society. He was not certain but it seemed that the carefree Dalton finally was concerned over something. It was intriguing to Cole. It seemed each of his companions had a soft spot in their heart for Byron, and maybe for one another.

"I have him right where I want him," insisted Byron.

Byron stood up, taking a few seconds to regain his balance.

"You ready wimp?" growled Timver as he twirled his bastard sword in a lazy loop.

Byron looked around the room as if lost. Genuine concern seemed to be on his face. "Wimp?" he asked. "I thought you were fighting me you lummox. Where is this wimp you're talking to?"

"He's you!" Timver shouted as he charged. He attacked high again and this time Byron didn't even have time to move his sword out of its guard position. The bastard sword smashed through Byron's guard and cracked against his head for the second time. Again, Byron found himself lying a few feet backwards on the ground.

Cole glanced down at Byron's prone body. He was still breathing but now there was a second nasty gash on his forehead. Jeron knelt down and gently lifted Byron's head up. A sheet of blood began to slowly trickle down his forehead.

"It's...a conspiracy," Byron gasped. "The...ceiling and...floor is spinning now too."

Cole wrung his hands at the response. Dalton cursed. A confused and then suspicious look spread across Jeron's face.

"You want me to stop the fight?" asked Dalton.

"No. I'm fine," said Byron as he began to stand, stumbling and swaying back and forth.

"But he'll kill you!" said a panicked Cole. "You can't take another shot like that!"

Byron smiled weakly back at Cole. "Good thing I don't plan to." He stood and his knees nearly buckled. He clapped Cole on his shoulder. "I'll be fine kid. Thanks for the concern."

Timver adjusted his gloves and rolled his neck. "You ready princess? Oh excuse me, prince. I forget sometimes due to your meager strength."

Byron chuckled. "Clever. Think that one up yourself? Who am I kidding? Of course you did. No one else could have such a staggering lack of imagination." Byron spat some blood out of his mouth. "Or, wait a minute. Did Barith have to come up with it for you while you were in the infirmary with your broken ribs?"

Timver's wiry body went even more rigid. Cole doubted that Timver could get any angrier. The veins in his neck looked like small mountain ridges and his eyes looked large enough that if Cole did not know any better, he would think Timver's totem was that of a flea.

Timver never did respond to Byron's question. He unleashed a roar that made Cole's hair tingle, and charged straight at Byron again. His hands had grown and could no longer rightfully be called hands. They more resembled paws, and engulfed the hilt of his bastard sword. Hair completely covered his exposed upper body as he embraced his inner bear. Timver growled and swung his sword at the unsteady Byron's head. The wooden practice sword was swung with enough force that it would crack Byron's skull when it landed.

But it never did.

Byron fell to the floor and rolled towards Timver. He sprang to his feet and unloaded a vicious uppercut to Timver's jaw. Bell guard met bone and the sound of the resulting crunch made Cole's breakfast try to rise up.

Timver's body thudded against the ground and his bastard sword slid out of his hand. He gasped for breath and tried to roll over but he could not make his body move in any sort of coordinated effort. Cole winced in sympathy at the skinny boy's pain.

Byron turned as if to leave. He stopped. He looked back at the writhing Timver and then back at the other trainees. "Oh yes. I forgot. Gotta touch him with my blade to score."

He walked back to Timver and with both hands raised his saber above his head. Byron swung with all his might and Cole winced in anticipation of the blow. The sword slammed into Timver's ribs and there was a loud popping sound as the slender boy's ribs broke for the second time.

Byron flipped his practice sword casually on to the groaning boy and sauntered over towards Cole.

"Was that last bit really necessary?" asked Jeron as he tossed Byron a towel.

"Nah," said Byron as he mopped a mixture of sweat and blood off his face. "But it sure felt good."

"But. How?" asked a puzzled Cole. "You could barely stand up. You said the room was spinning!"

"He lied," Jeron and Dalton said in unison.

Byron shrugged his shoulders and grinned evilly as he tossed an arm across Cole's shoulders. "I don't have Timver's innate strength, so I have to create my advantages where I can," he said. "Timver never was all that strong before he got his totem. He simply can't fathom how strong a person can be without one. It never entered his mind that I'm physically strong enough to knock him out with only my muscles."

"But why the wrist cuts then?" asked Cole.

Byron finished wiping his face off and tossed the towel into a pile of dirty rags. "To piss him off. I wanted him to get angry and overextend. He lacks imagination and that shows in his fighting. He left himself open and I seized the advantage, and probably what is left of his reputation. That knockout is something everyone here will remember, Cole."

Cole looked even more confused. "So it was all about humiliating him?" he asked.

"Politics," Jeron spat out the word like it was spoiled cheese.

"What?" asked Cole who clearly was confused by the direction the conversation was headed.

"Right now, everyone knows that Timver and Barith are physically stronger than Byron," explained Dalton. "And you'll find that many nobles who control military forces have totems that are predators. And when predators sense weakness-" Dalton slashed his sword through the air "-they strike."

"So all the fights you get into are to discourage predators?" asked Cole. Jeron snorted at the question.

"Sort of," said Byron. "I keep those two and their ilk at bay but I also remind everyone that I'm strong enough to beat them all without a totem."

"And when his totem actually bonds with him, they'll be loyal as no one will want to risk fighting him," interjected Jeron.

Cole let out a relieved sigh that he had been holding in for the past few minutes. "Whew. I thought you just wanted to piss Timver off."

Byron snorted. "If I only wanted to piss him off, I would've fought him with my left hand." Byron shook his head bemused. "You know the sad thing is that he'll never bring himself to admit that I have more talent and skill than him. He'll believe it was all a gimmick. It will drive him nuts."

Byron paused for a handful of seconds with a thoughtful expression on his face. The gesture did not last long as it was quickly replaced by a wicked grin. "In fact. I think I'll do exactly that next time. Use my left hand."

"Sounds like fun," said Dalton as he reclined against the training room wall. "As long as you're not expecting us to come bail you out when Timver gets angry and tries to tear your head off."

"Us?" said Jeron as he raised an eyebrow at Dalton.

"Ummm...yeah...you know...uh you and me," stammered Dalton. "We come running in and save the fearless hero here from fighting an entire gang of furious totem wielding boys."

"Oh, I understand the fighting part," said Jeron drily. "What I'm failing to understand is this 'we' business. As I recall, you ran from the last fight and by some miraculous miracle wound up in the mess eating pie."

The tall blonde boy ran his fingers through his hair, parted a small smile and had the good grace to blush.

"How'd you think he got there?" asked Byron. "An act of God?"

Jeron nodded his head. "Yeah. A legion of seraphim and whatnot whisked him away to the kitchen."

"The heavenly pie legion...works with me," said Byron with a slight strain to his voice. Jeron grunted his assent.

Dalton laughed and held his hands up in mock surrender. "Okay, okay, so I didn't fight this time." He stretched his lanky body and returned to slouching languidly against the wall. "But I did find our boy Cole here. I think I deserve some credit now."

"Please," said Cole as he closed his eyes and concentrated. "I *let* you find me."

"Hey!" exclaimed Dalton. "Whose side are you-what the...? Where the hell did he go?"

Cole smiled to himself as he phased his body to the point of near invisibility. "Hard to find me if you can't see me," he said. Cole tapped Dalton quickly on the shoulder and darted behind Jeron as Dalton flailed at where he had stood a moment ago. Byron and Jeron burst into laughter at Dalton's plight.

"I guess there goes that theory-OW!" screamed Jeron as Cole pinched him in the side which sent Dalton into a fit of laughter.

Dodging and ducking, Cole weaved his way between the three boys causing mischief. This was his haven. The part of the world where no one could see him. Cole enjoyed the silence and the anonymity. No one ever bothers someone they cannot see. His fingers snaked toward Byron's belt and the buckle that held his scabbard on. Byron's hand shot down and clamped onto Cole's wrist. Shocked, Cole unconsciously phased back into sight.

"How-how did you do that?" yelped Cole. A few heads nearby turned, shocked at the sight of hearing Cole's usually soft voice carry.

"You're nearly invisible Cole, not silent." Byron let go of his wrist. "If I can hear you, it's not impossible to find you once I know where to look." Byron inclined his head to the door. "Looks like Master Maxus has returned. That's our cue to get going Cole. I really don't want to see what Master Tyson will do to us if we're late."

"Agreed," said Cole.

"Take care," said Jeron as he clapped the two of them on their backs. Byron stumbled and regained his balance by grabbing hold of Cole, nearly sending them both tumbling to the ground.

"Are you okay?" asked a concerned Dalton.

Byron waved off his protests. "I'm fine." He gestured to Jeron. "Someone just doesn't know his own strength."

Cole and Byron left the training room and began to walk down the corridors to meet Master Tyson in the dungeon and catacombs beneath the fort. After they turned the first corner, Byron collapsed. He fell to his knees and bowed his head to the floor, breathing rapidly.

Cole bent down on one knee and lay a hand on Byron's back. "Byron? Are you alright?" Nothing. The prince did not say a word; his skin was drawn tightly across his face and had paled significantly. "Byron! Oh God, what do I do?" Cole felt the panic begin to rise within him. What would happen to him if the prince died and he was the only one there? Did Shadows have some sort of special sets of duties? Was a Shadow an actual position or a position that Master Tyson invented? Hopefully they did not have to join their charge in death.

"Okhuy, Cohle," gasped Byron. "I'm oh...kay." His face was still pale and the skin was still stretched tight over his muscles. But some of his coloring had returned. His body had broken into a full sweat. Byron took a couple of deep breaths.

It seemed to Cole that Byron was slowly regaining some of his strength. But then again, Cole was not a priest, and it could always be wishful thinking on his part.

Byron placed a pale, shaking arm around Cole's shoulders and Cole helped Byron to his feet. Cole grunted as his sore body struggled to lift the heavier boy. Despite Byron's insistence that he was fine, the prince was not able to support much of his own weight.

Byron smiled weakly at Cole, "I guess Timver hit me harder than I thought."

"Yeah. I guess so," said Cole as worry etched itself onto his face and burrowed into his mind.

"I'll be fine," said Byron as he regained his balance and began walking slowly under his own power. "Do me a favor and don't tell Jeron or Dalton. They'll both try to act like my mother."

"I thought you said he didn't hit you that hard," said Cole.

Byron smiled weakly, "I lied."

Cole nodded in assent as if the statement made all the sense in the world, and found himself wondering for the second time in as many days just what he had gotten himself into.

Chapter Eight

"You're late," said Master Tyson. He stated it as a simple fact like saying the sun would rise in the morning. However, the torches in the dungeon flickered casting their shadows over Master Tyson's face, lending him a sinister expression.

Byron glanced around the dungeon. It predated the creation of the Duchy of Antier by centuries. The hillmen who originally inhabited the area built a rudimentary defensive structure to protect their livestock from their less than friendly neighbors. The dungeon was a remnant of that structure, and its construction reflected their more modest means. The room they stood in was cramped, possessing a small ceiling. Apparently, the hill people had been shorter on average than modern day Antierians, or they were strong believers in making their prisoners uncomfortable.

A stairway from the main keep led down to the area where they were standing. New wood and polished stone clashed with the rough-hewn stone gathered by the hill people. The entry room had the layout common to bureaucratic functions. Small, tight, and whose only purpose was to achieve its designated function. The room was designed to process the prisoners whose cells lined the hall that branched off the far side of the room from the staircase. It did not need to be warm and spacious.

The cells had long since been deserted, at least decades before the fort was converted to the use of the Antierian military. The most use the cells saw these days was housing soldiers and trainees for drunkenness or other punishment.

Byron rubbed his lower back in remembrance. The cells were not designed for comfort or a good night's sleep.

The dungeon descended down multiple levels into the earth. Beneath the lowest levels of the abandoned dungeon lay the catacombs which were the oldest part of the fort. The hillmen had worshipped the land, and according to custom they built their catacombs deep into the earth so that their dead could rest deep in its embrace.

They never would find rest though. The souls of the dead never truly rested across the realm. At night, their spirits would rise from their graves and haunt the surrounding areas. According to the priests, the spirits roamed the earth as a result of strenuous, uncomfortable deaths, full of regret. Few were those who truly died in peace, content with their lives. Especially in a country where minor skirmishes occurred nearly every day.

The dead would roam through the night, slaughtering any of the living who were unfortunate enough to cross their path. Jealousy drove them. Jealousy of those who still possessed life. Jealousy of those who could still eat, breathe, love, and laugh. Or so the modern religions preached. Byron had not sought to confirm their teachings. There was little fun to be had in a graveyard at night.

Constructing graveyards that could contain the spirits took centuries, but finally, through a joint effort between the church and the temples, there was a discovery of a series of glyphs and wards that when placed around the outside of graveyards, would imprison the spirits inside. Naturally, both the church and temples took individual credit for the discovery, but the important thing was that large cities and castles were secure. Cities and nations grew as the spirits could not break through the barriers keeping them contained within their resting places.

Locked behind the wards, the spirits could not escape, but they could be heard. At night, the dead could be heard howling and shrieking, unable to escape their confinement, and unable to live as they were forced to tread upon the same ground every night.

Byron shuddered at the thought. Anyone who had spent a night in the dungeon had heard the screams of the dead echo and bounce off of the walls.

Fear of spending another night in lockup scared many soldiers sober and into what Captain Levren described as proper military discipline.

Byron despised the place.

"I thought I told you two not to get into any trouble," said Master Tyson sternly. He grabbed Byron's chin and twisted his head from side to side, inspecting the damage. "And just how did you get all these cuts and lumps?"

Byron rubbed his jaw before replying. "Morning paladin training, sir."

"I see. Now Cole, were you all practicing fist fighting today?" asked Tyson.

Byron glanced at Cole out of the corner of his eye. The kid was doing better. He was still the most shy and nervous person Byron had ever met, but he did not stutter nearly as much as he did when they first met. Cole had also improved his skills at fighting in that time. Byron wondered if there was some correlation between the increase in Cole's confidence and his improved ability to protect himself. Regardless from where the newfound confidence originated, Cole was becoming less of a liability and an increasingly dangerous man.

"No sir," said Cole. "We were practicing sword fighting."

Master Tyson chuckled and sat down on an old wooden stool next to the wall. "Well at least you were honest," he said. "Next time Byron, try not to break Timver's ribs again. He needs his training too."

Byron felt his jaw drop. There was no way Master Tyson could have known that he was fighting Timver. The young cavalier was not even supposed to be in the same training session. Byron looked over at Cole and even through the darkness he could see the shock mirrored on the other boy's face.

Master Tyson broke out into laughter. "I know more, and I'm capable of doing more than you boys think. You can try to puzzle out how later," he said. "Now onto our business. Do either of you know the purpose of the Brotherhood of the Dark Flame?"

The two boys exchanged glances and shrugged. "Spies?" asked Byron.

"Assassins?" asked Cole tentatively.

"Partly to both," said Master Tyson. He leaned against the wall and blew out a deep breath. "The original purpose was a little bit more than that. The original Brothers thought of themselves as keepers of freedom. A force to keep the nobles honest and in line. Things were worse back then. It was common for the nobles to let their totems control their actions and give into their more primal urges. Villages would burn, and the pact between noble and peasant wasn't honored. At that time the Brotherhood was formed and nobles who were terrorizing their subjects began to die unexpectedly."

Master Tyson paused and looked each boy in the eye. "This is important, so listen carefully. Never has a wraith killed a noble. Never. If nobles who abused their powers started dying at the same time the Dark Flame was formed, then that is just sheer coincidence. We have never taken credit for a noble kill, nor has one ever been successfully proven.

"When the nobles started dying, there were plenty of lands and titles available for a man of means and methods to seize. That's where we officially come into play. The nobles and the powerful who wanted to claim those titles needed information. They turned to those who were exceptional at moving through the shadows and worming their way into places they should not be.

"That's where we became spies true to our modern reputation. And from that day on. we've had numerous other jobs ranging from ambassadors, couriers, advisors, alchemists, advance units, and yes, assassins. We do the jobs that are required of us. That is our duty.

"It may sound corny and self-serving, but we see ourselves as preserving the light of justice from the shadows. Hence our standard is a dark blue flame surrounded by darkness. Any questions about what our purpose is boys?"

"Are we going to have to learn to do all of that stuff you just mentioned?" asked Cole. "I don't even know what alchemy is."

"Yes. And more," replied Master Tyson. "Now are you ready for your mission?"

"Whoa! A mission now?" Byron held up his hands in protest. "We just finished with training and you want to send us out of the fort on a mission now?"

Master Tyson arched an eyebrow, "Who said anything about leaving the fort?" he asked. "You're going to prove your worth. Both of you. You're going into the catacombs."

Cole gasped and his skin appeared to Byron's eyes, to turn a few shades closer to the color of the walls.

Byron closed his eyes and thought for a minute. It was always dark in the catacombs, and that meant that the spirits may be awake at any given time, as it was impossible to tell the difference between day and night underground. Master Tyson would not send them to their deaths. But he did just obliquely tell them some of the secret history of the society. Maybe he was trying to subtlety do away with them if they did not pass this test.

"Do we get weapons?" asked Byron.

Master Tyson laughed and it echoed down the corridor. "Do you think you'll be able to kill a ghost with them?"

Byron gritted his teeth. It was well known around the fort that when he had spent a drunken night in the dungeon that he had been heard screaming at the ghosts and challenging them to duels. "Maybe. I'd rather not go down there unarmed. I have no idea if it's possible to kill a spirit, but if they try to kill me, I'd at least like to have the opportunity to be able to attempt to return the favor."

"Fair enough," said Master Tyson. He turned around and pulled two belts out of the darkness. "Take these with you," he said as he tossed them at the boys. "At the very bottom depths of the catacombs is a symbol of our order. Bring it back to me to before the evening mess."

Byron slipped the belt around his waist and checked to make sure that the swords cleared their scabbards. His belt had two standard longswords and two dirks. All the weapons were of a plain yet sturdy build. Byron smiled to himself. Master Tyson must have done some research as to his preferred weaponry.

Cole slipped his own belt around his waist and carefully inspected his weapons. His armaments consisted of two short swords and two daggers. Cole moved the belt around in an effort to adjust the balance. "Sir, I'm not really familiar and comfortable with using two weapons," said Cole.

Tyson gave Cole what the boys had begun to consider his sinister smile, while he started climbing up the stairs back into the fort proper. "Well, you better become comfortable my boy. There are two very good reasons why you should learn to use two weapons. First, you're a wraith now boy. You better be able to fight with any given weapon as you never know what circumstances you'll find yourself in. And secondly, you're the Prince's Shadow. And he uses two weapons. You may need to impersonate him one day. So get used to it. No one likes a complainer."

Cole scowled at Byron as the last bit of light from the fort vanished behind the closing door. "See? It's entirely your fault that I have to do this," Cole said.

"Yup," said Byron. "Causing problems for people is my specialty. Speaking of which, care to go see if we can sneak past a bunch of angry ghosts?"

"Not really," replied Cole.

"Yeah, me neither."

The boys began walking down the passageway, careful not to make too much noise. The hinges on the cells had begun to rust long ago, and the pungent smell of the dead wafted out of the cells. After creeping past rows of cells, they finally came to a staircase leading down into the catacombs.

The staircase was hewn straight into the floor of the dungeon. It wound back upon itself and descended down into near darkness. A frigidly cold breeze blew up the stairway and carried with it the faint moans of the dead. Byron's skin prickled at the unnatural sensation. Breezes just should not exist underground.

Byron glanced over at Cole as the slender boy stared down at the staircase. His skin was pale and he stared at the stairs with the type of fear in his eyes usually reserved for a prisoner about to meet the gallows.

"Cole, I thought you only could blend in to the background and your surroundings. I had no idea you could make yourself resemble the local flavor," Byron said to the scared boy. Cole did not respond, he just looked up at Byron and his eyes shifted from terror to a blank confused look.

"I was making a joke," Byron explained. "You look like a ghost right now. Never mind. Just follow my lead and walk as quietly as you can. Quiet as a mouse. It'll all be okay." Byron reluctantly put actions to his words and placed a foot onto the staircase.

A pitched shriek ripped through the air and Byron fell to the ground clutching at his head. The pain was shooting through his brain, tearing apart any semblance of rational thought. It felt as if an invisible dagger was thrust into his skull through his left eye socket, and remained firmly lodged in the left portion of his brain. The pain radiated outward in a fashion that distantly reminded Byron of a time where he dropped a pebble into a pool of water. Except that instead of water rippling through his mind, there were little bolts of lightning wreaking havoc.

Byron could vaguely feel his body striking the stones of the staircase as he tumbled downwards. Luckily, with the exception of his head, his body was failing to register any pain. His blasted head felt like it was trying to both explode and implode at the same time. A cool breeze hit Byron as he could feel his tumbling body go airborne. A large impact struck his body, but he could not focus his mind to determine what had happened.

His head erupted again and his world burned with pain.

CHAPTER NINE

C ole tore down the stairs, but restrained himself from taking the steps two at a time. They could not afford for both of them to trip and fall. The stones were old and worn, yet still sturdy. Cole winced. They had to have hurt.

He tried to determine what caused Byron to fall, but could not for the life of him figure it out. One moment they were standing before the staircase, and then without warning, Byron began shrieking. He clutched his head and stumbled down the staircase. Cole tried to catch him, but it all happened too fast for him to react. A fall like that could easily break someone's neck. Cole swallowed at the thought of the prince breaking his neck with only Cole around to take the blame. He took a ragged breath and began taking the steps two at a time.

The walls disappeared near the bottom of the spiral staircase leaving only empty space. Cole peered around cautiously before venturing further. It appeared that the staircase emptied out into a large square chamber with exits branching off in all directions.

The walls in the catacombs consisted of a pale grey stone that at one time may have been polished to a near white. The walls glowed in a faint eerie light that tinged everything in a pale blue. The light was enough to see by, if just barely, and made obsolete any notion Cole had of carrying a torch. Symbols, glyphs, and strange characters covered the wall. Many of them depictions of burial and hunting scenes.

Byron was sprawled at the base of the wall opposite the foot of the staircase. Cole hurried over and tried to assess the damage. Byron's shirt had large tears in it revealing the battered body beneath it. Fresh scrapes and bruises lay side by side with the injuries from the morning, creating a lurid mural of yellows, reds, and purples across Byron's body. Fresh blood was streaming from gashes on both of his temples.

Cole used his shirt to wipe the blood off of Byron's face. He inspected the wounds on his temples and gasped. Cole picked up Byron's bloody hands and looked at the shape of the wounds on Byron's head. Cole groaned.

Byron had been gouging at his own temples.

Cole gently shook the unconscious boy, "Hey, Byron, wake up." Byron groaned and squinted up at Cole. Cole swore he could see the pain shining radiating behind Byron's eyes.

"We need to stop meeting like this," groaned Byron. "It's getting bad for my health." He stood up and wobbled more than after his previous tumbles that day. "Let me tell you something Cole. Never get a concussion. Hurts really bad. Guess Timver can hit harder than I thought. Never get a concussion. Hurts really...what was I saying?"

A faint moan echoed through the halls. Cole felt himself began to sweat despite the cool air. "Do you think you can go on?" he asked.

"I'm still breathing, aren't I?" snorted Byron. "Besides, I don't think this is the kind of mission that you can just stop." He let out a deep sigh. "Might as well get back to finding whatever it is that we're supposed to be finding."

"I don't suppose Master Tyson left it near the entrance?" asked Cole with a desperate hint of hope tinging his voice.

"I have no idea if he's even the one who left it, what it actually is, much less where it is at," responded Byron, irritation dripping with every word.

Cole helped Byron stand again, and the pair set off slowly down the widest hallway leading from the room. The hall was lined with a variety of sarcophagi and caskets. The stone this deep in the catacombs had long since been worn smooth from age with many of the tombs having empty sockets and grooves where gems and precious metals had been looted years earlier. However, not a single tomb's lid was ajar or breached. There were certain things a soldier just would not disturb when thieving from the dead. Especially when the dead might still be around to take umbrage to the theft.

Cole stopped at the mouth of a small hallway branching off from the main path. It seemed to extend as far as he could manage to see in the faint light. "Byron, could I ask you a few questions about Jeron and Dalton?" Cole asked as they ignored the smaller path.

Byron stopped and leaned against the wall next to a statue of a large burly man with a thick beard and a double-bladed great axe. The hallway was lined with numerous statues bearing identical great axes. It was most likely a family burial area for a one-time local lord, or whatever the hillmen had called their leaders.

"What do you want to know?" answered Byron in a soft strained voice.

"Umm, is the story Dalton told me about Jeron true? Being found alive surrounded by his family? Were they all dead?"

Byron slowly massaged the bridge of his nose. For the first time all day, it appeared to Cole that strain of the day's events were starting to show and wear on Byron. He looked tired, as if were about to collapse.

"Yes. That's true," sighed Byron.

"Then why did he want to become a knight? Wouldn't he prefer to have been a cavalier and avenge his family for what was done to them? I know I sure would have," said Cole, putting a great emphasis of certainty on the last sentence the way only a teenager could. He hoped Byron did not pick up on his false bravado. He did not have many friends, any actually, and he wanted the prince and the others to like him.

"His entire family died protecting him," said Byron. "From cavaliers, judging by the dead Loachian bodies found at the scene. A sacrifice and horrific event like that tends to make an impression on a man. There was zero chance he was ever going to join the society that murdered his family. He chose to follow a different path. One that forsook vengeance and instead made him happy. Oh, don't look so confused. He still hates Loach and would kill them all in a heartbeat if he saw them. He just doesn't plan on seeking them out. It's a complicated distinction, but a distinction nonetheless."

"Oh," said Cole flatly. His face flushed with embarrassment. "I see. I think? But umm, why did Dalton want to join the cavaliers?"

Byron exhaled a great breath, letting his lips make a series of loud flopping vibrations as the air rushed out. "Now that is a long story. One we don't have time to stand still and talk about. Oh, don't look sad, I'll tell ya while we walk."

They passed rows of tombs before Byron spoke again. "So ya want to know about Dalton do you? Very well. Jeron was with his family when they died. Dalton was denied that luxury.

"Dalton's from a small village out west, near the mountains. His father was squire of the area. Not a wealthy or influential position. Barely anyone lived out there at the time. I guess not much has changed in that regard.

"One night, a large fire consumed an outlying farm. It was a brilliant fire, and the blaze was easily visible from the village center.

"It was also an ambush. When his father and the village men reached the farm, the trap was sprung. Centaurs and satyrs leapt from their hiding places and pounced on the men." Byron paused to take a breath and ran his hand through his hair in frustration. "Cole, they never had a chance. Those men were armed to fight a fire, not to battle monsters. Buckets aren't any match for bows, clubs, and spears."

Cole grimaced as they passed the tomb of another forgotten lord. This one looked halfway between a modern lord and what Cole imagined a hillman to look like. The slight familiarity made the differences in the surroundings stand out that much more to Cole. While the foreign and inhospitable surroundings, and eerie pale light, made Byron's story seem that much worse.

"After they slaughtered the men, the creatures turned their attention to the village," continued Byron in a somber voice. "The village was defenseless without the men. Dalton's mother grabbed him and told him to run. That's when Dalton's totem manifested itself. You'd know more than me about how that works though."

Cole nodded. Many people's totems awakened in their youth under great stress and personal need. The event ingrained itself into one's memory. Cole shuddered. It was not an experience that you ever forgot.

"The cheetah came out of Dalton's soul and he ran," said Byron. "He ran for three days straight. He passed many farms and villages but he didn't stop.

Eventually, he collapsed on a road, and was found by a farmer and his family on their way to Antier on an errand or business of some sort. Dalton never says what it was. I doubt that he was in much of a physical or mental state to remember. Regardless, they cared for him until they reached Antier, where they dropped him off at the palace to be cared for.

"You see, Cole, that's why Dalton wanted to be a cavalier. He had to run while he heard monsters destroy his entire life and everyone he knew or loved. If someone had hunted the monsters down before they could attack his village, then his life would not have been ruined. He wanted that job. He wanted to prevent what happened to him from happening to some other poor kid. Dalton also wants to kill the beasts. Badly."

"I see," said Cole. He shivered in the dark. The prospect of staring down a charging centaur frightened him. Almost as much as creepy crypts and ghosts.

"Actually, I don't see," said Cole. "If Dalton wants to hunt down murderous beasts so much, why does he run from fights?"

Byron shrugged. "Byproduct of running before? I don't attempt to understand it. Just know that if you ever need to put your life on the line, that Dalton will be right by your side. He just happens to choose those moments rather carefully when his own life is in jeopardy."

They branched off into another passage, wandering aimlessly through the catacombs. "What about you, Cole? What was your life like? Have any interesting totem stories?" asked Byron with a tinge of bitterness.

Cole opened his mouth to speak, but a shriek tore through the air at that moment sparing him the discomfort. The noise made Cole's hair rise on end as he nearly leapt out of his skin. Suddenly, Byron was slamming Cole up against the wall and clamping a hand over his mouth for silence. If Cole could have let loose a sigh of relief or a scream, he would have. But he could barely breathe. At least now he would not have to embarrass himself by talking about his past. Embarrass himself? By the gods there were angry spirits around that would kill him in a heartbeat! And he was worried about being embarrassed? Cole's eyes widened in shock. What had happened to his priorities?

Byron's longsword made a soft scraping sound as it left the scabbard. Byron removed the hand covering Cole's mouth and made some hand gestures that Cole struggled to process. Cole stared numbly and tried to remember what to do. Follow and be silent. Oh yes. He could do that. He was good at being silent.

Cole gripped the hilt of his shortsword and quietly stalked after Byron as they neared the exit of the passageway. The hallway ended in an arch that poured out into a large cavernous chamber. The stone walls slowly gave way to packed dirt. They were in some sort of barrows now. The graves of the original hill people would be located down this far into the ground. Buried as deep under the earth as their meager technology permitted.

The surroundings, while interesting, were not the most compelling sight in the chamber. Ethereal beings floated past the arch at an incredible rate. Cole gulped. The room was full of spirits. And they were awake.

Cole nudged Byron on his arm. "Maybe we should head back now," he whispered. "They're awake now."

"No," said Byron. He shook his head in disagreement. "We haven't found whatever it is we were sent to find. Besides, we don't know if the dead are also going to rise behind us. We can't afford to be caught between two groups of them. So we move forward."

Cole sighed in exasperation, "You're crazy."

Byron turned and gave him a smile of all teeth in response.

By the gods, he really might be crazy, thought Cole in dismay. In the stories, princes were always honorable and virtuous. Why did reality have to be so different? And for what seemed like the hundredth time that day, Cole wondered how he had allowed himself to be entangled with a prince. He glanced at the spirits roaming around their graves. Whatever he was involved with, he was certain that he was not going to like it.

Byron motioned Cole to move forward, and the two slowly snuck down into the chamber. They were high up. At least twenty feet above the floor of the barrows. A large earthen ramp led down from the arch to the floor of the chamber. Unlike the previous passageway, there were very few adornments and ornamentations this far down. There were not any statues or fancy tombs. The only stone Cole could see was that of the biers, abscessed into the walls in a fashion reminiscent of a honeycomb.

There were not any bodies laid out to rest on those stone biers. They had long since faded to dust over the past thousand years. All that remained was the air, which was dank and moist and smelled of wet earth.

The same eerie glow pulsed from the walls down here as well. It was a very disturbing feature. Cole's mind latched onto the glow and tried to rationalize its existence as a means of dealing with his fear. He had little success, as his thoughts drifted to the wards placed by priests upon tombs. Cole's mind conjured images of those wards failing, or not existing, and a veritable horde of spirits waiting to come pouring out of the wall to slay the two of them.

However, despite Cole's fears, the ghosts did not attack. The spirits wandered aimlessly all throughout the chamber, oblivious to their presence. What was still recognizable in their worn ethereal faces and clothing, could be identified as a common warrior's garb of hides and leather.

Thankfully, most of the ghosts congregated and floated around the ceiling of the chamber, another twenty or so feet above Cole's head,. A few forlorn souls lay upon their biers or hovered closely nearby, seemingly resigned to their fate and wretched existence.

Byron motioned to a doorway along the far wall below. It was lined with granite which Cole took to signify some importance, considering the dearth of architecture in this area. If Master Tyson hid some item in the barrows, that door would be as likely a place as any other. However, the only way to reach that door without exposing themselves to every ghost in the room would be to move down the ramp and hug the chamber wall until reaching the door. They would need to move quickly and silently; careful not to alert or be detected by the wandering spirits.

It was as good a plan as any, Cole decided. Besides, he really did not fancy having to fight the ghosts of thousand-year-old dead hillmen. He still struggled with fighting living opponents. These ghosts were big, scary, and many still carried axes and clubs. Very large axes and clubs.

They moved steadily down the earthen ramp, with every fiber of Cole's being screaming in protest with each step. How could a pile of dirt possibly hold up under their weight? It had been here for so long that it had to be close to falling apart. Then they would fall, and then the ghosts would get them. Cole squeezed his eyes shut. If he could not see the danger, then it would not be real. That was rational. He would reopen them in just a second.

The next thing Cole knew his face smacked into a hard surface. He nearly yelped as he fumbled around with his sword. He glanced around quickly, looking to see if the ghosts were coming to kill him. But there had not been any shrieks, or ghostly visages appearing out of the wall, or any other sounds of impending doom. Only Byron, scowling at him.

Cole had walked into Byron's back. He had jumped at his own friend's presence. Cole blushed sheepishly. He had managed to keep his eyes closed for the entire way down the ramp. Byron rolled his eyes in exasperation and they continued on towards the granite lined doorway.

They passed within feet of a few of the ghosts that were loitering near their biers. The ghosts appeared disinterested and not focused on the world around them. They just remained still, moaning softly to themselves. Cole could not blame them. After hundreds of years of being stuck in the same room, it would be easy to lose interest in an unchanging world.

They were within ten paces of the doorway when a loud shriek cut through the melancholy moaning in the chamber. Above the doorway, a spirit was embedded into the soil and it was screeching while stretching its arms out in the direction of the boys.

Cole groaned inwardly as fear gripped his body. It was a guardian of sorts and it had alerted the spirits in the room to their presence. Whatever lay beyond the granite doorway must be of some importance to the spirits in the barrows. What in the name of the gods could be important to a ghost anyway? Cole paused for a heartbeat to ponder the question, his shortsword shaking in his hand. What *could* a ghost determine to be important and worth protecting?

He did not have much time to ponder the matter, as Byron grabbed him by the arm and propelled him through the granite lined door. Cole stumbled going through the door, but luckily kept his balance, and kept moving down the hallway beyond, anxious to put some distance between himself and the ghosts.

The hallway beyond the granite lined door was surprisingly crafted entirely of stone. A divergence from the packed dirt in the barrows. Ceiling, walls, and floor were all laid with crude granite stones, providing the area with a cramped claustrophobic atmosphere. There were sconces in the wall that had once held torches long ago, and the entire length of the ceiling and walls were covered in strange glyphs and runes.

The stone-lined path sloped down gently into the darkness. There were not any graves lining the walls. Only torches, glyphs and runes adorned the granite walls. Cole concluded that this particular corridor must be important. If the hillmen refused to bury their dead in this area, why else was there a passage even deeper into the earth? And why did the ghosts avoid this hallway? And why was there a guardian above the doorway? Cole turned around to tell Byron of his suspicions, and his eyeballs nearly popped out at what he saw.

Byron was standing before the doorway, a longsword in each hand, looking in each direction for vengeful ghosts.

"Byron! Get in here!" screamed Cole. His voice sounded raw and high-pitched to his own ears, and altogether too loud. He did not care though. The prince was acting reckless again, and was liable to get both of them killed. What was Byron trying to prove? Why fight a ghost when they could run?

"No! I can hold 'em off," shouted Byron as the spirits advanced in a semi-circle upon the doorway. Their faces were grim and their eyes shone with hate. The eyes captivated Cole. Many said the eyes were windows to the soul, or some other poetic phrase. Cole did not care about that. Eyes were interesting. The colors and how some people had eyes that seemed to dance, while others had a certain dullness lurking behind them. Cole tended to find that the latter almost solely belonged to those with somewhat slow minds.

The eyes on these ghosts however were terrifying. They were red, gold, orange, and purple, entirely the wrong colors for humans, and they were all terrifying. They glowed and pulsed in a rhythm reminiscent of a beating human heart. And they shone with hatred.

And all the eyes were focused on Byron. It was as if Cole were invisible to them.

"Byron! Get back in here! Now!" hissed Cole as loudly as he dared as an idea quickly formed in his head.

"I can't! They'll overwhelm us! Find a way out or whatever it is that we are supposed to find in this damn place!"

"Byron, they won't come in here!"

"What?" replied Byron as he swiped lazily towards an advancing ghost. The ghost hesitated briefly. Whether that hesitation was because the blade could actually hurt it, or some remnant of a human instinct, Cole could not tell. Nor did he particularly care. The specters were closing in on them and their angry eyes now had an additional emotion behind them: excitement. Cole doubted that they had been granted the opportunity to unleash their hatred of the living on anyone in an incredibly long time.

"There are glyphs and runes on the wall! No tombs! The ghosts don't come in here! They must be the same thing that the churches and temples place within the cities! COME ON! BACK UP!" screamed Cole. His voice rising in volume as the spirits inched closer and closer to Byron.

Byron hesitated for a second, gave one look at the approaching ethereal mass and dove through the doorway. His momentum carried him forward, rolling down the hallway past Cole.

Cole swallowed and tightened his grip as those glowing eyes advanced; their attention now focused on him.

The ghosts halted just before the doorframe, the volume of their shrieks increasing. Their eyes never left Cole. They stared straight at him, intense and angry. The spirits in the back of the pack kept pushing, trying to move past their brethren in the front. But they never made it past the doorway. Some force prevented the ghosts from crossing the granite threshold. The ghosts appeared to crash into an invisible wall and pile on top of each other like waves crashing against a cliff.

Cole sighed and sheathed his weapons. "It looks like we're safe for the moment."

Byron arched an eyebrow as he slowly picked himself off the ground. "Safe? Maybe. Have you considered what would be beyond this hallway that would need this sort of protection?" he said while gesturing to the glyphs on the wall. "Or if maybe these are here to protect the ghosts back there from whatever is down this way?"

Cole felt his anger rise as his hands fell back to his hilts. Byron always did that. He seemed to enjoy being contrarian. To point out what others missed, give an alternative theory. He always had to be right. It was infuriating. And Cole had not known him for that long. How Dalton and Jeron managed not to strangle him, he would never know.

The worst part was that Byron actually was right. This time.

Only a fool would assume safety in a place that had already proven to be less than hospitable. Cole's hands drifted back to his belt as he drew a sword and dagger. He did not particularly feel like being a fool today. "I take it you want to go deeper?" he asked.

"Better than staying here and seeing if those ghosts can find a way in here eventually, or find ourselves caught between them and whatever lies down this way. Besides, it may be fun."

"Fun? I think that blow to your head is starting to affect your brain," muttered Cole drily.

"Oh goody," said Byron as he began to walk down the corridor. "I've always wanted to be crazy. If I'm crazy then I can't be held responsible for my actions."

"I'm pretty sure that saying about fools and the fools that follow them applies here," said Cole, his voice sorrowful.

"Definitely," agreed Byron.

"So are you crazy or a fool?" asked Cole.

"Yup. Almost certainly."

Cole rolled his eyes and moved to slap himself in the forehead in mock aggravation. He stopped his hand just before his face. The dagger he had drawn moments before was inches from his eyes. He stared at it, astonished at his own stupidity. He had let his emotions get the best of him and lost his focus for only a moment, forgetting that he had drawn his dagger.

Cole closed his eyes and took a few breaths to calm his racing heart. He had almost joined the ghosts of his own accord, by doing something so bereft of common sense that not even a child would do it. At this pace Byron would not have a chance to get him killed. Cole would manage the feat all on his own.

"And I'm the fool," said Byron wryly.

Cole rolled his eyes, swore under his breath, and they resumed their march downward into the depths of the barrows in relative silence.

The glyphs and runes in the corridor slowly gave way to depictions of beings, part man, part animal, doing battle with each other and all manner of creatures. Were those depictions of how the hillmen came to grips with their totems, or did those creatures actually exist? Cole swallowed against the bile rising in his throat. The last thing he needed was to encounter some strange unknown creature down here. Much less the ghost of one.

The further down the corridor they ventured, the more decorative the trappings on the wall became. Crude bits of jade and uncut gems were strewn haphazardly against the walls, as if they had just been dumped in a pile and pushed out of the way. Figurines of gold and other precious metals began to appear embedded within the stone walls.

The corridor emptied out into a chamber the size of a noble's large bedroom. At least six granite pillars supported the ceiling, and an enormous pile of treasure was centered around an ancient stone tomb. Weapons, nuggets of gold, simple chalices, gemstones, and jewelry were included in the horde. It was a grand fortune fit to honor a great hillman warrior or king.

Sitting atop the tomb was the ethereal figure of a large skeleton. The skeleton stood a head taller than any man Cole had ever seen. The handle of a large claymore stuck up over its right shoulder. The skeletal spirit wore a suit of chainmail with a mantle of animal hides draped over its shoulders, cascading down its back and ending at the waist. The armor gave the spirit the appearance of being a refined warrior, while the furs lent it an air of a savage.

A crown of twisted iron rested upon its brow. Iron spikes fanned out in a circle from the top of the crown, and a large egg-shaped sapphire was set in the center of the band giving the appearance of a third eye, dark and merciless.

And its eyes drew Cole in. They were made of a pale flame. At first glance they appeared to be a shade of white. Then they flickered between what seemed to be a very light blue, then an orange, a red, a purple, and even a shiny black. They were decidedly too creepy and eerie; appearing to flicker in time with Cole's fluttering heartbeat.

And they were staring directly at Cole.

His heart raced even faster as he met that gaze. The spirit's eyes increased the pace of their flickering, matching the pace of his racing heart.

The rational part of Cole's mind was telling him that all the noise the spirits in the other room had made would certainly have put the skeletal ghost on alert to any intruders, and the ghost would naturally be on its guard. But that rationalization did not make coping with the being's gaze any easier. There was still a part of Cole's mind screeching at him to run and hide. He was familiar with that voice. It was a voice that had kept him alive in the city. It was just good common sense that even a ghost could not kill what it could not find.

The ghost rose from its stony tomb, its armor clinking as metal shifted upon bone. Its jaw moved, and its voice hissed out in what Cole imagined fog would sound like if fog could make noise. "Who are you to interrupt my rest?" the ghost demanded imperiously. It drew the sword from its shoulder, holding it nonchalantly before Cole. The sword seemed to be just out of phase with reality. It appeared to be solid while also simultaneously appearing to be ethereal and ghostly. "All I want is pea—Where did you go?!" roared the creature as it swung its sword in a wild arc. "YOU WILL NOT HAVE MY TREASURE!" bellowed the creature as he charged the boys' position, instantly switching personalities from detached weariness to a bloodthirsty jealous rage.

Stunned, Cole could only watch as the deceased spirit swiftly narrowed the gap between them. Fright had a firm grasp on Cole's mind and his cognitive functions slowly ground to a halt. Some dim portion of his mind was aware that he had shifted his body to blend into the granite wall. However, all his brain could manage was wondering why a ghost needed to run when apparently it could float wherever it wished.

His brief reverie was interrupted as his body was tossed against the wall, as Byron pushed past him to charge the creature. Byron met the skeletal ghost at the outskirts of the pile of treasure, their swords meeting in a shower of sparks. Byron attempted to dance around the creature, his blades snaking towards the ghostly warrior.

The spirit floated effortlessly through the fight, parrying Byron's blows and returning them with savage ferocity, its eyes flickering quickly. The skeletal ghost showed no signs of tiring and began to cackle during the fight. "Grave robber, this place will be your tomb. You'll join us for all eternity in your torment!"

Byron gritted his teeth and blocked a blow aimed at his head. "Isn't that a little overly dramatic for a dead person?"

The spirit never responded, it only shrieked and resumed its flurry of blows. Byron could not continue defending himself from the being for much longer. His body was already wounded and battered from the day's events. It was only a matter of time before he slipped up, even if it was only by a fraction of a second. And then he would be dead. Or worse.

Cole was not exactly sure what would happen if the ancient warrior struck Byron, but he was certain that it would not be pleasant. He gulped and forced down the bile that was rising higher in his throat. He knew he had to do something to help Byron, but had no idea where to begin.

How does one go about fighting a ghost that all the other ghosts appeared to be terrified of? Was he a king or an overlord? Why did he appear as a skeleton while the others retained flesh? Was it some sort of reflection on the spirit's mental state that the ghost was aware that it was long since deceased, and should by all rights be a skeleton? Did a ghost have a mental state? Why would a ghost care so much about treasure? Where would the weaknesses be in a hill king's armor, he wondered, as his mind raced to process the ongoing stream of information.

And would the ghost have the same weakness as a being of flesh? It probably lacked internal organs, especially if it was only a skeleton, but Cole did not want to get close enough to confirm that theory. The training at Raven's Perch did not include such creatures. Probably because not many people had ever attempted to solve that mystery, and fewer probably ever survived such an encounter.

Cole never had the chance to find his courage, as Byron's foot slipped on a stray golden gem-encrusted chalice, depositing the prince to the floor with a heavy thud and sending one of his swords skittering across the floor. The ghost howled in triumph and charged the fallen boy, its eyes pulsating a bright red. Byron weakly raised his blade in a feeble attempt to parry the incoming blow. The spirit beat Byron's blade to the side with its claymore, and its skeletal offhand darted towards Byron's exposed body.

Cole screamed in rage and frustration as he wildly tossed his dagger at the deceased hillman. The blade toppled end over end as it streaked towards the ghostly skull.

But it did not fly fast enough.

The ghost's bony hand plunged into Byron's left shoulder, his shirt and skin melting as they came in contact with the spirit's ethereal limb.

Pus and blood immediately started pouring forth from the wound. The skin around the specter's bony hand began to char and curl back upon itself at the entry site. There was a hissing sound as steam rose from the wound. Something, Cole did not know what, sounded and smelled like it was boiling inside of Byron's shoulder.

Meanwhile, the dagger struck home, the point piercing the spirit's eye socket. The spirit's sword evaporated and vanished from existence, as it yanked its hand out of Byron and clawed at the injury.

While it shrieked, Cole crept quietly towards Byron, ignoring the sounds of bone scraping loudly against bone. Cole grabbed Byron's uninjured arm and cautiously began dragging him towards the entrance to the chamber.

Cole strained with his back and legs as he pulled the muscled boy. Just a little bit farther and they would be away from the crazed spirit and its claymore.

Cole nearly fell as his foot slipped and kicked a small object off into the dark. His breath caught in his throat as the same chalice that Byron had previously slipped on, scuttled off through the chamber, bouncing off plates, coins, and other objects causing all sorts of a racket. A small anti-climactic *clank* signified the end of its trip as the chalice came to a rest against the stone wall.

The spirit whipped its head around searching for the offending noise. Cole tightened his grip on Byron's arm in white-knuckled terror. They were exposed, standing in the middle of the room without any cover. It was only a matter of seconds before the spirit's gaze drifted away from the wall.

"Show yourselvessss!", screeched the spirit, its voice trailing off into a hiss reminiscent of the stories the masters told Cole and the other trainees about creatures called snakes. "Where are you hiding you filthy grave robbers?"

Cole froze, not daring to breathe, ignoring the small cold bead of sweat dripping its way down his spine. The creature was swinging its sword at random, trying desperately to strike them while simultaneously yelling rudimentary curses. Cole slowly resumed dragging Byron towards the hallway. Remaining still was not an option. Eventually the spirit might get lucky and connect with its sword if they did not move. Glancing down at Byron's wound, Cole was certain that he did not want to share in that fate, or see what sort of wound the ghost's spectral blade would leave in its wake.

"Where are you?" bellowed the ghost as it slammed its blade into a pile of gold coins, showering the room in a cascade of tiny golden missiles. "Do you even exist? Or are you some sort of phantoms sent to haunt me!"

Cole stopped his dragging in the doorway. His heart was trying to lodge itself within his throat. What the hell was the spirit babbling about? It knew it was dead? Were *they* spirits? Was the thing insane? *It* was the spirit!

The spirit's blade dropped to the ground with a soft hiss. "I'm not mad yet," the ghost said softly. "I've survived this long, I'm not going mad yet, not while I still have my treasure! Do you hear me?! I'm not mad yet!" roared the ghost in defiance to no one in particular.

The creature collapsed into sobs, convulsions racking its skeletal form, but no tears came from its eyes. Cole stood transfixed in the doorway, dumbfounded by what he was witnessing. Who knew that the ghosts had feelings? Or that they could go insane.

Cole bent down and struggled to lift Byron. The boy was mostly shoulder and muscle. While Cole's training had made him stronger, lifting deadweight was a grueling feat to which he was still unaccustomed.

Eventually, Cole managed to heft Byron up onto his shoulder, careful that the two of them stayed in contact with each other. Cole did not know how he had kept them both hidden from that spirit, but he liked the results enough not to question them.

The tiny voice in his brain screamed that if he thought about keeping them both invisible, that he would lose the ability to conceal them both. He knew that it did not make any sense, but nothing so far today had made any sense. He needed to put his faith in something, and it might as well be his own instincts.

He glanced back once last time at the ghost in the burial chamber. It was vacillating between extreme sorrow and fits of rage. Insanity did not do the being justice.

Cole turned and hobbled back towards the earthen barrows teeming with mindless ghosts. If he could manage to keep the two of them hidden from one ghost, then he could hopefully keep them hidden from a horde of the ghosts.

At least that was what he was telling himself. Master Tyson's mission be damned; he just wanted to get out of the barrows alive.

CHAPTER TEN

Tyson swore under his breath for the umpteenth time as he paced the dungeon floor. He schooled his features into an outward expression of calm. Years of training and field experience prevented even a fleeting emotion from straying across his face. It was his personal and professional philosophy that people should not be able to read his thoughts from his features, and he made certain that not a single unwanted expression crossed his face without his consent. But if those two boys were privy to his thoughts at that moment, they would strongly consider fleeing to Nuqua and joining up with a buccaneer fleet.

Far above the stone foundations of Raven's Perch the day dragged on, and the sun light began to wan and fade, taking with it Tyson's belief that Byron and Cole were shirking their duties. Nevertheless, he slouched silently in the flickering torch light, patiently awaiting the return of his charges. Usually, Tyson enjoyed the serene moments that came with the job. Today, that peace of mind eluded him as the intermittent shrieks from the ghosts below punctured his thoughts.

He had charge of the Duke's son for only a brief period of time, and already the boy was proving to be more trouble than he was currently worth. It should not have taken the boys that long to accomplish their task. Tyson had set the medallions on the ground at the top of the staircase leading down into the barrows. It was a simple task to test their mettle, prove to him that they had the courage to overcome life threatening fears to accomplish their mission. The ghosts terrified everyone with any sense in Raven's Perch. The two lads merely needed to overcome their natural instincts to avoid the spirits, and take the first steps toward the crypts. He would not actually send them down into that death trap.

Laziness, Tyson could break through that flaw with hard work. Cowardice, however, was a completely different creature. A person either had bravery, courage, or whatever the bard's were calling it these days, or they simply did not. Sure, a coward may find something rise up within them in extraordinary situations and accomplish a feat that most would consider brave. However, in Tyson's experience, those situations usually were few and far between. People just did not change all that much. They were who they were.

Being a wraith meant having the strength of will in trying times that were not extraordinary situations. Situations where a person's life was not immediately at risk, but by doing one's duty, their own life would be placed in jeopardy. Getting people to take that first step was always the most difficult in Tyson's mind.

Thump. Tyson quickly scanned the area, his ears straining to detect the source of the noise emanating from the darkness. Nothing. Time and age were not being kind to his senses, and in his line of work, old age and retirement were not usually an option.

Tyson clenched his fists, and was startled to realize that he had drawn his dagger without consciously deciding to do so. He silently scolded himself as he sheathed the blade. Jumping at shadows was childish. Just because he was getting old, that did not mean he had to make Death's job any easier.

Thump. Twin daggers sprang into Tyson's hands. His senses were not deceiving him this time. Someone, or something was beyond the cells. Silently, Tyson chided himself for his own childhood fears of ghosts. The sigils holding the dead in their tombs had not failed in centuries. Meaning that whatever he heard had to be a living being. He shook his head trying to force his thoughts from the macabre path they had been on lately.

The noise continued, increasing in volume and proximity. Tyson stuck to the shadows, inching closer to the sound, his eyes unable to detect the source of the noise. Seconds passed and the noise crept inexorably closer. A strangled moan floated down the hallway, its raspy voice filled with pain. Sweat slowly slid down Tyson's neck, but the source of the voice eluded him.

Maybe it was a ghost, Tyson thought to himself as years of his mother's bedtime stories surged to the forefront of his mind. He tried to banish the idea, but the terror that gripped his mind would not let him. He was above the barrows, there were loud noises, creepy moans, and all without a visible source. Reason be damned, all the evidence pointed to a ghost stalking the dungeon.

Thump. The noise was almost upon him now. Tyson strained, pressing his back into the wall in an effort to give the spirit as much room to pass as possible. Staying silent and observing was usually the best course of action. How does one fight a ghost anyway? Can one even fight a ghost with mundane tools? Tyson did not know, so he held his breath, determined not to alert the spirit to his presence. If he managed to survive, the first thing he was going to do was ask a priest about battling ghosts.

Thump. Thump. Thump. The noise was nearly past him now. *Thump. Thump.* His lungs burned as the pained moaning drew even with him. *Thump.* He still could not see anything. *Thump. Thump.* The noise passed by him and Tyson slowly let his breath escape in a hiss, while his eyes attempted to track the noise. The attempt was fruitless, as his eyes could see neither man nor spirit. *Thump. Thump.* Whatever *it* was, it was heading for the door –*Thump*– and the fort full of trainees

Indecision gripped Tyson. He could not fight the creature, but how could one raise an alarm against an incorporeal being? Everyone be on the lookout for...nothing? And the racket from a raised alarm would certainly mask the creature's movements.

At the very least he could follow it and see where it went. With his decision made, Tyson lifted his foot to advance, and paused.

The room had gone silent.

The air shimmered, it looked like a layer of water was rippling around the source of the spirit's moans. The rippling suddenly vanished and two blood-soaked bodies tumbled to the stone dungeon floor. They bounced heavily, like a dead fish tossed on the dock.

Tyson peered at the bodies from his hiding place in the shadows. The bottom body was soaked with blood, dirt, and grime. It looked as if the blood originated from the head, although Tyson could not discern any visible wounds through the mess of blood and dirt.

The second body appeared to be much better off at first glance. There was a comparatively minimal amount of blood along its right side. Tyson carefully crept around the room and amended his evaluation of the second body. While the right side was relatively clear of blood, the left side was soaked through. The source of the blood appeared to be a deep pus-filled wound on the left shoulder.

Swallowing his fear, Tyson approached the bodies to inspect them. It struck him as odd that spirits would bleed, much less leave behind a body. The bodies appeared to be that of a pair of teenagers. Perhaps, a pair of hill-people ghosts deduced a way through or around the wards.

Ghosts of hill people? Walking dead? That could avoid the wards? Tyson shook his head in disbelief. There had to be a more reasonable explanation. It was just his nerves getting the best of him. He wiped the blood and dirt off of the second body's face, and felt the color rush out from his own.

Indeed. There was a simple, easy explanation.

The body was Byron's.

CHAPTER ELEVEN

C ole leapt back into the crowd, startled by the horse that had bumped into him. He quickly regained his balance before he was knocked to the ground by a hairy Nuquan sailor.

There were two things a small child could expect when walking through the streets of the city of Antier: people from every duchy in the kingdom, and being jostled by the uncaring crowd.

Cole struggled to stand up and regain his footing upon the rough cobblestones. His muscles ached and his body burned from dozens of cuts and scrapes. Cole staggered to his feet with the aid of a wooden hitch post, and immersed himself into the murmurs of the crowd as it went implacably about its daily business.

"Is he okay?"

The words cut through the drone of everyday life, but Cole could not grasp their meaning. A child getting knocked over in the overlap between the Merchant District and Center District was a common enough sight. But a person noticing, now that would be an uncommon sight. No one was that kind.

Cole scanned the faces of the crowd, searching out the concerned voice. His search was fruitless, as he knew it would be. The crowd simply did not care. Both the sizes of the people and the clothing that passed by him came in a wide variety, but every face marched onward, focused intently on reaching its own destination.

Sucking his scrapped knuckles, Cole gingerly maneuvered his way back into the flow of the crowd, careful to stay near its edges. Cole, despite his shorter legs, kept pace with the crowd, dodging the occasional hawker intent on peddling his wares to the masses. Eventually, Cole came upon one of the many markets in the city bustling with throngs of people intent on reaching their destinations as quickly as possible. People carried sacks full of goods and groceries, barking at everyone to get out of their way. Cole quickly scrambled onto an empty bench beneath a solitary tree, desperate to avoid being trampled by the crowd.

Gazing around the square, Cole tried to remember what errand brought him to the market. Did he need to visit the butcher? No. Mother rarely could afford food on most days. Cole rubbed his sore head. Apparently, the horse had knocked him harder than he realized. He could not remember why he came here, but he knew his errands were important. Someone had to put food on the table. By any means possible. Father taught him that lesson.

"-no, they are minor-"

Cole leapt off the bench, prepared to run from the voice following him. But his foot caught on the edge of the bench, and for the second time that morning, Cole's body slammed into the ground.

He crawled on his hands and knees, trying to regain his equilibrium. The city spun around him, oblivious to his discomfort. He pulled himself up with the aid of a wooden post supporting the eaves of a tailor's shop. The rough grain of the wood tore at his already scraped hands. Cole yelped as a splinter found its way into one of the open wounds on his hands. It was always the smallest pains that seemed to hurt the most.

The sun was still hours away from midday, and the market was packed with people going about their morning business. A butcher's shop, a cart selling meat pies, a cobbler, and none of them were what he was searching for. Not being able to remember his errand irked Cole. He had too much responsibility to forget simple things. Unfortunately, people depended upon him. Running his hands through his red hair, Cole decided to survey the market square one last time before continuing his search in a new location.

Upon closer inspection, there was nothing remarkable about this particular market. The buildings in this section of the city were made mostly of stone. Yet there were the occasional wooden beams on the structures, and wooden market stalls set throughout the square. However, they were rarely side by side. The layout of the square appeared to be designed to safeguard the buildings from the spread of fire jumping from one wooden structure to the next. Constructing stone buildings was not inexpensive, and many merchants forewent the expense as their wares were simply not worth the extra cost.

Cole frowned as he stared at the shops. He was not one to acquire expensive goods; they attracted attention, making it harder to blend into a crowd. However, he would not be in a market such as this one unless he needed an expensive item.

His gaze settled on a jewelry shop, and he felt a faint memory tug at his mind. Some distant memory danced at the edges of his consciousness, light, yet irritatingly insistent. Perhaps his mother had sent him to pick up a piece of jewelry, or maybe a gift for one of his sisters. Cole could not quite remember, but that felt wrong. Try as he might, he could not recall his mother or sisters wearing jewelry. Much less expensive jewelry. However, the tugging sensation on his brain increased, the sight of the jewelry store drawing him towards its entrance.

The jewelry store was on the far side of the market with a dense shifting throng of people laying between him and his destination. While sticking to the edges of the crowd would be safer, Cole was upset at having already wasted precious time trying to remember his errand, and decided to take a more direct route. He plotted himself a mostly straight path across the market, careful to steer himself clear of the group of nobles chatting beside a fountain. Their exposed fangs and claws marked them as predators. While they seemed genial while talking to each other, Cole had learned through experience that their kind was nothing but trouble for people like himself.

He stepped lightly off of the bench, dipping and spinning his way through the crowd, careful not to jostle anyone and draw unwanted attention to himself. Appearances in Antier could be deceiving, as even the smallest old lady could potentially be strong as an ox and toss Cole around without breaking a sweat.

Cole was halfway across the market square without attracting the attention of anyone in the crowd when he decided to brave a glance toward the fountain and the danger lurking around it. His timing could not have been worse as his eyes briefly locked with one of the noblemen. Cole felt a surge of fear shoot through his body. The man had dirt brown eyes that appeared to blend into his trimmed blonde beard. He wore mustard-colored clothes, with lace around the cuffs, and a thick belt strapped from his left shoulder to his right hip.

The man smiled at Cole, his lips pulled back showing off his two very large canines.

Cole swore under his breath. Any foolish hopes of avoiding notice vanished. He quickly stepped back into the crowd, breaking his line of sight with the mustard clothed nobleman. He focused his mind and forced his body to blend in, to take the appearance of its surroundings. It had required years of effort, but the act became a reflex. Learning how to change his clothing and hair color when blending into the surroundings was difficult, and took quite a bit of time to master, but the results were worth the investment. It was a simple matter of imagining his skin, hair, and clothing as being one continuous part of his body. Once that was locked into his mind, everything just seemed to merge into one. In the space of a breath, Cole vanished.

"-the hell did he go?"

Cole smirked at the sounds of confusion around him. He slipped through the crowd at a reckless speed while in his current state. He was already tired and sore, and as a result would not be able to hold his focus for very long. However, he did not have much of a choice. If he remained stationary it would not take long for someone to realize that just because they could not see him, that did not mean that they could not smell him, hear his breathing, or a slew of other clues available to their senses. Knowledge of his presence negated the advantage of near invisibility. His only option was to place as much distance between himself and his pursuers as he could manage.

Cole's heart pounded as he crossed the street without further incident, and entered the jewelry shop. The door closed behind him, muffling the voices in the square.

The store was modest in its layout. One long counter stretched from wall to wall. Jewels and precious metals gleamed beneath the glass panes of the display case. They were worth more money than he had seen in his short life.

The proprietor sat behind the display case. She was a middle-aged woman, with steel gray hair drawn into a single ponytail. She wore a dark blue vest over a plain white shirt. Cole was not a connoisseur of fine clothing, but even his untrained eyes could discern that her clothes were fashioned from silk. The woman wore a pair of silver framed glasses, and her gaze seemed to pierce right through the lenses.

The array of precious jewelry sparkled beneath the glass counter; various earrings, amulets, necklaces, lockets, bracelets, and rings of precious metals and all set with gems and stones. The inventory could easily bring his family out of the destitute state his grandfather had left them in. Perhaps his father had sent him here to steal some jewelry and sneak away? If that was the case, he would need to hold his focus for just a little longer. At least until he could pilfer the necessary pieces.

"-sent them to pick up two amulets."

Amulets? It did not sound wrong to Cole, but what would his father want with amulets? Cole peered over the counter and down at the amulets. There were about fifty amulets in the case of varying shapes and sizes, but one stood out to Cole. It was a sphere of onyx with silver and platinum threaded around and through the sphere. Sapphires were set inside the silver and platinum inlay, forming the shape of a small blue flame.

"He and Byron were supposed retrieve those amulets in his hand."

Byron and him? Why would Byron have been sent to the jewelry store with him? And when did he spend time with Byron in Antier? The last errand they had gone on together had been to the barrows. Cole's heart raced at the memory. He could still remember the sheer terror as the skeletal specter sunk its bony hand into Byron's shoulder.

But if Byron had been wounded, why would Cole be going on an errand to a jewelry store? Cole racked his brain but could not come up with an answer to the puzzle. Did Byron survive? Cole could not remember that either.

His head was throbbing from when he had fallen earlier in the day. Cole felt nauseated as the room began to spin and blur out of focus. He clutched his head in pain, as if that simple act could bend the world to his will and contain his out-of-control vision and lightheadedness.

Slowly, the room began to slow down. Cole removed his hands from his head and began to apologize to the storekeeper for his unusual mannerisms.

"Ma'am, I'm sorry for the commotion," said Cole as he raised his head. The storekeeper was staring straight into his eyes. Cole felt his voice taper off under her penetrating stare.

He held her gaze and slowly her eyes began to change color. Cole did not flinch. He could change his skin color, and in comparison, hers was not that impressive of a trick. That was until her face began to change shape. Cole was taken aback. He was not familiar with any animals that could change the structure of their bodies to such a degree.

The shopkeepers' face and body progressively became more masculine. Facial hair began to grow and fill in the face. As her body became thicker, her clothing began to change. The shirt and vest transformed into hides, and armor. Recognition slowly set in as the identity dawned on Cole.

It was the same hillman ghost that had attacked Byron. Except that now he looked alive and young.

Cole screamed, turned and fled through the store windows and into the daylight.

***

Strong arms restrained Cole as he struggled to flee. He was no longer in the strange jewelry store. He was in a plain stone-walled room, and if his senses were not deceiving him, he was lying in a bed. Four figures loomed over him.

"Easy, Cole, you're safe now," said the figure on the right. Cole squinted and the water cleared from his eyes. Dalton smiled down at him; his forehead wrinkled in lines of concern.

Jeron, Master Tyson, and a stern-faced woman were also huddled with Dalton over his bed.

"He is suffering from a severe case of fatigue," said the woman to Master Tyson. "What he needs is a few days rest to recover from the shock to his body."

Master Tyson nodded in agreement. "That's good to hear. Thank you, Priestess Jana. If you'll excuse me boys, we need to go check on the other boy."

"The other boy?" The words tore their way out of Cole's already ragged throat. "What happened to Byron? We were in the barrows, there was a ghost, it stabbed its hand into Byron-" Cole hurriedly explained. His voice was racing, the words tumbling out one over the other. "-Oh gods, it stabbed Byron! But then why was I in the city? There were voices following me-" his words began to run together as he reached a frenzied pace, his arms swinging around in his bed. Dalton and Jeron's efforts to restrain him were in vain, his right arm broke free, striking Dalton in the chin. "-and the men who chased me near the fountain- and the jewelry store! Yes! There was a jewelry store! And the woman behind the counter-"

Cole came to a sudden stop as his eyes came to rest on the woman standing near his bed. For the first time since gaining consciousness, Cole actually focused his attention upon her features, and his blood grew cold. She did not look like the woman from the jewelry store; she *was* the woman from the jewelry store.

Cole felt his already sore muscles try to clench up in fear, as his tired mind strained to phase his body into near invisibility. He never got the chance, as Jeron and Dalton took the momentary pause in his flailing to slam him back against his bed and restrain him.

"Quiet," hissed Jeron. "If you start swinging your arms again, I swear I'll slap you and see how much you like it."

"Again?" asked Cole, completely bewildered by the venom in Jeron's tone.

"Yes. Again," growled Dalton, his usual cheery face flushed red in anger. "We carried you to the infirmary, and you fought us the entire way."

"I did?" asked Cole. He thought back to his chase through the city streets of Antier and felt his cheeks heat up as comprehension dawned upon him. "Oh. Sorry. Umm I guess some things are making a little more sense now."

"S'okay, Cole," whispered Dalton as his expression softened in sympathy. "Just try to keep quiet. Maybe we'll be able to overhear something about Byron."

Cole nodded in agreement and took the following moments of silence to evaluate his surroundings. Judging from his apparent physical condition, and the sparse furnishings in his room, he had to be within the medical wing of the fort. Which meant Byron had to be nearby, and given everyone's solemn behavior, the youngest son of the Duke of Antier must have been in worse shape than Cole.

The Duke's son was near death, and Cole was the only person who had been with Byron. That could not be good for his immediate future. Cole swallowed, trying in vain to prevent the contents of his stomach from escaping.

"By God," muttered Dalton as he swiped at his sleeve. "I'm not cut out to be a medic."

"Sorry," said Cole weakly.

"Boys, if you are done," said Tyson from the foot of the bed. Cole glanced around, but the strange priestess had slipped out of the room while he was emptying his stomach. "Before we get started, let me say that I am displeased with how all of you handled today's events."

"But-" began Jeron.

"Quiet! I don't want to hear any excuses," snapped Master Tyson. Jeron clinched his jaw, and said nothing. However, Cole grimaced as Jeron's grip on his arm tightened noticeably. "Now, Cole, can you tell me what hairbrained reason you and Byron had for venturing down into the barrows?"

"Um, uh, sir," stammered Cole. "We were trying to find uhhh whatever it was you sent us down there to umm find...sir" finished Cole lamely.

"In the catacombs, I said," hissed Tyson. "Never did I say enter the barrows. The amulets were hanging right next to the staircase leading down to the barrows. You couldn't have missed them."

"Sir, right when we got to the staircase there, Byron let loose this loud shriek, grabbed his head, and went tumbling down the staircase. I followed after him. We never saw any amulets," said Cole.

"A scream. Explain," ordered Tyson, his face drawn into an expression somewhere between a thundercloud and a granite stone.

Cole took a deep breath, wincing at the pain in his side, and slowly began to tell his tale to the bedside assembly. He began with Byron's piercing scream that sent them down into the barrows, their trek through the ancient burial tombs, Byron's duel with the hill chief's ghost, Byron's subsequent wound, and their inexorably slow flight from the earthy tomb.

"And that's it. I don't remember anything after we reached the dungeon," finished Cole.

"I see," said Tyson as Cole finished speaking. "Well, you two were right about the assignment being a test of courage. However, you two exhibited a total lack of wits when you entered into the barrows. I expect all of you to think and analyze a situation before acting." He narrowed his eyes as he looked over Dalton and Jeron. "And I do mean *all* of you.'

"Why would I risk the prince's life by sending him into the barrows?" Tyson asked but did not wait for a response as he answered his own rhetorical question. "I wouldn't, and I expect you all to realize that. Had you and Byron thought before embarking on some mad impulse, you wouldn't be lying in that bed, and I wouldn't have to explain to the Duke why his son was aimlessly wandering around a ghost infested barrow.

"I expect the three of you to learn how to think for yourselves. It is going to take all three of you working together to keep up with Byron's mind. The boy is too smart for his own good. Even worse, he is aware of his intelligence. Get used to anticipating his every move, as well as those of anyone who might wish to harm him."

"I thought we just had to protect him from anyone who might attack him," asked Jeron. "Not protect him from himself."

"Of course you do," chuckled Tyson. "But you're bodyguards, not mindless lackeys. Get used to preventing situations where you need to knock someone's head in."

"I see," replied Jeron.

"No, I don't think you do," retorted Tyson. "Where is Prince Byron right now?"

Dalton rolled his eyes. "Obviously, he is receiving medical attention from the priests, in that room you won't let us in to," said Dalton sarcastically.

"I see," said Tyson. "So what you're telling me, is that you are unaware of where your charge is right now. But presumably, to the best of your *vast* knowledge, he is injured, maybe unable to defend himself, surrounded by strangers, and you don't think that is a problem?" said Tyson icily.

Jeron swore, and darted from the room nearly crashing into Tyson. The older man sidestepped adroitly, turned towards Dalton and arched an eyebrow questioningly.

"But there are already guards in this wing!" protested Dalton.

"Indeed there are," replied Tyson. "And two of them happen to be those boys that he is fond of fighting. I am sure they will be on their best behavior and won't seek any sort of retribution upon the prince."

Dalton's eyes narrowed, "Not even those two would stoop that low. And besides, the priests won't let us in!"

"Figure it out. Before they do," said Tyson as he gestured towards the door.

Dalton tossed his hands up in exasperation and exited the room. Cole sat up and tried to follow Dalton out of the room.

"Stop," commanded Tyson. Cole let his body sag back into the bed and readied himself for the worst. He had barely begun to be a wraith, and here he was prepared to be sent home in disgrace. That would not do his mother and sisters any good.

Tyson pulled a small stool from against the wall and settled in next to Cole's bed. "You did good, son," said Tyson. Cole struggled to keep his jaw from dropping. He did good? But the prince was wounded! And Master Tyson had just finished stripping off a piece of his hide.

"All things considered, you made the best out of a bad situation," continued Tyson as he tapped his chin thoughtfully. "But there is something I need to know. Jeron deduced right away that Byron was still in danger, despite the prince being watched over by a priest. But his upbringing has left him slightly paranoid.

"Dalton took a little prodding to figure it out," continued Tyson. "However, it is in his nature to try to avoid conflict. What I need to know," said Tyson as he leaned in closer to the bed, "is when did you figure out the potential danger."

"When you said he was alone with priests working on him," replied Cole.

"And you think priests are a potential threat?" asked Tyson.

"Everyone is a threat," answered Cole coldly.

Tyson threw back his head and laughed. It was a deep laugh, but not consistent, it cracked as if covered in rust from lack of use. "So cynical for one so young. You'll do," chuckled Tyson as he turned and headed for the door.

"Master Tyson, umm is that it?" asked Cole. Tyson arched an eyebrow at the boy. "I just assumed there would be uhh, more yelling, and screaming, and uhh why am I still talking?"

"Because you completed your mission," said Tyson as he gestured towards Cole. "If you would have looked in your hand, you'd have realized that one of you had the presence of mind to pick that up on your way back."

"Picked what up?" asked Cole as he glanced down at his hands. His left hand was clenched in a fist around a silver chain. Dangling from the chain was some sort of amulet or medallion made up of gemstones. Cole inspected the design closer; it appeared to be a blue flame. It looked eerily familiar. Cole flipped it over a few times as realization dawned on him.

It was the same onyx amulet with the blue flame from his dream.

Master Tyson slipped out of the room without another word as sleep slowly overtook Cole's body.

CHAPTER TWELVE

The minotaur bellowed, its nose ring swinging violently back and forth, as its axe arched towards Darik's head. Darik intercepted the blow with his greatsword, the shock of the strike reverberating up his arms. Darik gritted his teeth and shoved forward against the minotaur's axe. Hard.

Nine feet of bovine monstrosity tumbled backwards off of the fort's walls and into the teeming mass of the army below. Immediately a swarm of satyrs crested the wall, filling the void left behind by the fallen minotaur.

Darik inhaled deeply, his lungs filling with burning pressure, and with a minor effort, he expelled a torrent of fire at the advancing horde. The flames burned white hot, incinerating the advancing goat men into a pile of ash, and rendering the enemy's scaling ladders useless.

"Reserves advance!" Darik bellowed in a tone and volume that his sergeants could only dream of reaching.

Darik took a brief respite from the battle to catch his breath and survey the section of the wall where the monsters had temporarily gained control. Geoffrey had been in charge of this portion of the wall. He was the third son of a baron whose holdings lay in the east, along the border between Antier and the capital duchy of Ochandor. As a result of his proximity to the capital, Geoffrey had always concerned himself with political intrigue, and considered the legion of monsters to the west of the wall to be beneath him, as they were a distant threat and nothing more than simple savages.

Geoffrey's body lay sprawled against the east side of the wall, pulled away from the conflict by the soldiers in his command. His body had been mangled by the crude blunt weapons of the satyrs, his limbs contorted until they faced odd directions. Darik sighed as the reserves advanced past him, plugging the position vacated by Geoffrey's men.

"Captain, the enemy is beginning to retreat along the edges, and are pulling back from the wall," said Renaldo. "Looks like this battle is over."

"Thank you, Renaldo," replied Darik. "However, my memory must be a little fuzzy. I seem to remember ordering you to stay in the keep."

"Really?" said an aghast Renaldo. "I feel like I would have remembered that. You know, maybe you took a blow to the head from that minotaur."

"I'm fine," answered Darik drily. "I didn't take any blows to the head."

"You don't remember the injury?" asked Renaldo, mock concern etched on his face. "That's the worst kind of head injury! We better get you to the priests right away. It must have been a horrific injury to make you think that you ordered your best friend to stay behind in the keep. Why, if you had done that, you might have wound up doing something incredibly stupid. You know, like fighting a minotaur one on one, while a horde of satyrs tried to take the wall."

"You've made your point," said Darik.

"Have I?" asked Renaldo, blood dripping from his thin brown hair. "I would hate to deprive the women of the realm of the Jewel of Antier."

"The Jewel, huh," Darik said flatly through a clenched jaw, as he glowered at Renaldo. "Well we'd hate for that to happen. Clearly the stress must be getting to you for you to worry so much. Maybe you should go check with the priests. How about I throw you to the keep? Cut out some time from your trip?"

"You're too generous, Your Highness," said Renaldo with a stiff formal bow. "I suggest you save your strength, and we walk back to the keep. Leave the fighting to Emkario, and the rest of the men."

Darik nodded his assent, and the duo descended from the battlements, the clamor of battle fading behind them. Soldiers hurried past them in both directions. Some were carrying supplies to the wall, while others marched in the opposite direction carrying the wounded back to the keep.

The keep rested at the eastern entrance of Hope Pass, located at the western outskirts of Antier. Fort Hope, was situated in proximity to the only two paths leading into the monster inhabited lands beyond the western edge of Antier. One was the mountain pass itself, home of the keep and the battlements that they had fought upon, located at the western exit of the pass. The other pass was five miles to the south at a small gap between the mountain range and the cliffs above the River Irinin.

"We received a batch of messages while you were at the wall," said Renaldo calmly, as if the battle was simply part of his daily routine. "Some military in nature, some political, and one with your family's crest."

Darik took a long sip of water from his flask as they walked into the keep's courtyard. "What'd they say?" he asked.

"Reinforcements are coming. A few minor nobles and their retainers. A minor skirmish along the Loachian border over a merchant caravan," recited Renaldo from memory.

"And the message from my family?" asked Darik.

"How should I know? Do you really think I would open your personal messages? You wound me," said Renaldo as he dramatically pressed a hand to his heart.

Darik arched an eyebrow and grunted in response.

"Fine," said Renaldo as he tossed his hands up in exasperation. "You know you could at least let me have some fun with it." Darik grunted again. "Let's see, your father said that he is proud of you, and is thinking of setting forth some plan that the two of you have talked about. Your mother says that she loves you, and that she has picked out a few eligible ladies to dine with you the next time you are in town."

Darik gasped as he choked on his water. "Easy there m'lord," said Renaldo as he slapped Darik on the back. "I'm certain these fine ladies are actually interested in you and not your future prospects. Oh, and your brother joined the wraiths." Renaldo added the last bit a little too quickly and matter of fact. Subtlety was not his strong suit. He favored direct conflict, and was not terribly adept at political machinations. It made him a great friend and refreshingly loyal in a court full of people who all thought themselves cleverer than the next.

"Yup," agreed Darik.

"Wait, you already knew? Great," groaned Renaldo. "Now the little monster will be able to torment me without me seeing him."

"That's kind of the point," said Darik stone-faced. "And I'm pretty certain you started that feud. Byron does owe you one."

"Hmm maybe," mused Renaldo. "Who really knows how these things get started? These sorts of things get lost in the annals of time."

Darik gestured for a messenger as they passed into Fort Hope. "Please send Lieutenant Vincent up to my office once he arrives," ordered Darik. "And tell him to have a report ready." The soldier saluted and departed at a quick jog.

"The engineers?" asked Renaldo as they walked across the marshalling yard and into the keep proper. "Did the wall suffer structural damage?"

"I'm not sure," admitted Darik. "But given the recent increase in activity on the wall, I think it prudent to check. Better safe than giving the beasts a clear path into the duchy."

Renaldo's arm shot out and grabbed the nearest soldier rushing past, yanking the man clear off the ground, and placing the soldier before him. "You. Disregard whatever orders you have, and go find the quartermaster and send him to the Prince's office." Renaldo patted the confused solider, and gave him a gentle shove in the general direction of the storeroom.

Darik wound his way through the keep until he reached his office. He placed his hand on the heavy oak door and began to push it open. Before the door could budge, Renaldo pushed Darik out of the way, and opened the door, one hand resting on the haft of the giant axe strapped to his back.

"Excuse me," said Renaldo as he entered the room ahead of Darik. "All clear. I don't see or smell anyone."

Darik shouldered his way past Renaldo, and gently tossed his helmet on his desk before collapsing into his chair. It was a simple unadorned wooden chair, as was the rest of the furniture in the office. While Antier was universally considered the frontier, Fort Hope was essentially the wilderness, and extravagant furniture was not available, nor was it needed.

Renaldo unlimbered the great axe from his back and took a seat next to the door. "Tell me, how did you know that Byron joined the wraiths?"

"It was my idea," said Darik as he picked up the stack of letters and began reading.

"Your idea?!" sputtered Renaldo. "Great, now I won't be able to sleep whenever the little man is around."

"Byron is taller than you are," muttered Darik as he read a report on the troop displacements on the northern border with Loach. "And your lack of sleep was the entire point of the plan. I want every noble in the kingdom to not be able to sleep well when Byron is around."

"I don't follow," said Renaldo as he rocked the chair back and forth, nearly tipping it over every few seconds.

Darik lay the report down on the desk, and glanced up at Renaldo. "It's simple. As things currently stand, every noble knows that Byron hasn't found his totem, and as a result they know exactly what he is capable of. They believe him weak, and that they can exploit that weakness. The wraiths are shrouded in secrecy, and dark rumors. Now, no one will know exactly what Byron is capable of, and maybe just maybe those rumors will have them checking under the bed before they try to sleep."

Renaldo hummed as he drummed his fingers against the side of his head. "Well, that could work. But how could you guarantee that Byron would pick the wraiths."

"It was simple," said Darik as he picked up his father's letter. "I threatened to have the other society masters transferred here if they selected Byron. After that, well they didn't seem too enthused to extend Byron an offer. That left him only two options, become a wraith or the family-approved path of being a paladin, and you know how he hates being told what to do."

"Byron will be pissed when he finds out," said Renaldo with a small chuckle.

"I know," assented Darik as he picked up a blank piece of parchment, and began drafting a reply to his father. "But if it keeps him alive, I don't really care."

"So what are you going to say to your father?" asked Renaldo. "Dearest father, things are rough here. Please send more troops, even though you already know that we're stretched pretty thin, and please send some rations that don't taste like my belt."

"Something like that," answered Darik without looking up from his parchment. "We do need more troops, and there is a plan in place for that."

"Is there also a plan for better rations?" asked Renaldo a note of hope entering his voice.

Darik ignored him and continued writing.

A knock on the door forestalled any further response from Renaldo. "Who is it?" asked Renaldo, his hand tightening upon his axe's haft.

"Lieutenant Vincent," came a muffled reply.

Darik gestured, and Renaldo opened the door with a flourish. "Lieutenant. Welcome. Please come in. His Highness awaits your report."

"Thank you, Lieutenant," replied Vincent with a grin and a formal salute. "But there's no need for the axe. That thing has already done enough damage to my walls."

"Whoops," said an unapologetic Renaldo.

Darik cleared his throat pointedly. "If you two don't mind, we do have some matters to attend to."

"My apologies, my lord," said Vincent, his face flushed red with embarrassment. "My report. Yes. Um the wall. It sustained some damage in the battle. Mainly to the-"

Darik held up a hand halting the smaller engineer in mid-sentence. "First things first, Vin. I didn't ask you here to talk about the walls. What I want to know is how much time will it take to construct another barracks?"

"Another barracks?" asked Vincent incredulously. "Why would we need another? We're not exactly hurting for room. Besides, most of our engineers' time is spent on repairs to the walls."

"Forget about the wall, Vin," said Darik sternly. "How much time to build another barracks?"

"May I sit while I think about it, sir?" asked Vincent.

"Yes," answered Darik. "Renaldo, if you wouldn't mind?"

Renaldo hooked his axe head around a chair and pulled it over without standing from his own chair. Vincent sat down, staring into space and absentmindedly rubbing his nose while he ran the calculations in his mind, his fingers drawing imaginary numbers in the air while he did so.

"Another barracks?" asked Renaldo. "Couldn't we just fit any extra soldiers into the barracks we already have?"

"Perhaps," answered Darik without any further elaboration.

Vincent stopped rubbing his nose, and focused his attention back on the prince. "Sir, will my engineers be working on these barracks in addition to their normal duties at the wall?"

"I'm afraid so," replied Darik. "However, all the men stationed in Fort Hope will be ordered to give you whatever assistance you request."

"I am not building a barracks," grumbled Renaldo, as his fingers drummed on his axe haft.

"Perhaps, you'd prefer to work on the latrines," Darik replied drily. He rubbed his eyes, and stretched his back. "Vin, I'm getting tired over here, do you have an estimate?"

"Sorry, sir. I expect that it would take us at least a month, maybe two if the fighting gets worse." Vincent stood up from his chair. "May I be dismissed, sir? I'll need to get organized right away if you're to get those barracks."

"Yes. Thank you, Vin," said Darik. "Dismissed."

Darik resumed his letter while Vincent exited the room. Juggling events at Fort Hope and at home was proving more difficult than he anticipated.

Renaldo closed the door and leaned against the office wall, his axe between him and the door. "A new barracks, huh?" asked Renaldo. "You think we'll actually get that many reinforcements?"

"Yes, I do," answered Darik, his quill scratching quickly across the parchment. "My father and I have a plan in place in the event of a large assault on Fort Hope."

"What's the plan?" Renaldo asked.

"You'll see," replied Darik. He continued writing, nearly missing Renaldo rolling his eyes at his response. "It'll take time to implement the plan, but I can guarantee that no one is going to be thrilled with it."

"You always have such wonderful plans," said Renaldo.

"I know," said Darik as he signed the letter with a flourish. He was glad Renaldo focused on the plan and not the necessity for more troops. Darik had done the math when he was up on the wall. The monsters were setting up camp, but in such a way that the camp would accommodate much more of their forces. Numbers that the beasts clearly believed would be arriving.

Fort Hope needed to prepare for the massive siege that was coming. Antier would need every troop it could muster. And if Darik was right, one new barracks would not be nearly enough.

CHAPTER THIRTEEN

His first sensation upon waking was pain. Pure, simple pain. His back was stiff, he presumed from lying on a cot, and a muscle in his lower right back was spasming. He tried to sit up and shake some life into his body. However, his muscles refused to comply as they felt locked in place. A general sense of fatigue consumed his body. It was as if his body had refused to wake up along with his consciousness.

Byron managed to open his eyes and immediately regretted the decision. Daylight stabbed into his eyes causing them to sting and water. He struggled to look around at his surroundings as his neck muscles were rigid and painfully slow to respond.

The room was plain. Incredibly plain. So plain that even the most stoic of priests would think it needed some color and ambiance. It was decorated with simple wooden furnishings and plain white linens. Bandages and medical supplies were stacked neatly on a nearby table. A hospital then, maybe a medical ward in a military installation.

His bed had the same rough white cotton sheets that seemed common to all medical facilities. They were clean, but they made his beard itch.

A beard? Since when do I have a beard? Bryon thought.

"You're awake. Good."

The voice belonged to an elderly man. He wore blood red robes with swirling black stripes. A priest of Hiloth, the god of medicine. The man was bald, with a dark pointed beard starting beneath his ears and resting beneath his sternum.

The priest had dark skin, and dark brown eyes, a combination common to the people of Erlon, the duchy to the south and east of Antier.

The priest stopped next to the bed and pressed his fingers against his patient's neck. "Do you remember your name?" the priest asked.

"Byron," replied Byron with a raspy voice.

"Very good," said the priest as he forced each eyelid open. "And do you remember what happened?"

Byron rubbed his head and tried to focus through the sluggishness. He remembered being in the dungeon with Cole, and descending down a staircase. A twinge of pain shot through his shoulder, and the skeletal face of the hillman ghost flashed through his mind's eye.

"Not much," Byron lied. "I just remember that I was with Cole. Is he okay?"

"He is fine," answered Master Tyson as he entered the room. "But he won't be if you ever do anything that stupid again. Father, thank you for looking after him. How is he?"

"His physical health is fine," answered the priest. "His lying however could use some work."

"Thank you," nodded Tyson. "Is he able to get up from that bed?"

"Yes," said the priest as he stepped back from the bed. "It will take a few days, maybe a few weeks until he is back to his normal self."

The priest departed the room, and Byron stretched his arms trying to work some semblance of functionality back into his sore muscles. Before he could try to rise again, a hand restrained him. "Now that the priest is gone, why don't you tell me what you actually remember," said Master Tyson.

"Like I said, I don't remember anything," said Byron through clenched teeth.

Master Tyson glared down at Byron. His face never changed; his entire demeanor just shifted into what Byron could only describe as more intense. Like a snake coiled, ready to strike. "Do you think I wanted to kill you? Is that why you think I sent you into the catacombs?" demanded Tyson. With a quick flick of his wrist, a small thin blade was at Byron's throat. "Because believe me, if I wanted you dead, I could arrange that at any moment."

Byron grimaced, the blade was digging painfully into his skin, but not hard enough to break the surface. It was always like this with people who knew about him. Everyone always wanted to see how far they could push him. Make him do what they wanted because they knew he could not stop them.

"Fine. You want to know why?" growled Byron. "Because I was going to show you that I wasn't afraid. People like you always want to prove to me that I'm not as good as you, by putting me in a situation that I physically can't accomplish. You send me down into the catacombs without any clue what I am searching for, well you can bet that I am going to find it."

Byron grabbed hold of Tyson's wrist and forced the blade away from his throat. Slowly he forced his aching body out of the bed. "Quite frankly, *Master* Tyson," he sneered. "I am not afraid. Not of you, not of anything. You can assign me as many of these stupid missions as you want, but just know, I am not going to quit."

Tyson laughed, and gently pushed Byron lazily with two fingers on his off-hand. Byron tumbled backwards, his weakened body landing in his bed. With a quick flick of the wrist, the blade vanished back into Tyson's sleeve.

"You have spirit, strength, and intelligence," said Tyson as he leaned down into Byron's face. "But I need something more. I need you to develop judgment, and discipline. I am going to break you of your pride and arrogance. Get rid of that giant chip you are carrying on your shoulder. Teach you some humility and some responsibility. In short, I am going to turn you into a wraith. You think you can do that?"

Byron grunted sullenly in assent.

"Good," said Tyson, as a grin split his face. The expression looked completely foreign on him and rather horrifying. "Well, I'll depart for now, as your friends will be here at any moment to tell you the news from Antier. I'm sure it will provide you with more situations to prove yourself."

Byron rolled his eyes as the old spy departed the room. Boots slapped against the stones outside his room. Multiple people were running toward his room. Byron suppressed a sigh. It was annoying how much Tyson knew. The footsteps slowed for a brief moment. The muffled voices had a brief exchange, and the footsteps resumed their run.

Dalton, Cole, and Jeron burst into his room. "Byron!" Dalton exclaimed. "You'll never guess what happened."

"Girls," interjected an excited Jeron. "Your father ordered girls to be trained as soldiers. They just arrived hours ago."

Byron closed his eyes in resignation as he tried to sink deeper into his bed. Another situation to prove himself indeed. More people capable of thrashing him. And this time it would be girls doing the thrashing. Break him of his pride through humiliation no doubt.

Tyson was such an ass.

Chapter Fourteen

The sword slammed into the ground inches from Jeron's face, sending a spray of dirt into the air. Jeron leveled a kick at his assailant's legs, and then rolled to his side, clipping his shoulder on a root before finding his footing.

Jeron readied his axe and surveyed his opponent. She was a slender woman of average height and dark brown hair. Her skin was a burnt brown, a common feature in those from the duchy of Talendor. She wore the military tunic and trousers assigned to the trainees, and was carefully circling Jeron with a Talendorian saber in her left hand, and a round shield in her right.

She was quicker than Jeron anticipated, and he had not expected how strange it would be fighting someone who was left-handed. It should have been as simple as flipping his normal fighting style around, but it was not. He was accustomed to his weapon facing his opponent's shield and vice versa. It was strange having his opponent's weapon facing his unshielded side, and he was having to adjust to her attacks on the fly, while she was clearly accustomed to this style of fighting. Every action that was ordinarily an ingrained involuntary response from years of training now required thought. And it was slowing him down.

Jeron began the fight exercising excessive caution. He did not want to be the first male to lose to one of the girl trainees and bear the brunt of all the jokes. The end result of his hesitation was that his opponent had seized the offensive, and the entire rhythm of the fight.

She was good, but her fighting style suggested that she was accustomed to sparring against sabers, and their cousins, the rapier. In such fights, quickness and dexterity reigned supreme due to the lighter blades, while brute strength took a secondary position.

An axe fight on the other hand was a completely different animal.

Jeron swung his axe and predictably, she moved her saber into position to block his strike. Big mistake. She should have used her shield or dodged. Jeron's axe crashed down her slender blade with only the slightest resistance, the force of the blow tearing the weapon from her hand. Before she could recover, he swung his larger shield like a club into her smaller round shield. The impact of the blow flung her to the ground. Jeron pounced, pressing his boot against her left wrist and pinning her sword arm against the ground, his axe raised and poised; ready for the killing blow. The blood was rushing through his muscles, his chest was heaving, and every fiber of his being ached to finish his prey.

"And that's the match!" shouted Dalton his arms raised to the crowd of trainees. "Miss Calabella, I believe you owe Byron ten gold marks. Cole, please go collect his winnings."

Cole scampered over to a haughty looking girl standing next to the bear of a woman that Dalton addressed. The bear of a woman handed a small bag off to the haughty woman who promptly passed it off to Cole who was more than happy to relieve her of it. Jeron wandered over to a smug looking Byron. His coloring had not yet returned to normal, but despite his poor health he still wore that infuriating smirk on his face. All things considered, it was a relief to see him up and about again. Even with all of his irritating quirks.

"What the hell do you think you're doing?" Jeron asked instead.

"Well I thought I'd come see what all the fuss was about," drawled Byron. "I mean, it's not like the priests said I couldn't come."

"That's precisely what they said," growled Jeron.

Cole arrived and handed Byron a small stack of coins. "Here you go, ten gold marks."

"Thank you, Cole, take one for yourself," said Byron. "And Jeron, if I hadn't stopped by, how would I have made this extra money? I mean, I almost didn't because you fought so tentative. What was that about?"

"It was nothing," growled Jeron. "I was just playing it cautious because I didn't know what she could do. And stop changing the subject."

"You were taking it easy on me?" demanded a voice from behind Jeron.

Jeron turned to face his former opponent. He hated this part. No one took losing well and they always felt like they had something to prove. Apparently beating them with his axe or fists was never enough, he had to also defeat them with his tongue.

Instead of only his opponent waiting for him, there were three other girls flanking her, including the haughty one and the bearish woman that had lost her money to Byron.

"No. I didn't," growled Jeron, the mane of hair beginning to sprout forth from his face. He ignored it and continued to speak in as gruff and uncaring a tone as he could manage. "I approached it cautiously, because I didn't know what you could do or what you were capable of."

"What I could do?" demanded the woman as she shook her saber at Jeron. "Do you think I can't fight? Am I some delicate creature that you might break?"

"No, you stone-brained woman!" shouted Jeron. "I thought you might fight like him!" Jeron pointed at Byron, the mane of hair fully encircling his face.

"Like him?" snickered the haughty looking woman.

"Are you saying I fight like a girl?" asked Byron as he clicked two gold coins together. "That stings man."

"What's wrong with fighting like a girl?" retorted the Talendorian looking girl.

"What's this about fighting like a girl?" asked Dalton as he walked up to the group. "Is this something that can be settled with another bout?" His eyes lit up. "Maybe another wager?"

"Apparently Byron fights like a girl," confided Cole.

"Oh," said Dalton looking crestfallen. "Nothing new then. Pity. Another fight would have been fun."

"That is not what I meant. This guy—" Jeron growled in frustration, his finger pointing accusatorily at Byron. "—will surprise you with some stupid trick if you've never fought him before. And it's always something so simple that it winds up embarrassing you. That was why I was being cautious."

The Talendorian girl stared back at him, and eventually nodded, relenting. "I can accept that. I look forward to our next bout...."

"Jeron."

"Jeron. Very well. My name is Olivia. Until next time." Olivia spun on her heel and marched off. The gaggle of girls with her turned and followed suit, but not until the haughty looking girl shot a poisonous glare at Byron. He blew a kiss at her.

Jeron groaned and looked heavenward. "Was that really necessary?" he asked the prince.

Byron nodded gravely. "I assure you that it was. Gloating is an essential part of both gambling and sporting events."

"And is making more enemies that want to kill you also essential?" inquired Dalton.

"Nope," said Byron as he slipped the two coins he had been playing with back into the bag and began bouncing the bag of coins on his palm. "That's an added perk. Besides, that's why I have such vigilant bodyguards."

Cole paled visibly at the statement. "But what if she's dangerous," he whispered. "We can't protect you all the time."

"Nelly? Oh, she's harmless," assured Byron. "She might hiss and make faces at you, but she never acts. She's a schemer, but not one to take risks. That's why she had Calabella place the bet for her."

Dalton scratched his head in confusion. "Doesn't take risks? But didn't she just gamble on the bout?"

"And she lost," Byron said flatly. "Trust me on this. That's the biggest risk she will take, and she isn't likely to try it again anytime soon."

Jeron grunted without comment. If Byron knew this Nelly, then it had to be from before his own family died. Before Jeron was packed up and sent to Antier to be raised under the Duke's protection. Which meant that Byron's encounters with this Nelly had to have occurred before they were even teenagers. Jeron swore. People did change during those years. He certainly had.

He spun and grabbed Byron's arm. Hard. "You're basing your analysis of this Nelly off of something that happened before you hit puberty?"

"Ouch," said Byron flatly, as he pointedly looked down at his injured shoulder.

Jeron had the good the grace to blush. "Sorry. I forgot about that."

Byron shrugged his uninjured shoulder, dismissing the event. "It's nothing. And yes, I am basing everything off of my childhood interactions with Nellandra. People don't change, Jeron. And neither has she."

"They may not change, but they do get smarter," observed Jeron. He raised his hands warding off any objection from Byron. "I know. I'm just saying be careful. While her nature may not have changed since she was a child, her goals may have. Who says that she has any use for you?"

"A woman not having use for me?" Byron rolled his eyes in annoyance. He had an unfortunate habit of displaying sarcasm and contempt clearly on his face. It was more than a little aggravating. "Fine. I'll be more careful," he said.

Jeron surveyed the remaining groups of female and male trainees gathered for the evening. Talking, laughing, and demonstrating various combat maneuvers. Jeron could have sworn that Barith was flirting with a pleasantly plump girl. However, he had his doubts as to whether the boy was capable of something as subtle as flirting.

"Is this what you all have been doing while I've been injured?" Byron asked.

"Yes," confirmed Jeron. "We were ordered to treat the girls like any other trainee. And that is what we have been doing."

Byron furrowed his eyebrows in puzzlement. "But why?" he asked.

"Really?" asked a bemused Jeron. "The youngest son of the Duke, who lacks a totem, and has been made fun of and tormented by those stronger than him for years, would look down on someone becoming a soldier based off of their gender?"

"Huh?" replied Byron. "Oh no. Not that. I meant why now. What is happening out there that Antier needs more troops?"

Jeron shrugged as he watched the next group of trainees begin their bout. "Maybe the Duke and the rest of the nobles thought it was the just and moral thing to do?"

Byron shook his head sadly as he stared off to the west toward Fort Hope and his brother. "No," he whispered softly. "People don't change."

Chapter Fifteen

Twelve dead. Six more missing and presumed dead.

Darik rubbed the grit from his eyes as he pored over the report on his desk. The creatures' attacks had become fiercer over the past three months. Their forces gathered outside the pass had increased at least tenfold in number, while the number of humans manning the fort remained unchanged. He quickly amended his thinking. Unchanged with the exception of the slow drain of his men, as the beasts continued to press their siege against the fort. Eighteen more humans dead at their hands.

Too many men were dying. His defense of Fort Hope was balanced precariously on a knife's edge. Too aggressive in his counterattacks, and he would not have the numbers to hold the fort. Too lax and reserved in his defense, and the fort would be overrun when the monsters claimed the battlements.

He desperately needed reinforcements before the strain on his forces became too great. But Antier also needed those reinforcements if it was to keep its other borders secure.

Darik slammed his fist against his desk in frustration. The wood cracked under the force of his blow causing thin cracks to radiate out from the impact site.

He was slowly bleeding men, and was starved of information from the outside world. The few trickles he received hardly painted an accurate portrait of the political and military situation facing the duchy. For all he knew there could be another war with Loach already underway.

A knock on his office door drew Darik out from his report. He shifted the report to conceal the small crater on his desk's surface and took a deep steadying breath. He smoothed his hair and straightened his armor. Appearance was everything. In court and in the military. Rumors would start and spread quickly if his soldiers glimpsed him in any sort of disarray. And rumors led to poor morale. And poor morale got men killed. That alone was worth a few moments of preening.

"Come in," he said loudly. He projected his voice calm and firm, the voice of authority. Good.

Renaldo burst through the door shaking a fistful of papers. "What is this?" he demanded. "Duke Cedric approved female soldiers?" Incredulity laced his voice, his face was flushed, and his eyes were wide.

All things considered, Renaldo was not taking the news well, and Darik considered him one of the smarter nobles in the duchy. Hardly a good sign for the plan. Darik kept his face impassive, like stone, while fighting the mirth building up inside him.

"Are we supposed to trust women to watch our backs on the walls when those monsters charge?" demanded Renaldo.

Darik began drumming his fingertips against his desktop. He stayed silent and allowed Renaldo to continue his outburst.

"And how will they carry the wounded?" continued Renaldo. "What if we get put on half rations? Can their bodies sustain that? And what if –why doesn't this upset you?"

"Discipline," replied Darik calmly. He left the word dangling out there as if it answered everything.

"Discipline?" asked Renaldo. His right eye was partially closed, and his lip turned up to one side. It was Renaldo's usual face of confusion. "You think women are more disciplined?"

Darik remained silent and let Renaldo stand there, uncertain, his face scrunched up in bewilderment. He would have to break the news to his men eventually. If Renaldo reacted this poorly, then his men would certainly react worse. He would have to orchestrate his delivery carefully. Stress the importance of additional troops to his men. Given their plight, that might help ease the delivery of the news. Thoughts of reinforcements could give the men hope. Hope was a powerful thing, and it was in short supply lately.

He held his hand out and gestured for the papers in Renaldo's hand.

"Not their discipline, yours," answered Darik. Renaldo started blinking in a most gratifying manner. Darik pressed on.

"You're an officer under my command. And you lose your temper over news? News that we will be getting more soldiers to bolster our ranks?"

"But I-"

"I'm not finished," growled Darik. "What will you do if you receive bad news during a battle? Charge the enemy? Lead your men to their deaths without weighing the situation? Your rage is a liability. I can't have you acting like a berserker on me."

"But it's how I fight!" protested Renaldo. "It hasn't been a problem, and you can't really expect me to change it now."

"Yes, I can. You're an officer and a reflection of my own authority. The men follow your example. I can't have them all losing their minds and reacting out of passion. What I need is discipline. Starting with you."

Renaldo visibly deflated and sank into one of the office chairs. He exhaled deeply. "I guess I can work on it."

Darik grunted in assent. "Good. And the answer to your question is Brina."

"Brina? That cow?" asked Renaldo as his face crunched up again. "What does she have to do with women soldiers?"

"I distinctly remember her thrashing you all over the palace," replied Darik.

"She did not—"

"Yes. She. Did.," replied Darik, as he emphasized each word. "All throughout the palace. Broken nose and a cracked rib if I remember correctly. And she did that without training."

"We really do need the soldiers, don't we?" asked Renaldo softly.

Darik pushed the report to the side, revealing the damage to the desk.

Renaldo's jaw dropped in shock. He slowly rubbed his palms against his temples. There were fresh scrapes on his knuckles. He had been up on the wall during his shift off.

"I'll try to hold my emotions in check." Renaldo sat down in his chair, back straight, head held high, a small sad smile on his face. "Especially since I am not the only one who reacts poorly to bad news."

Darik smiled inwardly. At least Renaldo was making a short-term attempt at discipline. It balanced out with his ever-futile attempts at humor.

Darik picked up a coded report from the stack. It was a status update from Tyson on Byron's health. Apparently, his recovery was going nicely. Darik still could not believe that the boy had been that foolish. It was a new low, even for him. Hopefully, the female students would provide enough of a distraction to the other trainees to provide his brother with some breathing room to heal and grow his skills.

"So how is Byron doing?" asked Renaldo. "Oh, don't give me that look. I didn't open your messages this time. When your brother comes up in conversation your face always scrunches up in this concerned look usually reserved for use by grandmothers and priests."

"He's doing better," Darik replied, choosing his words carefully. "Hopefully enough of the other trainees will share your sentiment regarding girls in the military, and they won't have time to bother Byron."

Renaldo snorted. "That's doubtful. The kid has a nose for trouble."

A pounding at the door cut off any remark Darik may have had regarding the relatively narrow gap in their ages. A messenger darted into the room before Renaldo could open the door. The messenger was out of breath and panting. His uniform was torn, and a mixture of dirt, blood, and sweat dripped down his face.

"Sir," stated the messenger as he attempted to salute while bent over trying to catch his breath. In another place and time Darik would have found the situation mildly humorous instead of dread inducing. "The monsters launched a larger assault than usual. A small squad of satyrs have gained a foothold on the northern part of the walls."

Darik sprang into action and darted toward the balcony behind his desk. "Renaldo, lead an auxiliary force to the walls, and do it now!" he bellowed as he darted out into the night.

The captain's balcony of Fort Hope hardly deserved such an unassuming name. It was as much a balcony as a rose garden was a pasture. The balcony was a large stone platform that jutted out from the captain's office. It was designed to support the comings and goings of a person whose totem was a large airborne animal, or for ease of accepting airborne messengers. Generally, such a large creature would be powerful, and thus the person who controlled it would be in command. Such was the case with Darik.

Darik focused as he ran towards the balcony. His skin rippled and cerulean blue scales began to emerge, overlapping over his skin and armor. Bones crunched and tendons stretched as his body began to shift.

The growing of his body was not as disorienting a process as people always expected. He had done it so many times that the larger body mass felt just as comfortable as his human form. It was the extra non-human body parts that felt strange and awkward to him, not the size.

Darik's back began to stretch, and a pair of metallic blue wings rose out of his now enormous shoulder blades. His lower back pulled, and a thick tail smacked against the balcony causing small pebbles to rattle and hop.

Darik took a deep breath and let loose a blast of flame from his dragon's body into the night sky. The flame illuminated his scales giving them a lighter cerulean appearance, and with a surge of raw power shooting through his legs, he leapt into the sky and streaked towards the walls that were beleaguered by a horde of monsters.

He flapped his monstrous wings and picked up speed. They could not afford to lose more men. And they would not if he could help it.

The flight from the keep to the battlements was usually short enough that Darik chose to walk the distance instead. Tonight, that distance felt as if it stretched on forever. Each beat of his heart could be the last for one of his men.

The night was cool and the sky was blessedly clear, making flying easier. Torches and lanterns flickered like cicadas in the distance. Men scuttled atop the wall looking so much like tiny ants going about their business. Darik ignored them, intent on searching for his quarry.

Huddled along the northern section of the wall, the ants slammed against other specks with reckless abandon while a steady stream of mishappen figures hurdled over the wall towards the men.

Darik banked his wings and headed north of the wall. While speed and time was paramount, he needed to be smart about his actions. He could hover behind his men pouring a steady stream of fire at the satyrs, but at best that would be a stalemate. His men could not enter through the fire and the instant he stopped breathing flame, the satyrs would be back over the wall before his men closed the distance.

His best option was to assault the satyrs from the west side of the wall. Interrupt their scaling of the wall so that his men could regain their defensive position. He would need to be quick about his work. Only God knew what sort of ranged weapons or monstrosities lay hidden within the darkness of the monsters' camp. The longer he stayed airborne in one place, the greater the likelihood that he would find out.

Darik dove sharply, the flickering lights increasing in size as the ground rose up towards him. As he drew closer, the specks on the wall began to come into crisp focus. He could see the rage and fear on each weary face as they charged against the satyrs. Too many of the brave defenders had already given their lives, and they were trying desperately not to join their comrades.

Darik flared his wings at what seemed like the last possible moment, pulling up and halting his dive just shy of the ground.

A mound of bodies lay at the foot of the wall as the goat men climbed over them, both living and dead, desperate to get their cloven hoofs over the wall. Darik did not intend to let any more of them achieve that feat.

He exhaled and a stream of yellow-orange fire immolated the area. Screams and terrified bleats rose from those unfortunate enough to survive the blaze. Many of the goats turned outright to ash. The sight satisfied some distant part of Darik's mind.

Out of the corner of his eye, Darik saw his soldiers burst through the satyr line, taking advantage of the enemy's confusion and lack of reinforcements. Darik knew that encounter would be resolved in a matter of moments. There was little more that he could accomplish on this side of the wall without placing himself in mortal danger.

Darik took one last breath and spat flame contemptuously down on the beasts below before returning to the night sky. He would leave the defense of the wall to Renaldo and the men below. It would hold for the night.

It would have to hold. At least until aid reached them.

Chapter Sixteen

The summer sun beat down on Jeron as he lay sprawled on his stomach on the stone rooftop of one of the smaller storage buildings inside the fort walls. The stones were growing uncomfortably warm beneath his forearms but the heat was a necessary evil that did not outweigh the advantages of being on this particular rooftop.

The roof provided an unparalleled view of the events taking place in the courtyard below. He and Byron had needed to climb on top of a small wall and hoist themselves up onto the roof to gain the necessary vantage point. It had been difficult finding handholds on the hot stones, but the view was worth it.

The girls' weapons clashed against each other as Captain Levren led them through a variety of drills. Their bodies glistened with sweat as they exerted themselves beneath the summer sun. A grin split Jeron's face. It was a magnificent view.

"They really are quite talented," Jeron observed.

Byron snorted from behind him. He had become bored a little while ago and had stretched out to take a nap, his feet pointing towards the courtyard. "Why don't you kiss her already? Or at least ask her on a walk, or spend dinner with her, or something?" he asked.

"Wh-what?" stammered Jeron. He tried to turn his head to look at Byron while not losing sight of the courtyard. "I have no idea what you're talking about."

"I'm sure you don't," said Byron wryly. Even though he could not see him, Jeron could feel the smirk on his friend's face. "And you just happened to start training without a shirt recently."

"It's hot out. That's why," insisted Jeron while he pushed himself up, his face flushed. "Besides, Levren just left. Time to go."

"Okay," said Byron. "Have a nice chat."

Suddenly Jeron felt himself tumbling through the air, his arms flailing for purchase, before he landed face first in the dirt. The air exploded from his chest as he gasped for breath.

How had he lost his balance? The only explanation was that Byron shoved him off the rooftop. But why would he do that?

"Well, what do we have here?" purred a feminine voice.

Oh, that was why.

Jeron sprang to his feet and dusted himself off as he regarded the semi-circle of female trainees forming around him. Was it just his imagination or were their weapons angled ever so slightly in his direction?

"Ah ladies, excuse me, pardon me," said Jeron, the words tumbling out of his mouth faster than his brain could process them. He was babbling. Fantastic. "Have you all seen Byron around? He was simulating the assassin in our training exercise."

Why did he ask them about Byron? He mentally kicked himself. So stupid.

"Are we supposed to believe that you just happened to drop in on our training session from a roof, because of some convenient training exercise involving the prince?" asked a slender blonde-haired girl, as she bounced a mace against her palm.

"Yes," deadpanned Jeron. Years of keeping a straight face while Byron lied to every authority figure in sight was finally paying off.

"I'm not buying it," said the blonde-haired mace aficionado. Lucky for him, she was a noble girl, they probably all were now that he thought about it. That meant they all probably had some form of formal education. Great. His lies were going to have to improve if he was going to extract himself from this mess.

"I don't care what you do or do not believe," replied Jeron sternly as he shifted tactics. Since the easy going lie proved ineffective, he would have to try tough duty-minded solider. "I was given a mission, and I don't plan on failing it."

Olivia and her saber appeared at the front of the semi-circle. "Well sadly, my dear Jeron, there is no sign of Byron. That means you let your assassin escape, and failed in your mission." She strolled within a pace of Jeron, twirling her saber before her.

What was with these girls and spinning their weapons? Especially in his direction. Did they not know that was incredibly dangerous?

Olivia stood on the tips of her toes and leaned up placing her nose within an inch of his. Jeron could feel her breath upon his face, and his heart began beating faster. So much for playing it cool and under control.

"Fortunately for us, you just happened to drop in after finishing your training mission," she said. "And we all happen to need more practice fighting against men." Olivia grabbed him by his shoulders, spun him in the direction of the weapons rack, and smacked his rear as if she were spurring forward a horse. "Now be a good boy and grab a weapon."

Jeron felt his face flush with embarrassment. He was going to kill Byron.

***

Byron could not stop grinning as he climbed down from the roof. Jeron was going to kill him. Well, he would certainly try. But that squeal he had made while falling was extremely satisfying and worth the risk.

Byron peeked around the corner of the building, checking to see if the path was clear. Master Tyson had been very specific in his instructions. He had to spend time with either Jeron, Dalton, or Cole, and then leave without any of the other boys being able to follow. Master Tyson had said something about it being important to ingrain oneself into social situations and to be able to disengage without being pursued.

Judging by the position of the sun, he still had about a half hour until he had to meet Master Tyson by the gates. And he had managed to grab a small nap. All things considered, the day was going quite well.

Byron skirted through the shadows when he needed to, and blended into the crowd of his fellow trainees moving about the fort. Master Tyson had taught him how to loosen his shoulders, and hunch them in while he walked, thereby lessening his noticeable profile, and, more importantly, reducing the odds of him inadvertently bumping into someone in a crowd. Even if the trick did not work at avoiding detection, it was certainly going to be a boon at any court function.

Within minutes Byron arrived at the front gates to find Master Tyson talking with Captain Levren, and a man in hunter's greens. A trainee stood behind the man in green, clad in a similar green suit, and carrying a bow and two travel packs.

"Ahh, Byron. Glad you could make it," greeted Master Tyson. "Alone and on time. Well done. Allow me to introduce Master Sildun." The older of the two men in green, Sildun, inclined his head in a slight greeting.

"Master Sildun is in charge of training the scouts," continued Tyson. "With him is his trainee, Thiago." The solemn faced ebony skinned lad nodded gravely in acknowledgement. "You will be accompanying Thiago on a scouting mission. Consider it an opportunity to practice your skills in a wilderness setting. Sildun, if you would be so kind as to brief the lad?"

"With pleasure," said a grinning Master Sildun, a jovial light flitting in his eyes. "We have had reports of centaurs and satyrs in the forest to the west. While it is rare for the monsters to appear in this area, it isn't unheard of for a handful to sneak past our defenses and make it this far east. Most likely, it is probably farmers panicking at the shadows, but it is our job to be certain. Otherwise, Captain Levren here will probably lose his sanity, as well as what is left of his hair.

"Byron, you will be accompanying Thiago in this expedition. Thiago has packed you a travel sack, a longbow, and a shortsword. I understand you have been on hunting trips before?"

Byron nodded in assent.

"Good," continued Sildun. "That is one of the reasons you were picked. Neither of you has enough experience to go at this alone. You'll both need to rely on each other, find out where your skills differ, and where they overlap. That will be key to survival out in the wilderness.

"Now your mission is to search the forests to the west for any signs of centaurs and satyrs. If you happen to find any stragglers, kill them. If they are numerically superior to you, note their position, travel movements, and report back. You have provisions for a week, and the surrounding area is ripe for foraging.

"Do not be gone for more than two weeks. Byron, get changed into your greens, and the two of you will depart immediately. Hurry up lads, the Captain's hairline isn't getting any thicker."

Captain Levren glowered at Sildun. "Be careful, boys. If centaurs and satyrs have made it past our defenses, we need to know. That is of paramount importance. Every life in the area could depend on that knowledge." Without another word Levren spun on his heels and departed.

Master Tyson chuckled as Levren walked away. "Sildun, one of these days Mark is going beat the pine needles from between your ears." Sildun just grinned even wider and shrugged dismissively. "Hurry up and change Byron," said Tyson. "I'll bring your clothes back to your quarters. But don't expect this sort of personal service to continue."

Byron opened the sack and started stripping off his training clothes. An expedition to go find possible monsters, and Master Tyson left alone in his quarters? He did not know which was more terrifying. One thing was certain. No one could accuse him of having a boring life.

CHAPTER SEVENTEEN

S ummer in southern Antier was clothes-sticking hot. The forests were thick with growth while remaining barely navigable. Pine and oak trees dominated the scenery, with moss covering many of the stray stones scattered about the forest floor.

The terrain was hilly, and the numerous small streams slicing through the region supported a large amount of wildlife. In years past, small bands of thieves had called the forests home. These groups had vanished over the past generations as the Antierian frontier became settled, and garrisons of troops occupied the forts dotting the country side.

Byron's hunting greens clung to his skin as he followed Thiago through the forest. It had been five days without any sign of satyrs or centaurs, or any other variety of creature that could conceivably be called a monster, and Byron was beginning to suffer through the early stages of boredom.

His travel companion, Thiago, was a tall slender boy of few words, who did little to ease the monotony of the journey. He had dark ebony skin, which contrasted sharply with his bright white smile. Byron guessed that his family had originated in the nearby coastal duchy of Erlon, before settling in Antier.

"Any ideas?" whispered Byron. "Or are we just chasing rumors."

"Keep your voice down," hissed Thiago. "There has been scarcely any small game around for this time of year. Something is scaring it off. Could be predators, could be something else. Can you climb trees?"

Byron nodded, and cursed himself inwardly. He had not noticed the lack of small animals, just like he had failed to notice the amulets Master Tyson had placed in the dungeon. If he did not pay more attention to the little details, sooner or later he was going to wind up dead.

"Good," whispered Thiago. "We climb up the trees. Stick to different trees when possible. Reduces the risk of branches breaking underneath our weight. It also spreads out the sound, makes it sound more natural, like we are the animals that call these trees home. There is a stream to our west. Everything drinks. We're most likely to find some traces of life along the stream. Keep quiet, use hand signals."

Byron climbed up the nearest tree and quietly leapt from branch to branch. Thankfully, the trees in the south-western areas of Antier were very old and study, and able to hold his weight. More advanced civilization, and lumber harvesting had yet to extend its grasp into these lands, and as a result the woods remained strong. However, Byron doubted that in all its existence, the forest had ever experienced humans leaping from branch to branch.

Byron heard the stream well before he could make it out with his eyes. He and Thiago slowed their already snail like pace, and advanced upon the stream as stealthily as possible, trying not to rustle any branches. Byron estimated that it had taken them a half an hour to advance the remaining quarter mile to the stream. In that time, the sun had begun its descent. Byron hoped they found some sign of life relatively quickly, as he really did not want to sleep near the only close and readily accessible source of water, where any predator might be lurking. He also did not want to sleep up in the trees. He already had enough nightmares where he was falling. Usually, he woke up before he hit the ground. The last thing he wanted was to experience the ending of those dreams.

Thiago held up his hand, halting the pair at an opening in the tree canopy above the waters of the stream. Byron slid over to a branch on an adjacent tree and surveyed the clearing below to see what halted their progress.

It was quiet in the clearing, with only a few squirrels and what looked to be a rabbit running through the grass. Byron rolled his eyes and mouthed "little small game, huh?" to Thiago.

Thiago shot him a withering glare and held a finger up to his mouth silencing any further comment. Byron bristled at taking orders from the other boy, but the chain of command was clear. Thiago was in charge. Even then, it was hot and boring enough without having to deal with the stoic lad's orders.

To make matters worse, as if on cue, a satyr and centaur sprang out from the brush beneath Byron's tree and pounced on a squirrel and the rabbit. The creatures did not even bother to clean their kills or set up a fire to cook the animals. They tore into the small creatures, not even pausing to breathe as they shoveled meat and bones into their mouths.

Thiago ran his finger over his throat, gesturing to himself then the satyr to the left, and to Byron and the centaur on the right. Finally, he held up five fingers, signaling the timeframe in which they would launch a joint attack on the beasts.

Byron glanced down at the beast beneath him. Blood dripped down the centaur's mouth to its heavily muscled chest. The upper body was that of a large man. The type of man that could wear heavy armor and carry a lance without the aid of a totem. As far as Byron knew, centaurs lacked the ability to use a totem, thereby limiting their strength to that of a comparable human. Unfortunately, while the creatures lacked the ability to use a totem, they more than made up for the disadvantage as their lower halves possessed all the strength and power of a warhorse.

Thiago drew his bow and Byron moved to follow suit, but stopped. The centaur had changed positions while it ate, and it now stood directly beneath his tree. Neither he nor Thiago had an angle to shoot the beast with an arrow, and they could not afford to let the creatures wander this far east into Antier. But they also could not kill only the satyr. Nor could they outrun the centaur. In such a tight corridor, and so many miles away from the fort, the centaur would run them down easily. And a straight up fight against the creature without the aid of armor or polearms was not a splendid idea.

Byron silently swore to himself, drew the shortsword from his belt in a reverse grip, point facing downward, flashed Thiago a wink and a grin, and dropped from the tree canopy. The air rushed by his face as he plummeted with reckless abandon toward the centaur below.

The shock hit his arms first, as his sword plunged into the centaur's lower back, the impact of the strike yanking the blade from his grasp. Byron instantly forgot about the sword as soon as he finished his drop, as he discovered a new dimension of pain. He landed bareback on the centaur, his legs straddling the creature as if he were riding a horse. The pain rising from his groin was immediate and unrelenting. In the blink of an eye, he found himself torn between two competing and disparate desires: the need to breathe and the overwhelming urge to vomit.

He slid off the centaur with all the grace of a drunk at the end of a successful night. Panic rose in his chest as he groped blindly across the ground for his missing sword. His breaths came in ragged bursts, tears blurred his vision, and his heartbeat pounded in his ears. His desperation grew as he increased the pace of his frenetic search, not knowing if death was plunging down towards him at any moment.

The seconds felt like an eternity, but he found no weapon, only dirt, grass, and a small rock. His fingers closed around the rock, a pebble really, and he rolled onto his battered left shoulder, his right arm cocked and ready to throw his meager missile.

However, death did not wait for him in the meadow. The satyr lay motionless on the ground a few yards off to his left, an arrow placed through its right eye. A clean kill. Thiago apparently was much better than a fair shot.

The centaur however was not as clean a kill.

The creature lay in the clearing, its legs thrashing in obvious pain. A pool of blood was beginning to form around its lower back where Byron's sword remained lodged. The centaur howled in rage, swinging a spiked club around wildly with unnatural strength. There was no pattern or intent behind the swings, only blind fury.

It really is more beast than man, thought Byron as he lay panting on the ground. He reflexively backed himself away from the beast's flurry of movement so as not to accidentally catch a stray blow. Slowly, the pace of the blows began to die down as the centaur weakened as its lifeblood drained from its body.

Eventually, the creature's legs stopped thrashing, and Byron hauled his battered body across the meadow to retrieve his sword. The blow had wedged his blade into the centaur's spine but had not managed to completely sever the bone. Byron grabbed the hilt with two hands, braced one foot upon the centaur's back, and with a grunt, freed the blade from the carcass.

Dark red blood coated the sword's blade. It was darker than human blood. Strangely, that fact bothered Byron although he was not entirely sure why. It should not matter that a half-man half-animal's blood was different than that of a human, but it did. Curious, Byron studied the carcass of the creature. While the centaur's upper body resembled that of a large heavily muscled adult male, the face was all wrong.

It's the eyes. They look large, wild, and utterly lacking any sort of compassion. Although I doubt anyone's eyes carry emotion in death. Byron nodded in agreement to himself. *Indeed. The face appears to lack laugh lines, or wrinkles that would denote any sort of regular facial emotion. It's unsettling.* An involuntary shudder snaked its way down his spine at the sight.

"What are you doing?" asked Thiago his brow furrowed in either thought or confusion. He must have slipped down the tree while Byron had been studying the creature. "The centaur isn't going anywhere."

"Sorry. I was having a conversation with myself inside my own head," said Byron in a matter-of-fact tone, as if such an activity was ordinary. Byron's gaze stayed focused on those blank wild eyes. He turned and saw the dumbfounded expression on the other boy's face and chuckled. "It's nothing. Conversation is just the way I think things through. And if there isn't anyone nearby, I have to make do with myself." Byron shrugged his shoulders helplessly as if the explanation was that of a harmless but relatively common habit, like biting one's fingernails.

"You're a little bit off, aren't you?" asked Thiago, his eyes narrowed in concern.

Byron shrugged. "Who isn't?"

Thiago grunted. It could have been assent, Byron thought. Maybe. "Should have figured that out the moment you dropped from the tree. Damn near gave me a heart attack. Almost missed my satyr. Clean your kill and get ready to carry it back to the fort," said Thiago as he gestured to the centaur.

"You want me to carry that beast back to the fort?" demanded Byron. "Are you mad?"

"Look who is talking. And it's rule number one of being a hunter. You carry what you kill," stated Thiago with a complete deadpan. "What are you staring at? Quickly now."

"I'm trying to determine how much you weigh," grumbled Byron.

CHAPTER EIGHTEEN

J eron removed the last splinter from his calloused hands and casually flicked
it off of the top of the newly constructed lookout tower. The sun beat down
heavily on his bare back and sweat dripped off of his olive skin with every step
he took, leaving what seemed to be small puddles in his wake.

According to the good Captain Levren, constructing the wooden outposts
was his punishment for losing track of Byron. Something to help him lookout
for Byron's return the captain had said. Captain Levren had even smirked at his
own pun. It was the first sign that Jeron had seen of any sense of humor from
the gristly man.

Master Maxus said that the punishment was useful. It would provide Jeron
a skill, while also providing the fort with some needed defensive structures.
Punishment without purpose was wasted punishment, according to Maxus.
Jeron agreed in theory. However, punishing him for Byron's behavior, which
could not be changed even through an act of God, did seem to be useless and
futile.

A strong wind blew across the hills and ruffled Jeron's black hair. The winds
were particularly strong this far south, but he was not worried that a strong gust
would blow the wooden tower over. The tower was sturdy enough to withstand
anything but the fiercest of thunderstorms. After all, he had built the structure.

He stared vainly out into the distance, scanning the western horizon and
waiting for any sign of Byron's return.

If that bastard had not pushed him off the roof and given him the slip, he
would not have to build these towers on top of his already abnormally grueling

training. He could have instead spent his minuscule amount of free time with Olivia.

Then again, if Byron had not shoved him off of that roof, he would not have been spending any of his precious free time with Olivia. It was an interesting line of thought and something he would need to consider further.

Perhaps he would not be too hard with Byron. Perhaps.

Jeron slipped back into his shirt and scuffled down the wooden beams of the tower. Agility and climbing were not exactly his forte, so the way down was accomplished with something a little less than alacrity. Physicality and brute strength were always where his talents lay. Useful skills when holding onto a tower for dear life.

His feet hit the ground and with a sigh of relief, he began to jog back towards the fort. He estimated he had another hour before Master Maxus's axe combat lesson started. After weeks of practicing with swords, he did not want to miss the training session with his weapon of choice. A chance to excel in front of the knight would be a welcome respite from all the punishment. And, if he hurried, with a little bit of luck, he might be able to steal a few minutes of free time with his friends.

Roughly a quarter mile from the fort Jeron could hear the commotion. It was not shouting, which meant Raven's Perch was not under attack. No, it was more of a buzzing sound like an agitated hornet's nest. The fort was simmering with pent up energy. Something, most likely trouble, was occurring.

Jeron broke into a sprint and was at the front gate in less than a minute.

Trainees were swarming across the yard, running back and forth, a flurry of frantic useless energy. But while at first glance it appeared they were moving fast, on a second glance it did not appear as if their actions were actually accomplishing anything of use. It was orderly chaos. Their actions lacked any sort of overarching purpose or objective.

"They're frightened," said a soft voice off to his side. "Maybe for the first time in their lives. And they don't know how to deal with it. So they seek a haven in the familiar."

Jeron started at the voice and looked around for it. Calmly. He looked around calmly. He certainly did not jump.

In the shadows of the gate was a slight distortion where the stones seemed to ripple like pond water after a pebble was tossed in. It was barely perceptible, and if he had not heard the voice and been searching for its source, he never would have found the distortion.

"Cole, did you have to try and startle me?" he asked with a long-suffering sigh.

The younger man shrugged apologetically as he eased back into focus. "Yes, actually. Master Tyson said that being able to hide doesn't do me any good if I don't know *how* to hide."

"Well, you seem pretty good at it to me," grumbled Jeron as they walked through the mass of hysteria. "What's all the commotion about?"

Cole dodged adroitly around a young man darting past carrying an arm full of arrow quivers. The red-haired boy moved lightly on his feet, spinning in a half-circle without breaking stride. "Byron and Thiago arrived while you were out working on your ahh...projects. And they came back with a centaur and a satyr."

Jeron stopped dead in his tracks. He could feel the blood draining from his face. "Where were they searching?" he asked.

"In the forests southwest of here," whispered Cole. "But that's not exactly common knowledge."

"If a few of those beasts slipped through, then more of them are likely to be coming," Jeron leaned close and gripped Cole's shirt. "More like an army of them, Cole. Those would be advance scouts."

Cole gently brushed Jeron's hands off his shirt and continued walking. "I know. I have been in the meetings with Byron, as has Dalton. You will be too if we quit stopping."

Jeron grunted and began walking again. He knew he should apologize for grabbing the younger man, but how was a man supposed to apologize for something like that? Umm sorry that I got caught up in the moment and was an asshole? He just did not have Byron's easy self-deprecating humor, or Dalton's carefree attitude that seemed to patch things over with most people effortlessly.

"Jeron!" he turned at the sound of the female voice shouting at him across the yard. Olivia and the other girls were marching towards him and Cole, their faces set in determined expressions. They were already armed and did not appear to have the panicked mannerism that was permeating through the young men at Raven's Perch.

"What is going on here," she demanded. "And don't tell me you don't know. This all started when Prince Byron came back, and this little one-" she pointed at Cole "-has been locked in a room with Byron, Captain Levren, and the other masters all day."

Jeron paused and took in the girls' appearances. Red faced, and chests heaving as if they had been running from place to place. Clearly, they were tired, and angry. No one was telling them anything and they were about to take that frustration out on him. Lovely.

He sighed. "I've been outside working on the lookout towers," he said. "I'm sorry, but I actually don't know anything. I just walked through the gate when Cole here grabbed me-"

"*I* grabbed *you*?" whispered Cole under his breath incredulously.

"-and was leading me to Byron so I could find out what is going on around here," he finished. "You're welcome to join us of course."

"Not armed they're not," said Cole in an authoritative voice.

Jeron looked at the redheaded man in shock. The outburst was completely out of character for the smaller man. Not only had he spoken up, but he did so strongly, and while voicing an unpopular opinion. His posture was slightly changed. Cole stood with a straightened back and embraced his full height with his shoulders held wide. It made him look like a confident man. And Cole had displayed his newfound courage before the girls, whom he had been shy and quiet around since Byron had left. The world really had gone mad.

"Excuse me?" asked Atrisha, a young blonde woman. Jeron winced at the tone of the statement and felt sorry for Cole. While she may have phrased it as a question, the fire in her eyes clearly stated otherwise.

Cole just shrugged. "Sorry Trish, not my call. Byron is a prince and I'm not about to bring a bunch of angry armed strangers into the same room as him.

Unlike muscles over here, I don't have any intention of spending every waking moment building wooden towers."

Jeron paused and looked at Cole thoughtfully. Maybe he was still as afraid and nervous as he had been, only that that fear was now of Tyson. What sorts of lessons had the old spy been teaching Cole while Byron had been gone? Jeron was not privy to those lessons, and try as he might, he could not remember Cole saying a word about his training.

Jeron motioned for two of the younger boys who were wandering around aimlessly to come over. "You two, take the girls' weapons and bring them to the female barracks. You don't need to clean them, or store them, just bring the weapons to the barracks. No jokes, and no pranks. I will be checking on both of you. Got it? Good. Now go."

The girls disarmed themselves, with only minor grumbling, and the two boys departed with arms stacked high with an impressive variety of weapons. Jeron gestured for Cole to lead on, and the man darted off at a quick pace deeper into the fort.

Jeron dropped back a few paces so that he was walking with the girls and letting Cole have some room to lead the group. It would not do to have the girls swarm over Cole asking him questions while they walked. The poor boy was so quiet, they would overwhelm him in no time. Jeron would just have to subject himself to that particular treatment.

Olivia walked next to him and slipped her arm between his as they walked. Jeron felt his back stiffen and tried to bear the girl's attention with a stoic face.

"Tell me, Jeron. Now why should I believe that you were outside building lookout towers when your shirt is barely sweaty and is not covered in dirt?" she asked in a dangerously sweet voice. "Where were you really? You can tell me," she whispered in a not so soft or conspiratorial voice.

Jeron nearly missed his next step. He looked down at Olivia who was batting her eyelashes and had a mischievous grin on her face. Jeron's world seemed to slow at the sight of the young woman, and just as quickly as it had slowed, time seemed to snap back to normal in a rush, and he became painfully aware of the smirks and stifled grins etched on the other girls' faces, as well as Cole struggling to muffle a laugh behind a cough.

He ignored them and the blush he felt creeping onto face, and answered the insistent girl. "Olivia, it's as I told you earlier, I was building the lookout towers as per my orders. As to the state of my shirt," he said as he gestured down at the garment with his right hand while leaning his head toward her conspiratorially. "Well, I don't wear my shirt while I work."

They rounded a corner and Jeron felt a grin trying to tug at the corners of his mouth. People always underestimated his wit, and it felt good to land a barb for once.

Olivia arched an eyebrow at him and purred "Well then, maybe I'll have to come out and watch next time." Jeron felt his heart lurch forward, and reminded himself to be cold, emotionless. That was the best way to handle the situation. Olivia's hand moved towards his face, and time seemed to slow again. His breathing paused and a small trickle of cold sweat slid down his back.

Her hand stopped just shy of his cheek and grabbed a fistful of hair. "But please do something about this mane of hair. It makes you look like a wild beast." She released the hair and patted his cheek gently as she disengaged her arm from his, and slid back into the pack of girls who promptly dissolved into giggles and suggestive catcalls.

When did his mane decide to pop out? So much for playing it cold, he thought. He cursed inwardly at himself as he tried to think of a quip to extricate himself from the increasingly awkward situation. Try as he might, his brain could not come up with anything witty on such short notice. That was more Byron and Dalton's territory.

"We're here," said Cole as he came to a stop, mercifully ending Jeron's torment before he could stick his foot further into his mouth.

Cole had led them to the entrance of the conference room. It was located a few doors down from Captain Levren's quarters. For convenience's sake, Jeron assumed. Jeron had been in the room on only a few occasions. It had a large rectangular table in the center upon which sat a map of the surrounding area. The map was regularly updated to reflect whatever logistical, scouting, and intelligence reports that reached them out in the wilderness. Normally, it was a quiet room. Neat and orderly as not much of note happened this far away from society.

Cole nodded to the two men-at-arms standing guard before the door. Both of them were actual soldiers and not trainees at the fort. The guards nodded back, and the rightmost knocked on the double doors before opening them inwards.

"-and you're sure it was this body of water?" asked Captain Levren as his voice floated out into the hall. It sounded different to Jeron. Less harsh, more polite, and more strained.

Cole entered the room and slid silently to the right of the doorway, keeping close to the wall. He motioned for the group to follow him and lifted a finger to his mouth indicating silence. Jeron nodded and he and the girls joined Cole on the wall at the outskirts of the conference room.

"Yes, sir. I am certain," replied a young tall dark-skinned boy that Jeron did not recognize. He was garbed in hunter's greens and was standing at military attention on the opposite side of the conference table from Captain Levren.

Beside the lad stood another scout clad in hunter's greens. He was shorter than the dark-skinned boy, but had a thicker, more muscular body. The second boy turned his head to glance at Jeron and the other new arrivals.

It was Byron. But why was he in hunter's garb? Jeron really had not given much thought as to where Byron had gone after he had pushed him off of the roof, and slipped out of Jeron's sight. He knew his friend had left the fort, but he did not know for what purpose. The Captain and the masters had kept him so busy that he only had time to curse Byron, while his brain usually spent its idle thoughts on Olivia.

Jeron frowned as he quickly studied Byron's features. The boy appeared, not leaner, that was not the right word, maybe more chiseled? No. That also was not right. He looked like his skin had been drawn tight across his entire face and body, and his muscles were straining to come out. It reminded Jeron of a nocked bow whose string was pulled tight before an arrow was loosed.

Their eyes met and for the second time in a space of minutes Jeron's breath caught and his stomach turned to ice. Byron's gaze was intense and piercing, like he was staring into your soul. And his eyes, they were impossibly both fiery and icy cold.

Jeron recognized the stare. It was less a stare and more of a glare. It was also the default expression of both Byron's brother Darik, and his father, Duke Cedric. The members of the Villa family all seemed to possess the same stare to some degree. Jeron could remember walking through the castle in Antier and gazing at the portraits of Byron's ancestors. Even in paintings, their eyes all carried that same intense stare. It was a deeply unsettling familial trait.

However, Byron's features generally took more after his mother, as evidenced by his lack of black hair. And while Byron's brother and father could summon the Villa family stare at will, Jeron knew that Byron could not. That stare only came onto Byron's face when he turned all his focus and attention on one thing to the exclusion of all else in the world.

Or, when Byron was furious.

Judging by the clenched muscles around Byron's jaw, and the presence of Captain Levren, Jeron was betting it was the latter.

Captain Levren motioned down at the map, "Did you two search anywhere else along the water before returning?" he asked.

"Yes, sir" answered the tall lad. "We followed the water for approximately six miles north of the encounter before turning back east. We did not encounter any other monsters. And, if I may sir, judging from the actions of the ones we did encounter, they seemed starved, almost...feral, sir? Like animals really. My best guess is they were among the first to make it across and have not been able to establish a foothold for foraging or the storing of supplies."

Foraging and the storage of supplies? And who or what did the two of them encounter? Cole had mentioned something about a centaur and satyr. Jeron shifted his weight and looked around at the faces in the conference room, aware that the girls were doing the same thing. He glanced at Cole, but the boy was standing rigid straight as if the conversation was not revealing any news to him, and the only matter of any import was looking the part of a dutiful soldier while in the presence of the masters. Jeron's eyes focused across the room, and saw Dalton leaning against the wall a few feet off to Byron's left.

While Dalton may have been slouching against the wall, Jeron saw that Dalton's knuckles were white from grasping the spear in his hand tightly. The boy's usually jovial face was drained of mirth and he gave a tight curt shake of his head to Jeron, indicating that, no, Jeron should not interrupt to ask any questions.

Jeron leaned back against the wall and looked on in puzzled silence. What was going on in here?

Captain Levren ran his hand back through his remaining short bristly gray hair and stared down at the map, concern etched upon his face. In this environment he almost appeared human to Jeron. Stripped away was the demanding instructor, and all that remained was a tired solider.

"Thiago, Byron, good job both of you," said Levren. Jeron felt his eyebrows shoot up. Levren complimenting Byron? The world had truly gone mad.

Levren waved his hand to the door. "Now you two go get some rest. You've earned it, and you'll certainly need it in the days to come. And Byron, take your friends with you from this council. They shouldn't be here."

The taller lad saluted and turned to leave, as did Jeron and the girls. No reason to test Captain Levren's patience. It was better to leave before he regained his usual temperament.

"No." The word stopped all motion in the room. It was not angry, it was not passionate, it was merely stated as a fact.

Once again, Jeron's stomach turned to ice, and he could feel his hairs standing on end. Byron stood before Captain Levren impassive, unmoving.

"Excuse me?" demanded Captain Levren as his face flushed red with anger. "Do I need to repeat myself Byron? Because by the gods, I do not have the patience to deal with your bratty attitude today boy."

Byron did not budge. "Prince," he said flatly.

Levren stared at him bewildered, "What did you say boy?"

"Prince Byron," replied Byron in a clipped measured tone. "I am still a Prince of this duchy and kingdom, and as you are aware, recent events have occurred which greatly concern all of Antier. I am staying."

Captain Levren slammed his hands on the table causing the markers placed upon it to shake. But before he could speak Master Maxus stepped forward and lay a calming hand upon Levren's shoulder.

"Thank you, Prince Byron," stated Maxus with an acknowledging nod. "Everyone in this room greatly appreciates what you and Thiago have accomplished." Maxus drew his eyebrows down and met Byron's stare head on. "But we are not in a war right now, and we are not in the capital. Here you are a trainee as well as a prince. And at this moment, the trainee needs to rest his body, or Antier may find itself short one prince in the coming days."

Byron stared silently at Master Maxus, but the knight did not so much as blink as he stared back at Jeron's friend. The room seemed to be holding its breath at the standoff. Jeron noticed Dalton across the room, still appearing to be slouching, but his right leg was clenched, ready to push off the wall and leap forward at a moment's notice.

Dalton felt it too, Jeron thought. The conference room had the same feel to it, the same energy to it as a tavern did before one of Byron's brawls broke out.

"Very well, Maxus," said Byron as he nodded at the man while purposefully omitting his customary honorific. "Carry on, and send word of what we found to both Antier and Fort Hope. My father and brother both need to be apprised of what happened here."

Byron spun on his heel and marched towards the double doors. The room exhaled and the gathered officers and masters all glanced around nervously, unsure of what to make of the exchange.

Dalton slid calmly off the wall, face grim, and marched a pace behind Byron on his right-hand side, spear ready. Cole slid past Jeron, gently grazing the larger boy as he nonchalantly adjusted his belt with two hands. Without a word, Cole joined Byron on his left hand, Thiago dropped in behind Byron, and the foursome departed, leaving a befuddled Jeron in their wake.

Jeron growled under his breath to himself, turned, saluted Master Maxus, whose gaze had returned back to the map, and exited the room, Olivia and her friends a half step on his heels.

"Byron!" Jeron hissed in an attempt not to shout outside the conference room. Byron stopped, and turned towards Jeron as the double doors of the conference room creaked shut. "What was that? And what was with that whole 'prince' thing? You hate being called prince," accused Jeron.

Face emotionless, yet still somehow filled with implacable fury, Byron stared silently at Jeron, seemingly choosing his words carefully. "I am a prince. Whether I enjoy it or not. And that Jeron, that was a war council."

Hushed mutters broke out amongst the girls, and Jeron felt the color drain from his face again. "A war council?" he sputtered dumbly at his friend. "What war? What am I missing here?"

A small smile cracked the impassive mask on Byron's face, and the fire appeared to die from his gaze as he lowered his voice before answering. "A lot. But more accurately, the war that happens because on our patrol Thiago and I discovered and killed a satyr and centaur. They had made it through the mountains, past Fort Hope, and into the woods beyond."

The muttering ceased and Jeron stood there stunned. Atrisha stepped forward and glared at Byron. "And what are you going to do about it?" she demanded.

"Me?" asked Byron innocently as he pointed a finger back at his chest. "Well, I'm just a trainee who is going to go eat a nice meal and then get some sleep. Care to join me?"

Atrisha silently glared daggers at Byron. "No?" he smirked playfully at her, a touch of ill-concealed scorn upon his voice. "Pity. Well, if you'll excuse me."

Byron turned to leave and Jeron reached out and grabbed his friend's arm. Byron stumbled momentarily in his grasp, and Jeron took a closer look at his friend. While just earlier Byron had looked focus, determined, and angry, the young man now just looked bone weary and exhausted, and so very young.

"Sorry," Jeron said. "No one meant any offense. It's just a lot for all of us to process. And please let us join you for that meal. I uhh really can't afford to let you out of my sight again."

Byron arched an eyebrow inquisitively at him and Jeron let out a deep sigh. "Punishment from Master Maxus for letting you out of my sight. I'll fill you in," he answered with a sigh.

Byron shrugged back at him. "Fine. You're all welcome to join us, and Jeron—" he reached out and tugged at the mane of hair surrounding Jeron's head. "—you can tell me on the way how you managed to show up to a war council sweaty, stinky, and looking like a crazy person."

CHAPTER NINETEEN

Matlin pushed open the door to the Swarthy Miner Inn and surveyed the carnage as he strode through. Half the chairs and tables in the inn lay scattered in piles of smashed jagged chunks of wood. The other half was soaked in what smelled like a combination of blood, wine, and some sort of stew. Lamb perhaps.

Bodies, both men and women, lay strewn haphazardly across the floor in various stages of undress. Many bore the telltale scars of a night of revelry. Bruises scattered on various parts of their bodies, and random tears to their clothes. Matlin stepped over the unconscious body of a barmaid, and the pool of partially dried red wine that surrounded her from the bottle she was still clutching in her hand.

"Fan out. Check for any dead and see that any wounded are tended to," ordered Clara, taking charge of the situation as she entered the inn. Matlin allowed her to issue her orders. She knew her business. He would take care of the rest. "Take any nobles to the castle. The Duke will have words with them when they are sober."

The men of Matlin's house guard fanned out immediately to inspect the bodies. Their chainmail and leather armor squeaked and creaked as they went about their business, making enough of a racket that Matlin was certain only the dead could truly sleep through it.

Matlin ignored the commotion in the common room and climbed the stairs of the once respectable inn. Despite the raunchy name, the Swarthy Miner Inn was patronized by both wealthy merchants and the nobles who profited from

Loach's many diamond, gem, and precious metal mines. Now the inn was in tatters. Matlin had stood on battlefields that had witnessed less chaos.

The two of them had gone too far this time.

The upstairs of the inn was nearly a mirror of the chaotic mess in the common room. Except instead of a slew of bodies spread throughout the hall, the upstairs denizens had the decency to collapse inside one of the many rooms lining the hall that reeked of booze, sweat, and sex.

One man had managed to remain conscious throughout the reverie. He stood rigidly before the door at the end of the hall, his posture betraying the fact that he was a military man accustomed to standing guard for long periods of time in less than comfortable situations. Over his armor he wore the divided black robes of a holy man in service to House of Loach with silver and teal piping sewn into the neckline, cuffs, and hems of the garment marking his devotion to Bollian, the god of negotiation, diplomacy, and peace.

As Matlin approached, he could discern the flecks of blood on the chainmail visible beneath the robe, as well as on the mace hanging from the thick leather belt around the cavalier's waist. It appeared negotiations had turned sour and somewhat final.

Matlin came to a halt before the younger man. He liked to think that his large height and frame commanded respect as he loomed imperiously over others. He unsheathed the claws on the fingers of his right hand and used them to snip some of the straight brown hair laying flat upon his temples. That movement always unsettled people.

To the young cavalier's credit, he did not flinch. He stood at attention, gray eyes staring coolly back at Madlin.

"Cavalier Toran. Report," stated Matlin icily.

The young cavalier ran a hand through his dark hair and gave the hallway a once over. "The situation is under control, Your Highness," he replied.

"Under control?" asked Matlin incredulously. He leaned down, acid dripping from his every word. "Three squads of troops back in the city after spending two years in the northern passes couldn't cause destruction and havoc on this scale. Now where are my little brothers?"

Toran inclined his head to the door behind him. "In there, Your Highness."

Matlin shouldered past Toran and thrust his arm into the door causing splinters to fly through the air as the door flew off its hinges. The bedroom was a tableau of passion, the type that might even make Panyea herself blush. Clothes were strewn everywhere, and two of his younger brothers lay sprawled upon the massive bed they currently shared with three older women, who by Matlin's eyes were pushing thirty. Given the quality of the clothing scattered around the bedroom floor, they were most likely the wives or daughters of wealthy merchants.

Fantastic. As if this morning could not possibly get any worse. The last thing House Loach needed was the merchants, and all of their wealth, angry with the ducal family. While revolts were not common among the Loachian populace, it still would not be ideal to have to put one down because the twins could not keep it in their pants. Not to mention the impact it could have on the finances and business interests of House Loach. It was a headache he could ill afford at this point in time.

Matlin walked to the bed and loomed over his twin little brothers. Edlin's knuckles were raw. Likely he had his fun beating on one of the men, or women, in the inn. While Dedlin's feet lay off the edge of the bed, his horizontal positioning leaving his unconscious head buried beneath a blonde lady. Matlin reached down to grab Dedlin's leg to throw the irresponsible lout onto the floor, but a hand grabbed his arm, restraining him.

He turned and rounded on the offending party, prepared to level Toran with a punch backed by all the rage he felt towards his brothers. Instead, he found Clara's gray eyes staring back at him, a cool rage simmering beneath them.

"Excuse me, cousin," she said, the calm in her voice bearing stark contrast to the venom behind her eyes. "If you'll allow me?"

Matlin nodded his assent and grinned with all of his teeth. Clara was a stern iron-willed woman who did not tolerate foolishness. The twins were going to get exactly what they deserved for instigating this mess.

She calmly extended her arms out before her, stretching her fingers out wide, a wicked grin on her face – she always had a twisted sense of humor. Five small sparks of lightning sprang from her fingertips, but from which fingers Matlin could not tell. The light was simply too bright to distinguish Clara's fingertips. The white globes shot forth across the room, striking the five sleeping figures. Their bodies spasmed as they were jolted back to consciousness. A lovely chorus of yelps and groans sang through the air as they tried to untangle their groggy bodies from one another.

"What the fuck was that," cursed Edlin. "I'll fucking—" he stopped as a second burst of electricity struck his body.

"Now, now, dear cousin, is that any way to speak to a lady?" lectured Clara mockingly.

"You bitch. I'll fu—"

"Excuse me? You'll what?" asked Clara as another burst of lightning arced through Edlin. "I can't hear you. I assume what you were saying, was that you will be watching your tongue from now on, as befits a prince. That you'll no longer be spewing that vile filth from your mouth. Especially in the presence of three godly ladies of cloth like we have here."

"Ladies of the cloth?" asked the blonde girl groggily. "We're not priestesses."

"Really," questioned Clara with an arched eyebrow. "That is terribly unfortunate. A cynical person might think you were trying to find a way to bear a prince's child, and force your way into the nobility through the back door." The girl opened her mouth to protest, but wisely shut it as Clara continued. "A priestess on the other hand has no use for titles, she serves the people, and her children are wards of the temple."

The girls were openly weeping, but Clara continued, ruthless, merciless. "It's the temple of Illis is it not?" Clara nodded in agreement with herself. "Yes. A good choice. The Sisterhood of Illis allows a one-year trial period for its new sisters. Chastity just isn't for everyone, and the sisters do frown on that sort of scandal happening with their older members. That first year can be so very difficult, I hear. Luckily for you three, I will be checking in on you to see how far along you have come on your path to enlightenment."

The girls' weeping had turned into the staggered gasps of a person has who was trying to stop themselves from crying. Reality was setting in on them, as they recognized the slim opportunity and the threat Clara had provided them. Matlin did not think he had ever seen women hope so hard that they were not pregnant. He could not help himself; he started chuckling in delight.

"Guardsman Nial, please come in here," Clara called out. The guardsman entered into the room and saluted. "Please escort these three pious women to the temple of Illis. Take a squad of your men with you. Confirm that they take their vows and report back."

He saluted and gestured for the three women to follow him. They all departed from the room wordless, but not silent. Matlin could hear the sobs and wailing trailing down the hall.

"Now as to you two," continued Clara as she rounded on the twins. "Carousing at night, shirking your duties, and not being in the castle when you were called to an important council, thereby necessitating your brother and I to come searching for you. Which of these activities sounds like the proper conduct of a prince?"

"Listen you witch," growled Edlin. Sparks began to fly from Clara's fingertips. Edlin held up his hands in supplication. "I'm sorry, Clara. Clara! Please. I'm sorry." The sparks died away and Edlin breathed a sigh of relief. "Thank you. What I meant to say was that we were just blowing off some stress. How were we to know that there would be an unscheduled meeting on the same morning?"

"Because it's your duty," said Matlin in a quiet firm voice.

Edlin opened his mouth to protest, but his younger brother spoke before he could form any words. "We're sorry, brother," said Dedlin smoothly. "You're right. We acted poorly and didn't mean to worry you and cousin Clara. Now what news from Antier came in that was so urgent?"

Matlin suppressed the smile that was struggling to break free from the stoic look he was trying to maintain before the twins. Dedlin had always been the more cunning of the two. He had a good soul and thankfully lacked the cruel streak that plagued his brother.

"What makes you think there is news and that it is about Antier?" asked Matlin curiously and with a forced tone of irritation.

Dedlin smiled wryly and said nothing.

Matlin could not help himself; he grinned at the slender boy. "Fine. I won't insult your intelligence. Get dressed and return to the palace. Antier has requested aid from all of the duchies. It appears that the monsters are launching a heavy invasion campaign focused at Fort Hope, and we're going to help. Pack your weapons and armor and prepare to march."

"Huh. Why would we help those Antierian ingrates," asked an incredulous and bewildered Edlin.

Dedlin rolled his eyes. "Because they're better neighbors than a horde of monsters would be, brother. And it's better for us to fight the monsters in Antier than in Loach."

Matlin smiled broadly this time. Both at Dedlin's cleverness and Edlin's consternation. "Correct. Very good. Now go get packing. It's a long march to western Antier."

"March?" sputtered Dedlin. "But..." his voice trailed off as the blood left his face.

Clara grinned wickedly at the twins. "But what, my dear boys? You thought because you deduced the obvious that we would be letting you two off the hook? We had plenty of time to formulate the proper punishment as we tracked you down," she said. "Now cover yourselves up. We leave after lunch. Try to get some food into your stomach too. Marching can be quite stressful on the body."

Edlin groaned, "Ugh. Cuz please don't mention food. Between the pounding in my head and the shakiness of my stomach, I don't think I could manage it."

"You'll manage it," stated Matlin flatly. "You'll be eating on the army's schedule now, and I won't have you passing out while on the march. I'll see you back at the palace."

Matlin marched out of the room, and he leaned in close to Toran on the way out. "See that they make it back to the palace within an hour's time cavalier," he whispered. "I'm counting on you."

"Understood, Your Highness," replied Toran.

Matlin descended the stairs and tossed a pouch of gold coins to the innkeeper who was telling his story to one of the guardsmen. The pouch bounced off of the portly innkeeper and landed on the floor with a thud. Without looking back, Matlin exited through the front door. The squad of soldiers waiting outside snapped to attention and fell into formation around him. Clara, slipped between the guardsmen and fell into an easy glide at his side, turned and called out over her shoulder to the innkeeper, "For your trouble, master innkeeper."

Chapter Twenty

The wave of foes felt endless to Darik. There simply was no end to their number. He opened the next one up with his blade and reached into the belly of the beast to claim his prize.

Darik placed the letter opener down precisely halfway between the stacks of opened letters and unopened letters. Operating a military installation like Fort Hope while also enduring the steady stream of probing attacks from the beasts, felt like he was fighting a battle on numerous fronts. And not the simple kind of battle that he could address with his sword.

Analyze how the enemies are arrayed, formulate a battle plan, carry out the battle plan, calculate the remaining weaponry, adjust the battle plan, worry about provisions, plan the resupply, find time to read the mountain of dispatches, and after all of that, find time to draft responses to the letters, issue orders to the garrison, and manage logistical reports and requisitions from various units.

Darik rubbed his sore eyes and picked up the freshly opened parchment from his desk. The document was well-worn and weathered, bearing the marks of being exposed to moisture. Clearly, the letter had travelled quite a distance, and must have originated from outside of Antier.

He began to read and groaned quietly under his breath. Loach was sending an army of reinforcements. While he was thankful for the aid, and the extra bodies, he was not sure if the benefit was worth the price of hosting the Loachians.

The two duchies had never been on the best of terms with each other. Numerous battles and skirmishes were fought along the border, with each side trying to claim extra land, mainly for the prime forests, perfect for logging, and for the iron mines strewn about the area.

Most of the men in the two armies would have had family members or friends that had died at the hands of the other duchy. Tensions would undoubtedly be running high, and more than a few bodies were bound to drop as a result.

Worse would be the logistical nightmare of the Loachians even making it to Fort Hope. There was zero chance the Antierian nobility would allow a Loachian army to march freely through the duchy without an escort. The suffering inflicted upon the countryside and its inhabitants would be too great. Therefore, a significant number of soldiers would need to be spared from the war effort to escort the Loachians to Fort Hope. Soldiers that would have been a great boon on the battlefield, and would have arrived at Fort Hope much sooner than the Loachians. Instead, with their absence, his men would suffer heavier losses due to fatigue and dwindling numbers.

"Hey man," called a voice from the doorway. Darik looked up as Renaldo sauntered into the office, a parchment in either hand.

"Tell me oh glorious Captain Prince, which you prefer first, the bad news or the not quite so bad news," Renaldo asked, waggling his eyebrows and both parchments. "Come on, it's your lucky day."

Darik knew that most people would have laughed or rolled their eyes at his friend. Not Darik though, that just was not in his nature. Instead, he titled his head sideways and rested it on his right shoulder staring flatly in exasperation at his friend. One of them would break first and laugh, and it was certainly not going to be him.

After a brief pause Renaldo rolled his eyes and held out the parchment in his left hand. "Fine then, the bad news. Seems like the paladins and cavaliers, knights and cavaliers, whatever you want to call 'em, are nearly at each other's throats throughout the kingdom. And it has even spilled over to Fort No Hope. Out past the border of civilized lands. Dissention in the ranks, holy war brewing. You know, insufferably stubborn, the lot of them."

Darik sighed and this time he did roll his eyes. "I want you to check yourself into the medical bay. Get your head examined."

"Your pardon, Your Highness," asked Renaldo, not even trying to hide his mirth.

"Clearly you have amnesia. Forgetting I'm a paladin," stated Darik. "The damage to your brain must be serious, and sadly, you have so little to begin with."

Renaldo grinned and flopped himself into one of the wooden chairs before Darik's desk. "Now where would the fun be in that?" he asked. "I assume you'll be sitting them down for a nice little pep talk?"

"No," growled Darik. "I just don't have the time. Tell Emkario to pair them up with each other on the battlefield. Make them have to depend on each other for their lives. Have him hint that if their partner dies, there will be extreme punishment for the survivor. Be vague. Let their imaginations conjure up the punishment. And stamp out the talk of Fort No Hope. The name is a detriment to morale. Fix it."

Renaldo winced in mock pain. "Ouch. I think I'd rather take the pep talk." Darik arched his eyebrow in the direction of the unread parchment. "Oh yes yes. Continuing on, Oh Exalted One. It appears your brother killed a centaur that was part of a scouting party. Good for him."

"And that's the slightly better news?" Darik asked incredulously.

Renaldo tossed the parchments on the table before responding. "Uhh yeah? He killed a centaur? You know how tough that is. Vicious beasts. Kid is either getting smarter, or maybe he is finally getting in contact with his totem."

The headache hit Darik like a knife being jabbed into his brain. His head felt tingly, and his vision blurred at the sudden onset of the migraine. "No. Not that," he growled, steam rising from his mouth. "If a centaur is that far east of Fort Hope, that means that the battle here is worse than we thought. This isn't one of their random probes, or a just a normal siege. Renaldo, it's the beginning of a full invasion. That's why they're scouting so far past the fort and the mountain range. They aren't planning on stopping, or being stopped."

Renaldo's face went ghostly pale, and he closed his eyes as recognition dawned on him. "Lovely, we're all going to die before help can get here."

"Don't be so glum," said Darik as he picked up the next letter from his desk. "They can still only attack with a small fraction of their numbers at any time. That's the benefit of having walls."

At that moment horns blared out from the fortress's walls, signaling another assault. Darik ignored the headache and swept up his greatsword as he darted out the door. His boots smacked on the stone floor in rhythm with his headache. At least he would get a reprieve from the army of dispatches.

"Well think on the bright side, man," said Renaldo as he grinned maniacally from ear to ear. "At least the constant fighting should keep the paladins and cavaliers from tearing each other's throats out."

Chapter Twenty-One

D arik cleaved a minotaur from navel to collarbone. The beast wailed its death cry, its arms flailing and knocking over the wall two unfortunate satyrs that were trying to gain purchase on the Antierian side of the fortress walls.

He ignored the spray of blood that splashed on his cheek, as well as the pools of blood forming upon the ramparts. Blood from both beast and man had stained the stones of the fort's walls for over a century, and more blood was bound to be shed before the day was over.

Darik leaned over the walls and breathed fire down upon the beasts seeking to take the fort. The stream of flame was not as wide as when he transformed into a dragon, the downside of having a smaller human head, but nonetheless it served its purpose. Flesh melted off of bone as the smell of cooking meat mixed with the screeches of pain filled the air.

It had been a day and a half since the horns announced the most recent assault. In that time Darik's blade had struck down dozens of monsters that had tried to crest the wall. While Fort Hope was not in any immediate danger of falling, it could not hold out at this onerous pace for much longer.

The defenders were only men after all, and men get tired, sore, and injured. Fatigue was the real enemy once it set in. Fatigue and lack of sleep would kill most of his men. The more it set in, the more his men would die. They would get sloppy as their reflexes became just a little bit slower than they had the day before. It would be a cascading effect, and casualties would mount exponentially over time. Sieges, at their core, were mainly a matter of time.

Darik stepped back to catch his breath as soldiers swarmed around him, manning the void in the defense he left behind. He took the pause from action to survey the defense of the fortress. To his right, Renaldo was bellowing out orders, sending his troops on an all-out assault to repel an attack on the walls. An effective tactic, but only in the short term. It was reckless and that rashness would lead to casualties. Casualties which they could not afford.

To his left, Emkario was leading his men in a more sedate defense. Cautious. Ordering his archers forward to keep the beasts from swarming against the wall in large numbers. Also effective, but costly. They only had so many arrows, and replacements were hard to come by this far from civilization.

Behind him, Vincent was ordering the ballistae and catapults to fire. It was a measured and methodical approach with the tools granted to him. While effective, again, they only had so much ammunition, and the enemy had superior numbers. The siege weaponry, while devastating on the beasts that were more akin to normal human infantry, were not as effective at stopping the larger creatures that actually could punch a hole in their defenses and breach walls.

His men were doing their best with the resources they had. There was no easy solution or salve that Darik could apply to their defense. Quite simply, time was not on their side. They did not have enough men, enough supplies, or enough hope. The men had sullen grave expressions on their faces. The truth of the situation was evident to them. They expected to die out here. Far away from their loved ones. Murmurs of the name Fort No Hope spread throughout the ranks. But the men held firm. Not because of an overwhelming sense of duty. They held because they knew there was nowhere for them to run, and if they did flee, there were not any defensible positions between Fort Hope and the more populated areas of Antier. The horde of beasts would face little to no resistance as they tore through the countryside like locusts, destroying everything in sight.

The men knew that, and they stood firm. For their families, their friends. Those who would die if they failed. The soldiers stood bloodied, battered, and prepared to die.

Time was running out. The more that time passed without reinforcements, the more Fort Hope lived up to its reputation as Fort No Hope.

A loud shriek from overhead drew Darik's eyes skyward. A swarm of harpies was descending upon the battlements. Their beaks protruding hideously out of their all too human faces, grayish feathers jutting from their arms, and the talons on their feet stretched out, preparing to rip into the soldiers below.

The harpies had recently begun serving as irregular aerial units for the monsters below. Their appearance and apparent coordination bothered Darik. The beasts were showing an apparent aptitude for tactics and coordination which they never demonstrated before. Despite their twisted appearances, with many exhibiting somewhat human expressions, the beasts had always acted like primitive animals. At their best, they occasionally demonstrated what resembled tribal behavior, not anything approximating advanced military tactics.

The apparent change in the monsters' normal behavior only reinforced Darik's belief regarding the inhuman army. This siege was certainly not a normal raid put together by the creatures. It was something more.

Darik let loose a primal roar up to the heavens and he felt his body begin to shift. Scales covered his plate mail, and his limbs began to grow. He felt his spine stretch, bones thicken, and muscles grow. He gritted his teeth against the pain from the change. Wings sprouted from his back and he stretched them wide and flexed. The force generated from his wings tossed a handful of nearby satyrs off the wall, the goat men bleating as they plummeted to their deaths.

Darik took to the skies, pushing his body as fast as he could to reach the harpies before they could strike his men. The power surged through his body as his speed increased. A toothy dragon grin was on his face. Even under the circumstances, there was something absolutely liberating about being in his dragon form. Flying into the sky, so fast, so strong, and free. Free of his responsibilities.

In the sky, there were not any issues with logistics, politics, or potential marriages. Here, he could just be himself. Do his job. Protect his men. Be Darik. He felt overjoyed and tried to savor the moment. The sensation was fleeting as within seconds he was upon the harpies.

Breathing in deep, he felt the fire swell within his lungs. Darik exhaled and reduced the opening wave of harpies into cinder and ash that sprinkled down upon the battle raging below. His claws flashed, shredding into the secondary ranks of harpies, their shrieks filling the night sky.

Given time, he could methodically slaughter all the harpies. Their claws were not much of a threat to him as they were not sharp enough to pierce his scales. The men below? That was another question. His race was against time, always against time.

Could he kill enough of the harpies before the remaining birds joined their ground-based comrades on a joint assault upon the wall's defenders? The fewer harpies that reached the battlements, the easier it would be for his bowmen below to drive off the satyrs, reducing the casualties that the fort's inhabitants would suffer.

With a chorus of shrieks, the remaining harpies descended upon the fort. Darik dove after them, a hail of arrows rising up between him and his prey. The arrows struck the harpies and his scales. While the arrows bounced harmlessly off Darik's scales, the harpies did not share in his good fortune. The arrows pierced their skin, sending winged bodies plummeting to their doom. Their death howls echoing through the air.

Darik was pleased to see that none of his men had transformed into an avian and taken flight at the harpies. At this point, arrows were more easily replaced than men. He would save and shield his aerial units for as long as he could. They made great scouts and messengers in a pinch. However, there was little need to scout out an opposing force that was conveniently massed into a large encampment. He could shoulder the burden of keeping the skies clear by himself. It was the wise tactical decision.

Only a handful of harpies reached the battlements, too few to cause much harm, and too stupid to realize that they no longer possessed any tactical advantages. Darik smiled as the harpies perished quickly against the humans below.

Darik pulled up from his dive and soared above the plains west of Fort Hope. The threat posed by the army of monsters amassed upon the plains seemed insignificant from this height. Tiny specks moving aimlessly about fields of grass.

On and on he soared, and on and on he encountered packs of the creatures lined up in ranks and marching towards Fort Hope. Their numbers did not lie. They had more than enough troops to overwhelm the defenders in time.

The exhilaration fled from Darik's heart, his mood shifting to maudlin as he surveyed the tableau below. An army at least four times larger than the largest force the beasts had ever brought against mankind lay sprawled across the plains beyond the pass. Death and despair bore down upon his unwitting men, and the only hope they had was that their sworn enemies, and any other allies that his father could muster from the realm would arrive in time.

Darik shook his head sadly as he looped back through the empty skies towards the fort. One way or another the defenders were about to discover the true name of Fort Hope.

Chapter Twenty-Two

Byron groaned inwardly as the disaster played out before him. It was just too tragic to watch.

Jeron and Olivia were openly flirting, and awkwardly holding hands. Each was smiling confidently at the other, but their eyes looked terrified. Jeron wore the expression of a man who caught a wolf with his bare hands, and now had no idea what to do with the creature.

And then there was Cole and Atrisha. The willowy blonde girl had both her arms entwined around Cole's left arm in a death grip. She was talking rapidly and barely pausing for breath. Poor Cole looked like he had just seen a ghost, again. His eyes were darting around, looking for a place to bolt.

Which one will screw things up first? Byron thought to himself. Either way, it was bound to be somewhat entertaining.

Dalton flopped down on the grass next to Byron, stuffing a chunk of bread into his mouth. "Fife gawld coins saysh Cole phases invisible in the next five minutesh," said Dalton around the mush of bread in his mouth.

"No deal," said Byron as he danced a dagger between his fingertips. "Kid is exhausted and barely thinking as it is. Given his awkwardness around most people, and add a girl into that? Nah, he'll panic."

Dalton tore off a piece of bread and offered it without taking his eyes off of the tragic romances. Byron snatched it and tore into the bread with his teeth; smiling as the warm sun beat down upon him. It was nice to have a break from the intense training sessions Captain Levren and the masters were hoisting upon the trainees.

Since the discovery of the satyr and centaur, training sessions were doubled for both regular military training, and the more specialized society training. The masters grumbled about the schedule, but not too loudly, and rarely in range of the trainees. And certainly not where Captain Levren could hear. Apparently, a dead satyr and centaur tended to change everyone's opinions as to what was and was not acceptable.

Byron was not sure who spread the news of the monsters, but word of the dead beasts had escaped from Levren's war councils. It was bound to happen sooner or later. Secrets never stayed buried for long.

All the extra work had been good for the other trainees. It kept their minds off what was to come, and provided them something to focus on.

It also gave me a little peace. Everyone is too worried at the moment to fight or play at politics.

Two blasts of a horn brought Byron out of his reverie. Two blasts. Time to assemble in the courtyard. Which most likely meant an announcement of some sort.

Maybe we're all heading to war. Or away from it.

Byron lurched to his feet, his sore muscles straining at the simple effort. A hand grabbed his arm steadying his balance. Byron looked over at the hand's owner and found Dalton shrugging helplessly, his mace swinging at his side.

His mace? When did that happen?

Byron nodded down at the mace at Dalton's side. "When did that happen?" he asked. "Where is your spear?"

Dalton absently rubbed at a sore spot on his shoulder. "Master Maxus made me switch it up," he answered. "He didn't want me becoming too comfortable with only one weapon. Said I wasn't using all of my muscles with a weapon whose primary purpose was thrusting. Said I was neglecting my body." He winced as he rubbed his shoulder again. "So he made me practice with a mace. Use different muscles, different motions. Train my body to move differently, and my mind to think different tactically. Sadly, my body doesn't feel neglected any longer."

"Hmm that must be difficult for you," said Byron as he patted his friend on the back.

"Thanks," replied Dalton drily as they headed for the courtyard. "My body hasn't exactly agreed with the new exercise."

"Your body?" asked Byron innocently. "I was referring to using your mind."

"You ass," said Dalton as he playfully swatted Byron in the back of his head.

"That's royal ass, thank you very much," chuckled Byron. "And what kind of bodyguard strikes the person he is supposed to be protecting?"

"The type who is trying to preemptively knock some sense into your head before we hear whatever Captain Levren announces."

"Me? Do something senseless?" asked Byron as he spread his hands palms upward before him in a show of innocence. "When have I ever done anything senseless?"

Jeron walked up beside him and tossed an arm around Byron's shoulders. "What sort of timeframe are we talking about here?" he asked. "In your life, the past year, the past month, or this morning? Either way I'm sure between Dalton and I we could write a book on your misadventures."

"Not that anyone would read that dreck," scoffed a feminine voice behind him.

Cole, and the gaggle of the girls had caught up with them and looked slightly out of breath. Byron gave a walking half bow to the stragglers. "Ahh Calabella. I am pleased to hear that you have mastered the art of reading," he said switching into the pleasant melodic voice he was forced to use at court. "It warms my heart. But I simply must know, when did your coven start giving out reading lessons?"

"We are not a coven!" protested Calabella in near rage.

"Oh please, God. Not this crap again," said Dalton as he cast his gaze towards the heavens. "Does anyone happen to know what this whole assembly is about?" he asked as he tried to change the subject.

"Maybe," said Byron and Jeron in unison.

"Well, what is it?" asked Atrisha impatiently as Cole tried to wriggle his arm out of hers.

The two friends exchanged a look and just grinned in response.

Good for Jeron. Figuring out the why. But does he expect what will happen next? Not likely, but I'll need to prepare for that.

Byron glanced down at his friend's belt and saw the axe slipped through a loop on it.

Maybe he does have more than an inkling of what is going to happen. I should give him more credit from here on out. Well here's hoping he doesn't have to use the axe on anyone. At the very least things should be interesting.

Byron ignored the buzzing of speculation and theories rising from his companions, and took stock of his surroundings. A wooden platform had been erected in the courtyard underneath a large oak tree. The tree provided shade to the speaker, while those in the crowd would have to bake underneath the hot sun. It was a small power play, but an effective one. Not to mention the implied threat of a platform placed under a sturdy tree.

A makeshift gibbet, huh? I guess it looks like it's going to be one of those speeches.

Byron slid over towards the left side of the platform, nearest the shade, as the crowd began to slowly fill into the courtyard. The trainees and soldiers were anxious, but there were also pockets of excitement. Scanning the faces of the crowd, Byron could see as many yearning for glory against the monsters as those that looked like they were about to be sick.

Those must have something to lose.

Captain Levren did not waste any time making his entrance. He strode up onto the platform without any fanfare, flanked by his lieutenants. All the men wore the much too serious expressions on their faces of men attempting to convey strength and discipline. However, the show was not very convincing. The officers were trainers, not garrison soldiers. They resembled brittle iron ready to crumble rather than hardened soldiers.

"Men," began Levren without preamble. "We have received orders from the capital. Most of you, in my opinion, are not ready for what is coming, but orders are orders."

Such a charismatic and inspiring leader. Knock them down first. Maybe he'll actually try to build them back up.

"As you all are most likely aware by now, the monsters have begun a large-scale assault upon Fort Hope," continued Levren. Scattered gasps and murmurs spread throughout the crowd. Apparently, everyone had not heard. Or perhaps they chose not to believe. Byron shrugged his shoulders helplessly at Cole. He had made quite a ruckus bringing back the centaur's severed head and its massive club after all. How they managed to remain ignorant of events around them truly boggled Byron's mind.

Levren raised his hand and the chatter slowly began to subside. "Our orders are simple. Many of us will be travelling to Fort Hope to augment our forces there. We will serve mainly as an auxiliary force, fighting where needed. The rest of you will be returning to Antier to aid in the war effort there."

The response from the trainees was less than subdued. Protests rang out from the crowd, even from the fearful. No one wanted to appear relieved that they were not going to war while their peers marched towards possible death.

It's almost time. Hopefully, I'm not completely stupid. Well. It's definitely stupid. Maybe just settle for not being incompetent?

"Silence!" roared Levren, his face flushing red. His pretense at calm strength vanished quickly as the angry training captain reappeared. "You all may be nobility of some kind, but right now you are soldiers in my army. And my soldiers follow orders whether they like them or not!"

And there we have it. Stupid plan it is.

Levren gestured to the two lieutenants on either side of him. "You'll receive your orders from the lieutenants. Pack quickly. We all leave Raven's Perch in five days' time."

Here goes nothing.

Byron pushed Cole gently to his left and leapt up onto the platform. "No, Captain we will not be leaving in five days," he said as the stunned officers turned to look at him. He continued on before they could interrupt him. "We leave tomorrow." Byron turned and addressed the audience. "Pack quickly, and wait for your instructions from the lieutenants. We'll be moving fast."

Levren stormed across the platform toward Byron, the sunlight sparkling on his sweaty forehead.

He looks like an angry tomato. Wrong man to lecture me about my temper.

"What in the hell do you think you are doing, *Your Highness*," sneered Levren as he grabbed Byron's shoulder and began to squeeze.

Byron gritted his teeth and ignored the pain radiating out from the old stab wound. Damn thing still was bothering him. He plastered a smile on his face which bordered on being an insolent smirk. "Yes. Your Highness. I am so glad you remembered my rank, Lieutenant Levren."

"Lieutenant?" Levren sputtered. "Why you little spoiled piece of-" he broke his sentence off as the blood drained from his face.

"Yes, that's correct my dear sergeant," continued Byron cheerfully as he lowered Levren's rank again. "We're in a time of war. You said it yourself. We're soldiers. Meaning this whole charade of trainer and trainee is over. I am the prince, and I am in command. Now remove your hand from my shoulder before you find yourself a corporal."

"I'd be happy to help with that," piped up Dalton who had finally recovered enough of his wits to leap up onto the stage next to Byron. He calmly bounced the head of his mace into the palm of the left hand. "More than happy in fact."

Levren calmly and very slowly removed his hand from Byron's shoulder. "You have no idea what you're doing, boy" he whispered darkly.

Jeron, who must have been a hair slower than Dalton in reacting to Byron's usurping of command, laid a restraining hand on Byron's other shoulder. But Byron did not so much as budge at Levren's words. "Perhaps," Byron said flatly. "But we'll find out together now won't we, Sergeant?"

A silence had fallen upon the crowd as Byron and Levren confronted each other. Shouts and cries of confusion and anger quickly shattered the silence. Evidently, Byron was not going to be the most popular of commanders.

"Silence!" roared Jeron as his mane popped out around his face. Surprisingly, the crowd went silent. "You all have your orders. Now act like soldiers and follow them. Dismissed."

With less-than-ideal military self-control, the crowd darted off towards their respective barracks, surprisingly complying with the order. Byron noticed a few of his less than ardent supporters, sulking and dragging their feet as they went about preparing for war.

Byron closed his eyes and breathed slowly as a headache swelled up behind his eyes.

Lovely. I'm in command of a force of boys. Many of whom have hated me for years. Just lovely.

Levren's two lieutenants quietly escorted the newly minted Sergeant Levren off the stage. By their gentle treatment of Levren, the poor men obviously did not know how to react. If the demotion was not permanent, they could easily find themselves in a very uncomfortable situation, and on the wrong side of Levren's infamous temper. Byron winced in sympathy.

In a matter of minutes, the courtyard was silent and Byron stood quietly, taking it all in. Thankfully his gambles had both paid off.

"Hey. Has anyone seen Cole?" asked a flustered Atrisha as her head swiveled around looking in vain for the quiet boy. "He just vanished during the speech. I could have sworn he was standing right next to me."

"I am right here," assured Cole's soft voice.

Atrisha and the others looked around in bewilderment, searching vainly for the red-haired youth. "Right where exactly?" she asked.

"Right here," Cole said again as he shifted into focus roughly where Levren had been standing.

Atrisha's brow pulled down as she frowned at him. "What are you doing over there?"

Cole shrugged his shoulders, but his usual sheepishness was absence. "My job," he said flatly.

Dalton scratched at his scalp, thankfully with the hand not holding the mace. While Dalton claimed to enjoy the finer things in life, he tended to have a few moments where his brain parted ways with common sense. "Your job? Shouldn't you be standing right here with Jeron and I? What were you doing over there?"

"Stacking the deck," said Byron softly. Cole grinned and walked a dagger between the fingers of his right hand, and with a small flick of his wrist the blade vanished. Byron turned and looked at Dalton before speaking. "You didn't think I went through that without a plan, did you? And the brass knuckles would have been way too obvious. Besides, I needed to put on a good show."

Dalton gaped at Cole in bewilderment while Jeron groaned in understanding.

Without another word, Byron hopped off the platform and began walking in the direction of the council room. Only Cole followed him as the others were still standing in shock. Or horror.

Now to keep the show going without everyone winding up dead. Especially me. No problem.

Chapter Twenty-Three

"**W**hy is there a giant hole in the ground?" asked Edlin as he yawned in his saddle. "Do these stupid Antierians not know how to dig a mine shaft?"

Dedlin rolled his eyes heavenward, while faithful Toran remained ever stoic. Matlin ignored the blithering of his younger brother and scanned the countryside.

They were roughly five miles past the border, and were well on their way into Antier. Decades earlier the two duchies had fought a large battle upon these grounds. The current Duke of Antier's father, a relatively young man at that time, perished before the conflict could escalate further into a full-blown war. The young duke died violently, and all the power from his considerable totem had built up, and was flowing within him and had nowhere to go at the time of his death. His corpse was unable to contain the energy, and it had erupted from his body, causing a massive explosion which claimed an untold number of lives on both sides of the conflict.

The result of the explosion was the crater off to Matlin's right. The explosion had sent dirt and debris all over the battlefield. Sadly, no precious metals or iron had been thrown loose in the blast. The area was completely unfit for mining, and not worth fighting a war over.

The duke's death ended the skirmish, and Matlin's family had lost all the ground it had seized in the conflict. Loach had fallen back, unsure of what caused the explosion, worried that the Antierians had developed a new weapon. It took years for the Loachani to deduce the cause of the crater.

Now, years later, all that remained was a scar upon the earth, and a legion of ghosts that swarmed the battlegrounds at night. Matlin shook his head sadly. Such a waste.

"It's what happens when young nobles with more power than sense get themselves killed," said Matlin drily.

"Brother, is it wise for us to stay on the road?" asked Dedlin. "Even if our help was requested, what is to stop some local lord or garrison from attacking us? We don't exactly have any reinforcements nearby."

Matlin shook his head in the negative but kept silent as he surveyed the countryside. It was a good question, but Dedlin needed to work some things out with his own mind. He had the brains for it.

"Cousin, that's a good question with a relatively simple answer," said Clara from her horse to Matlin's left side.

Matlin sighed inwardly. His beloved cousin was far too softhearted for her own good. He motioned his assent with a slight flick of his left wrist.

"The heathens didn't ask for only our aid in repelling those vile beasts," lectured Clara. "They sent the request out to the entire kingdom. And so every other duchy will be looking on the road for us, or waiting for us to arrive. If we show up on the backroads, it makes it look like we are engaged in one of those nefarious plots the Antierians always accuse us of being involved in. If any town gets robbed by bandits, we'll be blamed. Because the Antierians certainly have had people watching us since before we reached the border, and an honor guard I'd assume is waiting to guide us through their land."

The twins nodded along. Dedlin thoughtfully, and Edlin as if he just wanted the lecture to be over.

They finally left the crater in their wake, and Matlin spoke up to the boys. "And more importantly, our army is larger than any local lord could feasibly challenge. That, and any fighting would result in taking us longer to get to Fort Hope," he said flatly. "And the longer it takes us, the more humans will die to the monsters."

Edlin snorted and started laughing. "Who cares?" he barked. "Let the monsters kill the bastards. We're better off without them." Dedlin snickered along with his brother. How disappointing.

Clara smacked Edlin on the shoulder on account of him being closer. "Listen to your brother," she hissed. "Or I'll have you back marching instead of on a horse. The political ramifications of Antier falling will land squarely on our shoulders. Everyone will-"

"That's not what I mean," interrupted Matlin as he glared at his cousin. "I've fought those monsters before, and believe me when I tell you that there is not another choke point in Antier or beyond, besides Fort Hope, that will keep those monsters from swarming into the realm." The laughter and snickering had started to titter off. "We call them monsters for a reason. They. Are. Monsters. And they have no mercy. They are not human, and no man should have to suffer at their hands. Believe me. Whatever your problems are with Antier, the monsters would make significantly worse neighbors. On a scale you cannot even fathom."

Toran nodded his assent. Matlin revised his evaluation of the lad. He definitely had potential, and might make a good soldier yet. He would have to give the lad more responsibility and see how he handled it. However, Toran's presence appeared to serve as a check against the twins' worst impulses. Perhaps if Matlin removed Toran from duty with the twins all three would have the opportunity to thrive. It would be worth monitoring.

A small village appeared on the horizon, and Matlin could pick out the banners belonging to an Antierian cavalry honor guard. Smart. Horses would not be as useful on the walls of Fort Hope. Time to see how inhospitable these neighbors of his could be. It would only be a matter of time before the knives came for their backs. Of that he was certain.

CHAPTER TWENTY-FOUR

J eron burst through the door, causing the wooden frame to protest loudly against the hinges. Puffs of sawdust heralded his entrance into the room. In three quick strides he was at the desk with his fists closed around the front of his antagonist's shirt.

"What do you think you're doing?" roared Jeron.

"I could ask you the same thing," said Byron softly, his face blank and cold.

Something cold and sharp pressed gently and insistently against Jeron's side, and he froze. Someone cleared their throat from the other side of the room and reality seemed to rush back into focus.

Dalton was gripping his spear, his usual slouch abandoned, his face grim. To Jeron's surprise and mortification, the room was full. Master Maxus's face looked equal parts ashamed and enraged, while Master Tyson's features stood in stark contrast, blank and unreadable. Levren, once again a captain, had a contemptuous smirk on his face, and Cole's face was blurred like the rest of his body, his dagger pressed sharply against Jeron's side. Also standing next to Jeron before Byron's desk was a middle-aged man, with salt and pepper hair, a plain boring face, and horror reflected in his blue eyes.

Jeron felt his breathing slow as the anger fled. He felt the heat flush through his neck and into his face, the mane of hair around his face standing on end.

"Sorry," he apologized halfheartedly to the room. "It appears I've interrupted something." He begrudgingly released Byron's shirt, smoothed it over and patted Byron's chest like his own mother used to do when dressing him as a child.

Jeron eased himself back from the desk, and slowly retreated to the wall of the room; his discomfort never left him, nor did Cole's dagger in his side.

The salt and pepper haired man adjusted his woolen brown robes and shifted his weight as he stood before Byron. "If I may continue, Your Highness?" he asked, his voice shaky.

Byron nodded and gestured with two fingers in a rolling fashion at the man. He rested his cheek on his other hand; boredom etched on his face.

"Right, yes. Umm. Indeed," the man stammered, but not solely because he was nervous. He seemed to be the type of man who did not enjoy speaking with others. "This timeframe to move and pack our things is just unacceptable. We have too many books and magical artifacts to transport. Proper care must be observed if we are to transport them to Antier safely. Not to mention my new students. I cannot allow them to go along to Fort Hope this early in their training. It would stunt their growth. They must be permitted to accompany me back to Antier."

The man stopped abruptly and just stood there, oblivious to the fact that he had not finished his line of thought. Perhaps he just assumed that everyone would be able to follow along with his reasoning, and that he did not need to vocalize his actual request to Byron. Or, Jeron mused, maybe the safety of his students was not as important to the man as he insinuated.

"I see," said Byron flatly as he drummed his offhand fingers on the desk's worn surface. "I sympathize with your problem Master Richard. Luckily for both of us, you are mistaken, and therefore the situation is easily remedied."

"Oh, yes. Very good," said a relieved Richard. He paused for a moment, his brow furrowing in concentration. "Wait. Mistaken? I'm afraid that I do not understand."

"Sir. You do not understand, sir," corrected Byron. "Or 'Your Highness' or 'Prince' or maybe 'Prince Byron'. All are acceptable. I don't actually have a preference which you choose to use."

Richard's demeanor seemed to shift instantaneously to Jeron's eyes. Gone was the slouched posture and downcast eyes, and in its place was a simple elemental fury, and an air of arrogance born from years of assumed superiority over others.

A lazy contemptuous smile spread across Byron's face, only slightly distorted by the heel of his palm pulling at his mouth. "There it is," drawled Byron, boredom interjected into his voice. "Did you know Richard, that I was at court the day you had a screaming match with both the Church and the temples? I was just a child then, easy to miss, but I witnessed it all. The terrifying wizard and his mystical powers–" Byron waggled his fingers, eyebrows, and eyelids around with mock melodrama, "—against the power of the faiths. Sadly, it was a disappointment. But I never forgot you."

Byron leaned forward; hands planted on the desk. "Let's cut through the nonsense then and speak honestly to one another. You're not a simpering fool, and you're not going to Antier."

"I'm not?" hissed Richard with a hint of defiance in his voice. "Then where precisely am I going?"

Byron grinned maliciously at the older man. "Why my dear Richard, you're going to Fort Hope."

Naked hatred was written all over Richard's face. Jeron had seen that expression on many men's faces in many taverns, and usually that expression was leveled in Byron's direction. For some reason Levren was smirking broadly.

"I will not," Richard declared vehemently.

"Oh yes you will," chuckled Byron. "It's an order. Failure to comply..." his voice trailed off and he drew a finger across his throat.

"Well, not a slit throat," continued Byron. "We're in the military. We hang people here. Right, Levren?" The smirk seemed to freeze on Levren's face, before the old military man could school his features into stoicism. The implied threat was not lost on the old soldier.

"That is correct, Your Highness," replied Captain Levren through a clenched jaw.

Byron picked up a piece of parchment and made a point of studying it intently while ignoring the older men. "Anger is good. It means you have energy," he said, speaking into his parchment. "You'll need that energy since you'll be training myself, Cole, Dalton, and Jeron how to use magic while we travel."

"Absolutely not!" roared Richard as he lunged towards Byron.

Jeron took a step forward to intervene but stopped short after one step for two very important reasons. The first being that Dalton moved in a blur, channeling his totem and crossing the distance from the wall to the desk in a breath, slamming the shaft of his spear into Richard's chest and placing the point of his spear against Richard's throat.

The second reason, was Cole's hand restraining his shoulder, while he kept his dagger pressed insistently into Jeron's side.

"Easy now," whispered Cole into his ear. "Things are under control."

"Tsk tsk tsk," admonished Byron as he shook his head in disappointment. "And everyone always calls me the rash one. Assault on the royal personage and your superior officer. Such serious charges. What to do, what to do."

Richard stood up proudly, ignoring the spear point to his throat. "There is more than one way to assault someone, boy. I could hurt you in ways that you could never see coming," he intoned.

Byron stood up slowly, the smile gone from his face. A bead of sweat slowly trickled down his forehead. A small flame flickered above his palm. "Maybe my father's court wasn't the only function I sat in on as a child," he said. "Maybe you should have checked the vents and crawlways in the castle before conducting your lessons."

The flame vanished and Byron slowly sank back into his chair. "And you make a valid point, Richard," he said slowly. "My friends and I are not equipped to handle a magical attack. I could be assassinated and never see it coming. Well, you're going to remedy that."

Byron scooped up a bottle tucked away behind his desk and took a swig of it. Jeron prayed it was water. "Or you could hang," he said drily. "Your choice."

Richard stood there silently. Fuming. He said nothing. Minutes passed, and he said nothing. Byron continued sipping calmly at his bottle, a nonplussed expression on his face as the silence dragged on. Jeron's breath came in bursts.

It felt like a giant hand squeezing his chest while simultaneously, his heart was also trying to burst forth.

The minutes dragged on. The room silent except for the *tat tat tat* of Byron's fingers drumming on the desk.

"This would betray everything I believe in," Richard whispered.

Byron arched an eyebrow at the man. "Perhaps," he said. "But honestly, who would believe that you actually taught us? In the middle of a war? Please."

Richard exhaled slowly. "Very well. Every day then." His eyes scanned over the four boys. "It requires immense discipline though. If you all shirk your training, I stop. No questions asked."

Jeron exhaled, and tried to silently gasp for air, unaware that he had stopped breathing during the showdown. He was vaguely aware of nodding his head in agreement, the hairs of his mane tickling his chest. Jeron took a deep breath and focused on forcing his mane of hair to retreat. At the very least he could try not to look like a wild man in the presence of the masters.

Byron nodded in agreement. "That is acceptable. Masters Richard, Tyson, Maxus, and Captain Levren, you are dismissed. Thank you for coming, go about your business. And make sure that business includes never uttering a word of what transpired here."

The elder men saluted and silently exited the room, the doors shutting softly behind them.

Byron sagged back into his chair and carefully pulled a thin rod out of his right sleeve and gingerly placed it onto the table. "Well, that went well," he muttered.

Dalton flopped down on the corner of Byron's desk. "Right. But it worked," he said. "The plan went through relatively clean."

Jeron looked around befuddled. Plan? That whole thing was a plan? Nearly pushing a master to commit murder and then blackmailing that same master? That was Byron's idea of a plan? When had this foolish plan been hatched and why was he not told about it?

"Would anyone like to clue me in on this plan?" he asked irritated.

"Nah," said Dalton as he casually tossed his spear back and forth between his hands.

"Byron?" asked Jeron.

Before the prince could answer, a knock came from the door. Byron gestured to Dalton who sprang up from the desk and sauntered to the door. Dalton opened the door and Olivia stormed past him with Atrisha and the other girls right on her heels.

Olivia glared at Jeron, fury etched on her face. "Well?" she demanded. "What did he say?"

Jeron felt his temper flare up and the mane of hair sprout again with it. The thought of Cole's dagger stopped him from moving toward her in anger. He really needed to get his mane of hair in control. Maybe he would keep it out to avoid the embarrassment its sudden appearances kept causing him.

"We have not had a chance to talk about it," he said with forced calmness.

"Really? You didn't find us being forced to return to the city worth talking about?" Olivia snapped rhetorically.

Jeron gritted his teeth and remained silent. He would not lose his temper for a second time in only a matter of minutes.

Olivia threw her hands up in the air in disgust and rounded on Byron. "And you," she snarled, her finger pointed at the prince in accusation. "What right do you think you have sending us off? We can fight just as well if not better than the boys you are taking with you!"

Byron rubbed at his face. Whether his eyes or temples, Jeron could not tell from his angle. "Doesn't anyone follow orders around here without questioning them first?" he asked wearily.

"They learned from you," quipped Dalton happily.

Byron grunted in what might have been assent and turned his head towards Jeron. "Is this what you barged in here about?" he asked.

Jeron nodded his head in acknowledgment. "Yes. It's not right," he answered.

"Right has nothing to do with it," replied Byron. "I don't have that luxury. I do what is necessary."

"Necessary?" hissed Atrisha as she pushed past Olivia. "How is any of this necessary? We'd be better used in the field!"

"How did you reach that conclusion?" Byron asked calmly in a soft voice. "Let's go over the facts shall we? Fact one. Girls training in the military is a new idea, and you all are the first group. Fact two. Not every noble in the duchy is thrilled with this change."

"Who cares what they think?" retorted Olivia.

Dalton grin faded from his face as his expression turned serious. He lowered his spear so that it stood between Byron and the girls. "The prince was not finished speaking," he said in a very un-Dalton-like serious tone. "Do not interrupt him again."

Byron nodded his thanks to the blonde boy and resumed counting facts out on his fingers. "Fact three. Many of those nobles, not all from Antier by the way, will be travelling to Fort Hope to fight and risk their lives. Fact four. Their forces will most likely, and hopefully, outnumber those from Raven's Perch. Fact five. Our group would make fantastic hostages for our allies even before we factor in the possibility of female hostages. Fact six. If taken hostage, many of our dear noble allies would seek to force the female hostages into marriages to improve their family's standing and holdings. Fact seven. If we have to fight our own allies, even for a good cause, we waste men and resources that would be better spent fighting the monsters assaulting Fort Hope.

"Now what conclusion can we draw from these facts?" he asked rhetorically. "That we need all the help we can get, and in order to avoid a potential fight with our allies, and the political backlash that will certainly follow, we send the small number of girls that we have here back to Antier as quickly as possible. Odds are that it will save lives and help us achieve our objective. Easy decision."

Byron's explanation seemed to take some of the fight out of the girls. Although to Jeron's eyes they still looked quite furious.

"What happens if they run into allied groups on the way back to Antier?" asked Jeron. "Wouldn't they run the same risk as if they had stayed with us?"

Byron waved his hand dismissively. "No. Not the same risk. They'll be travelling north and any force heading to Fort Hope should be taking a road heading west. As long as they're careful they should be able to avoid any conflicts. Scout ahead at areas where roads intersect and so forth. It can be done. And they won't be a party of only women. I'm also sending the younger boys back with you. I am also sending some of the boys who are the only children in their respective families back with them. Try to prevent their houses from ending. You'll have additional fighters with you." Byron glanced up at Olivia. "You'll be in command, and you Atrisha, her second. It's the best I can manage in this situation."

Jeron nodded his assent and an awkward quiet seemed to settle upon the room. The girls shifted their weight and looked around the room, Dalton started whistling, Byron stared stonily ahead, and Jeron stood rigidly still.

Atrisha broke the silence first, puzzlement and concern on her face. "Where is Cole?" she asked. "I don't see him anywhere. He is always vanishing like that now."

Jeron turned around and sure enough the nimble man and his dagger were gone. But when? The blade had been at his back for the entire conversation. Hadn't it?

"He's taking care of a matter for me," replied Byron.

"A matter?" asked Atrisha. "When will he be back? Will I be able to see him before we leave?"

"If everything goes to plan, yes," answered Byron.

CHAPTER TWENTY-FIVE

C ole peeked around the corner and tried to slow his racing heart. Which proved to be more difficult in practice than in theory. He was already fixated on shifting his body out of focus, while keeping pace with his targets, and also remaining silent. The entire ordeal was physically and mentally taxing. And to top it all off, his heart was pounding so loud that he was certain that it would betray his presence.

His targets were moving quickly through the fort and were already exiting the hallway and entering the audience hall. Cole slipped down the hall and pursued them as quietly and swiftly as he dared. He peeked through the doorway to the audience chamber, quickly scanning the area. No one was looking in his direction. Cole breathed a quick sigh of relief before ducking behind a suit of platemail armor displayed in the audience hall as if it were some sort of martial artwork.

The armor fit the room well as the audience chamber at Raven's Perch was at its core a more militarized version of a noble's audience chamber. Instead of a throne, tapestries, and fancy portraits of deceased relatives, the fort had suits of armor. Both had banners of course. Some things just remained the same.

Cole flipped over a short waist-high wall and scrambled up a nearby pillar into the rafters. The layout of the fort's audience hall was also different than that found in castles and palaces. It had minor fortifications designed to bleed invading forces and provide cover for the defenders. But not too much cover. Any visiting noble would still expect some modicum of accommodations that were familiar and pleasing to the eye.

Cole's heart beat faster as he climbed, and he hoped the sound of his targets' conversation would drown out any noise caused by his boots scraping against the stone. Cole pulled himself onto an archery platform and crouched down as he continued eavesdropping on his targets. So far, they appeared none the wiser to his presence.

"Now that was a marvelous disaster," said Levren with a sigh. The group of masters stopped in the center of the audience chamber and looked around for any eavesdroppers before continuing.

No one ever looks up, thought Cole. Why was that?

"It went according to plan," replied Maxus sternly.

"Plan?" asked a wide-eyed Richard. "What part of the plan involved that brute threatening to kill me and then extorting me into training him?" Richard shoved his finger into Maxus's face. "And don't tell me that it is just the plan. We were supposed to offer the idea to them! Make them reliant upon us!"

Master Tyson stepped forward and lay a hand upon the wizard's shoulder. "Easy Richard. As much as it may pain us, we achieved our goal and the plan moves forward," he said. "True. It may not have gone exactly how we desired, but the end result is the same. Those four boys will learn some magic, and the prince is the undisputed commander of our forces here."

Richard jerked his shoulder free from Tyson's grip. "And if those boys talk?" he demanded. "What happens then? My society will surely kill me for spreading its secrets to outsiders."

"Death would be the easy way out for all of us," Maxus said softly.

"Ain't that the truth," swore Levren. "The kid better be worth it."

"He is," assured Tyson. "And if he isn't, Antier will be torn apart by a succession war when his brother takes the throne. A war almost as bad as the one the kingdom is heading towards. If only the king had a viable heir. This wouldn't be necessary then."

Richard threw up his hands in disgust. "I know! Gods know that I know," he said as he vacillated between anger and deflation. "I just wish we didn't have to be involved in all of this. Ten years we've spent on this plan in some form or another. Ten years."

"It has been a long time," said Maxus sadly.

"We're just lucky that no one has remembered that we were friends growing up," said Levren.

"Indeed," said Tyson. "And we should keep it that way. We all need to go on our separate ways before people see us together."

The men nodded and said something Cole could not discern from his perch. Cole leaned back against the archery platform and pondered what he had overheard.

At least three masters were in collusion with each other and had formed some sort of cabal. A plan that involved Cole and his friends being taught magic? Byron becoming a duke? And Darik becoming king? And somehow Captain Levren was a part of it all?

Had any of their schemes actually been their own? Byron's plan to take control of Raven's Perch? Was Byron right and things had been just a little too easy? That was the reason why Byron had forced Richard's hand earlier. To see how far he could push the masters.

Cole shook his head and tried to focus. He could think more on matters later. Right now, his immediate concern was to return and report back to Byron. It would not do for him to be seen exiting this room. Word of that would reach the masters, especially Tyson. The man had an uncanny knack for knowing everything that happened in Raven's Perch. Cole would need to stay invisible until he could return to Byron or some other part of the fort where his presence would not be of any particular note. He sighed inwardly and silently made his way down from the archery platform.

***

Tyson smiled to himself as he stalked through the halls of Raven's Perch. It appeared that Cole had improved during his training. Who knew that the meek boy would have the audacity to trail them. Tyson had not noticed Cole's presence until some time after they arrived in the audience hall. The boy was good. He felt a flash of pride tinged with some minor annoyance. He should have picked a less obvious hiding place than an archery platform though. It stuck out too much and drew people's eyes to it.

The boys were showing a streak of cleverness and cunning that they had not demonstrated before. Good, thought Tyson with some measure of conviction. They all might just survive what was to come, and his carefully laid plan might work after all. If not, well, that was why he made contingencies.

Chapter Twenty-Six

The river Irinin marked the southern border of Antier. It flowed east, beginning from a point beyond the border of the land the monsters called home, and eventually curved southeast into the duchy Biona, establishing Biona's western border.

Large cliffs ran along the Irinin's northern banks, with the river lying hundreds of feet below the cliffs. Along the southern bank lay nothing but swampland. Antierians never ventured into the swamp due to the difficulty of navigating up and down the cliffs. Cole had heard rumors that the Bionans avoided crossing into the swamplands because no one that entered ever came out alive. But surely those were just local superstitions.

Cole grabbed at his leather armor and tried picking his soaked shirt from his skin. The humidity in this area of Antier was downright oppressive. Cole assumed it was the byproduct of being adjacent to the river and the swamplands. If no one truly ever came out of the swamplands the reason most likely was that they drowned on the air there.

To Cole's right, Byron rode on his horse, humming softly, apparently unaffected by the humidity. And...was he dancing? Cole blinked in confusion. He could have sworn the prince's shoulders were shaking in rhythm with his horse's cantor. Surely no one could actually be enjoying the horrid weather.

It had been a week since their force departed Raven's Perch, and Byron was pushing a rather hard pace during that time. From what Cole could gather, Byron wanted to reach his brother at Fort Hope as soon as possible, while avoiding being caught from behind by any larger allied forces.

Cole's legs ached from the march. He had never ridden horses much before, and never for an extended period of time. His inner thighs and the muscles therein felt like they were being stretched to the point of snapping.

While it hurt, Cole did not mind the pain and discomfort as much as he thought he would. It kept his brain occupied from other difficult subjects. Many of those subjects being related to Atrisha.

Before the girls departed Raven's Perch for Antier, Atrisha had pulled him aside. She had kissed him, and if that alone was not too much for him to process, she then told him that she loved him. How was he supposed to react to that? He had barely spoken to her and found her forwardness incredibly intimidating and perplexing.

Then she told him that they could not be together and then she had kissed him again before leaving. Were all women this confusing? Cole would have asked his friends about it, but Jeron had been in a mood since they left. Apparently, he and Olivia had a similar talk, but judging from Jeron's ever shifting mood between happy and depressed, Cole could not guess what exactly transpired between the pair.

Dalton was growing increasingly fidgety, agitated, and temperamental as the days passed; making him a less than an ideal candidate for a conversation. Cole had not known the blonde boy very long, but from what he had been told by Byron, Dalton had been born closer to Fort Hope. They could be near his hometown for all Cole knew. Heading back to that area had to be drudging up all sorts of bad memories for his friend.

His friend. Cole shook his head ruefully. All those years of being the shy and lonely kid who did not have any friends at all, and now he had three of them, more if he counted Atrisha and the other girls. He could scarcely believe it. Sometimes it felt like a dream.

Dreams. Cole tried to suppress a shudder. The dreams had returned and were occurring every night of the march. Each night he was chased and hid from herds of strange men. And every morning he woke up feeling exhausted.

Cole took a deep breath and tried to clear his mind with the exercises Master Richard taught them. Master Richard said that magic was merely an application of a person's willpower combined with the knowledge of how the world interacted with itself. The gadgets and devices that the public was familiar with were simply explanations for commoners, nobles, and the various religions. Apparently, people had a difficult time accepting that which they did not understand, and were prone to ascribing nefarious intentions to the deeds of those that did.

Therefore, a physical explanation was provided through wands, glyphs, runes, and other devices. However, they were far from necessary for a wizard. Merely tools.

Cole took to the magical training quicker than his friends. Years of channeling his inner chameleon had taught him mental focus. His time at Raven's Perch had strengthened that focus, and taught him how to divide his mind between various tasks. Coincidentally, all of those skills happened to be helpful and crucial in the use of magic.

Imagination was the other crucial component to magic. It was all well and good to have the focus and willpower to use magic, but it was another thing to know what to do with it. Byron had excelled in that area. He was always trying to do new things with what they learned. The results however were inconsistent at best. Byron's attempt at giving himself a haircut by freezing his excess hair and shattering the frozen strands with his hand, resulted in him needing a much shorter than anticipated haircut.

Jeron and Dalton turned out to be competent but disinterested scholars. Sure, they studied and went through the drills like he and Byron did, and they participated in the same training and were actually learning. But after each session, they collapsed with usually Dalton complaining about being physically and mentally drained. It was a valid complaint. All the training they were undergoing was beginning to take a toll on them all.

Things were only going to be more difficult as they drew closer to Fort Hope. Who knew what awaited them there? War, soldiers, and nobles; any of whom may want to kill them.

Cole suppressed a shudder and turned his attention back upon the road ahead. He focused his mind and pushed a low hanging tree branch out of his way with a gentle gust of air. Small enough to be unnoticed by the other soldiers on the march, or if it was, to be attributed to the actual wind. Their secret training would still remain a secret.

He sighed in contentment. Using magic was just plain fun. There was joy in doing something that you knew had to be physically impossible, yet still doing it anyway. Cole doubted that feeling was ever going to get old.

"Your Highness!" a voice called out from behind.

Cole craned his head over his shoulder and scanned the area looking for the disturbance. A rider was approaching quickly from the back of the column. No, not a rider, only a horse.

A horse narrowed the newcomer's identity down drastically. It had to be one of Sildun's other scouts, Atticus, channeling his horse totem. Byron had ordered Atticus to cover the force's rear, and to keep an eye out for any forces pursuing them.

"Sir," said Atticus, his nostrils flaring from exertion. Saluting would have been problematic for the boy in his current form, so Atticus settled for a nod of his head, his brown mane bouncing in time with his gait. If Cole was not mistaken, Atticus in his human form, was a brown haired, slender youth with small shoulders yet strangely large hands.

"There is a force approaching from the east, sir," he reported.

"Bandits?" Byron asked skeptically, and maybe with a tinge of hope.

"No, sir. Military," Atticus reported. "Judging by their banners it is Baron Mavon and his troops."

"Walter Mavon," sighed Byron. "Atticus, ride ahead and inform Thiago that we are going to be needing to a place to stop and rest. Make sure it is easily defensible."

"Yes, sir," said Atticus. The boy nodded again and galloped on ahead, his hooves kicking up dust and dirt along the road.

Dalton turned around in his saddle; he was riding point for the prince's group today. He claimed the position would make it easier for him to use his spear in battle. From Cole's perspective it made it more difficult for Cole to do his job. It would be harder for Cole to slip out of sight without leaving a glaringly obvious gap on Byron's shield side. Not that there was really anywhere to duck off to on a march. "Mavon?" Dalton asked. "Doesn't he live out near the Bionan border?"

"He does," said Byron. "And that should make you a little nervous. Biona's border is a lot closer to the baron than the city of Antier."

"And we all know how nebulous borders can be," said Jeron bitterly.

The masters had chosen to ride directly behind the boys, and apparently the mention of nobility and politics loosened their tongues.

"If I may, Your Highness," said Master Maxus as he pushed his horse up alongside Byron. "I have known Baron Mavon for years. We trained together and joined the same society. He is a godly man, and a man of honor. You can trust him."

"I don't trust him, Sir Maxus," said Byron. "Trust is earned, not given. And I have never met the baron personally. While I value your assessment of the man, I am not prepared to risk the lives of everyone here on blind trust."

Maxus bristled at the response. Cole did not think it was possible for the man to look more rigid in his full platemail, but he had been wrong before. Looking at Maxus, Jeron, and Dalton in those metal frying pans, Cole considered himself blessed to only be wearing leather armor in this forsaken heat and humidity.

"What do you intend to do about it then?" asked Maxus.

Byron arched an eyebrow at the older man. "Really? Well first I thought I would serenade him under the moonlight. After that, I'll invite him back to my tent for some wine. See where things go from there." Byron waggled his eyebrows at the paladin while Jeron and Dalton snickered. Cole thought he even saw a hint of a smile appear on Master Tyson's face.

"And well if he is as godly and honorable a man as you say, well then I'm sure I won't have to worry about my honor being sullied," said Byron as he patted the knight's shoulder in mock reassurance.

"Be serious boy," snapped Levren from further back.

Byron rolled his eyes. "Fine. I'll be serious," he said. "Hopefully by that time you'll have found some semblance of a sense of humor."

Cole's friend turned back to the knight. "And if I'm being serious Master Maxus, I plan on meeting him with strength and measured respect. See how he responds," said Byron.

"And if you don't like how he responds?" Maxus asked.

"Then I'll do what I must," replied Byron harshly. "Consider me skeptical. The man catches up to a smaller force from behind? While we are pushing ourselves rather hard? Doesn't that sound the least bit suspicious to you?"

Levren let loose that evil snicker that still made Cole's heart skip a beat in fear. "You're turning into quite the little diabolical tyrant aren't you, Your Highness?" he sneered.

Byron stared back over his shoulder at the man; eyes narrowed into a glare. "I'll be whatever I need to be to survive."

Cole reached down and touched the dagger he kept hidden behind his belt. Hopefully Baron Mavon did not choose the second option. Cole hated doing what he must. But, he too did whatever he needed to survive.

***

They stopped two hours later in a small clearing along the road. While the layout was not ideal, it was the first place where they could gather their force into a cohesive group, and the baron's forces, if hostile, would not be able to do the same with his superior numbers.

And then they waited.

Half of Cole's adult responsibilities seemed to involve waiting on one thing or another. But that waiting was apparently indispensable to his superiors.

So, he waited. And waited some more.

Cole checked both swords and daggers attached to his belt for the fifth time. All four drew easily from their sheaths. While the habit probably made him look nervous and fidgety to others, Cole did not care. The routine brought him comfort. It also provided him an opportunity to test out various other hiding places for the third dagger that he kept hidden behind his belt.

His goal was to transfer the dagger surreptitiously to another location on his body each time he checked his weapons. Richard's magic was not the only type of magic in the world. Cole greatly enjoyed using Tyson's magic, the magic of sleight of hand. The lack of an obvious explanation always made the sleight of hand seem more mystical and impressive. Cole liked that.

Cole's experiments did not end with just manipulating his hold-out dagger. He also experimented, and trained, at extending his natural chameleon camouflage to envelop the blade. Similar to what he did with Byron back in the barrows.

He was having some measure of success with the project, but it was draining. Disguising the appearance of an inanimate object, which was not clothing, took some extra measure of focus on his part.

Cole suspected that it had something to do with the nature of the items and the way his brain interpreted them. The clothing and armor rested upon his body, like it was part of his skin, and that was probably how his brain viewed it. The blade on the other hand was more of an extension of his body and not a physical part of it.

He would need more practice to surpass that mental block. He could not rely on always having to wait to draw his blade. His work may even require him to run with the blade drawn and a shiny floating piece of steel was sure to stand out to any observer.

"Checking your weapons won't make time go by any faster, Cole," said Jeron as he walked up and clapped Cole on his shoulder.

Cole rolled his eyes and picked at the shirt that seemed to be permanently stuck to his skin. "I'm just practicing," he replied. "Seemed like a good use of my time. What else should I do?"

Jeron swept his arm at the camp and gestured grandiosely like some sort of showman. "Why Cole, this is a military camp! There is always something to do! Why I'm sure you could help dig a latrine pit if you really wanted to do something."

"What do you really want?" sighed Cole in exasperation.

"Dalton," replied Jeron soberly. "We're getting close to his village. He's already starting to act differently. Acting a little darker. More depressed. Moody." Jeron pinched the bridge of his nose before continuing. "I need your help, Cole. I can't keep an eye on him all the time, and Byron has too many responsibilities to be roped into this."

"Again. What do you want me to do?" asked Cole.

"Just keep an eye on him, okay?" said Jeron. "Try to cheer him up when you can. Make a joke. Hell, maybe just talk to him. Let him get lost inside of his own mind, and our friend may not return for quite a while. And we need him at his best for what is coming."

Cole spun one of his daggers delicately between his fingers, silently, before answering. He did not know Dalton that well. Was it really his place to intervene? But then again, Dalton had been a friend to him. Should he not return the favor in Dalton's hour of need?

It was all so new and complicated to him. What would Atrisha want him to do? She would want him to help. She always was so kind to others. Well, others not named Byron. He slipped his dagger back into its sheath with finality. It was decided.

"Very well," said Cole. "I'll do my best, Jeron. But I'm not very good with people. But I'll try."

"Who is?" laughed Jeron. "So do you know anything about this baron?"

"Not really," replied Cole. "You've heard as much as I have."

Thiago walked up at that moment, his dark skin blending in with his green and brown leather armor. His entire outfit seemed to maximize his ability to blend in with the local terrain. Cole found himself nodding in approval, appreciating the camouflage effect that others had to work so hard to achieve.

Thiago crouched down next to Cole, seemingly unwilling to fully relax. "Didn't mean to overhear you all talking about the baron," he said. "I don't know much about what he has done in the past, but I can tell you what he is doing now."

"Really? And why would you do that?" asked Jeron.

Thiago chuckled lightly. "My, you are a paranoid one," he said. "Well, the answer to that is easy. I can't find the prince, and I need to head back into the woods as soon as possible and get back to work. It would appear that you two would be my best bet of relaying a message to the prince."

"What is the message then?" Jeron asked curtly.

"Heh. Easy man," said Thiago. "The baron is sending small parties of men into the woods on each side of the road. I doubt they're simply scouting given the timing. By this time, they have to know that we're here and are planning for either a surprise attack, or a flanking action if things go poorly."

"Not much of a surprise attack if we know they're there," observed Cole.

Thiago sprang up from his crouch. "That's cause I'm good at my job boys. Now please tell the prince what I said. I have to go plan some surprises for our dear friends. You know, just in case they aren't our dear friends."

The scout vanished into the woods and Cole stood up, surveying the camp for Byron. With Jeron nearby, that meant only Dalton was guarding the prince. Cole thought he may as well find Byron before Master Tyson found something else for him to do first. That and it was not like he could continue practicing with his hidden blade in Jeron's presence. He already had to draw it once on his friend, and if he was forced to draw it a second time, he did not want Jeron to know where it was coming from.

The camp was apparently acceptable by military standards. Men were grouped together by unit, horses were picketed, and camp fires lit. There was a clear separation between the noble trainees and the soldiers from the Raven's Perch garrison. The soldiers looked more at ease than the trainees. Their groups were larger and their chatter seemed natural and unforced.

The young nobles however were tightly bunched and huddled together in smaller groups. Less chatter escaped from the young boys, and everything about their groups looked less crisp.

While it appeared like the men were setting up for the night, a closer inspection revealed that the soldiers had not put down their arms and armor, the picket lines were too close to the soldiers, and not one tent, bedroll, or cooking pot had been taken out for use.

As far as mummery went, it was a poor job, but it was a polite fiction. Any decent scout would see that they were ready for a fight. However, if the baron's forces did not attack, then the camp would finish setting up for the night, and both sides could pretend that nothing had happened, and they were and always had been friends.

Politics. Cole rolled his eyes.

Byron and Dalton were in the rear of the camp, close to where the baron's forces would be arriving if they stuck to the road. The prince was surrounded by a coterie of society masters and military officers. Most would be offering their opinions on all sorts of minor issues, or merely hanging around so as to look important. It was more politics and posturing. Cole resisted the sudden and intense urge to spin his dagger. Barely.

Cole stayed back and observed the crowd. He would be of more use out of the way, watching everyone, than he would be in interrupting a strategy meeting.

Jeron had other ideas. He pushed past Levren and one of the lieutenants and took position opposite of Dalton. He did it as if it were the most natural thing in the world, and to Cole's surprise, no one said a word in protest. The men acted as if being pushed aside without a word of apology was appropriate. Byron did not even acknowledge Jeron's arrival, he just continued listening to Master Sildun speak.

Cole could not hear everything that was said, but he could make out a little bit about the placement of something in the woods. He assumed that it involved whatever Thiago had left in a hurry to do. Maybe some of his surprises.

Master Sildun finished speaking, and Jeron whispered something into Byron's ear. Most likely relaying Thiago's message about the baron's men being in the woods. Byron nodded and resumed his conversations, gesturing and pointing in various directions while he spoke.

"You should be over there," said a voice from right next to his ear.

Cole nearly jumped out of his skin. He had not heard or seen anyone walk up next to him. Which meant it could only be one person.

"Hello, Master Tyson," said Cole as he tried to speak calmly and force the fright out of his voice. "I didn't see you leave the group." Which was true. One second Tyson was standing next to Richard, and the next he was standing next to Cole.

"Trade secret, son. Now why aren't you over there? You can't hear much from over here," observed Tyson.

Cole shrugged. "Jeron and Dalton are over there. I'm not needed to guard Byron."

Tyson clucked his tongue against the roof of his mouth. A habit the older man had to signify his displeasure. "Are you a bodyguard or a wraith?" he asked.

"Umm, both?" answered Cole hesitantly.

"Indeed," nodded Tyson. "And what is a wraith's most important weapon?"

"Knowledge," said Cole reflexively.

"Correct. Now what are you doing over here when there is a whole host of knowledge to be had in the prince's presence?" Tyson asked.

"I'm not much for tactics," said Cole. "Most of the conversation would be lost on me."

"True. Information without the proper context to understand it is not that useful," said Tyson. "However, no one was born a master tactician. You need to learn, and one of the best ways to do that is by listening and observing those who know more than you do. Most nobles' plots involve some sort of use of force. Either large or small. You need to be able to differentiate between solid plans, poor plans, and misleading bullshit. Otherwise, all the information and knowledge in the world will be useless to you, the duchy, and your fellow wraiths."

Two horn blasts blared throughout the camp interrupting Master Tyson's sermon. Soldiers leapt to their feet, gathering their weapons and assuming defensive positions facing the road and the woods. The prince and his counselors lined up behind the soldiers and their walls of shields and waited. The signal was only supposed to be sent when Baron Mavon's forces were a mile away.

Cole began to move towards the assembling lines when Tyson's hand restrained him.

"Where do you think you're going, Cole?" he asked.

"Umm, to Byron's side?" responded Cole uncertainly.

"Nope. Not your job in this interaction," replied Tyson.

"What is my job then?" asked Cole bewildered.

A surge of humanity rushed past the two men as soldiers bustled around the duo while they stood still in the chaos. Tyson clapped Cole on the back and darted towards the woods. "We get to have some fun boy."

Cole sighed in resignation and took off after the master. Tyson said it was going to be fun, but Cole could not help but notice that the man did not smile.

CHAPTER TWENTY-SEVEN

D alton shifted restlessly upon his horse as they waited for the baron's arrival. Byron had insisted they mount up to meet the baron, who would undoubtedly be riding. He said that he was not going to be looking up at the man during their first meeting.

Dalton agreed. It was best not to show anyone weakness, even if it was merely perceived, or they would pounce. He just wished that showing strength did not require him to sit still on a horse in full platemail in the sweltering heat and humidity.

The smell alone was driving him crazy. He reeked of his own sweat mixed with steel, and with the added aroma and spice of a sweaty horse mixed in. They never mentioned the smell in the stories. If they had, no one would ever willingly choose to be a knight. Byron was lucky. He was wearing chainmail and leather. He did not have to roast nearly as much as Dalton did.

Dalton sighed and resumed his waiting. Why was there always so much waiting? It did beat the alternative though. So long as they were staying still, they were not heading west, heading towards home.

Home was a subject he tried hard to avoid. If he closed his eyes, he could still smell the burning buildings of his village. He could hear the words of his mother telling him to run. The voice was hers, but not hers. Try as he might, he could not clearly remember the sound of her voice, only a partial recollection of it. Like a shadow. Her face was clearer, but he did not trust his memory of it any longer.

That more than anything else bothered him. It was why he was dreading heading back. He had already lost his family, but if he had lost their memory as well? Then they would be truly gone, and Dalton did not know how he would react to that.

To make matters worse, he was not entirely sure how far away from his village they actually were. His flight from the village was a blur. He ran for what felt like days. Trees, bushes, and the road all flashed by. Time and distance ceased having any meaning for him. He barely registered seeing the sun rising three times during that period. But he had no recollection of how far he actually travelled. They could travel past the charred remains of his village and he may not even know.

Master Maxus reined his horse in beside Dalton and squinted down the road. "You've changed," he said softly, while never removing his eyes from the road. "In a few months all four of you have changed."

"Sorry?" said Dalton confused. Changed? Him? What was Maxus talking about? He was the same as he had ever been.

"You all don't curse and swear as much as you used to," continued Maxus.

"And that qualifies as a change?" grumbled Dalton. He hoped this line of conversation ended soon. He would rather suffer in silence and the sweet aroma of horse before listening to another lecture.

"Indeed it does," said Maxus with a faint smile appearing on his face. "It shows maturity and responsibility. Shows that you can act like an adult." He took his eyes off the road and looked over at Dalton. "Why a few months ago Cole was incredibly timid. He would never have put a dagger to a man's side. Much less do it twice. Our young prince has borne his duty without thrashing at the bit. And you, well, you are standing still, ready to face a fight instead of running from one."

"I've already thought of six different ways to get out of here," Dalton shot back.

"Ahh, but you haven't," said Maxus.

"What makes you think we won't all revert once this is all over?" Dalton asked.

Maxus burst out into a fit of laughter, his body shaking with the force of it. The laughter cut through the tension of the camp. The sound was so out of place and unexpected that soldiers turned around from the line to gawk.

"Son, it'll never be over," said Maxus. "And you'll never go back to the way you were. That's just how life and time works."

Dalton shook his head sadly at the older man and bore Maxus's life lessons in silence. His wait was blissfully short as the baron's banner, a green iguana upon a yellow field, approached steadily in the distance.

The column moved at a relatively slow pace which Dalton took as a good sign. If there was to be a fight, the baron's cavalry would be charging, right?

"Aerial scouts report that their weapons are not at the ready, Your Highness" reported Master Sildun.

Byron nodded his acknowledgment. "Thank you. Nothing changes though."

They waited for another quarter hour with Dalton glancing to the woods every minute. If the baron turned hostile, he was grabbing Byron and darting into the forest for safety. Between his speed and the tree cover, no one would not be able to catch them.

Eventually, the baron and his troops arrived. Baron Walter Mavon was a man of approximately forty-five years of age. He was a bald, barrel-chested man with scaly skin. Dalton had no idea of the nature of the baron's totem, but judging from his skin and family crest, he felt it safe to assume that it was reptilian in nature.

Baron Mavon rode without a helmet, a decision that Dalton considered wise and enviable. He had narrow eyes with thin slits, but a large warm smile with thick sparkling white teeth. The effect made Dalton feel uneasy, and he found himself gripping his spear tightly.

Maxus rolled his shoulders while patting his horse's neck. "Easy boy, it's almost time," he said softly. Dalton was not sure whether the admonition was directed to him or the horse.

The baron raised his hand and the column of troops came to a crisp halt. Dalton suppressed a whistle. It was a good show of coordination.

"Heh, pretty," snickered Levren from behind the prince. "Wonder if they'll be that pretty in a fight with the monsters."

Dalton wrinkled his brow in confusion, thankful that his helmet obscured his facial features. Why was Levren insulting them?

"Antier and Biona are on friendly terms, son," explained Maxus. "Unlike our northern neighbors, many of the border lords near Biona have family and commercial interests in the neighboring duchy. Their garrisons aren't as seasoned as those who serve out west or on the Loachian border. They mainly perform in parades and ceremonies."

Dalton shifted uneasily in his saddle. How the hell did Master Maxus know what he was thinking?

"Body language, son" Maxus supplied. "Learn to control it. Any fool could read your thoughts without seeing your face."

The baron's bannerman rode forth and calmly surveyed the Raven's Perch soldiers before slamming the banner into the ground. "Hello the camp," he announced. "You are blocking the path of Baron Walter Mavon of Loral. The baron rides to do battle at Fort Hope. Be ye friend or foe?"

"Who talks like that?" muttered Jeron.

"Way too pretty," agreed Levren.

"Captain Levren," said Byron. "Would you please do the honor of announcing us to the ahh most impressive baron?"

Levren arched an eyebrow at Byron, but a wolfish grin slowly spread across his features. "With pleasure, Your Highness."

Dalton nearly fell off of his horse. Levren being respectful to Byron? If they were not careful, soon Timver and Barith would wind up squiring for the prince.

Captain Levren trotted his horse through the line, the pikemen creating and closing a gap for him. Dalton had never witnessed a horse canter arrogantly, but it was the only way to describe Levren upon his white steed. Both rider and beast seemed to be cut from the same cloth, their manner treating the approaching forces with nothing but disdain.

"Why hello there my good man," hollered Levren in an exaggerated pompous manner.

Good man mouthed Dalton silently to himself. When had Levren ever demonstrated anything approaching a sense of humor that was actually funny?

"You have the honor of addressing Prince Byron Villa and his forces from Raven's Perch," continued Levren. "We are also travelling to Fort Hope and are glad to have you join us. Please set up camp along the road. His Highness looks forward to the baron's company over dinner tonight."

Captain Levren bowed to the baron's forces with an exaggerated flourish and sauntered his horse back towards the prince's forces. He had the grace to wait until his back was turned to the baron before snickering.

"I thought you were supposed to be the one giving sarcastic responses to authority figures," Jeron said to Byron.

The prince shrugged nonchalantly. "It's unit policy. A fighting force has to have an attitude."

"We are blessed to have such a sophisticated and urbane leader then," said Richard drily.

The baron's troops broke formation and began setting up camp alongside the road. Dalton could feel the tension release from the camp as the prospect of battle and death departed.

Byron gazed at the apparently allied forces. "Yes, Richard, it seems we are blessed." He turned his horse away from the gathered forces, Dalton and Jeron matching his movements while removing their helmets with sighs of relief. "Please instruct Cole and Tyson to see me when they return. Captain, please prepare a tent to receive Baron Mavon. Master Sildun, have our men stay hidden near our surprises in the woods until we are certain there won't be any trouble. Have them disassemble the traps before we march in the morning. It wouldn't do to set the forest on fire."

The men nodded and the three boys continued deeper into camp. "So where are Tyson and Cole?" asked Dalton.

"Are you seriously asking where two spies are when an armed force shows up?" mocked Jeron.

Dalton rolled his eyes heavenward. "Okay. So maybe it wasn't the best question. I assume you were wanting me to be the one to let you know when they arrive?"

Byron nodded. "That, and to keep your eyes open for any spies the baron will send in. I highly doubt he'd be the first noble who didn't want to test me. See what the Duke's disappointing son looks like with his own eyes."

Jeron spread his arms up to the sky while laughing. "God, I've turned into the only person not wallowing in self-pity around here. Some help please?"

Dalton and Byron scowled at Jeron in unison. "I am not wallowing in self-pity," growled Byron. "I'm suffering the burdens of leadership in relative silence."

"Well, I am," said Dalton. "And will continue so long as I'm roasting in this armor."

"Get used to it," said Jeron with a sigh. "It's going to be a long journey."

CHAPTER TWENTY-EIGHT

M atlin swore under his breath as the ghosts took another of his men.

Things had all gone to hell at a village a few days south of the border. According to Dedlin, it was caused when one of the Loachani soldiers argued with a blacksmith over a dagger. The type of dagger that soldiers liked to secrete on their persons as a backup weapon. The argument had blossomed quickly and one of the Antierian soldiers escorting his men tried to intervene.

Matlin could not ascertain who had thrown the first punch, or drew the first blade, and he supposed that it did not matter anymore. The results were the same: three Loachani, one blacksmith, and two of their Antierian escorts dead. The remainder of their escorts fled south on their horses to the capital carrying news of the incident.

Despite the protests of his siblings and cousin, Matlin had ordered his forces west, off of the road and into the wild Antierian frontier. It was not much of a choice. If they continued south, they would have clashed with Antierien soldiers and entered into a full-blown war. By heading west, Matlin would preserve lives, and hopefully make it to Fort Hope without instigating a war while his men were already deep inside enemy territory, without hope of timely, if any, reinforcements.

Frontier was a generous way of describing the landscape. The grass was tall and thick, blowing lazily in the wind. Forests covered the land to the north, and also appeared in large clumps on the southern horizon. Signs of civilization were non-existent. They had yet to encounter any roads, villages, farms, or any other signs of human habitation.

Which also included graveyards, wards, and any of signs of the faiths laying the dead to rest, pacifying their spirits, or containing them. As a result, at night the land really became a literal wild frontier.

Ghosts roamed the land, their souls tethered to the spot in the world where they perished. The spirits killing his men had to be ancient due to the lack of civilization or any ruins in the area. The lack of any ruins had so far been a boon at night. Large clusters and cities worth of ghosts had been a common problem in the initial settling of Antier. A problem Matlin did not want to hurdle after encountering only bands of stray phantoms.

The claiming of new land, and the creation of the Antierian duchy, required the aid of priests to clear the land of hostile ghosts by binding their spirits behind holy wards and glyphs. The Church had spearheaded the drive into Antier as the institution was more unified in its goal, purpose, and funding than the individual temples.

By the time the temples reached some semblance of an understanding between them, the damage had already been done. Antier had been settled by followers of the Church, and hostilities soon erupted between the Antierians and the temple settlers from Loach. And as a consequence, Matlin found himself pacifying lands that should have been settled by good Loachian men of the temple generations ago. Instead, Antier was a horrid amalgamation of temple faiths and the Church heathens.

Matlin's priests were attempting to ward as much of the camp as they could manage each night, but the encampment was just too large and the time and energy required to set up the wards was too taxing on his priests. Their only option was to have the priests banish each individual hostile ghost that was unfortunate enough to materialize in the camp.

The priests said that the ghosts would only be temporarily banished without a permanent ward. Most likely for the night, maybe an additional day at most. Either way, the ghosts would be the problem of any Antierian pursuit that chose to follow his forces through the wilderness.

While aggravating, the losses had been manageable, and fighting ghosts was always good training for his men. Tonight would be no different. If the gods were willingly, hopefully they would not leave too many new ghosts behind in this unholy land.

"Toran, what have the scouts reported today?" Matlin asked.

"Your Highness, they estimate that we are only a few days away from the mountain range marking Antier's western border. Once the mountains are in sight, they say we should be able to follow the range south to the pass at Fort Hope. Reports indicate that game is abundant and plentiful out here, and there are numerous bodies of water for our forces to replenish our supplies," answered Toran, his tones precise and his manner respectful.

Toran was the very image of the perfect cavalier. Strong, respectful, and loyal. His reports were concise, and he did not editorialize with his personal comments. He impressed Matlin and earned his respect during their travels. Respect however, was different from trust. Matlin questioned where the perfect cavalier's loyalties lay. The duchy, the temple of Bollian, his society of fellow cavaliers, or Matlin's twin brothers.

"We'll be late," stated Matlin flatly.

"Yes, Your Highness."

"Clara, can you instruct the scouts to bring along extra men to trailblaze?" asked Matlin. "Have the men store their arms and armor with the quartermasters. We need to move faster."

"It will be done," responded Clara. "You mean to be there before the fighting ends?"

"Indeed."

"Why?" asked Dedlin. "Would it be that bad politically for us to miss the battle?"

Matlin arched his eyebrow at his younger brother's question. "Little brother. The king is not well and he does not have any children. A new king will need to be chosen. That's why everything, our future, depends on us arriving before the fighting ends."

"You really think the other dukes will choose Darik?" asked Edlin.

Matlin glowered at his little brother. "We ride at first light. Pass the word."

"Okay, but you think-" continued Edlin.

Clara grabbed the young man by his shoulders and shoved him away. "We ride at first light," she said menacingly. "You have your orders. Now follow them."

First light. Time seemed to be working against Matlin. He studied the bare bones map of Antier that his scouts provided, as if he would be able to divine some of the frontier's secrets from the scant lines on the parchment. There was so little time, and so much of his plans for Loach and himself depended on reaching Fort Hope in time for the battle. He would be king. Even if the gods saw fit to keep delaying him with ancient ghosts.

And all over a cheap dagger.

Chapter Twenty-Nine

D arik stood with a smile plastered painfully on his face as he stared down the road waiting for the column of soldiers to reach Fort Hope. By design the rear of the fort did not have any walls or a gate. The monsters were too dangerous. If Fort Hope ever fell into their hands, even temporarily, the fort's defenses could be turned against the Antierians, and the price of recapturing the fort, and the pass it guarded would be astronomical.

Darik had been greeting arriving nobles for days. Earls, barons, counts, and squires had all arrived. Thankfully, many brought along more than just token forces. Their camps and tents scattered around the roadway. The Antierian force could now rightly be considered an army, and more were on their way. Messengers had flown in reporting that both Biona and Loach had dispatched forces.

The Bionians, were known mostly for their navy, as were the other three southern duchies. Darik's reports stated that the Bionians only sent a token force. With most of their might at sea, they could not spare much of their garrisons without leaving their own lands ripe for invasions or banditry.

The Loachians on the other hand? Darik suppressed a sigh and kept the smile plastered on his face. He had to keep a polite face on and be a gracious courteous host for the arriving lords after all. Not even the missing Loachian army could alter that. He assumed they turned around and fled back to Loach after the killings in northern Antier. He held little hope that they were actually going to honor their word and fight the beasts. Generations of conflict assured that.

Emkario tapped his foot nervously as he waited beside him. Like, Darik, he too wanted to be back on the wall. However, meeting the nobles and securing their support, for now and in the future, was more important. Renaldo could handle the defense of the wall for a few hours. Darik doubted Renaldo would actually abandon the wall to lead an all-out assault upon the enemy forces, but anything was within the realm of possibility if Renaldo lost control. Which was the main reason why Renaldo was not greeting the arriving nobles.

"That looks like Baron Mavon's banner," said Emarkio as the column of troops drew closer.

"Decent man," remarked Darik. "Doesn't he have Bionian relatives? If so, we should use him as a buffer between our two forces. Try to keep diplomatic relations running smoothly. Also, they're less likely to fight one another."

"Agreed," said Emkario as a frown developed on his face. "But doesn't that seem to be a lot of men for Baron Mavon?"

"Hmm. It does seem to be that way," said Darik with the smile still painfully engraved on his face. "Maybe he met up with the Bionian forces that are en-route?"

"It's possible," grumbled Emkario. "I guess we'll just have to wait. And I hate mysteries."

The baron and his troops made decent time, and Darik was only once interrupted by a messenger. The monsters launched another attack on the walls. Only satyrs. No centaurs, cyclopes, or minotaurs. Renaldo could handle the goat men.

"Umm, Your Highness. That isn't Baron Mavon leading that force," said Emkario. "Unless the baron found a way to turn back time, that is someone else, and he is much younger."

"Byron," whispered Darik under his breath.

Emkario jerked upright in surprise. "You can't be serious? Your brother? Your Highness, from what I've heard, and what you've said, a group of soldiers would not follow him, much less a baron. And he wouldn't want to lead them."

Darik should his head in amazement, the smile replaced on his face with a look of amazement. "Nevertheless, that's him. If you'd ever met him, you'd easily recognize him. And trust me, I'd recognize him anywhere."

Byron waved jauntily from the front of the column. Despite the dirt and weariness on his face, he looked nothing so much as a young boy giddy to be playing soldier. Fort Hope would beat that attitude out of him quickly.

Darik surveyed the party surrounding Byron. He recognized Jeron and Dalton, even if the latter looked especially pale and morose, as if he had not slept for days. Captain Levren and Master Maxus, his own trainers from his days at Raven's Perch were also present. The large, older, scaly looking man accompanying them was most likely the baron. He had no clue who the flame haired youth was. That bothered him immensely. Darik made it his business to be aware of anyone of particular note within the duchy. Especially someone in close proximity to his little brother.

Darik waved back at his little brother and made sure the smile was securely fastened on his face.

Byron held up a fist and the column came to halt. Emkario looked over at Darik with raised eyebrows. Apparently, his little brother was in command after all.

"Brother. Baron," greeted Darik as he spread his arms wide. "Welcome to Fort Hope. Those of us here greatly appreciate you riding to our aid. Baron Mavon, it is a pleasure to make your acquaintance. I look forward to fighting by your side. That soldier over there will direct your men to where they may set up camp and picket their horses. My apologies for the lack of a roof, my lord, but we are a little short on beds here at Fort Hope."

"Byron," continued Darik. "If you don't mind, please walk with me. I'd like to catch up with you."

Byron nodded his assent, the boyish grin still on his face as he handed his reins over to Captain Levren. He dismounted, as did Jeron, Dalton, and the flame haired boy. Darik furrowed his brow but said nothing.

Despite his jovial expression, his little brother looked ragged. The skin around the corners of his eyes was tight, his eyes were bloodshot, and his entire body seemed as rigid as a drawn bowstring.

Darik drew his little brother into an embrace. A big manly bear hug of an embrace. "You okay little brother?" he whispered.

"Yeah," Byron answered while laughing. "Tired and stressed from not knowing who may or may not want to kill me. It is good to see you, big brother."

Darik clapped him on the shoulders. "That's good. I don't believe you have met Lieutenant Emkario before? No? We'll have to remedy that. Jeron. Dalton. Pleasure to see the two of you again. By the looks of it, you're knights now. Congratulations. Welcome to the family."

Darik finished his handshake with Dalton and stopped before the flame haired boy. He eyed the boy with skepticism without letting the suspicion reach his face. A difficult skill to learn, but one he had mastered over the years. There were some advantages to spending time in court, he begrudgingly admitted to himself.

"I don't believe we have met," he said extending his hand to the boy.

"I'm Cole, Your Highness," the boy said softly.

The response drew arched eyebrows and looks of surprise from the other three boys.

"So now you're meek again?" asked an incredulous Jeron.

"He didn't look that meek when he held his dagger to you, or Levren for that matter," Dalton pointed out.

Darik nearly crushed the Cole lad's hand in surprise. "You drew a dagger on Captain Levren?" he asked shocked. "And on Jeron?"

The boy at least had the gall to look sheepish. "Umm. I was just doing my job, Your Highness," he replied. "Umm. May I have my hand back?"

Darik released the boy and turned to walk back to the fort. "Walk with me gentlemen. And start from the beginning."

Byron shrugged helplessly. "Well for each of us, there was a moment when a man loved a woman–"

"Not that beginning," snapped Darik.

"—okay. Long story or short story?"

Darik sighed. "The accurate version, please."

Byron shrugged and began to tell the story. "Well, we received the news and orders from the capital that Fort Hope needed reinforcements and then I seized command."

"You seized command?" interrupted Emkario with his jaw hanging agape. Darik remained impassive and allowed Emkario to provide the commentary. His brother was prone to telling a story in such a manner as to set the listener up for a joke, and Darik was not prepared to give him the reaction that he wanted.

"Of course," said Byron nonplussed. "I'm a prince. It was a time of war, and we were asked to be soldiers, not trainees. And the chain of command is quite clear in a time of combat. A prince outranks a captain."

"If he has been given a military command," snapped Emkario.

"Which you weren't," Darik interjected.

"Uhh are you sure?" asked Byron, a flash of nervousness quickly streaking across his face. Cole looked like he was going to be sick.

"Yes," answered Darik and Emkario in unison.

Byron assumed a fake look of shame. "Whoops," he said drily and without conviction. "Guess I need to brush up on the law some."

Jeron raised his hand before speaking and stared aghast at the limb as if it had betrayed him, unsure of whether to leave it up or take it down. "Why did Captain Levren give in to Byron then?"

Emkario snorted in derision. "Making your point by having a point stuck into you isn't a very good strategy, boy. Neither is making enemies of the Duke by attacking his son. It was the safe decision."

"Ohh," said Jeron lamely.

Byron continued his story and Darik nodded along. His brother's decisions were not that bad under the circumstances. Sending potential hostages away, securing the bloodlines of vassals, and treating Baron Mavon's forces with caution. All good decisions. Darik might not have made the same decisions, but they were acceptable. Frankly, it was more than he could have hoped to expect.

"Your plan was to burn the forest down around the baron's men?" Darik asked.

Byron's three companions' eyes all widened in shock. Apparently, they were unaware of that part of the plan. "Yes, it was," he answered.

Darik sighed and composed himself before answering. He wanted to give the impression that he was thinking the plan through before responding. Otherwise, Byron would take any answer as a judgmental response from his older brother and dig his heels in. The boy was stubborn and would pretty much always do the opposite of what he was told in an argument. However, if Darik handled him carefully, he could try diverting his brother into the proper course of action.

After a few steps, Darik decided it was safe to reply. "And how were you planning on your men breathing through all the smoke and flames?" he asked.

"Umm. I hadn't thought of that," Byron replied.

Darik grunted. "Risky. Could have got you all killed."

Byron nodded in agreement. "It could have. But I didn't see any other options. All my options were bad. And a bad chance was still better than allowing his larger force to hit us straight on and from the woods. I didn't have the luxury of fighting fair."

"True," acknowledge Darik. "But there's always another option."

"Your Highness!" a man shouted. He was bloodied, dirty, and running down the path leading from the battlements. A messenger then. Darik groaned inwardly.

"Yes?" answered Darik and Byron simultaneously.

"Sorry," said Byron with a grin that said otherwise. "New habit."

Darik ignored his brother and addressed the messenger. "What's the news solider?"

"Minotaurs...joined...the fight...sir," he said as he gasped for breath. "Need...more...men."

"Understood," nodded Darik. "See that your wounds taken care of. Emkario, go grab some of our reserve forces. If the minotaurs clear some space on the battlements, things are going to get nasty quick. I'll go see what I can do until then."

Darik tore off down the pass towards the battlements at a sprint. A leader had to lead after all. He was almost to the stairs leading up to the battlements when Byron overtook him. His little brother had always been faster.

"Where do you think you're going," yelled Darik as he took the stairs two at a time.

"Fighting," replied his brother. "You didn't order me to go elsewhere, and I won't listen anyway. I'll be careful. I promise."

Darik could feel the headache pounding away at his brain. If it was not one thing, then it was another. "Fine," he said. "But how about letting me head out there first. And please be careful. The last thing I need is for mom and dad to kill me."

"Okay. Fine," said Byron as he slowed down allowing Darik to pull even.

"Your Highness," called Dalton from a few steps behind. "I just wanted to let you know that it is a real pleasure to enter battle with the Jewel –"

"Finish that name and I'll throw you down to the monsters myself," snarled Darik.

Jeron and Dalton started chuckling and the headache started pounding worse. Children. He was entering battle with children. Commander and babysitter. Things just kept getting better and better.

Darik burst out onto the battlements and began bellowing orders over the battle cries. It was just one more thing he needed to deal with, and it would have to wait.

Right now, he had monsters to kill.

CHAPTER THIRTY

C alabella peered over the ridge of the hilltop at the bandits below. Ten men armed with a variety of weapons. She saw axes, bows, longswords, short swords, and dirks. No shields though. Evidently, the bandits preferred to carry multiple weapons. Most likely it was easier to carry a replacement weapon, than it was to buy one. It was not like bandits could just walk into any town or village and get their weapons repaired. She did not see any large two-handed weapons either. They probably were too heavy and difficult to replace.

She only spotted a few bandits that were sporting patches of fur, but not enough to identify any particular totem. Good. That meant the bandits most likely did not have a freakishly strong member amongst their ranks. Those sorts of men usually liked to show off and display their animal features upon their body for all to see.

Earlier that day, their advance scouts discovered a small trail crossing paths with the main road. The trail snaked between two small hills making it the perfect location for an ambush. Olivia had ordered Calabella on ahead to further scout out the area around the road.

Olivia assumed command of their little band when they left Raven's Perch. One of the boys had tried to wrest control from her and she had knocked him flat on the ground with one punch.

Calabella had a flash of pride thinking back on the moment. Olivia was such a strong and virtuous woman. After she asserted her authority, it did not take long for the other boys to fall into line. Not one of them had the temerity to challenge her authority again.

If only Oliva had punched that insufferable ruffian of a prince. Maybe then they would not have to travel back to the capital.

Calabella pushed the thought out of her head and made her way back to the group. She would have to tell Olivia that they could either go days out of their way to avoid the bandits, or they could attack the would-be highwaymen.

She was fairly certain would option Olivia would choose.

Calabella moved quickly, staying low to the ground, and moving between cover whenever possible. She was not a scout, although she thought that she would be quite good at it. None of the women were permitted to select or be invited to join a society. They arrived at Raven's Perch too late for that. Very convenient timing to say the least.

Not that any of the societies would have let the women join anyway. Calabella gritted her teeth in anger and picked up her pace. The sooner that she would be able to hit someone, the better.

Calabella trekked back through the light woods and hills to Olivia's encampment. It did not take long as Olivia kept their forces fairly close by. They numbered fewer than thirty women, and outside of a few wagons carrying supplies, there was not really any place to hide those that were too young for battle.

Calabella saluted as she approached her friend. "Vivi, I counted ten bandits over the hill in quick striking distance of the road. It is almost certainly an ambush. I don't believe they have any idea that we are here, but there will be little chance that they fail to hear us when we pass."

"Thanks, Ella," responded Olivia. "Is it possible that there are more hiding?"

Calabella thought about it before responding. "Yes, maybe up in the trees or closer to the main road. It would make sense for them to have a runner. But I didn't get close enough to check. I didn't want to give away our position."

"Good," said Olivia. "We attack right away then. One group travels up the road and strikes up the path, a second group charges down that hill from above their camp at the first sound of fighting. The younger children stay with the wagons on the main road."

Calabella leapt up onto her horse. "I should lead the second group. I'm familiar with the terrain, and know where we can charge the horses down the hill without getting woman or beast killed."

Atrisha adjusted the strap that secured a sword to her waist. "I'll go with Ella," she said as she pulled her long blonde hair back into a tight knot.

Calabella grabbed a few more women, raising her party to a group of fifteen. She decided to avoid bringing the boys with her since the whole purpose of bringing them back to the capital was to prevent their houses from being heirless. She assumed Olivia would keep them towards the rear or with the wagons.

They set out at a slow trot, careful not to make too much noise and alert the bandits to their position. Olivia's group would be making much more noise upon the road and moving at a slower pace than normal. She would draw the bandits' attention, while providing Calabella and her women more time to navigate the brush and get into position. If things went to plan, the bandits would fail to notice Calabella's approach.

If they spotted Calabella's group, well, then she would still retain a numerical and mounted superiority over the bandits.

Calabella led her group into position on the south side of the hill and waited for the signal. She readied her mace and felt her tusks exit from her skull. She doubted that she would have much use of them in a cavalry charge, but she assumed that seeing boar tusks charging at you had to strike at least a little bit of terror into a person.

She checked her group, and the other fourteen women were also tapping into their totems and altering their bodies. Wings, claws, talons, beaks, fangs, feathers, and fur all began to appear. Atrisha looked simply radiant on her white horse with her sword drawn, blonde hair pulled back beneath her helmet, and large white wings spread out behind her. She had left her face unchanged, although Calabella was fairly certain she could grow a beak and feather the rest of her body if she so chose.

They did not have to wait long for the signal. There were a series of loud shouts off to their left, soon followed by the pounding of hooves. Calabella did not hesitate. She dug her heels into her horse and charged the bandits' camp.

She crested the hill and glanced down and tried to survey the scene while at a near gallop. The bandits had arrayed themselves in a loose line across the road, with two bowmen behind them. A bald bearded man burst into the camp from the direction of the road breathing heavily. A lookout then. Olivia's forces should be there soon barring the man having an absurdly quick totem.

Calabella aimed her horse at the bowmen and tightened her grip on the mace. The bowmen were the real threat. The men on foot might get lucky and strike one of the women, but they were more likely to be trampled by the mounted riders. The bowmen on the other hand would have time to get at least one arrow off before Olivia's forces could strike at them. One arrow that could find one of their women.

But not if Calabella reached them first.

The lookout's eyes widened in fear as he saw her group of horses charging down the hill towards the camp. He shouted a warning causing the bandits to panic and hesitate, unsure of which direction the attack was coming from. Calabella smiled grimly. She was about to give them the opportunity to gather their senses.

She braced herself before making impact with the first bowmen. She gritted her teeth and swung her mace downward in a low arced pendulum swing.

Time seemed to freeze as the mace connected with the bowman's face. She could see every detail of the man's face from his light blue eyes, the salt and pepper stubble of his beard, his long greasy black hair, and the small canines in his mouth. The mace connected above his left cheekbone, caving in his face and eye socket in a bloody mess.

The collision nearly tore her from her saddle, and almost wrenched the mace out of her hand. But in a moment, it was over and she was past the bandits. Calabella steadied herself and turned her horse to the right and back up the path, away from Olivia's charging force. She completed her loop and looked back at the camp. Her cavalry charge was successful. The bandits were all laying upon the ground, their blood soaking the soil.

Olivia reined her horse in, signaling the women behind her to stop. There was no longer a need for them to strike the bandits. Olivia met Calabella's gaze, her expression and eyes full of sadness.

Calabella glanced down at herself and for the first time noticed the blood spattered across her chain mail and tabard. She had killed a man. The crunch of his skull giving way echoed in her mind. She could still feel the warm spray of his blood hitting her face. Her arm more than ached, it hurt. She gingerly reached up and touched her face. It was wet. Blood dripped slowly from her tusks.

She leaned over the side of her horse and emptied the contents of her stomach. Behind her she could hear a chorus of unpleasant sounds as some of the other women reacted similarly.

Calabella spared a glance behind her and took stock of the sight of her sisters. Most of them were, like her, spattered with blood. Their faces were grim and in every set of eyes she saw a mixture of horror and resolution.

She felt the surge of pride rise within her again.

Atrisha brought her horse up next to her, her blade scarlet, and strings of blood splattered across her face and wings. She resembled an avenging angel that walked out of one of the Church's paintings. "No injuries," she whispered softly to Calabella.

Olivia trotted her horse over to them. She sat rigidly upon her horse, face calm and emotionless. Yet somehow not cruel. "Any injuries?" she asked the bloodied women. Silence greeted her. "Very good. Then we'll return to the road and continue north. And if we happen upon any other bandits, we'll kill them too."

Cheers answered her.

Chapter Thirty-One

Tyson howled in pain as the beast's crude club slammed into his shoulder with a sickening crunch. The satyr bleated a furious cry and raised his club again for a deathblow.

Tyson raised his sword weakly in a feeble attempt to block the blow. Well, at least he tried to lift his sword. His shoulder would not let him raise the blade high enough to save his life.

A greatsword flashed horizontally above his head, removing the satyr's upper body at the pectorals. Tyson tried to scoot away from the falling body, but his muscles and brain just were not on the same page.

Sure, stick him alone in a hostile palace in the dead of night and he was an ice cold operative. Calm, in control, and in his element. However, put one repugnant satyr before him and he froze. If he could have laughed, he would have.

Suddenly, he was forcibly dragged backwards away from the conflict. Tyson looked up at Maxus pulling him away with one hand as if Tyson were a child. The other hand effortlessly gripped a bloodied greatsword, and the knight managed to be shouting orders while in the midst of rescuing Tyson.

Tyson could not make out the words. For all he knew his old friend was either shouting out orders, encouraging the men, or even trying to talk to Tyson.

The fighting had grown more intense in the week since they had arrived at Fort Hope. Everyone pitched in to fight while at Fort Hope. Whether it was by order or necessity, Tyson was uncertain. Either way, it made doing his job much more dangerous but, in some ways, simpler.

All of these nobles were gathered together in one place. The fort was ripe with intelligence and plots. However, instead of snooping around and seeing what he could uncover, he had to pitch in defending the fort. Which did grant him the opportunity to be close to those nobles and overhear conversations that they did not record on paper. It also provided mindless satyrs with the opportunity to nearly kill him.

Yet it also permitted him to monitor Prince Byron. He had already invested too much time and energy into that young man. He was not prepared to see it all fall apart because the prince lost his footing, or some satyr got lucky.

Maxus scowled down at him. "What did you think you were doing back there?"

"Fighting," growled Tyson.

"Idiot," growled Maxus. "Stay out of the way or help with the supplies. There are very few reasons for you to be out here swinging a sword on the battlements. It's a waste of your talents."

Tyson closed his eyes as he let his head fall back onto the warm cobblestones. "I'll see what I can do."

"You better," growled Maxus. "We have too much riding on this plan of yours."

Tyson groaned and pulled himself up to his feet. "Quiet," he hissed. "Never say that in public again. Now I'm going to go get my shoulder looked at. Take care of yourself, Maxus."

He hobbled down the stairs, cursing to himself. Maxus was right, it had been a risk. Was his spying really why he was up there courting death? Or was he just trying to justify himself? Prove he was just as much of a warrior and a man as the others.

Tyson sighed, once he was out of sight of the battlements and rolled his shoulder, the pain gone, and walked briskly down the stairs of the fort. A priest was no longer necessary. He just did not have the time for that particular charade. There were too many plots in motion for him to waste time being injured.

CHAPTER THIRTY-TWO

C ole leaned lazily back against the stone walls of the fort and allowed his body to blend with the stones. The boys and soldiers from Raven's Perch had drawn duty guarding the extreme left edge of the battlements. The majority of the fighting was concentrated along the middle of the wall. Cole was unsure whether that was because the monsters naturally gravitated towards the middle, or for some tactical reason. Regardless, he was happy not to be in the thick of the battle.

The monsters' assaults did not seem to occur in any discernible pattern. Sometimes they struck during the day, and other times during the night. The random nature of the beasts did not shock Cole after he saw what passed for their camp.

The creatures' camp sprawled for what looked like miles across the plains on the western side of the pass. While the Antierians made camp in orderly units around fire pits, with areas designated for horses and supplies, the monsters possessed no such order or discipline.

Fires popped up randomly, some within feet of each other. There was no apparent shape to the camp, nor did there seem to be set paths to walk throughout the camp. The ground was beaten brown, and the beasts seemed to swarm in every direction making it looks like ants crawled over the land.

Luckily, it did not appear that they were preparing to mount a major assault any time soon. If they were fortunate, it would not happen until after he had been replaced on guard duty.

Cole did not think he was a complete coward, but he did not share the passion for battle professed by many of the other soldiers and nobles. His instincts screamed to stay back and watch. Cole trusted his instincts. They kept him alive. He acted when he needed to, but he did not mind admitting to himself that he feared death. Leaping into the thick of battle while swinging his sword just sounded like a terrible idea to him.

Barith and Timver were two of the men in their squad, anxious and eager to engage the creatures. Battalion? Unit? He still was not certain on the nomenclature. Perhaps he would need to follow Master Tyson's advice and pay more attention to how the military functioned.

However, that would be difficult as Fort Hope had turned into a mishmash of soldiers from different areas. Orders were just bellowed out by location. Raven's Perch to the battlements, Mavon to reserves, et cetera. It was organized chaos at best, unorganized madness at worst.

Cole shook off the thought and focused his mind back to Barith and Timver. The two had been standoffish ever since Byron took command back at Raven's Perch. They had not spoken to Byron or caused any disturbances that Cole had seen or heard about. It was what Cole had not heard that concerned him. Cole had yet to determine whether the two brutes were plotting against the prince, or if they were merely concerned for their own lives now that Byron was in command and had the ability to make their lives miserable. Either option was probable, and monitoring the situation was one more matter added to his list of responsibilities.

The two boys were sorely disappointed when they had the opportunity to meet Prince Darik. They had tormented Byron under the impression that he was a disappointment to their idol, only to find out that their idol loved his little brother very much. Cole smiled thinking back on that meeting. The looks on Barith and Timver's faces when Prince Darik knew them by name, and did not need an introduction was priceless. Darik had not said a word beyond that. He only glared at the two of them and continued being introduced to the other noble sons. Barith and Timver had been awfully silent around Prince Darik after that meeting, and generally made themselves scarce whenever he was around. It was quite a pleasant turn of events.

Maybe they feared some sort of retribution from the elder prince. Cole did not know Prince Darik well enough to make that assumption, but Jeron and Dalton were fairly certain that Darik would react quite violently if he found out the full truth of their treatment of Byron.

Based upon the prince's reaction, Cole deduced that Darik's information sources were either less than fully reliable, or had edited their reports in an effort to soothe the prince's temper. Cole frowned. That seemed highly unlikely. It was always possible that Jeron and Dalton were wrong in their assessments. He would need to observe and draw his own conclusions about Prince Darik.

Cole sighed and added another matter to his growing list of responsibilities.

Byron strode down the battlements, patting men on the shoulders and exchanging words with each of them. Cole frowned as Byron laughed and said something that seemed kind to Barith and Timver. The two also appeared thunderstruck and did not know what to make of the situation.

Byron stopped an arm's length from Cole and stared out at the plains. "Anything interesting happening?" he asked quietly as he hummed to himself.

Cole scowled. "No. And how do you do that? There is no way you could have seen me that time."

The prince chuckled. "I knew you were on duty here, and this was really the only secluded portion of wall where no one else was standing. It was an educated guess."

"Uh huh," said Cole skeptically. "Nothing else?"

Byron grinned evilly in his direction. "Trade secret," he intoned in a fair impression of Master Tyson.

Cole rolled his eyes and looked back towards the keep in time to catch Jeron and Dalton's arrival. They were flanking an averaged sized man with light, thin, brown hair that blew easily in the wind. A greataxe was strapped to his back, causing him to walk with his shoulders and head slumped forward just the slightest bit. His lips were pursed as if he were trying to hold back a smile from a joke that only he could hear. Judging by the lines beginning to form around his eyes and mouth, it was a common expression for the man.

As the trio drew closer, Cole could make out the unmistakable sound of someone whistling. It was a merry little tune and it seemed to match the light in the stranger's eyes.

Jeron and Dalton on the other hand were clearly telling the man a story as they were laughing and gesticulating wildly.

"Byron, who is that man?" Cole asked.

"Huh?" asked Byron as he broke out of his reverie and glanced around. "What man? Oh. Renaldo!" The prince started laughing and waved at the whistling man.

The whistling man waved back before embracing Byron, laughing wildly. "Good to see you, little brother. Is half of what these two idiots tell me true?"

Little brother? Cole mouthed to himself. He thought Byron only had one brother. Maybe a bastard? And why were Jeron and Dalton grinning? This Renaldo fellow just called them idiots and they looked thrilled at the moniker.

It was moments like this that Cole regretted growing up poor without much to his name, besides that family name. He was hopelessly behind the other boys in terms of knowledge on the other noble houses and their family trees. As well as developing social relationships with all of those people.

Not to mention military tactics. There had to be another way to learn those besides participating in actual battles. Knowing his luck? He probably was in line for more battles.

"Depends what they told you," Byron said. "But it's probably true. Maybe only a hint of embellishment on their part."

Cole watched silently as the four joked and swapped stories. For a moment there on the wall, they did not look like soldiers facing down a horde of nightmarish beasts. They looked like young men. Happy to see their old friends. Talking, joking, and teasing each other as if they did not have a care in the world. As if a horde of monsters was not hundreds of feet away, eager to feast on their corpses.

Cole smiled sadly to himself. He did not have any old friends to catch up with. Most died early trying to scrape together a living day by day. And at the pace they were going, he probably was not going to live long enough to develop any old friendships. Forever the outsider, unnoticed, forgotten. That was who he was.

And he was content.

"What are you doing up here man?" Byron asked. "It's good to see you and all, but I bet you have a ton on your plate here. Probably could use some sleep."

Jeron snorted. "On his plate." He jerked his head towards Renaldo. "This guy waylays – yes, yes, you waylaid us – waylays Dalton and I in the mess while we were enjoying a nice lamb pie. He starts talking about the old days, telling stories, and then he completes the ambush."

"Ambush?" snorted Byron.

"New orders," supplied Dalton.

"Ahh," said Byron. "And you couldn't have sent a runner?"

A merry light sparkled in Renaldo's eyes. "And miss seeing you?" he asked as he reached up and mussed the prince's hair. "It's been way too long." He looked around before lowering his voice into a conspiratorial tone. "And the rationale behind the orders is way too sensitive to trust to a messenger."

Byron nodded gravely, but kept the smile firmly planted on his face. He had been doing that a lot recently. Cole learned to look at the man's eyes if he wanted to figure out his mood.

"What are the orders?" Byron asked.

"Aerial scouts spotted the Loachians approaching through the wilderness to the north, not from the road," Renaldo explained. "Your brother doesn't want both of you to be at the same place when they arrive. Too dangerous. You're to take your men south to the small pass above the River Irinin.

"Our scouts and men at the river have reported some small amount of enemy movement there. I doubt there will be heavy fighting. The gap between the mountains and the cliffs above the river is just too narrow to move a force through quickly. It'd be easy to get bottlenecked. The beasts rarely bother trying it. You probably won't face too large of a force, if any. Most likely it'd just be a token force to occupy some of our soldiers and keep them off the wall.

"You'll have to leave your society masters here. The fighting will be thicker on the battlements, and their knowledge and power will do more good here," explained Renaldo.

Byron winced at the news. Cole knew that the masters provided Byron with good counsel since he assumed command. And that would also signal the end of Cole's magic lessons. Cole suppressed a sigh.

"Anything else?" Byron asked.

"Yes. Your brother suggests you send out rear scouts. Keep an eye out for any Loachians. And do not keep any men that you think are untrustworthy near you," said Renaldo. "If it were me, I'd mix in the untrustworthy men with the rear scouts. Send them out individually so that they can't plot against you."

Byron nodded. "When do we leave?"

"As soon as possible," said Renaldo. "Gather your men and keep your friends close. I'd hate to see anything happen to you. Good thing you have these two strong bodyguards here." Renaldo elbowed Jeron and Dalton as he said it.

"Three," said Cole suddenly, as he let his body shift to normal.

Renaldo nearly jumped out of his boots and over the wall in surprise. Jeron and Dalton jumped as well, but sadly not as high.

"What the hell!" exclaimed Renaldo.

"Damn it, Cole!" shouted Jeron and Dalton in unison. They looked at each other, surprised at their shared reaction.

"Oh God," breathed Byron. "I forgot you were there."

Jeron smacked himself in the head with the heel of his palm. "Of course. I should have known," he complained. "There is no way you would have left Byron alone up here."

"Forget that," said Renaldo in a tone just beneath yelling. His breathing started to slow down, and his tone of voice was dropping in time with it. "Will someone tell me who the hell this is?" he demanded.

"I'm Cole," said Cole simply.

"He's Cole," said Byron, Jeron, and Dalton in unison.

Renaldo stared blankly at them and his chest seemed to collapse as he exhaled. "Yes, I figured that much," he said while barking out a laugh.

"Cole is our friend," Byron said. "And he makes it a point to look out for me."

"Good," said Renaldo. "Keep him close then. Good to see you, Byron. Boys," he nodded to the three of them. "Keep my little brother safe, or we're going to have words."

Renaldo spun around and stalked back towards the keep, muttering something under his breath before resuming his whistling.

"So how did Byron manage to be alone for such a long time," Cole asked Jeron and Dalton pointedly. "I was up here where I was supposed to be."

The boys blushed sheepishly before Dalton answered. "Well, we heard they were serving pie," he said. "And we figured we'd sneak off and have some. We had no idea it'd lead to getting new orders."

"You went to the mess instead of the battlements?" Byron glared at them.

"Oh, don't give us that look," said Jeron dismissively. "You know we occasionally have issues with authority, and as a result, a few small lapses of judgment. It's part of our charm."

"Your charm," said Byron flatly. "I think you're getting us confused. I'm fairly certain I'm the one everyone calls irresponsible."

Dalton nodded with faux dignity. "That's true, but then you started trying to act like a commander. We had no choice but to keep the universe in balance and pick up some of your old habits."

"Well how can I be upset with that?" asked Byron. "Who am I to interfere with the universe?"

The boys laughed for a brief moment before Byron continued. "Dalton, round up the men, we need to head out as soon as possible. Jeron, I want Thiago in charge of our rear scouts and assign Timver and Barith to him."

Cole glanced out one last time over the wall and to the teeming horde of monsters beneath. He doubted he would ever miss being on the wall.

CHAPTER THIRTY-THREE

C ole missed being on the wall.

It was one thing to fight a satyr in hand-to-hand combat after it had finished a decent climb to reach the top of the wall. It was quite another thing entirely to see a pack of centaurs, supported by minotaurs, and a cyclops charging straight at you.

The ground seemed to shake with the fury of their charges. Their shrieks and bellows rattled in the air. The sound alone made Cole think that the battle was hopeless. Cole knew that he was being irrational. Jeron told him that the enemy's numbers were not that large, these were merely probing attacks to test their defenses.

But the creatures were just so large and terrifying. There was not any humanity lurking behind those eyes. Only a wild angry animal.

At least when he was on the battlements, he did not have to worry much about centaurs and cyclopes. They were either too big, or physically incapable of scaling the walls in large numbers. The river pass offered an entirely new set of nightmarish possibilities for his dreams. Assuming he lived long enough to have more dreams.

The river pass was a relatively narrow open patch of ground resulting from the sudden end of the mountain range where it met the River Irinin. The southern portion of the pass ended in a cliff approximately four hundred feet above the raging waters of the Irinin. The elevated cliff extended for miles on the Antierian side of the pass, and coupled with the dense swampland below, made it impractical, if not impossible, to move an army into Antier any way other than through the two passes at Fort Hope.

So far, they had only dealt with three charges, but that was three charges too many in Cole's opinion. The shield he carried, while unwieldy, and not well suited to stealthy movement, had saved his life in the last charge. A centaur had swung a club at his head and he had managed to intercept the blow with his shield just in time to prevent his head from being cracked open. Had he attempted such a maneuver with a short sword or dirk in his left hand, the centaur would have opened his skull like a rotten melon dropped on cobblestones.

A howl echoed through the pass. It was full of fury and caused Cole to shudder, his skin prickling at the sound. More howls answered the original. They were louder than a band of the duke's trumpeters, and the sound swept through the pass like a gale of wind, and reverberated off the mountains before fading out.

A shudder, more like a coldness that sank into a person's bones, swept through the camp. An uneasiness went through the men as they started shifting their feet. The answering howl was larger by magnitudes than any they had heard.

This next charge was going to be the largest yet. Cole could feel it in his bones. The men were nervous, and Cole did not blame them at all. They were mainly noble born, and were being asked to do something outside of their comfort zone. They were being forced to defend the river pass on foot, without the horses that people of their station were accustomed to riding in battle. The presence of the centaurs frightened the horses, and in the narrow confines of the pass that could prove disastrous. That, and the footing was uneven and treacherous. Even if only a handful of horses were frightened, men could be trampled, and horse and rider could plummet into the Irinin below. Antier simply could not afford the loss of either man or beast, and so they fought on foot.

Cole did not mind being on foot that much. It was much easier to blend into the surroundings that way. But judging from that last howl, he was not going to be provided with the opportunity to utilize his gifts any time soon.

"Hold your ground!" bellowed Jeron. "And show them we can be louder!" He roared causing his mane of hair to appear and pebbles to bounce and rattle down the mountainside.

The men cheered and responded with a wide range of primal roars. Cole detected everything from human voices, to feline roars, and reptilian hisses.

"Umm Byron, I have a question," asked Cole.

"Really? Right now? What is it?" Byron asked while he spun his longsword in his right hand. He had also chosen to employ a shield in this battle although he still carried the second sword strapped on his back.

"Is Renaldo actually your brother?" Cole asked. "It's been bothering me for a while now."

"You're asking that now?" asked Dalton incredulously. "Right before a battle?"

Cole shrugged. "May not get an opportunity later."

"No, he isn't," said Byron. "He was like a second older brother to me growing up though, but he isn't a blood relation. You good to fight now? Anything else on your mind?"

"Umm. No?" answered Cole hesitantly.

"What about me?" said Dalton as he rested on his spear shaft. "I've got plenty of questions about a whole lot of things."

"Shut up," growled Jeron. "They're coming." There was a strange sort of focus to his eyes. Eyes that were showing too much white. Eyes that did not blink. Mouth turned up into a snarl. It was a frightening visage.

The ground seemed to shake again, and the group of centaurs charged closer towards the pass. The creatures started every attack with a centaur charge. Cole conjured up varying reasons for that. Maybe the centaurs were just faster than the others, or maybe they just had more centaurs to spare because they were of little use climbing a wall. Perhaps the beasts had figured out the importance of cavalry. Cole still did not fully grasp the importance of horses in battle, but he gathered that they were very important.

Cole felt the sweat trickling down his face and decided that the beasts' reasoning did not matter all that much. This attack looked to be at least three times larger than any of the others. It appeared the probing attacks were over. Cole swallowed and gripped his sword tighter.

"Pikes and spears forward!" shouted Byron. "Archers...fire!"

Arrows streaked through the sky towards the charging horde. Centaurs began to fall, but not enough to stop the charge. The beasts collided with the spearmen. Hooves met shields carried by totem-strengthened men in a crushing impact. Screams filled the air, and bodies flew.

A centaur landed face first before Cole, its body sending up a spray of soil into the air. Cole did not hesitate. His blade darted out and pierced the centaur's throat. Its blood poured out quick and easy.

The battle lines could not really be called lines after the initial collision. It looked more like an all-out brawl with amorphous shifting sides that Cole distinguished as merely "ours" and "theirs".

Cole raised his shield out of reflex and waited for a blow that never came. Cole quickly glanced around trying to locate the beasts. Off to his right, Jeron and Dalton dispatched a pair of centaurs that broke through during the initial push. Cole, looked to his left and saw Byron regaining his feet a bit to the south of the initial impact. The force of the collision must have thrown him in that direction.

The prince was barking out orders and rallying the surrounding men to create a concentrated defense near the cliffs. Cole gritted his teeth and began making his way through the battle towards Byron.

Naturally, that was when the next wave of creatures joined the fray.

Satyrs swarmed into the melee crying out with their warbleats. Cole intercepted a kick from the nearest satyr's cloven hooves with his shield. The impact of the kick staggered him slightly and left a dent in his shield.

Cole ducked under a vicious backhand from a crude machete and ripped his sword through the goat man's kidneys. The beast bleated in pain and collapsed to the ground howling in agony. Cole reversed his blade and brought his sword down in a deathblow to the back of the satyr's neck.

Cole slew two more satyrs, driving his blade into their backs while they were engaged with their human counterparts. He rolled past a centaur and sprang up behind it, and with two quick strokes hamstrung the beast.

He ducked, dove, and slashed his way through the battlefield, but it was not dumb luck that kept him safe. Cole kept himself partially blended, fading in and out of view. Enough that he still looked human and would not catch a blade from his fellow man, but obscured to the point that maybe it would confuse the animalistic senses of the creatures.

Embracing his full chameleonic powers would be preferable to navigating the battlefield, but his heartbeat and emotions were out of control. There was no way he would be able to find the focus to maintain the deception in his current state.

Cole skirted around a pair of men fighting a minotaur. The beast roared in rage as it swept its axe at one man and then turned to try to strike the other. The pair seemed to be using some sort of tactic where they each switched off between offense and defense to counteract the sizeable brawn of the minotaur by using its simple brain and lack of intelligence against it. It seemed like a wise strategy to Cole. That axe the beast wielded was large enough that the word 'axe' hardly seemed to fit it. A massive halberd covered in human blood was probably a fairer description.

The flow of battle seemed to be pushing the prince just out of Cole's reach. He should have reached Byron by now, but each time he had to stop and fight, the battle took the prince further away from Cole and closer to the cliffs.

Cole swore under his breath as another goat man jumped into his path. Of course, Jeron and Dalton were nowhere to be seen. They were lost elsewhere in the battle. Cole swore again. They were most likely debating the merits of meat pies versus fruit pies, instead of protecting Byron.

The madness on the battlefield was not really that different from the madness of the markets. Only there were more weapons bared. Luckily, Cole had years of practice navigating that madness in the flesh as well as in his dreams. He would just have to do it at a faster pace than usual if he was to be of any actual use to Byron.

He hamstrung another centaur, but before he could regain his balance a large impact struck his shield and flung him from his feet. Cole slammed face first into the ground. He rose slowly, wiping dirt and blood from his eyes. He gasped for breath as his chest convulsed in agony.

Cole squinted up at the monstrosity before him. The beast stood roughly twenty feet tall, and was humanoid in appearance, with thick flabby muscles covering its body. Its gray green skin glistened in the sun as it roared in defiance. The creature lowered its head from its roar, and one single large eye glared down upon the battlefield.

A cyclops.

Its massive club dripped with blood from its most recent victims. Bits and pieces of oddly colored and textured material still clung to the club. Cole tried not to think of what they were, or what had put the newest dent in his shield.

Cole gritted his teeth and he felt something strange happen inside of him. The constant fear vanished, and he felt a great rage burning inside of himself.

He stretched his left hand out, concentrated, and flung his anger at the cyclops. A column of fire nearly as tall and thick as himself sprang forth from his hand and raced towards the beast's head, engulfing it.

The smell of burning flesh filled the air, and the cyclops's battle cries turned to shrieks of pain. Man and monster alike appeared unsettled by the sound, as the fighting around Cole took on a slight momentary hesitation. But it was only momentary, man and monster quickly forgot the shrieks and fought on, desperately trying to cling to their own lives.

The cyclops fell to the ground in front of Cole. It smacked its head against the ground repeatedly, and rolled aimlessly trying to put out the flames.

Cole stepped forward in a calm, cold, rage and thrust his sword into the cyclops's eye. The beast howled as it twitched in agony. Cole savagely twisted the sword and the cyclops shuddered and ceased moving.

He stepped back from the beast's carcass and quickly appraised his wounds. Cole was not bleeding, but the cyclops's glancing blow was going to cause his chest, ribs, and left shoulder to be sore for the foreseeable future. A small bit of flame remained stuck to his leather bracers, dancing madly. Cole focused and a small stream of water appeared and extinguished the flame.

Cole stumbled through the thick black smoke billowing up from the cyclops's corpse. It stank of a mixture of charred rotten meat and old eggs. The smell alone could have been used as a weapon. Hopefully, the smoke would help mask that he used magic on the battlefield. He vaguely remembered somewhere in the back of his mind that he was supposed to keep that fact a secret. Cole would rather stay alive than worry about secrecy.

He did not have time to worry too much about it as he was forced to block a wild swing from a satyr's morningstar. Cole kept his footing and tried to hide behind his shield until the beast made a mistake. Satyrs normally did not use such a sophisticated weapon as a morningstar. They preferred clubs and blades of simpler construction. The monster must have scooped the morningstar up off of a fallen human's corpse. Cole hoped that it did not know how to employ it effectively.

He did not have to wait long to find out. The beast leveled a backhand blow at Cole. The weapon struck Cole's shield and at the moment of impact he braced his body and pushed his shield and the morningstar to the side.

With the goat man's torso exposed, Cole's sword darted out in two quick strikes. The first punctured the beast's exposed stomach, and the second sliced open a deep wound from its upper sternum to its larynx.

Blood squirted out of the wounds and the satyr bleated in terror. It dropped the morningstar and fell to the ground. Its hands vainly trying to staunch the flow of blood.

Cole pushed past the dying beast. Fatigue had fully set in. His arms felt heavy and weak. They still worked, they were just sluggish and did not respond as effectively as they had five minutes earlier. Cole groaned. By the time he found Byron, he doubted that he would be able to protect either of them from an armed child.

Multiple impacts shook the ground and Cole looked up and felt his blood turn to ice. Three cyclopes swung their clubs and bellowed their war cries as they ran behind a line of centaurs charging the human forces. The ground continued to thunder and shake in protest.

Another centaur charge. Fantastic.

Cole sighed and joined a small group of men who were trying to set up a shield wall. He would just have to take care of one more matter before he could resume his search for the prince.

CHAPTER THIRTY-FOUR

Darik swiped his claw and batted a flight of harpies out of the sky. The sun could barely be seen through the mass of bodies tangled in combat in the skies above Fort Hope.

His fears had finally come true today. The probing attacks and half-hearted assaults had ceased. The monsters no longer received reinforcements. They had not for the past few days. And therefore, they no longer had a reason to wait.

The assault began in earnest shortly after the sunrise. And he too began killing shortly after sunrise.

The monsters only had so many harpies. From what he could see, the majority of their forces, like the human defenders, were ground based. They would have to stagger their aerial assaults. Which was a relief for the human defenders. The monsters would not be able to overwhelm them at the wall and simultaneously attack the fort defenders from the air and the rear.

However, he also did not have a limitless supply of men with aerial totems, and for those that they did have, night battles would prove difficult if not impossible. Most of the humans did not possess totems of nocturnal birds. Hopefully, harpies, griffons, and chimeras suffered from the same limitations. But basing a battle plan off of hope was foolish.

Darik's mission was simple then. Take out as many of the harpies, griffons, and chimeras as they could during the day so that the beasts could not mount effective assaults at night.

A gout of flame burst forth from Darik's mouth roasting a crowd of chimeras in his path. He swept his dragon breath back and forth through the enemy ranks, destroying those that stood before the inferno.

Darik swung his prodigious body around and flew back towards the thick of the fray, and his allies. While he was immensely strong, he needed his allies in this fight. With his large size, the beasts could theoretically swarm over him and destroy him bit by bit. He had once witnessed a colony of ants systematically devour the carcass of a rabbit. The carcass had been unrecognizable beneath the shifting swarm of ants. Darik had no desire to emulate the fate of that rabbit. He would stay near to the humans in the sky. The men had their orders and knew their duty. They would watch his back.

He spared a glance down at the battle raging on beneath him. The creatures no longer had what could be considered a camp. Merely a mass of bodies lunging forward and surging against the wall. If any of the beasts reached the top of the battlements, they would be shoved off, and the process would repeat.

He had left his own men in charge of Fort Hope's defense, not the recently arrived nobles. His men knew the defenses better and they had his trust. Darik had ordered the society masters from Raven's Perch to stay inside the fort and off of the battlements. He deemed them capable administrators, and a few did have battle experience. But he did not trust them to assume a command position over most of the combined forces of the duchy.

Darik doubted the nobles would stand for it either. Most would buck at having someone of lower birth being in command of Fort Hope.

Command meant anticipating problems and countering them. The issue of the masters was one problem he had addressed. Nobles would listen to them as administrators, but not as commanders. The fort would run at a higher efficiency rate, and he could spend more of his focus upon the battle instead of personnel squabbles.

Not to mention that it would also reduce the masters' influence upon Byron. While he did not doubt that they were decent men, they had too much of his little brother's ear. Byron needed to learn how to make decisions on his own. Especially in the heat of battle. Otherwise, they would not be his decisions, but theirs. The last thing they needed was for the soldiers and nobles of the duchy thinking that Byron was a puppet, or could easily be manipulated as one.

Darik swatted another harpy out of the air, breaking its wings, and circled the skies looking for another. The dogfight was incredibly dense in this area. Man, animal, and beast limbs were completely entangled in aerial combat. Blood and feathers sprayed throughout the sky. The airspace was so tight and congested that his effectiveness was rapidly diminishing. It was true that he could pick off harpies one by one, but it was incredibly ineffective. It was akin to killing individual ants with a catapult.

Darik chuckled at the thought and turned his attention to a problem where a catapult would be effective.

He roared in fury, startling the nearby harpies, and pulled his wings back into a dive. The air blew past his face and pushed against his scales as he plummeted towards the earth.

Under different circumstances Darik would consider the dive fun. However, when an army of monsters was waiting at the end of the dive, fun tended to be replaced with a bit of dread.

Darik pulled out of the dive about thirty feet above the ground. He took a deep breath and unleashed fiery hell upon the monsters below. They howled, screamed, and shrieked as muscles and bone melted, some being incinerated completely to ash. Darik strafed over their forces, burning a swath of death through their ranks.

One more pass while he still retained some element of surprise would have to be enough. The monsters would adapt if given the time and opportunity. Arrows, spears, and other makeshift projectiles might overwhelm him. Harpies would try to pull him down out of the sky.

He had done what he could in this form for the time being.

Darik finished his pass and pulled up gaining more altitude. His flight killed quite a few monsters, but it still was not enough. Their force remained enormous, and what would cause monsters to surrender? It was not like they could engage in diplomacy or peaceful negotiations. Were they going to have to slaughter the beasts until they turned and ran? And if so, would they have to chase the beasts down on the plains to prevent them from returning?

The point was an academic one at this juncture. The arduous task of defeating the monsters remained. And their success was not guaranteed.

Darik landed outside the keep in a puff of dirt and dust. He was already shifting back to his human form as he landed. Scales were replaced by skin and platemail. He resisted the urge to take off running before he looked fully human again.

It just would not be appropriate for the prince and commander of the fort to run through a warzone looking like a crazed half-human half-animal monstrosity. It would be bad for morale, and bad for his health if some unfortunate soldier shot him with an arrow thinking that he was a monster. Also, the identities of his guests ensured that any unflattering stories would spread throughout the entire duchy and beyond, just like that accursed jewel tale.

Sildun was racing out of the keep towards him. Darik held up a hand instructing the master to wait until he was finished transforming.

Darik took a deep breath with his significantly smaller human lungs, and motioned for Sildun to join him as he made his way to the battlements in a restrained and dignified manner benefitting a prince.

"The battlements hold, Your Highness," Sildun reported. "The monsters reached the top a number of times and were repelled quickly in each instance. Our supplies and man power remain adequate. We are in no fear of being starved off of the wall."

"And the other matter?" Darik asked.

Sildun hesitated before answering. "Reinforcements are expected today, sir."

Darik rubbed at the headache that seemed to be his constant companion lately. "Show the reinforcements every possible courtesy. We'll need their assistance before this is all over."

"Understood, Your Highness. It will be done," confirmed Sildun. "I'll make sure the men know every courtesy is to be extended per the orders of the Jewel of—"

"Sildun," interrupted Darik. "Are you a court lady?"

"Umm, no I am not, Your Highness," Sildun answered with a confused expression on his face.

"Good," answered Darik. "Because that name is only used by court ladies and gossips. Neither of which we have in Fort Hope. See that you don't use it again."

Darik drew his greatsword and exited onto the battlements before Sildun could respond or excuse himself. Darik could have sworn that he saw Sildun grinning once he had started to turn his back. The man must have received the reaction he was expecting. Darik mumbled a prayer and a curse under his breath.

Always another problem when you were the commander. Big or small. Luckily, Sildun's jest hardly qualified as even a minor issue. Just another headache that came with the command.

At least morale remained high.

CHAPTER THIRTY-FIVE

J eron roared in anger as his axe removed a satyr's head. His backhand slash detached the arm of another nearby satyr. He let the rage wash over and consume him as he prowled across the battlefield. It energized him and gave him purpose.

In his mind the pass was his hunting range, and he was the apex predator. These lands were his, and these monsters were interlopers upon his territory. His purpose was to eliminate them and reestablish his dominance.

He roared in fury, a primal challenge that caused many of the monsters nearby to cringe away. He flung himself at the nearest minotaur, his canines bared, sweat pouring through his mane. His axe rose and fell, biting into the minotaur's flesh. His shield was less a defensive instrument and more of a club at this point, and he employed it for that purpose. The cold metal smashed into the minotaur's head, cracking its skull and breaking one of its horns.

Jeron pounced to his feet and braced himself as another satyr charged his position.

A spear flashed in a blur past him and the satyr fell to a quick death, blood gushing from the hole in its throat.

Dalton. The memories came back to him, and his fury at being denied a kill subsided a little bit, allowing his thoughts to clear.

The opening charge of the battle scattered their ranks and caused he and Dalton to become separated from Byron and Cole. The pair had battled through the horde of creatures, searching, but had failed to find their friends.

The rage surged through Jeron again. He was a failure. He could not protect his friends if he could not find them. That failure led him to pursue a different course of action.

The monsters could not kill Byron if they were all dead.

Following that logic, Jeron had his purpose. He would destroy the monsters, scatter their herd. Because that was all their army was. A large herd, grouped together to protect them from him. He would hunt each and every one of them down. And his people would be safe from peril.

While he and Dalton hunted scores of the beasts down, Jeron hungered for even more. Luckily for him, the beasts were in abundance.

A column of fire shot off to his left, engulfing the head of a cyclops in flame. A growl rose up from Jeron's chest at the sight. A new challenger to his dominance had entered the field. And someone else had killed the cyclops, clearing the field of battle of his prey. The fury nearly boiled over.

"Look, more cyclopes!" exclaimed Dalton.

Jeron scanned the field and saw them. Three more. Sheltered behind a line of charging centaurs. His teeth pulled back into a vicious grin. He snarled and charged towards his challengers.

In one breath he swung his arm and broke a centaur's back. Another breath, another slash, and a satyr's intestines began spilling out onto the grass. Another breath, and his teeth ripped into a minotaur's throat. Another breath, two more goat men had their arms removed at the shoulders.

And suddenly gray green flesh lay before him. Jeron roared and his axe bit into the cyclops's calf in a spray of blood. He roared in triumph and swung his axe again. Knee. Ankle. Shin. Knee. Calf. He kept moving and striking swiftly at each opening. The cyclops howled in pain and swung its club blindly at him. Out of the corner of his eye he saw Dalton darting in and out of attacking range of the second cyclops, his spear dancing like a mad tempest.

A cyclops was large, and strong. But it was no hunter. Its reflexes were not tuned to catching prey. It was just too slow.

A fist landed next to Jeron sending up a spray of dirt. He growled and his next strike severed the tendons in the beast's wrist. The cyclops staggered backwards and the damage Jeron inflicted upon its legs finally took its toll.

The cyclops crashed to the ground landing on its back, its useless hand unable to break its fall. Jeron pounced on the monster and his axe cut deeply into its throat. He sprang into a forward flip, the weight of his own armor barely an obstacle. He bellowed as he brought his axe down upon the thrashing creature's eye.

Blackish fluid spurt forth from the wound, and Jeron danced out of its way. It smelled horrible and he did not want to try removing it from his mane.

A large crash signaled the death of Dalton's cyclops. Before Jeron could look for his next challenger, his brain processed the sound he heard during his battle with the cyclops.

Hooves. And a lot of them.

He glanced to the west but did not see a fresh wave of centaurs charging down from the plains.

Jeron spun back to the east and saw Cole staring at him, mouth agape. He wanted to grin at the red-haired boy, but the sight from the east chilled his blood.

Cavalry was charging into the pass out of the east. Judging by their colors, red, silver, and a tinge of black, Loachian forces. The Loachians charged over man and monster alike, their steel failing to discriminate between friend and foe.

"Traitors!" howled Jeron. "Kill the murdering Loachian bastards!"

He burst into a sprint and sped past a stunned Cole who was just beginning to recover from the shock of the treachery.

Jeron's axe flashed as he ran towards the Loachians, his rage claiming more monsters. Every beast he could kill would matter in this battle. The monsters did not care whether the humans were from Antier or Loach, but Jeron did. Stopping the Loachians would not matter if they lost the river pass.

And he would stop the Loachians.

A minotaur's axe swung towards him and some forgotten corner of his mind remembered to bring his shield up to absorb the blow. The impact knocked him off of his feet and onto the ground. He growled and rolled to his feet in time to see Dalton's spear arm return from its trip to the minotaur's throat.

Dalton's blonde hair was streaked with red, and his face locked into a grim expression. The expression did not extend to Dalton's chemistry though. Jeron could smell the waves of terror pouring off of his friend. But finally, the only running Dalton did was towards the enemy.

Jeron nodded in appreciation at Dalton and sped towards the horsemen. Three satyrs and two centaurs perished to his axe before he reached the first Loachian.

His axe bit into the horseman's leg, severing it at the knee and slicing into the horse's flank. Man and beast shrieked at the blow and crashed to the ground. One murdering Loachian dead.

The second horseman's horse shied away from the battle, and Jeron felt his lips pull back in a feral grin. The Loachians rarely ever engaged the monsters. The Loachians did not share a border with them, and therefore had no way of knowing that horses were terrified of the monsters' blood. Blood that was spattered all over his body and throughout the pass. Many horses began to panic and their riders were spending just as much time fighting their mounts as they did their opponents. Jeron took advantage of the opportunity and waded deeper into the chaos.

His axe rose, fell, sliced, cleaved, and hacked as he administered years of past-due justice to the Loachani forces. Two. Three. Six. Nine. Jeron buried his axe in the chest of a blue eyed Loachian who wisely had abandoned his mount. Ten. He removed his axe and looked for his next target, but there were none in sight.

His charge took him straight through the Loachani ranks and to the eastern edge of the river pass. A line of thick foliage met him as he reached the forests that surrounded the path leading back to Fort Hope.

"Where to now?" asked Dalton. Apparently, he was able to keep pace with Jeron through the charge against the Loachians. And judging by the red human blood covering his spear and armor, he also managed to keep pace with Jeron in more than one way. Jeron nodded his head in approval.

"We find Byron before the Loachani do," replied Jeron. "See if we cannot salvage this position, or barring that, our lives."

Dalton nodded in agreement. "That's great, but where do we start? All I see are Loachians and monsters. Not that there is much difference between the two I guess."

"The cliffs," answered Jeron. "It's the only place on the battlefield that we haven't been to yet."

"Yeah," agreed Dalton. "Umm. Where's Cole? I thought he was right behind us?"

Jeron looked around but did not see his friend. A wave of guilt washed over him. Cole was not nearly as strong as he and Dalton. Cole would not be able to match Jeron's pace, and Jeron had abandoned him because he had let his rage take control of him.

"I don't see him," Jeron said. "Maybe he had the same idea regarding the cliffs? I hope he is okay."

"Yeah. Maybe," said Dalton flatly. He sounded unconvinced.

Without warning a pair of arrows streaked over their heads and buried themselves in the backs of two Loachian riders. A second volley streaked silently out of the woods and two more riders fell.

Jeron turned towards the woods, his shield raised to protect himself from the next group of arrows. The archers may not discriminate between Antierians and Loachians, and he was not in a trusting mood.

"Easy, Jeron," a voice called from the woods. "We aren't going to shoot at you."

"Who's there?" called Dalton. "We don't exactly have time for guessing games."

Two shadows appeared in the tree line and stepped forth silently from the wood, their green and brown leather armor making them difficult to spot. Thiago and Atticus had their bows out and their eyes were constantly shifting looking for new threats. Bowmen never liked feeling exposed on a battlefield, and apparently scouts were even more paranoid. Jeron assumed it was a result of spending most of their time alone in the woods.

"Thiago, what the hell is going on?" demanded Jeron.

"The Loachians split this group off from their main column and rode to the river pass. The remainder of their forces continued onto Fort Hope," the dark-skinned man said calmly. There were tears in his armor and fresh cuts on his face. The two boys must have seen some fighting before reaching the pass.

"But why?" hissed Dalton. "Why would they do that? It doesn't make any sense!"

Thiago sighed and Jeron noticed the dark circles under his eyes. The man probably had little sleep in the past few days.

"Well. It's a guess, but I would assume that Barith and Timver told them about the river pass and the men holding it," Thiago replied.

"What?!" demanded Jeron and Dalton in unison.

"I can only tell you what I saw," Thiago said. "And that was the smaller force of Loachians breaking off the main force with Barith and Timver riding on horses alongside them. And when we left on our scouting assignments, we didn't leave on horses. Do the math."

Jeron gritted his teeth and felt his knuckles pop from gripping his axe tightly. "Barith and Timver both come from lands close to the Loach border," he said. "The traitors probably have connections on the other side and sold us out."

"Timver is a cavalier," Dalton pointed out. "Loachians worship only at the temples. We should have expected them to side with their own kind."

Jeron made a noise that was half grunt, and half disgust. "We were so concerned about keeping them away from the prince, that we gave them the perfect opportunity to stab us in the back."

"What do we do now?" asked Atticus, his fingers strumming nervously upon his bow string.

"We find Byron, and Cole if we can," said Dalton. "And then we get the hell out of here."

"Are you seriously suggesting that we run?" hissed Jeron angrily.

Dalton nodded. "Yes. I think it is safe for us to assume that the rest of the Loachians aren't heading to Fort Hope to be friendly. We have to get the prince away from this betrayal and murder trap. That means we'll need to escape from here and pass word of the Loachani betrayal to the rest of the kingdom."

"The roads will be watched," Thiago pointed out. "You don't plan this sort of thing without having a net of scouts out to catch the runners."

"Is that a guess?" asked Jeron. "Or are you basing that off of your scant weeks of experience?"

"Not a guess," Thiago said angrily. "Both Atticus and I saw signs of the scouts out in the woods. We avoided them when we could, killed them when we couldn't, and tried to get here as quickly as we could."

"We need to move," said Dalton anxiously. "We're wasting time. As we're talking our friends are fighting and dying."

Jeron nodded in agreement. "Right. Towards the cliffs then. Find Byron, and rally any of our men that we can."

They took off towards the cliffs, fighting as they went. Jeron's axe struck out time and time again, but the vast majority of the time it only found Loachians. The number of monsters and Antierians in the pass were dwindling rapidly. Humanity would win the battle at the pass, but in name only. The concept of humanity was dead at Fort Hope. Those clad in red and silver saw to that.

They cut a path as quickly as they could through the chaos. The two scouts had eschewed their bows in favor of short swords. The four moved effectively, but Jeron knew the odds of success were low. The battlefield was congested and full of chaos. Not to mention they were running in the direction of the setting sun which was beginning to affect his vision.

"This isn't working," panted Dalton as he drove his spear through the back of a Loachian who was too preoccupied with his butcher's work to notice their approach.

"Keep going," said Jeron as he slew two more soldiers. They were so slow and weak compared to him that it was almost unfair. Almost. Under different circumstances that may have bothered him. Today, he merely dispatched another Loachian without feeling any guilt, only immense satisfaction.

A minotaur roared a battle cry and Jeron felt his rage spike at the new challenge. His heart raced and he bared his teeth and glared at the beast in the distance.

The minotaur was engaged with an Antierian who had lost his shield. The beast swung its axe at the man who dodged nimbly away, his back to the cliffs and his profile exposed towards Jeron.

"Byron," Jeron whispered.

The minotaur's axe swept down and Byron blocked it with his sword. The minotaur snarled, and Jeron sprang into motion, Dalton right beside him. The minotaur drew its axe back for another strike.

The blow never came. Two arrows struck the minotaur in its back. The beast threw its head back howling in pain which provided Byron with the opening he needed. His blade swept forward in a quick two-handed strike, removing the minotaur's throat.

"Good job, Thiago," said Jeron.

"Umm what?" asked Thiago as he breathed heavily, a bloody sword still in his hands. "What did I do?"

Jeron stared at the bloody blade in disbelief. The other boy was still running with them. "But the arrows," he protested. "If those weren't you...oh no."

Two Loachians reined their horses in roughly ten yards or so from Byron. They could have been twins from what Jeron could make out. They were astride fine sleek black horses. Their armor appeared to be well-crafted, most likely from the metals of the famous Loachian mines. And they both carried short recurve bows in their hands.

And they were flanked by Barith and Timver.

One of the Loachians said something to Byron, but Jeron could not decipher the words over the distance and din of battle. The other Loachian merely smiled cruelly.

And then they fired.

Two arrows slammed into Byron's chest. The prince staggered backwards, struggling to keep his balance and remain upon his feet. He looked up, defiance and sheer stubbornness etched onto his features. His eyes moved past the Loachians and locked onto Jeron's.

"Run!" Byron screamed as blood began to leak out of his mouth. His voice was still strong enough to carry over the din of the battle.

Two more arrows slammed into the prince. Jeron could feel both blows as if he were being punched in the chest. The force of the impact cost Byron his balance and he tumbled over the edge. His eyes widened in horror before he fell over the cliff and dropped out of view, plunging downward towards the raging waters of the Irinin.

Jeron lunged in the direction of the murderers, but before he could finish his first step he was yanked in the opposite direction.

"You heard Byron!" Dalton screamed while dragging Jeron along with him. "We run!"

And the four, no seven, Antierians sprinted towards the trees. When did they become seven? Jeron wondered to himself in stunned silence. Thiago and Atticus must have gathered a few remaining soldiers while they fought.

Jeron spared a glance over his shoulder towards Byron's murderers. Timver and Barith were pointing in his direction and screaming. The Loachian with the cruel smile was bellowing orders while pointing in Jeron's direction.

Jeron's rage ignited again as he tried to struggle against Dalton's grip. Those murdering whoresons would pay for what they did. He would rip their throats out; he would tear their –

An explosion rocked the battlefield. A giant fireball, larger than the keep at Fort Hope, shot up into the sky from the direction of the Irinin and the swamplands below. Men and horses screamed, riders were thrown from their mounts as the horses panicked at the sudden heat and sound of the explosion. The ground shook, and chunks of the cliffside started crumbling as sections of earth broke off and plummeted into the river.

Jeron pushed himself up from the ground, spitting chunks of dirt out of his mouth. Strong hands grasped his arms and he was dragged to his feet.

"Come on," pleaded Thiago. "This is the perfect distraction to escape."

His legs and body ached all over. Heavy did not even begin to describe how his limbs felt. It had been a long day of battle, and it looked like it was going to be followed by a long night of running. Part of him wanted to give in. Stop and make a stand against the remaining Loachians. Kill as many of them as he could.

Instead, Jeron let Thiago guide him until his body was moving somewhat smoothly. The six of them ran as fast as they could. Six? Jeron felt a wave of sadness at the loss of the unknown soldier, and kept running.

Fortune graced them a slight bit of luck as the concussion from the explosion prevented the Loachians to mount any sort of coordinated pursuit. The battlefield had devolved into complete and utter madness. Loachian soldiers wandered around without direction, while the few remaining monsters bolted back towards the west. Running away in fright from the giant fireball. Jeron ignored them and stayed his axe. Every second was precious, and they needed to stay alive.

They reached the forest and kept running. Thiago and Atticus took the lead. Their scouting expeditions and training made them more familiar with the terrain, and a better choice to lead. Dalton grabbed Jeron's arm, his feline eyes narrowed in fury as tears slowly dripped down his face. He exchanged a grave nod with Jeron and they followed after the two scouts.

They had no choice now but to survive. They had to let the rest of the kingdom know of Loach's betrayal. It was the only way they would be able to extract their vengeance. The only way to make Byron, and the others deaths have any meaning.

Chapter Thirty-Six

"Well this is fun!" shouted Renaldo as he used his greataxe to clear the battlements of the five satyrs that reached the top.

"Your version of fun scares me," said Vincent as he swung his war hammer at the nearest beast. "I'd prefer a nice ale. Maybe a steak."

Emkario deftly removed a minotaur's arm with his falchion. "Well if history has taught us anything, it is that the monsters cannot continue the assault after this battle," he said. "They won't have the numbers once the Loachians reinforce us, or the coordination to sustain another assault. They'll have to leave or be wiped out."

"We'll see," said Darik as he cleared his section of the battlements of satyrs. "I think it may be prudent to focus on defeating them today, before we speculate as to whether they can mount another attack tomorrow."

The monsters were gaining footholds on the wall much more frequently as the day went on. Yet the defenders of Fort Hope repelled each assault, although they were slightly slower each time. Every surge of the beasts' forces against the wall brought more of them to the top and inflicted more death upon the defenders.

It was a battle of attrition and one Darik believed that they could win. It was butcher's work from here on out. Granted, his belief in their victory hinged upon the Loachians keeping their word and arriving in time to provide aid.

Their delay in arriving had already cost Antier many of its soldiers, and quite of a few of its more powerful nobles. It would take a few generations for Antier to fully recover from the losses it had suffered today. Heaven only knew how much of an impact the battle had on the monsters' forces.

With the sun beginning to set in the eastern sky, the fort's aerial defenders were grounded. Any aerial assault by the creatures would be met with bows, arrows, and what scant magic they had available.

However, the creatures did not appear interested in another aerial assault. The damage Darik inflicted upon them with his previous flights must have deterred them. At least that is what Darik hoped as wave after wave of the beasts kept cresting the walls with single-minded determination. Another aerial attack would stress his juggling of the fort's defenses to a breaking point.

Darik moved up and down the battlements, filling in at gaps in the defenses wherever he was needed, repelling monsters where needed, and boosting men's morale as he fought. Years earlier, during his first battle, he learned that merely seeing the commander fight, and fight well, had a positive impact on the ability of soldiers to fight. It was human nature to become resentful if a person thought that the leader did nothing, while they broke their backs working. That was why Darik pushed himself so hard. He would have the loyalty and the respect of his men, and they would fight that much harder for him. That way they would all have a country and homes to return to.

"Your Highness!" called out a blonde-haired man. He was bruised, dirty, and had lost his helmet at sometime during the battle. A good soldier.

"Yes, soldier?" Darik replied as he backed away from the wall.

"Lieutenant Emkario asked that I find you," the soldier said. "A cyclops is aiding a unit of minotaurs trying to capture a section of the wall. Renaldo engaged the beasts, but the Lieutenant requests your presence."

Darik nodded. That sounded like Emkario. Pragmatism to balance out Renaldo's recklessness. Renaldo probably thought that he could take out the beasts all by himself, and the entire enemy force in a single charge. It was why Emkario reached the rank of lieutenant before Renaldo.

Renaldo had balked at that decision. Saying it was a command decision had not helped much either. It was Byron who had gone about repairing Darik's relationship with Renaldo, albeit unintentionally.

His little brother was standing in the doorway, eavesdropping, one of his favorite habits, and heard the entire exchange as Darik denied Renaldo a lieutenant position. Byron cracked one of his famous bad jokes. The type where he tried too hard and relied on crass inappropriate humor.

Renaldo acted as one might expect out of him. He charged Byron and leapt at him. Byron sidestepped to the side of the doorway and Renaldo's knee crashed into the doorframe with a loud crunch.

The three of them collapsed into a fit of laughter as Renaldo lay on the floor grabbing his knee. The situation was too absurd not to. Darik had not been able to breathe for a good ten minutes after the collision without laughing. It had been one of the best laughs of his life. Stupid, yet simple.

He smiled at the thought. It was good to have his little brother close by. The joker took it as a personal challenge to make Darik laugh every single day. If Darik was being honest, Byron succeeded more times than not.

The smile faded a little as Darik reminded himself where they were. Byron was facing an army of monsters without Darik there to protect his little brother. True, Darik and his father's plan to give Byron the training he would need to survive with his particular skill set had succeeded up to this point. But so much could happen in a war for which Darik could not account.

Case in point, Renaldo was charging the door frame again, only this time the door consisted of vicious beasts armed with terrible strength and weapons. And they would inflict upon Renaldo much more than a bruised knee.

"Thank you, soldier," Darik said as he hurried off towards the other end of the battlements. Hurried was a poor way to describe it he thought. It took every bit of restraint he had not to break out into a full sprint. At the very least, that sight would cause his men to gawk at him, and take their concentration off of the fight. In the worst case scenario, that could cause a panic which they could ill afford right now.

Darik did not have to dodge around his men. They all parted before him, whether they acknowledged his presence or not. The fort was his and everyone there acknowledged that fact on some subconscious level.

The far end of the wall was pure pandemonium. The beasts had seized upon the confusion caused by the cyclops, and satyrs had joined their minotaur brethren upon the battlements. Larger groups were gaining purchase on the walls, and the defenders were desperately trying to push them back and throw them off the battlements.

The situation was growing desperate, but not desperate enough to where Darik felt that he needed to call the reserves up from below. In a battle of attrition, fatigue would play as crucial a role as sheer manpower.

Thankfully, the cyclops had not tried to actually climb the wall. Instead, the monster was standing a few feet away from the wall and was swinging its club at the humans from a distance. Vincent was organizing a cadre of archers to shoot at the beast's eye, but was finding little success as a result of the chaos of the battle raging around him.

Darik frowned. The situation seemed improbable at best. Cyclopes were tall, but they were not giants. He stopped a few yards away before he reached the brewing melee and dared a peek over the wall. His jaw dropped at what he saw.

The cyclops that was attacking the wall was standing on the shoulders of another cyclops. The sight would be absurdly comical if it was not downright petrifying. Darik pulled his head back from over the wall and tried to wrap his head around what he had witnessed.

Were the beasts developing tactics? He felt an arctic chill rush through his intestines. If that were true, holding Fort Hope would become that much more difficult. Now and in the future. Maybe even impossible.

They would need to destroy the top cyclops and all of the beasts that reached the top of the battlements. Utterly. Any of the monsters who witnessed the success of the tactic needed to perish. Too many Antierians would die if the knowledge of that tactic spread amongst the creatures.

Darik unsheathed his sword and began clearing the wall of the creatures. He had not been able to find Renaldo or Emkario in the madness. Hopefully, they were still safe. The only sure way to ensure their safety was for Darik to kill as many of the monsters as he could, before Renaldo tried to take on the cyclops by himself.

Renaldo did not carry many, if any, ranged weapons. His only tactic would be to leap at the creature, and they did not have the numbers to launch a rescue operation over the wall and into the middle of the monster horde.

A minotaur swung an axe at him which he parried easily and knocked away the follow-up slash meant to decapitate him. A quick flick of his wrists and the minotaur's corpse lay twitching on the stones.

Five satyrs, and three more minotaurs stood in his path before he could reach the segment of the wall besieged by the cyclops. The beasts surged at him and he swung his greatsword repeatedly. It felt like he was holding back a tidal wave all by himself.

Darik was breathing heavily as he held his sword up in a guard position; staring out at the cyclopes. The top beast roared and swung its club in a horizontal blow meant to knock Darik off of his feet. Darik casually moved his sword to intercept the blow and braced his arms for the impact.

The blow hit with the force of a stampeding horse, but Darik did not so much as flinch. The club stopped an arm's length away from crushing every bone in his body. He held the club locked in place with his sword. Every muscle in his body straining, his biceps and shoulders feeling as if they would pop.

A cheer erupted from the men on the wall as they witnessed his exchange with the cyclops. Darik gritted his teeth and glared at the cyclops. If the men enjoyed that show, they were going to love what he had in mind for an encore.

The cyclops's singular eye stared at him, stretched wide in disbelief. It held that expression, stunned, its limited brain capacity trying to process what it had seen. A sole man having the strength to not just block its strike, but halt it completely. And with only a sword, not a shield. Fear must have been a new sensation for the beast.

The lower half of the cyclops tower glared up at Darik, bellowing a wordless challenge at him.

Flames burst forth out of Darik's mouth in response. An inferno enveloped both creatures, their howls of rage quickly shifting to shrieks of anguish. Darik swept his mouth left and right over the area, blanketing the ground in dragon fire and broiling those below.

He stopped to catch his breath and looked down at the flames. His breath had also heated the stones of the wall as the sound of cooking meat over hot stones was audible over the crackle of the flames. The heat would force the beasts to halt their assault on that portion of the wall. Neither flesh nor scaling ladder would fare well pressed against the heated stones.

Darik stumbled back from the wall and looked up just in time to see the blow that would kill him. The club streaked towards his head, the satyr bleating loudly in triumph as the weapon descended. Darik gasped for breath, his tired body unable to raise his sword in time. A part of his brain refused to accept that this was the end. Done in by a goat.

The blow never landed. A greataxe sank into the beast's collarbone, and a second later, the axe's wielder crashed into the beast, knocking man and goat to the ground.

Renaldo drew a dagger from the sheath on his belt and savagely sliced the monster's throat. He wiped off the blade, stuck it back in its sheath, yanked his axe out of the satyr's corpse, and smirked at Darik. "You're welcome," he said as he extended a hand to Darik.

"I don't recall thanking you," answered Darik drily as he took Renaldo's hand and regained his footing. "Actually, I remember coming this way to rescue you."

"Me?" asked Renaldo innocently as he pointed a finger at himself. "I have no idea what you're talking about."

"Hmm. Someone charging a cyclops, leading an attack all by himself?" Darik asked. "Sound familiar?"

Renaldo did not have the decency to blush. He hefted his axe and slammed it into a nearby minotaur's back. "Nah. That doesn't sound like me at all." He swung the axe again, slaying a satyr. "Now beating back a cyclops attack. Saving the battle and everyone at the fort? Yeah, that sounds like me."

Darik rolled his eyes. Renaldo did not share Byron's gift at making him laugh. The cyclopes' attack had failed and this section of the fort's defense was not going to fail any time soon. That alone was enough to merit a small smile though.

Darik turned his attention back to the battle, and to the sounds of men screaming as they fought and died. He paused and frowned. Something was not right. The sound was wrong.

Too many men were dying.

More men were in the process of dying at this instant than in the past few weeks combined. Something was terribly wrong. The monsters should not have been able to gain such a large foothold on the battlements.

"Men, be alert!" shouted Darik. "Something is wrong." He whispered the last to himself. No need to alarm the men.

Emkario appeared next to Darik's left arm. Blood of varying colors was spattered at random over his armor. He had been putting that falchion of his to work. "What is it?" he asked.

"I'm not sure," said Darik in as soft a voice as he could manage while still being able to be heard over the fighting. "But something is killing our men. Massacring them judging by the sounds."

"Loachians!" cried Vincent from his position back with the archers. "Fire! Fire!"

A volley of arrows flew over Darik's head as the first batch of Loachians burst into view. They were clad in red and black tabards over chainmail that had been crafted to gleam almost silver in color. A clear reference to the mines that were ubiquitous throughout Loach and were the backbone of the duchy's wealth.

The Loachians were quite literally stabbing his men in the back as they spread like a plague throughout the battlements. Darik swung his sword at the nearest soldier, anticipating the Loachian's movements. The northern man did not have a chance. Darik's sword cut through his chainmail as if it were hot butter, and cleaved the man in two before he had the opportunity to register Darik's presence.

Chaos reigned throughout Fort Hope. Men from both duchies shouted and died all along the battlements. Darik, flanked by Emkario and Renaldo, held out against the traitorous northmen from their defensive position on the northern edge of the wall. They swung their weapons time and time again, but it was a losing fight.

The Loachians were going to take Fort Hope and slaughter every Antierian there. It was inevitable. The defenders were exhausted, and did not have the numbers or a defensible position.

Darik's stomach collapsed in on itself. He had left Byron all alone. His brother would not stand a chance against the Loachians. Unless...maybe the Loachians were not aware of the river pass.

Darik clung to that hope. It was a faint hope, and he knew it. But he only had one brother.

He did not dare use his dragon breath or transform again. Darik knew his death had to be one the Loach's primary objectives. It is what he would do if he were in their place. Cut off the enemy general's head, and discipline and morale would crumble. The second a flash of fire announced his presence, the Loachians would descend upon his position with their full force like vultures on a carcass.

"Your Highness, we need to fall back," shouted Emarkio.

"Where to?" shouted Renaldo. "We're kind of on top of a fort if you haven't noticed!"

"We jump!" shouted Darik. "North-Northeast portion of the wall! Down the mountains and regroup away from the fort!" Darik sliced a few a more Loachians, but not before one of them raised a shout of "Prince Darik."

"Vincent! Covering fire!" Darik ordered as loud as he could. "And then get your men out of there!"

More arrows streaked over his head. Darik could not help but notice that there were fewer arrows than in the previous volley. He prayed that some of the archers must have already retreated. He could not say that he blamed them. Most of the Antierians were going to die upon the battlements, and many more would perish trying to escape down the mountainside.

Darik was staring at the Loachians when the sky exploded. A fireball rose from the south, a giant ball of flame streaking into the sky. It was a sight to behold, and a frightful herald for what came next. Tremors shook the ground as a deafening explosion rocked the area. Men on the wall were thrown from their feet, and howls filled the air as the monsters plummeted off of the wall.

Tears welled up in Darik's eyes. He knew of only one thing that could cause an explosion such as that. Byron had died, and the power inside of him exploded outward causing untold destruction, just like what happened when their grandfather perished near the border with Loach.

Darik howled in pain, his heart having dropped and vanished somewhere beneath his stomach. There was only a cold void where his heart was. But nature abhors a vacuum.

The dam he built to hold back all his ignoble feelings and his anger came crashing down. Rage and a lust for vengeance came pouring in to fill the void inside of him.

Darik swung his greatsword down with all of his strength. In two quick blows he beheaded two Loachian soldiers who had yet to regain their senses. A third Loachian began to find his footing. A third strike sent his head flying beyond the battlements into the monsters below.

Someone grabbed him from behind and started pulling him away. Darik roared and struggled to gain free. He had yet to meet someone stronger than him, but whoever was pulling him was coming close, and they had caught him off balance.

"Your Highness, we must retreat," pleaded Emkario as he pulled on Darik's shoulder. "There is nothing more than can be accomplished here."

"Dammit Darik!" shouted Renaldo as he yanked on the other shoulder. "We need to go now!"

Darik thrashed against them half-heartedly for a few seconds and exhaled, the exhaustion washing over him. The pain did not vanish though. It merely dulled as he forced his more animalistic tendencies back behind the dam where they belonged.

"Alright," he panted. "I'm fine now. Let's get moving. Full retreat. Let's go. Over the wall."

Darik put actions to words and sprinted down the battlements and vaulted over the wall into the cold night. Tears streaked down his face as he skidded down the mountainside. His little brother. Dead.

He shook his head in denial. Byron was not the only person he had lost to the Loachians. An entire army of dead Antierians could be laid at their feet. An entire army that was his responsibility. Family lines were extinguished. A generation of orphans and fatherless children.

Tonight he could not afford to think of them. Tonight he could only think about survival. Tomorrow he would turn his mind to vengeance. If he lived to see tomorrow.

Chapter Thirty-Seven

Matlin polished the blood off his blade as he gazed out at the retreating horde of monsters. The creatures did their reputations justice. They truly were terrifying beings. He had seen the horrors up close before, but there was no comparison between his previous encounter and the horde of monsters he saw retreating. That would be comparing a candle light to a wildfire. Mothers were right to frighten their children with stories of the beasts.

The massive explosion that had sown chaos throughout the battlefield had shattered whatever cohesion it was that held the enemy forces together. Their sense of purpose vanished and the beasts entered a panic, fleeing into the sunset.

His men of course believed it was their appearance that scared off the beasts. They walked around with a swagger and puffed out chests. They had dealt a massive defeat to Loach's enemy as well as the enemy of all of humanity.

Matlin knew better, but he refused to quash the rumors. Let the men think they were the impressive and superior fighters. Heroes out of some story. The boost to their confidence would do them well in future battles.

The blast and tremors originated from the south, in the general direction of the river pass. He would have to wait for his brothers to return from the pass and report actual confirmation of what caused the explosion. But he was fairly certain he deduced the cause.

The image of the crater kept surfacing to the top of his mind. Prince Byron was reportedly at the pass, and his death would be the most likely source of the explosion.

Which left only one remaining prince of Antier. The one the mattered. The one who was his only obstacle to becoming king.

Matlin gnashed his teeth in anger. They had been so close to pulling off the plan too. But Darik escaped the trap. His men reported seeing Darik and some of his men before the explosion. Afterwards? It was as if he vanished into the night.

They had searched the corpses but did not find any that resembled Darik's description. No one had seen a dragon take flight during their attack. That would have been impossible to hide. Darik had to have leapt off of the battlements. It was the only conclusion that made any sort of logical sense. A man could not simply vanish.

But on which side of the wall did he leap? Surely, he did not leap off into the west and the horde of monsters. That would be suicide. Darik had to have chosen the east, towards Antier.

Matlin had ordered aerial scouts, and more conventional scouts out to hunt Darik. They could not cover every route, but they could cover the main roads and trails to Antier. If the prince made it home...well Matlin would not like his own position very much in that event. Stuck behind enemy lines, without hope of reinforcement, in a fort that lacked any defenses from the direction the Antierians would be striking? Not an enviable position.

He merely had to ensure that Darik did not reach the capital before the Antierian reinforcements arrived to replace the men lost at Fort Hope. The best-case scenario would be capturing or killing Darik, but beyond that, he just needed to get himself and his men home to Loach before the entirety of the kingdom could be alerted of their treachery.

The Antierians had lost too many men to win a war with Loach that was fought on the border. Once his forces returned home it was all but an assured victory. Whether in a year, or a generation. Antier's army would not be able to replenish its manpower enough to challenge Loach any time soon.

As to the matter of who would be the next king, well that was more difficult, thought Matlin. If news of today's events leaked out, some of his support from the nobles of other duchies would evaporate. However, not everyone was bound by honor. Fear of reprisals from Loach, both militarily and economically would keep most of the nobles in line. Most of the kingdom just did not want to fight a war, and so Loach could keep pushing because the others would not fight back.

"Cousin," called Clara as she glided through the corpses strewn across the battlements. "The keep has been purged of the Antierians."

"Good," said Matlin gruffly.

Clara hesitated. "There was a complication, cousin. There were Bionians amongst the dead. A few were nobles from what we could ascertain."

Matlin swore as he brought his fist down upon a stone crenellation causing spiderweb cracks to appear in the stone. The plan was simple enough, but like every plan, variables in the execution had muddied it. Their delay in reaching Fort Hope had allowed some Bionian forces to arrive first. Their deaths could pit an entire duchy and its allies against him in his bid for the throne.

Militarily, if the truth were to reach Bionia, it would be two duchies at war with Loach. That numerical advantage Loach enjoyed dwindled with every second.

"Any word from the twins?" he asked dreading the answer.

Clara's eyes hardened to the appearance of cold steel. "Yes. They confirmed the death of Prince Byron. The twins personally shot him with four arrows to the chest. His body fell backwards and down into the river."

Matlin clenched his fists in frustration. Every bit of good news he received seemed to be balanced with bad news. "They shot him with arrows?" he hissed. "From what we know, the monsters do not use arrows, or if they do, they are nowhere near the quality of arrows made in Loach. One look at his body will disprove our story rather quickly."

"I know," said Clara softly.

"They were supposed to make it look like the monsters killed Byron!" Matlin protested. He sighed in frustration. One dead prince whose body his brothers had lost, one destroyed army, and one prince for whom he could not account. Far from a masterful stroke, but the damage could be contained if they moved quickly.

Well at least no one should be able to find the body if it fell into the river. "What about our two...ahh new friends?" Matlin asked with contempt dripping out of his voice.

"Barith and Timver?" Clara smirked as she spoke. "Those fools are willing to sing whatever tale we instruct them to. The skinny one keeps talking about how much of an honor it was to aid his brother cavaliers."

"Lickspittles," spat Matlin with disgust. "They have no honor. Typical Antierians. Have Toran keep an eye on them."

Clara frowned. "Cousin, you did attack the Antierians in the rear when they thought you were their allies," she said cautiously. "Many might find that dishonorable."

Matlin waved a hand dismissively. "That's different. They would have done the same to us, and were probably already planning to do so. Besides, the Antierians are just like our two *friends*," he sneered. "They all have no honor. They turned on their own."

Clara bowed her head in acknowledgment. "There is more, cousin," she said. "Our two friends informed us that they witnessed a small group of Anterians fleeing from the river pass before the explosion."

"Inconsequential," Matlin said. "A small group of soldiers are of no concern. Their words will bear no weight."

"Apparently they were Prince Byron's close friends and personal retainers."

Matlin squeezed his eyes shut in pain. Gods, the plan kept springing leaks at every turn.

"Add them to the list to hunt down," he ordered. "At the very least, make sure they cannot reach Antier itself. Block off any route that would allow them access back to the capital. That is where their allies will be concentrated, and I doubt many people outside of Antier would recognize Byron's retainers on sight. If we can keep them from Antier, their tales won't carry any weight, or will at least be heavily doubted. We can make time our ally in this."

"And so, we sit here, waiting, giving the Antierians a chance to evade us?" she asked.

Matlin shrugged his shoulders helplessly. "We don't have much of a choice. We have to play our part and guard the realm for a few days at most. If we leave, the rest of the kingdom will view us with disfavor. That could cost us the crown. Consider it a head start." He smiled at her in a predatory fashion. "Then we unleash more of our men on the hunt, while we return to Loach to put the rest of our plans in motion."

Clara nodded coolly. "I pray to the gods that you are correct."

Matlin said nothing in response. He merely gazed out at the monsters retreating over the plains. It had been a risk, one that he willing took, and a risk that kept growing at every turn. Hopefully they would live through its consequences to reap the rewards.

CHAPTER THIRTY-EIGHT

Tyson gripped the cloth around Maxus's mouth tight and pushed down on the makeshift muzzle as hard as he could. Any concerns he had regarding suffocating his comrade were offset by his concerns for their survival.

The Loachian attack on Fort Hope had been sudden and without mercy or warning. Tyson assumed that their rear scouts must have been murdered by the Loachian forces. The Loachians had swept through the keep killing men who were resting, sleeping, eating, and recovering from battle.

He wished he could claim that the Antierian forces put up a valiant defense. But that was not the case. He would be shocked if the Loachian forces suffered a dozen casualties taking the keep.

Tyson had been in a meeting with the other masters when the first cry of treachery was raised. The masters fought briefly, with Maxus being wounded in the struggle, although Levren slew Maxus's assailant. That action bought them a brief respite in the battle, and some time to determine their next move.

They quickly decided that their only feasible option was to try and hide from the Loachian betrayers.

It was not a brave, honorable, or very dutiful thing to do, but it was their only choice. Dying without a purpose could not be considered a reasonable choice. Luckily, Maxus was wounded and had been teetering on the edge of consciousness. Otherwise, the stubborn knight's pride would never have allowed him to be convinced to go into hiding. He would have preferred dying proudly for his liege lord.

Their options at hiding were rather limited given the circumstances. Tyson regretted his choice, but he had not seen any other option at the time. He appropriated a strategy from Byron and Cole's repertoire.

He only wished the barrows were a more hospitable place.

The dead were supposed to find peace and rest in these places. Tyson wondered how anyone could rest comfortably in a place like this. Cold dirt was hard packed everywhere, broken up only by stone monuments and the remaining crude mausoleums which had not crumbled over the years.

Wards were placed throughout the barrows, creating an impression of a prison with each ghost and spirit restricted to its own cell.

No wonder ghosts were always surly and unpleasant.

Not that the present human company was much better.

"Hold him down," hissed Levren as he used one of Richard's flame devices to heat a needle. "This is going to hurt, and we can't afford him screaming or kicking about and ruining what few supplies we do have."

Richard snorted in disdain as he held down Maxus's upper body while Sildun attempted to restrain the paladin's thrashing legs.

The wound was shallow, but the location was troublesome. The Loachian soldier sliced Maxus along the left upper quadriceps. None of their little merry band of survivors were priests, but from what they could tell, the wound was not life threatening, as it had stopped gushing blood. However, the wound needed to be stitched and cleaned to prevent infection. Levren swore that he had seen numerous wounds throughout his career, and if they quickly took the proper precautions that Maxus would not permanently lose much, if any, of his mobility.

Maxus strained against his meager restraints, but he did not use his totem. The man was in pain, but was not stupid, even if he was making enough noise to wake the dead.

Levren finished his work in relative silence. As he finished wrapping a bandage around the wound, Maxus seemed to unclench his body for a brief moment, before convulsing slightly in pain.

Tyson winced in sympathy. He disliked stitches. It was a strange and obtrusive feeling, the thread pulling one's skin together while not having any sensation or control over the actual thread. If possible, he would rather forego the stitches and take a jagged scar.

Maxus stopped straining against the gathered masters, and Tyson carefully withdrew the makeshift muzzle.

"Thank you," Maxus whispered. His skin was pale and drawn tight against his face in discomfort.

Levren made a rather noncommittal grunt. "Don't mention it," he said.

Sildun sat down wearily on a chunk of stone that had broken off a rather plain looking mausoleum. Salt and pepper stubble covered his face, and his entire body looked weary. The man had just returned from two days of scouting only a few hours before the Loachians had arrived. He must be exhausted.

"What now?" asked Sildun. "We barely have any supplies, food, or drink. I suppose Tyson and I could sneak out and forage what we need from the fort's supplies. But assuming we can do that, it still begs the question of where do we go?" He gestured to Maxus. "We can't go far carrying Maxus, and leaving him behind is not an option. The Loachians are certain to have patrols throughout the area searching for survivors. Too much time has passed for me to be able to successfully guide a group of untrained woodsmen through such a web."

"We stay," said Tyson firmly.

"Are you mad?" hissed Richard in what could only be described as part whisper and part shriek. "Why would we stay here? Amongst the dead and restless dead?" He did not even bother to suppress a shudder.

"Because the Loachians are not likely to look in the crypts," said Tyson. "What sane person would hide out down here? And think it through Richard. There is no reason for the Loachians to hold Fort Hope long term. Right, Levren? Only a few days before more Antierian and Bionian forces arrive?"

"Correct," spat Levren. "And Fort Hope is intentionally not defensible from an attack on the Antierian side, due to fears that the monsters would one day seize it. And the Loachians will have to expect that they will be blamed for the attack. They will have to depart as soon as they possibly can. Probably immediately, after the first reinforcements arrive to hold the fort."

"Right," nodded Tyson. "That gives us time for Maxus to heal up and then make our way back to the capital in the wake of their rear scouts."

Maxus grimaced at the mention of his healing. Undoubtedly, the idea of spending time in a grave was unpleasant to a wounded man. "The duke will be receiving late intelligence then. Our enemies will be out of reach."

"Better late intelligence than no intelligence at all," stated Tyson as if he were a teacher repeating a favorite phrase.

"I'm all in favor of that," said Richard.

"Besides," said Sildun as he leaned backwards against the mausoleum. "After today, I doubt Antier is in any shape to conduct a war, and simultaneously defend Fort Hope from the monsters. A little time to regroup and calm tempers may be what is best."

"Gods is that the truth," said Levren. "Well, we should at least make the best of our grave situation."

Tyson groaned as he lay back to catch a few minutes of sleep. Who knew Levren had a sense of humor?

CHAPTER THIRTY-NINE

D arik's men numbered fifteen as they set a breakneck pace away from Fort Hope. Their flight had taken them more northerly than northeast than he originally planned. But it was a few days after the betrayal at Fort Hope, and he and his men were still breathing.

At least they still had that much. It could have been much worse.

Byron.

Darik gritted his teeth as he pushed through the overgrown foliage of the Antierian wilderness. Sadly, their group did not number any trackers or scouts. It mainly consisted of men comfortable with a weapon in their hands. While they may not be able to track an animal, they could certainly kill one quickly if they chanced upon it. Cooking the beast might also prove a difficulty. None were great at starting a fire; not that they dared light a beacon for their pursuers.

Without a forward scout the group stuck together as one, lest they become separated. Darik was pushing them forward at a rather fast pace. There were enough of them that an enemy scout would not be able to assault them by himself, yet few enough that they would be able to outrun any pursuit from a large army.

"So where are we going boss?" asked Vincent. Somewhere along the way he had picked up a large weed and decided that he would chew on it while they walked. It was highly unprofessional and not the sort of behavior Darik would prefer his soldiers engaging in. However, they had suffered a catastrophic defeat of historical proportions, and he needed to keep morale up for his men and himself. If that meant looking the other way while his men engaged in some harmless fun after staring down death, then that was what he was prepared to do.

"We can't head back to Antier," said Darik. "It is the first thing the Loachians would expect, and we'd run into their forces well before we got to the city. No. We have to go elsewhere. Somewhere we can expect to find aid. Talendor." Darik schooled a neutral look onto his features and waited for the response.

Most of the men looked nervous, some physically ill. Those who were not on a first name basis with Darik did not say anything. Darik groaned internally. That lack of initiative may get them all killed if his plan was to work.

"Umm, Your Highness," said Emkario hesitantly. "Doesn't that mean we'd have to travel through Loach, and uhhh...there?"

"Yes," said Darik simply.

Renaldo snorted. "And they say I'm the reckless one."

Darik leveled a glare at Renaldo. Now was not the time for jokes. "My father has long been friends with the Duke of Talendor," he said. "They fought together, and he will believe what we say. And if we play our cards right, the duke will help us march on the Loachians."

"If you say so big man," said Vincent while affecting a faux drawl.

Sometimes, friends can be a real pain.

Emkario looked frustrated. "But that means we'll have to travel through Kelon!" he protested. "The entire duchy is deserted! It's nothing but ruins which are overrun by the ghosts! We'd be better off facing Loach's army!"

Darik shrugged unconcerned. "I'm not afraid of any ghosts."

"Well, I am boss man," said Vincent now with a nasally accent. He jerked his head back. "So are some of the boys. Although they may be more concerned about travelling through Loach in Antierian colors." He shrugged. "But maybe that is just me."

A valid point. Darik smiled. At least someone's brain still worked. Now he just had to tell them the second part of the plan.

"I don't relish the idea either," he said. "Which is why we won't be wearing Antierian colors. Our tabards go into the next body of water. Any piece of equipment that screams Antierian soldier goes in the water. From here on out we are a mercenary band."

"You're going to be trashing that fancy armor then boss?" said Vincent.

Darik grimaced. "No. I'm going to char it so that the colors are unrecognizable. Wear a cloak once we can get our hands on one," he said. "But I also can't lead our mercenary group. Everyone always looks at the leader, and I am too recognizable. Someone else will have to be a decoy leader."

"And who dat gonna be," asked Vincent in an unrecognizable accent.

Darik grinned ruthlessly. "Who do you think boss?" he said. "Be sure to stand up straight, Vin. They always shoot at the leaders first."

The weed fell from Vincent's mouth. "What?! Really?" he asked in his normal voice.

"No," laughed Darik. "You clearly have your brains rattled from the battle. Emkario, congratulations on your new command."

Emkario let loose a long-suffering sigh as he looked to the sky seeking relief. Receiving none, he faced a group of grinning, blood stained, and battered men. "Very well. Captain, no, Commander Emkario, reporting for duty sir."

"Which is higher?" Vincent whispered loudly to Renaldo.

"Who cares?" whispered Renaldo back even louder. "We're all going to call him Captain anyway."

Emkario slumped his shoulders in defeat. "Very well. I guess I can suffer the burdens of command," he said solemnly to Darik. "But until then, where to boss man?"

Darik rubbed at his constant companion of a headache. It was not easy being the boss.

Chapter Forty

D alton reached out and grabbed Atticus before he could trip over a tree root. The night was incredibly dark with only the moon providing illumination. Dalton was using his feline gifts to navigate in the darkness. However, not everyone possessed that ability.

He found himself busy trying to prevent his companions from tripping and falling, while also focusing his exhausted mind and body on running. Keeping his focus proved difficult. Running, especially running at a challenging pace, while wearing armor, was an extremely mentally demanding activity. Dalton constantly focused on forcing his legs to travel quickly. Otherwise, his body would subconsciously slow itself down to an easier pace. A pace that would undoubtedly result in his death.

They had not yet paused to rest, and Dalton had already seen the sun rise and set once. After fighting in the battle, he doubted his body had much left in it, and, unlike the others, he was accustomed to running long distances. The others must be exhausted. However, with the exception of Jeron, they were not wearing platemail. Lucky them.

Their group would need to rest soon, and he doubted anyone retained the energy to stand watch. They would just have to sleep and pray that there was enough distance between themselves and any Loachian pursuit. And if there was not, pray that the pursuing Loachians did not find them.

"Where are we headed?" Dalton gasped between breaths.

"East," gasped Thiago. "At the moment."

"We need to stop soon," said Jeron.

Dalton frowned and looked at his friend. He did not even sound tired. Jeron's chest was heaving, just like the rest of theirs. Exhaustion was plainly visible all over his body, with the exception of his eyes, which were still feline and shining bright. He barely blinked, and with his mane and constant snarl he looked terrifying. But his voice did not waiver at all.

Thiago slowed the pace but did not stop. "I haven't been this far east while scouting," he said, while breathing a little easier. "I can't guarantee that we'll find any decent places to rest. Out here we could run for hours more and not find anything."

"Then we stop now," said Jeron. "We need some rest, and we aren't fighting anyone in this condition."

They came to a merciful stop and Dalton slumped down next to a large tree of...something. He was too tired to identify it, and just did not care to waste the effort. Dalton could faintly hear the sound of running water. He assumed it was the Irinin. They must not have strayed too far north while fleeing from the fort.

"So where are we going?" repeated Dalton.

"Talendor," said Jeron.

"Why Talendor?" asked Atticus.

Jeron glared at the boy. "Because that's where Duke Cedric always told Byron to go if he was in trouble," he snarled. "Apparently the dukes are old friends."

"Why don't we try to get back to Antier?" Dalton asked.

Thiago shook his head in the negative. "As it is right now, I doubt we are that much farther east than the Loachian scouts. East puts as much distance between us and them as possible. And reaching Antier means crossing the roads. And heading north. And the Loachians have horses. It won't be long until they have mounted scouts out patrolling the roads."

"So we would be discovered," concluded Daltion in disappointment.

"East it is then," said Jeron. "Any questions?"

There were none however. Everyone else had already fallen asleep, even Thiago.

"You okay?" Dalton asked Jeron.

Yellow eyes focused on him through narrow slits. Dalton tried his best not to swallow. Jeron was still his friend after all.

"I saw my oldest friend, a brother to me, get murdered before my eyes," Jeron said. "I should have been there to protect him. Both of us should have. But we weren't. And now he is dead."

Dalton felt the lump begin to rise in his throat as his own grief and guilt threatened to overwhelm him. "We tried," he said meekly.

Jeron shook his head, his mane shaking wildly. "No. We didn't," he said forcefully. "We got caught up in the fight. Don't deny it. I saw the look on your face. We enjoyed killing the monsters. Me? Cause it made me feel powerful. You? Because you enjoyed the revenge."

"And we weren't there for Byron," Dalton whispered. "Or Cole."

Jeron closed his eyes and his body began to quiver. "Cole. Damn it all. Dalton, I ran right past him when the Loachians attacked," he said. "I knew he couldn't fend for himself against them. But I wanted *my* vengeance. And I left another friend to die."

"He could have lived," protested Dalton. "We never saw him die."

Jeron kept shaking his head. "No. You know that's not true," he said. "In that battlefield? Through that explosion? Even if he was camouflaged, his focus would have wavered at some point. There is no way he would get far enough past their scouts. He's dead, Dalton. And he may not have been if we had focused on protecting Byron during the fight."

"Suppose I buy that theory," said Dalton. "And I'm not sure that I do. Why go to Talendor? What can we actually accomplish there?"

"They would help Byron," said Jeron stubbornly.

"Neither of us is Byron," retorted Dalton. "And how would they recognize us? I doubt either of us has even met anyone from Talendor."

"I don't know," said Jeron.

"But-" said Dalton.

"I said I *don't know*," snarled Jeron. He slumped back against his tree as his body seemed to deflate and the fire died down from his eyes. "We'll figure it out as we go. We have to go somewhere, don't we? And we can't go home."

Dalton's eyes seemed to close on their own accord. The last thought that crossed his mind was a familiar one.

He could never go home.

Chapter Forty-One

C alabella stormed through the palace in a fit of rage. It was happening again. After Raven's Perch she thought things would be different. Her skirts said otherwise.

Their group disposed of a total of four different bandit groups on their way to the capital. They had not suffered a single casualty outside of a few scrapes and bruises. The duchy was safer as a result of their actions.

And their reward? Their training was discontinued. The duchy's military decided to postpone their training until such time as the duchy was not under imminent threat, and the army was replenished. The unspoken word was that it was not going to happen again.

The nobles were spooked at the news of the monsters gathering west of Fort Hope. The thought that their little girls may be hurt by some monstrous creatures was the real reason behind why their training ceased.

She charged through a solid oak door, knocking it off of its hinges as she worked her way towards the duke's court.

Calabella was furious. How dare they think that they could force them to remove their arms and armor and replace them with fine magenta silk dresses, and not expect them to be upset. Once they had a taste of real freedom and power, did they honestly expect them to don pretty chains willingly?

Another door connecting to a separate wing, bowed and exploded out into Calabella's hallway. Atrisha glided through the newly made opening looking stately in an elegant gown of an almost white color, more reminiscent of cloudy crystals or diamonds. Her wings were out, and her eyes were frozen dark blue gems of righteousness.

Even without her arms and armor, Atrisha effortlessly managed the avenging angel look. Calabella squealed with glee at the sight of her.

"Hi Ella," beamed Atrisha. "Heading to court today?"

"Hi Trishy," replied Calabella. "Of course. I'm tired of waiting for them to decide where I belong. I am going to tell them what I am going to do, and they can shove off if they don't like it."

"Agreed," said Atrisha frostily.

The pair squared their shoulders and strode confidently to the audience hall. As they approached, the guards on duty opened the double doors while executing the formal court bow customarily required by soldiers who served at court.

"They look too dainty when they do that," grumbled Calabella. "It makes them look less like soldiers and more like court dandies."

Atrisha smiled softly in response and entered the audience hall. The duke's majordomo stood on the steps just beneath the dais holding the duke's throne. The man cleared his throat and made public note of their arrival.

"Lords and Ladies, Lady Atrisha Melango, daughter of Lord Stellin Melango, Earl of Falcon's Hollow, and Lady Calabella Lorezzini, daughter of Lord Pompello Lorezzini, Earl of Munaris," he announced.

They strode into the room determined to make an appearance before the duke. They made it about two strides before a strong hand gripped Calabella's shoulder and pulled her into the crowd.

"Not today, baby girl," growled her father, his bull horns glistening.

"Like hell," Calabella snarled.

A thin graceful man with fine delicately sculpted facial features placed a hand lightly and firmly upon her father's shoulder. "Easy, my friend," said Lord Stellin, Atrisha's father. "Ladies, what he means is that terrible news has reached the duke today. Now is not the time to broach the subject of female warriors in court."

"What news?" asked Atrisha much too calmly. Her eyes were crinkled at the corners with worry.

Lord Pompello's grip loosened on Calabella's shoulder and his arm dropped to his side. "News from Fort Hope. The Loachians betrayed us and their forces struck ours from the rear. So far there are not any reports of survivors. The duke mourns both of his sons."

"No survivors?" whispered Atrisha, tears slowly dripping down her face. "No. Not Cole. He was so...sweet."

Calabella gingerly hugged her friend, offering whatever meager comfort she could under the tragic circumstances. "I'm so sorry, Trishy," she whispered quietly in Atrisha's ear.

Calabella turned and addressed their fathers. "How did the news get out if our forces were destroyed to a man? Did someone make it out?" she asked with a tinge of hope in her voice that caused Atrisha to look at her father like a drowning woman seeking a life raft.

Lord Stellin shook his head sadly. "One," he said. "An owl. He was the first to take to the skies on evening watch duty. The man was supposed to be on the lookout for an aerial attack on the fort. Instead, he witnessed the Loachian treachery from the sky. Apparently, there was a large explosion that threw the Loachian forces into disarray for a few minutes. The man seized the opening provided by the explosion and flew day and night back to the capital to report it." He shook his head sadly. "The man pushed himself beyond his limits, and has been in a coma since shortly after he arrived."

"There will be war," her father said firmly. "There is no other response appropriate to this betrayal."

"I agree," said Atrisha with a sniff. She raised her head and composed her features into proud determination. "And we will be the ones who fight it."

Lord Stellin shook his hands in disagreement. "Don't be foolish sweetie," he said. "We are talking about a war here."

"We've already fought and killed," Atrisha said calmly. "And we are quite good at it. Also, father, if what you say is true, then Antier needs the soldiers. And we are all willing to fight."

"Just put weapons in our hands, and we'll see that the war is won," said Calabella matter-of-factly. "I guarantee you the women of this duchy will fight. Especially to avenge their brothers, sons, and loved ones."

"Do you know what will happen if you lose a battle?" protested Lord Stellin. "The Loachians will rape you!"

Atrisha icily regarded her father. "I'll castrate anyone who tries," she said emotionlessly. "And maybe those that don't."

Lord Stellin looked shocked while Lord Pompello let loose a bellowing laugh that pierced the pall that was cast over court. Nobles looked on aghast at his breach of decorum.

"I'll give her this," said Lord Pompello. "She has spirit. And, well, it's not a bad plan."

"Pompello! You can't be serious," said Lord Stellin.

Calabella's father nodded slightly. "But I am, old friend," he said. "They are right. We don't have the numbers otherwise. The Loachians have no choice but to declare war now that the truth is out."

"They'll be in harm's way," protested Lord Stellin.

"And they won't be if the Loachians roll right over us?" Pompello asked.

Stellin sighed in acquiescence. "That is certainly true."

"Father. I can take care of myself," said Atrisha firmly, yet kindly.

The delicate man smiled sadly. "I know that sweetie," he said. "But you'll always be my baby, and I'll always try to protect you from harm."

Atrisha hugged her father fiercely. "I know that daddy," she said. "But this is something I have to do."

"I understand," Stellin said. "And I truly believe you can do it. You convinced me of that years ago."

Calabella looked at her father who tried to affect a roguish grin on his burly face. The effect looked frightening, but Calabella smiled at her father's silliness anyway.

"Well, I certainly won't be the one to try and stop you my dear," he said. "If you're even the slightest bit as hard-headed as your mother, I may not survive this conversation with both of my horns intact. We'll speak to the duke on your behalf," he said. "He may be in mourning but he'll see the sense of the plan. The training of you girls did receive, originated from him after all."

"Or maybe the duchess," supplied Lord Stellin. "But enough about politics. Go gather your friends and see if you can find any others willing to join you. Training will need to be accelerated if you all are to fight, and you'll need to get the word out."

Calabella hugged her father tightly and pressed a large kiss against his cheek before rushing off to the door.

What would she wear to war she wondered to herself.

"I am going to kill every single Loachian that I can," whispered Atrisha softly, the tears gone from her eyes.

Black. They would wear black.

TO THE READER

I would like to acknowledge you the reader, and thank you for reading. I hope you enjoyed the story. Please consider leaving a rating and review for the book. Both help the book achieve visibility for other readers.

This book is part of a trilogy. All three books are finished and slated to be released within months of each other. If you're interested in these books, or in other future projects, please consider signing up for the Author Newsletter here: https://calixtowayne.com/newsletter/.

ABOUT THE AUTHOR

Calixto Wayne is a fantasy author who enjoys telling fast-paced stories. The goal of every story should be to create characters with whom the reader enjoys spending their time. Calixto builds worlds where the reader can daydream about inserting themselves into the action.

He currently resides in Florida. You can find more about the author and his works at https://calixtowayne.com/